T

Hans

NOVELLE

NACHWORT VON
WALTHER HERRMANN

PHILIPP RECLAM JUN. STUTTGART

Der Text folgt bei geringfügigen Modernisierungen der
Orthographie und Interpunktion der Ausgabe: Theodor
Storm. Sämtliche Werke in acht Bänden. Herausgegeben
von Albert Köster. Sechster Band. Leipzig 1920

Universal-Bibliothek Nr. 6035
Alle Rechte vorbehalten. Gesetzt in Petit Garamond-Antiqua.
Printed in Germany 1978. Satz: M. Storz, Echterdingen. Druck:
Reclam Stuttgart
ISBN 3-15-006035-4

Auf einer Uferhöhe der Ostsee liegt hart am Wasser hingelagert eine kleine Stadt, deren stumpfer Turm schon über ein Halbjahrtausend auf das Meer hinausschaut. Ein paar Kabellängen vom Lande streckt sich quervor ein schmales Eiland, das sie dort den »Warder« nennen, von wo aus im Frühling unablässiges Geschrei der Strand- und Wasservögel nach der Stadt herübertönt. Bei hellem Wetter tauchen auch wohl drüben auf der Insel, welche das jenseitige Ufer des Sundes bildet, rotbraune Dächer und die Spitze eines Turmes auf, und wenn die Abenddämmerung das Bild verlöscht hat, entzünden dort zwei Leuchttürme ihre Feuer und werfen über die dunkle See einen Schimmer nach dem diesseitigen Strand herüber. Gleichwohl, wer als Fremder durch die auf- und absteigenden Straßen der Stadt wandert, wo hie und da roh gepflasterte Stufen über die Vorstraße zu den kleinen Häusern führen, wird sich des Eindrucks abgeschlossener Einsamkeit wohl kaum erwehren können, zumal wenn er von der Landseite über die langgestreckte Hügelkette hier herabgekommen ist. In einem Balkengestelle auf dem Markte hing noch vor kurzem, wie seit Jahrhunderten, die sogenannte Bürgerglocke; um zehn Uhr abends, sobald es vom Kirchturme geschlagen hatte, wurde auch dort geläutet, und wehe dem Gesinde oder auch dem Haussohn, der diesem Ruf nicht Folge leistete; denn gleich danach konnte man straßab und -auf sich alle Schlüssel in den Haustüren drehen hören.

Aber in der kleinen Stadt leben tüchtige Menschen, alte Bürgergeschlechter, unabhängig von dem Gelde und dem Einfluß der umwohnenden großen Grundbesitzer; ein kleines Patriziat ist aus ihnen erwachsen, dessen stattlichere Wohnungen, mit breiten Beischlägen hinter mächtig schattenden Linden, mitunter die niedrigen Häuserreihen unterbrechen. Aber auch aus diesen Familien mußten bis vor dem letzten Jahrzehent die Söhne den Weg gehen, auf welchem Eltern und Vorfahren zur Wohlhabenheit und bürgerlichen Geltung gelangt waren; nur wenige ergaben sich den Wissenschaften, und kaum war unter den derzeitig noch studierten Bürgermeistern jemals ein Eingeborener dagewesen; wenn aber bei den jährlichen Prüfungen in der Rektorschule der Propst den einen oder andern von den Knaben frug: »Mein Junge, was willst du werden?«, dann richtete der sich stolz von seiner Bank empor, der mit der Antwort »Schiffer!« herauskommen durfte. Schiffsjunge, Kapitän auf einem Familien-, auf einem eignen Schiffe, dann mit etwa vierzig Jahren Reeder und bald Senator in der Vaterstadt, so lautete der Stufengang der bürgerlichen Ehren.

Auf dem Chor der von einem Landesherzog im dreizehnten Jahrhundert erbauten Kirche befand sich der geräumige Schifferstuhl, für den Abendgottesdienst mit stattlichen Metalleuchtern an den Wänden prangend, durch das an der Decke schwebende Modell eines Barkschiffes in vollem Takelwerke kenntlich. Auf diesen Raum hatte jeder Bürger ein Recht, welcher das Steuermannsexamen gemacht hatte und ein eigenes Schiff besaß; aber auch die schon in die Kaufmannschaft Übergetretenen, die ersten Reeder der Stadt, hielten, während unten in der Kirche ihre Frauen saßen, hier oben unter den andern Kapitänen ihren Gottesdienst; denn sie waren noch immer und vor allem meerbefahrene Leute, und das kleine schwebende Barkschiff war hier ihre Hausmarke.

Es ist begreiflich, daß auch manchen jungen Matrosen oder Steuermann aus dem kleinen Bürgerstande beim Eintritt in die Kirche statt der Andacht ein ehrgeiziges Verlangen anfiel, sich auch einmal den Platz dort oben zu erwerben, und daß er trotz der eindringlichen Predigt dann statt mit gottseligen Gedanken mit erregten weltlichen Entschlüssen in sein Quartier oder auf sein Schiff zurückkehrte.

Zu diesen strebsamen Leuten gehörte Hans Adam Kirch. Mit unermüdlichem Tun und Sparen hatte er sich vom Setzschiffer zum Schiffseigentümer hinaufgearbeitet; freilich war es nur eine kleine Jacht, zu der seine Mittel gereicht hatten, aber rastlos und in den Winter hinein, wenn schon alle andern Schiffer daheim hinter ihrem Ofen saßen, befuhr er mit seiner Jacht die Ostsee, und nicht nur Frachtgüter für andre, bald auch für eigne Rechnung brachte er die Erzeugnisse der Umgegend, Korn und Mehl, nach den größeren und kleineren Küstenplätzen; erst wenn bereits außen vor den Buchten das Wasser fest zu werden drohte, band auch er sein Schiff an den Pfahl und saß beim Sonntagsgottesdienste droben im Schifferstuhl unter den Honoratioren seiner Vaterstadt. Aber lang vor Frühlingsanfang war er wieder auf seinem Schiffe; an allen Ostseeplätzen kannte man den kleinen hageren Mann in der blauen schlotternden Schifferjacke, mit dem gekrümmten Rücken und dem vorüberhängenden dunkelhaarigen Kopfe; überall wurde er aufgehalten und angeredet, aber er gab nur kurze Antworten, er hatte keine Zeit; in einem Tritte, als ob er an der Fallreepstreppe hinauflaufe, sah man ihn eilfertig durch die Gassen wandern. Und diese Rastlosigkeit trug ihre Früchte; bald wurde zu dem aus der väterlichen Erbschaft übernommenen Hause ein Stück Wiesenland erworben, genügend für die Sommer- und Winterfütterung zweier Kühe; denn während das Schiff zu Wasser, sollten diese zu Lande die Wirtschaft vorwärts bringen. Eine Frau hatte Hans Kirch sich im stillen vor ein paar Jahren schon genommen; zu der Hökerei, welche diese bisher betrieben, kam nun noch eine Milchwirtschaft; auch ein paar Schweine konnten jetzt gemästet werden, um das Schiff auf seinen Handelsfahrten zu verproviantieren; und da die Frau, welche er im Widerspruch mit seinem sonstigen Tun aus einem armen Schulmeisterhause heimgeführt hatte, nur seinen Willen kannte und überdies aus Furcht vor dem bekannten Jähzorn ihres Mannes sich das Brot am Munde sparte, so pflegte dieser bei jeder Heimkehr auch zu Hause einen hübschen Haufen Kleingeld vorzufinden.

In dieser Ehe wurde nach ein paar Jahren ein Knabe geboren und mit derselben Sparsamkeit erzogen. »All wedder 'n Dreling umsünst utgeb'n!«, dies geflügelte Wort lief einmal durch die Stadt; Hans Adam hatte es seiner Frau zugeworfen, als sie ihrem Jungen am Werktag einen Sirupskuchen gekauft hatte. Trotz dieser dem Geize recht nahe verwandten Genauigkeit war und blieb der Kapitän ein zuverlässiger Geschäftsmann, der jeden ungeziemenden Vorteil von sich wies; nicht nur in Folge einer angeborenen Rechtschaffenheit, sondern ebensosehr seines Ehrgeizes. Den Platz im Schifferstuhle hatte er sich errungen; jetzt schwebten höhere Würden, denen er nichts vergeben durfte, vor seinen Sinnen; denn auch die Sitze im Magistratskollegium, wenn sie auch meist den größeren Familien angehörten, waren mitunter von dem kleineren Bürgerstande aus besetzt worden. Jedenfalls, seinem Heinz sollte der Weg dazu gebahnt werden; sagten die Leute doch, er sei sein Ebenbild: die fest auslugenden Augen, der Kopf voll schwarzbrauner Locken seien väterliche Erbschaft, nur statt des krummen Rückens habe er den schlanken Wuchs der Mutter.

Was Hans Kirch an Zärtlichkeit besaß, das gab er seinem Jungen; bei jeder Heimkehr lugte er schon vor dem Warder durch sein Glas, ob er am Hafenplatz ihn nicht gewahren könne; kamen dann nach der Landung Mutter und Kind auf Deck, so hob er zuerst den kleinen Heinz auf seinen Arm, bevor er seiner Frau die Hand zum Willkommen gab.

Als Heinz das sechste Jahr erreicht hatte, nahm ihn der Vater zum ersten Male mit sich auf die Fahrt, als »Spielvogel«, wie er sagte; die Mutter sah ihnen mit besorgten Augen nach; der Knabe aber freute sich über sein blankes Hütchen und lief jubelnd über das schmale Brett an Bord; er freute sich, schon jetzt ein Schiffer zu werden wie sein Vater, und nahm sich im stillen vor, recht tüchtig mitzuhelfen. Frühmorgens waren sie ausgelaufen; nun beschien sie die Mittagssonne auf der blauen Ostsee, über die ein lauer Sommerwind das Schiff nur langsam vorwärtstrieb. Nach dem Essen, bevor der Kapitän zur Mittagsruhe in die Kajüte ging, wurde Heinz dem Schiffsjungen anvertraut, der mit dem Spleißen zerrissener Taue auf dem Deck beschäftigt war; auch der Knabe erhielt ein paar Tauenden, die er eifrig ineinander zu verflechten strebte.

Nach einer Stunde etwa stieg Hans Kirch wieder aus seiner Kajüte und rief, noch halb im Taumel: »Heinz! Komm her, Heinz, wir wollen Kaffee trinken!« Aber weder der Knabe selbst noch eine Antwort kam auf diesen Ruf; statt dessen klang drüben vom Bugspriet her der Gesang einer Kinderstimme. Hans Kirch wurde blaß wie der Tod; denn dort, fast auf der äußersten Spitze, hatte er seinen Heinz erblickt. Auf der Luvseite, behaglich an das matt geschwellte Segel lehnend, saß der Knabe, als ob er hier von seiner Arbeit ruhe. Als er seinen Vater gewahrte, nickte er ihm freundlich zu; dann sang er unbekümmert weiter, während am Bug das Wasser rauschte; seine großen Kinderaugen leuchteten, sein schwarzbraunes Haar wehte in der sanften Brise.

Hans Kirch aber stand unbeweglich, gelähmt von der Ratlosigkeit der Angst; nur er wußte, wie leicht bei der schwachen Luftströmung das Segel flattern und vor seinen Augen das Kind in die Tiefe schleudern konnte. Er wollte rufen; aber noch zwischen den Zähnen erstickte er den Ruf; Kinder, wie Nachtwandler, muß man ja gewähren lassen; dann wieder wollte er das Boot aussetzen und nach dem Bug des Schiffes rudern; aber auch das verwarf er. Da kam von dem Knaben selbst die Entscheidung; das Singen hatte er satt, er wollte jetzt zu seinem Vater und dem seine Taue zeigen. Behutsam, entlang dem unteren Rande des Segels, das nach wie vor sich ihm zur Seite blähte, nahm er seinen Rückweg; eine Möwe schrie hoch oben in der Luft, er sah empor und kletterte dann ruhig weiter. Mit stockendem Atem stand Hans Kirch noch immer neben der Kajüte; seine Augen folgten jeder Bewegung seines Kindes, als ob er es mit seinen Blicken halten müsse. Da plötzlich, bei einer kaum merklichen Wendung des Schiffes, fuhr er mit dem Kopf herum: »Backbord!« schrie er nach der Steuerseite; »Backbord!«, als ob es ihm die Brust zersprengen solle. Und der Mann am Steuer folgte mit leisem Druck der Hand, und die eingesunkene Leinewand des Segels füllte sich aufs neue.

Im selben Augenblicke war der Knabe fröhlich aufs Verdeck gesprungen; nun lief er mit ausgebreiteten Armen auf den Vater zu. Die Zähne des gefahrgewohnten Mannes schlugen noch aneinander: »Heinz, Heinz, das tust du mir nicht wieder!« Krampfhaft preßte er den Knaben an sich; aber schon begann die überstandene Angst dem Zorne gegen ihren Urheber Platz zu machen. »Das tust du mir nicht wieder!« Noch einmal sagte er es; aber ein dumpfes Grollen klang jetzt in seiner Stimme; seine Hand hob sich, als wolle er sie auf den Knaben fallen lassen, der erstaunt und furchtsam zu ihm aufblickte.

Es sollte für diesmal nicht dahin kommen; der Zorn des Kapitäns sprang auf den Schiffsjungen über, der eben in seiner lässigen Weise an ihnen vorüberschieben wollte; aber mit entsetzten Augen mußte der kleine Heinz es ansehen, wie sein Freund Jürgen, er wußte nicht weshalb, von seinem Vater auf das grausamste gezüchtigt wurde.

– – Als im nächsten Frühjahr Hans Kirch seinen Heinz wieder einmal mit aufs Schiff nehmen wollte, hatte dieser sich versteckt und mußte, als er endlich aufgefunden wurde, mit Gewalt an Bord gebracht werden; auch saß er diesmal nicht mehr singend unterm Klüversegel; er fürchtete seinen Vater und trotzte ihm doch zugleich. Die Zärtlichkeit des letzteren kam gleicherweise immer seltener zutage, je mehr der eigne Wille in dem Knaben wuchs; glaubte er doch selber nur den Erben seiner aufstrebenden Pläne in dem Sohn zu lieben.

Als Heinz das zwölfte Jahr erreicht hatte, wurde ihm noch eine Schwester geboren, was der Vater als ein Ereignis aufnahm, das eben nicht zu ändern sei. Heinz war zu einem wilden Jungen aufgeschossen; aber in der Rektorschule hatte er nur noch wenige über sich. »Der hat Gaben!« meinte der junge Lehrer, »der könnte hier einmal die Kanzel zieren.« Aber Hans Kirch lachte: »Larifari, Herr Rektor! Ums Geld ist es nicht; aber man sieht doch gleich, daß Sie hier nicht zu Hause sind.«

Gleichwohl ging er noch an demselben Tage zu seinem Nachbaren, dem Pastoren, dessen Garten sich vor dem Hause bis zur Straße hinab erstreckte. Der Pastor empfing den Eintretenden etwas stramm: »Herr Kirch«, sagte er, bevor noch dieser das Wort zu nehmen vermochte, »Ihr Junge, der Heinz, hat mir schon wieder einmal die Scheiben in meinem Stallgiebel eingeworfen!«

»Hat er das«, erwiderte Hans Kirch, »so muß ich sie einsetzen lassen, und Heinz bekommt den Stock; denn das Spielwerk ist zu teuer.«

Dann, während der andre zustimmend nickte, begann er mit dem, was ihn hergeführt, herauszurücken: der Pastor sollte seinen Heinz in die Privatstunden aufnehmen, welche er zur Aufbesserung seines etwas schmalen Ehrensoldes einigen Kostgängern und Söhnen der Honoratioren zu erteilen pflegte. Als dieser sich nach einigen Fragen bereit erklärte, machte Hans Kirch noch einen Versuch, das Stundengeld herabzudrücken; da aber der Pastor nicht darauf zu hören schien, so wiederholte er ihn nicht; denn Heinz sollte mehr lernen, als jetzt noch in der Rektorschule für ihn zu holen war.

Am Abend dieses Tages erhielt Heinz die angelobte Strafe und am Nachmittage des folgenden, als er zwischen den andern Schülern oben in des Pastors Studierzimmer saß, von Wohlehrwürden noch einen scharf gesalzenen Text dazu. Kaum aber war nach glücklich verflossener Stunde die unruhige Schar die Treppe hinab und in den

Garten hinaus gestürmt, als der erlöste Mann von dorten unter seinem Fenster ein lautes Wehgeheul vernahm. »Ich will dich klickern lehren!« rief eine wütende Knabenstimme, und wiederum erscholl das klägliche Geheul. Als aber der Pastor sein Fenster öffnete, sah er unten nur seinen fahlblonden Kostgänger, der ihm am Morgen Heinzens Missetat verraten hatte, jetzt in eifriger Beschäftigung, mit seinem Schnuptuch sich das Blut von Mund und Nase abzutrocknen. Daß er selbst an jenem Spielwerk mitgeholfen hatte, fand er freilich sich nicht veranlaßt zu verraten; aber ebenso wenig verriet er jetzt, wer ihm den blutigen Denkzettel auf den Weg gegeben hatte.

Der Pastor war des Segens eines Sohnes nicht teilhaftig geworden; nur zwei Töchter besaß er, einige Jahre jünger als Heinz und von nicht üblem Aussehen; aber Heinz kümmerte sich nicht um sie, und man hätte glauben können, daß auch er der Bubenregel folge, ein tüchtiger Junge dürfe sich nicht mit Dirnen abgeben, wenn in dem Hause dem Pastorgarten gegenüber nicht die kleine Wieb gewesen wäre. Ihre Mutter war die Frau eines Matrosen, eine Wäscherin, die ihr Kind sauberer hielt als, leider, ihren Ruf. »Deine Mutter ist auch eine Amphibie!« hatte einmal ein großer Junge dem Mädchen ins Gesicht geschrien, als eben in der Schule die Lehre von diesen Kreaturen vorgetragen war. – »Pfui doch, warum?« hatte entrüstet die kleine Wieb gefragt. – »Warum? Weil sie einen Mann zu Wasser und einen zu Lande hat!« – Der Vergleich hinkte; aber der Junge hatte doch seiner bösen Lust genuggetan.

Gleichwohl hielten die Pastortöchter eine Art von Spielkameradschaft mit dem Matrosenkinde; freilich meist nur für die Werkeltage und wenn die Töchter des Bürgermeisters nicht bei ihnen waren; wenn sie ihre weißen Kleider mit den blauen Schärpen trugen, spielten sie lieber nicht mit der kleinen Wieb. Trafen sie diese dann etwa still und schüchtern vor der Gartenpforte stehen oder hatte gar die jüngste, gutmütige Bürgermeisterstochter sie hereingeholt, dann sprachen sie wohl zu ihr sehr freundlich, aber auch sehr eilig. »Nicht wahr, kleine Wieb, du kommst doch morgen zu uns in den Garten?« Im Nachsommer steckten sie ihr auch wohl einen Apfel in die Tasche und sagten: »Wart, wir wollen dir noch einen mehr suchen!« und die kleine Wieb schlich dann mit ihren Äpfeln ganz begossen aus dem Garten auf die Gasse. Wenn aber Heinz darüber zukam, dann riß er sie ihr wohl wieder fort und warf sie zornig in den Garten zurück, mitten zwischen die geputzten Kinder, daß sie schreiend ins Haus stoben; und wenn dann Wieb über die Äpfel weinte, wischte er mit seinem Schnuptuch ihr die Tränen ab: »Sei ruhig, Wieb; für jeden Apfel hol ich dir morgen eine ganze Tasche voll aus ihrem Garten!« – Und sie wußte wohl, er pflegte Wort zu halten.

Wieb hatte ein Madonnengesichtlein, wie der kunstliebende Schulrektor einmal gesagt hatte, ein Gesichtlein, das man nicht gut leiden sehen konnte; aber die kleine Madonna aß gleichwohl gern des Pastors rote Äpfel, und Heinz stieg bei erster Gelegenheit in die Bäume und stahl sie ihr. Dann zitterte die kleine Wieb; nicht weil sie den Äpfeldiebstahl für eine Sünde hielt, sondern weil die größeren Kostgänger des Pastors ihren Freund dabei mitunter überfielen und ihm den Kopf zu bluten schlugen. Wenn aber nach wohl bestandenem Abenteuer Heinz ihr hinten nach der Allee gewinkt hatte, wenn er vor ihr auf dem Boden kniete und seinen Raub in ihre Täschchen pfropfte, dann lächelte sie ihn ganz glückselig an, und der kräftige Knabe hob seinen Schützling mit beiden Armen in die Luft: »Wieb, Wiebchen, kleines Wiebchen!« rief er jubelnd; und er schwenkte sich mit ihr im Kreise, bis die roten Äpfel aus den Taschen flogen.

Mitunter auch, bei solchem Anlaß, nahm er die kleine Madonna bei der Hand und ging mit ihr hinunter an den Hafen. War auf den Schiffen alles unter Deck, dann löste er wohl ein Boot, ließ seinen Schützling sacht hineintreten und ruderte mit ihr um den Warder herum, weit in den Sund hinein; wurde der Raub des Bootes hinterher bemerkt und drangen nun von dem Schiffe zornige Scheltlaute über das Wasser zu ihnen herüber, dann begann er hell zu singen, damit die kleine Wieb nur nicht erschrecken möge; hatte sie es aber doch gehört, so ruderte er nur um so lustiger und rief: »Wir wollen weit von all den schlechten Menschen fort!« – Eines Nachmittages, da Hans Kirch mit seinem Schiffe auswärts war, wagten sie es sogar, drüben bei der Insel anzulegen, wo Wieb in dem großen Dorfe eine Verwandte wohnen hatte, die sie »Möddersch« nannte. Es war dort eben der große Michaelis-Jahrmarkt, und nachdem sie bei Möddersch eine Tasse Kaffee bekommen hatten, liefen sie zwischen die Buden und in den Menschendrang hinein, wo Heinz für sie beide mit tüchtigen Ellenbogenstößen Raum zu schaffen wußte. Sie waren schon im Karussell gefahren, hatten Kuchenherzen gegessen und bei mancher Drehorgel still gestanden, als Wiebs blaue Augen an einem silbernen Ringlein haften blieben, das zwischen Ketten und Löffeln in einer Goldschmiedsbude auslag. Hoffnungslos drehte sie ihr nur aus drei Kupfersechslingen bestehendes Vermögen zwischen den Fingern; aber Heinz, der gestern alle seine Kaninchen verkauft hatte, besaß nach der heutigen Verschwendung noch acht Schillinge, und dafür und für die drei Sechslinge wurde glücklich der Ring erhandelt. Nun freilich waren beider Taschen leer; zum Karussell für Wieb spendierte Möddersch noch einmal einen Schilling – denn so viel kostete es, da Wieb nicht wie vorhin in einem Stuhle fahren, sondern auf dem großen Löwen reiten wollte –; dann, als eben alle Lampen zwischen den schmelz- und goldgestickten Draperien angezündet wurden, waren für sie die Freuden aus, und auch die alte Frau trieb jetzt zur Rückfahrt. Manchmal, während Heinz mit kräftigen Schlägen seine Ruder brauchte, blickten sie noch zurück, und das Herz wurde ihnen groß, wenn sie im zunehmenden Abenddunkel den Lichtschein

von den vielen Karussellampen über der Stelle des unsicht-
baren Dorfes schweben sahen; aber Wieb hatte ihren silbernen Ring, den sie nun nicht mehr von ihrem Finger ließ.

Inzwischen hatte Kapitän Kirch seine Jacht verkauft. Mit
einem stattlichen Schoner, der auf der heimischen Werft
gebaut worden war, brachte er für fremde und mehr und
mehr für eigne Rechnung Korn nach England und nahm
als Rückfracht Kohlen wieder mit. So war zu dem Korn-
nun auch ein Kohlenhandel gekommen, und auch diesen
mußte, gleich der Milchwirtschaft, die Frau besorgen. Um
seinen Heinz, wenn er bei seiner Heimkehr auf die kurze
Frage »Hat der Junge sich geschickt?« von der Mutter eine
bejahende Antwort erhalten hatte, schien er sich im übrigen nicht groß zu kümmern; nur beim Quartalschlusse
pflegte er den Rektor und den Pastor zu besuchen, um zu
erfahren, wie der Junge lerne. Dann hieß es allemal, das
Lernen sei ihm nur ein Spiel, es bleibe dabei nur zuviel un-
nütze Zeit ihm übrig; denn wild sei er wie ein Teufel, kein
Junge ihm zu groß und keine Spitze ihm zu hoch.

Auf Hans Adams Antlitz hatte sich, nach Aussage des
Schulrektors, mehrmals bei solcher Auskunft ein recht un-
geeignetes und fast befriedigtes Lächeln gezeigt, während
er mit einem kurz hervorgestoßenen »Na, na!« zum Ab-
schiede ihm die Hand gedrückt habe.

Wie recht übrigens auch Heinzens Lehrer haben mochten, so blieb doch das Schutzverhältnis zu der kleinen
Wieb dasselbe, und davon wußte mancher frevle Junge
nachzusagen. Auch sah man ihn wohl an Sonntagen mit
seiner Mutter nach einem dürftigen, unweit der Stadt belegenen Wäldchen wandern und bei der Rückkehr nebst
dem leeren Proviantkorbe sein Schwesterchen auf dem
Rücken tragen. Mitunter war auch die allmählich auf-
wachsende Wieb bei dieser Sonntagswanderung. Die stille
Frau Kirch hätte Gefallen an dem feinen Mädchen und

pflegte zu sagen: »Laß sie nur mitgehen, Heinz; so ist sie doch nicht bei der schlechten Mutter.«

Nach seiner Konfirmation mußte Heinz ein paar Fahrten auf seines Vaters Schiffe machen, nicht mehr als »Spielvogel«, sondern als streng gehaltener Schiffsjunge; aber er fügte sich, und nach der ersten Rückkehr klopfte Kapitän Kirch ihm auf die Schulter, während er seiner Frau durch ein kurzes Nicken ihren Anteil an seiner Befriedigung zukommen ließ. Die zweite Reise geschah mit einem Setzschiffer; denn der wachsende Handel daheim verlangte die persönliche Gegenwart des Geschäftsherrn. Dann, nach zwei weiteren Fahrten auf größeren Schiffen, war Heinz als Matrose in das elterliche Haus zurückgekehrt. Er war jetzt siebzehn Jahre; die blaue schirmlose Schiffermütze mit dem bunten Rande und den flatternden Bändern ließ ihm so gut zu seinem frischen braunen Antlitz, daß selbst die Pastorstöchter durch den Zaun lugten, wenn sie ihn nebenan im elterlichen Garten mit seiner Schwester spielen hörten. Auch Kapitän Kirch selber konnte es sonntags beim Gottesdienste nicht unterlassen, von seinem Schifferstuhle nach unten in die Kirche hinabzuschielen, wo sein schmucker Junge bei der Mutter saß. Unterweilen schweiften auch wohl seine Blicke drüben nach dem Epitaphe, wo zwischen mannigfachen Siegestrophäen sich die Marmorbüste eines stattlichen Mannes in gewaltiger Allongeperücke zeigte; gleich seinem Heinz nur eines Bürgers Sohn, der gleichwohl als Kommandeur von dreien Seiner Majestät Schiffen hier in die Vaterstadt zurückgekommen war. Aber nein, so hohe Pläne hatte Hans Kirch doch nicht mit seinem Jungen, vorläufig galt es eine Reise mit dem Hamburger Schiffe »Hammonia« in die chinesischen Gewässer, von der die Rückkehr nicht vor einem Jahr erfolgen würde; und heute war der letzte Tag im elterlichen Hause.

Die Mutter hatte diesmal nicht ohne Tränen ihres Sohnes Kiste gepackt, und nach der Rückkehr aus der Kirche

14

legte sie noch ihr eigenes Gesangbuch obenauf. Der Vater hatte auch in den letzten Tagen außer dem Notwendigen nicht viel mit seinem Sohn gesprochen; nur an diesem Abend, als er auf dem dunkeln Hausflur ihm begegnete, griff er nach seiner Hand und schüttelte sie heftig: »Ich sitze hier nicht still, Heinz; für dich, nur für dich! Und komm auch glücklich wieder!« Hastig hatte er es hervorgestoßen; dann ließ er die Hand seines Sohnes fahren und trabte eilig nach dem Hof hinaus.

Überrascht blickte ihm Heinz eine Weile nach; aber seine Gedanken waren anderswo. Er hatte Wieb am Tage vorher wiedergesehen; doch nur zu ein paar flüchtigen Worten war Gelegenheit gewesen; nun wollte er noch Abschied von ihr nehmen, sie wie sonst noch einmal um den Warder fahren.

Es war ein kühler Maiabend; der Mond stand über dem Wasser, als er an den Hafen hinabkam; aber Wieb war noch nicht da. Freilich hatte sie ihm gesagt, daß sie abends bei einer alten Dame einige leichte Dienste zu versehen habe; des ungeachtet, während er an dem einsamen Bollwerk auf und ab ging, konnte er seine Ungeduld kaum niederzwingen: er schalt sich selbst und wußte nicht, weshalb das Klopfen seines Blutes ihm fast den Atem raubte. Endlich sah er sie aus der höher belegenen Straße herabkommen. Bei dem Mondlicht, das ihr voll entgegenfiel, erschien sie ihm so groß und schlank, daß er erst fast verzagte, ob sie es wirklich sei. Gleichwohl hatte sie den Oberkörper in ein großes Tuch vermummt; einer Kopfbedeckung bedurfte sie nicht, denn das blonde Haar lag voll wie ein Häubchen über ihrem zarten Antlitz. »Guten Abend, Heinz!« sagte sie leise, als sie jetzt zu ihm trat; und schüchtern, fast wie ein Fremder, berührte er ihre Hand, die sie ihm entgegenstreckte. Schweigend führte er sie zu einem Boot, das neben einer großen Kuff im Wasser lag. »Komm nur!« sagte er, als er hineingetreten war und der auf der Hafentreppe Zögernden die Arme entgegenstreckte; »ich habe Erlaubnis, wir werden diesmal nicht gescholten.«

Als er sie in seinen Armen aufgefangen hatte, löste er die Taue, und das Boot glitt aus dem Schatten des großen Schiffes auf die weite, mondglitzernde Wasserfläche hinaus.

Sie saß ihm auf der Bank am Hinterspiegel gegenüber; aber sie fuhren schon um die Spitze des Warders, wo einige Möwen gackernd aus dem Schlafe auffuhren, und noch immer war kein weiteres Wort zwischen ihnen laut geworden. So vieles hatte Heinz der kleinen Wieb in dieser letzten Stunde sagen wollen, und nun war der Mund ihm wie verschlossen. Und auch das Mädchen, je weiter sie hinausfuhren, je mehr zugleich die kurze Abendzeit verrann, desto stiller und beklommener saß sie da; zwar seine Augen verschlangen fast die kindliche Gestalt, mit der er jetzt so einsam zwischen Meer und Himmel schwebte; die ihren aber waren in die Nacht hinausgewandt. Dann stieg's wohl plötzlich in ihm auf, und das Boot schütterte unter seinen Ruderschlägen, daß sie jäh das Köpfchen wandte und das blaue Leuchten ihrer Augen in die seinen traf. Aber auch das flog rasch vorüber, und es war etwas wie Zorn, das über ihn kam, er wußte nicht, ob gegen sich selber oder gegen sie, daß sie so fremd ihm gegenübersaß, daß alle Worte, die ihm durch den Kopf fuhren, zu ihr nicht passen wollten. Mit Gewalt rief er es sich zurück: hatte er doch draußen schon mehr als einmal die trotzigste Dirne im Arm geschwenkt, auch wohl ein übermütiges Wort ihr zugeraunt; aber freilich, der jungfräulichen Gestalt ihm gegenüber verschlug auch dieses Mittel nicht.

»Wieb«, sagte er endlich, und es klang fast bittend, »kleine Wieb, das ist nun heut für lange Zeit das letzte Mal.«

»Ja, Heinz«, und sie nickte und sah zu Boden; »ich weiß es wohl.« Es war, als ob sie noch etwas andres sagen wollte, aber sie sagte es nicht. Das schwere Tuch war ihr von der Schulter geglitten; als sie es wieder aufgerafft hatte und nun mit ihrer Hand über der Brust zusammenhielt, vermißte er den kleinen Ring an ihrem Finger, den er einst auf dem Jahrmarkte ihr hatte einhandeln helfen. »Dein Ring, Wieb!« rief er unwillkürlich. »Wo hast du deinen Ring gelassen?«

Einen Augenblick noch saß sie unbeweglich; dann richtete sie sich auf und trat über die nächste Bank zu ihm hinüber. Sie mußte in dem schwankenden Boot die eine Hand auf seine Schulter legen, mit der andern langte sie in den Schlitz ihres Kleides und zog eine Schnur hervor, woran der Ring befestigt war. Mit stockendem Atem nahm sie ihrem Freunde die Mütze von den braunen Locken und hing die Schnur ihm um den Hals. »Heinz, o bitte, Heinz!« Der volle blaue Strahl aus ihren Augen ruhte in den seinen; dann stürzten ihre Tränen auf sein Angesicht, und die beiden jungen Menschen fielen sich um den Hals, und da hat der wilde Heinz die kleine Wieb fast totgeküßt.

– – Es mußte schon spät sein, als sie ihr Boot nach dem großen Schiff zurückbrachten; sie hatten keine Stunden schlagen hören; aber alle Lichter in der Stadt schienen ausgelöscht.

Als Heinz an das elterliche Haus kam, fand er die Tür verschlossen; auf sein Klopfen antwortete die Mutter vom Flure aus; aber der Vater war schon zur Ruhe gegangen und hatte den Schlüssel mitgenommen; endlich hörte Heinz auch dessen Schritte, wie sie langsam von droben aus der Kammer die Treppe hinabkamen. Dann wurde schweigend die Tür geöffnet und, nachdem Heinz hineingelassen war, ebenso wieder zugeschlossen; erst als er seinen »Guten Abend« vorbrachte, sah Hans Kirch ihn an: »Hast du die Bürgerglocke nicht gehört? Wo hast du dich umhergetrieben?«

Der Sohn sah den Jähzorn in seines Vaters Augen aufsteigen; er wurde blaß bis unter seine dunkeln Locken, aber er sagte ruhig: »Nicht umhergetrieben, Vater«; und seine Hand faßte unwillkürlich nach dem kleinen Ringe, den er unter seiner offnen Weste barg.

Aber Hans Kirch hatte zu lange auf seinen Sohn gewartet. »Hüte dich!« schrie er und zuckte mit dem schweren Schlüssel gegen seines Sohnes Haupt. »Klopf nicht noch einmal so an deines Vaters Tür! Sie könnte dir verschlossen bleiben.«

Heinz hatte sich hoch aufgerichtet; das Blut war ihm ins Gesicht geschossen; aber die Mutter hatte die Arme um seinen Hals gelegt, und die heftige Antwort unterblieb, die schon auf seinen Lippen saß. »Gute Nacht, Vater!« sagte er, und schweigend die Hand der Mutter drückend, wandte er sich ab und ging die Treppe hinauf in seine Kammer.

Am andern Tage war er fort. Die Mutter ging still umher in dem ihr plötzlich öd gewordenen Hause; die kleine Wieb trug schwer an ihrem jungen Herzen; nachdenklich und fast zärtlich betrachtete sie auf ihrem Arm die roten Striemen, durch welche die Mutter für die Störung ihrer Nachtruhe sich an ihr erholt hatte; waren sie ihr doch fast wie ein Andenken an Heinz, das sie immer hätte behalten mögen; nur Hans Kirchs Dichten und Trachten strebte schon wieder rüstig in die Zukunft.

Nach sechs Wochen war ein Brief von Heinz gekommen; er brachte gute Nachricht; wegen kecken Zugreifens im rechten Augenblick hatte der Kapitän freiwillig seine Heuer erhöht. Die Mutter trat herein, als ihr Mann den Brief soeben in die Tasche steckte. »Ich darf doch auch mit lesen?« frug sie scheu. »Du hast doch gute Nachricht?«

»Ja, ja«, sagte Hans Kirch; »nun, nichts Besonders, als daß er dich und seine Schwester grüßen läßt.«

Am Tage darauf aber begann er allerlei Gänge in der Stadt zu machen; in die großen Häuser mit breiten Beischlägen und unter dunklem Lindenschatten sah man ihn der Reihe nach hineingehen. Wer konnte wissen, wie bald der Junge sein Steuermannsexamen hinter sich haben würde; da galt es auch für ihn noch eine Stufe höher aufzurücken.

18

Im Deputierten-Kollegium hatte er bereits einige Jahre gesessen; jetzt war ein Ratsherrnstuhl erledigt, der von den übrigen Mitgliedern des Rates zu besetzen war.

Aber Hans Adams Hoffnungen wurden getäuscht; auf dem erledigten Stuhl saß nach einigen Tagen sein bisheriger Kollege, ein dicker Bäckermeister, mit dem er freilich weder an Reichtum noch an Leibesgewicht sich messen durfte. Verdrießlich war er eben aus einer Deputiertensitzung gekommen, wo nun der Platz des Bäckers leer geworden war, und stand noch, an einem Tabakendchen seinen Groll zerkauend, unter dem Schwanz des Riesenfisches, den sie Anno Siebenzig hier gefangen und zum Gedächtnis neben der Rathaustür aufgehangen hatten, als ein ältliches, aber wehrhaftes Frauenzimmer über den Markt und grade auf ihn zukam; ein mit zwei großen Schinken beladener Junge folgte ihr.

»Das ging den verkehrten Weg, Hans Adam!« rief sie ihm schon von weitem zu.

Hans Adam hob den Kopf. »Du brauchst das nicht über die Straße hinzuschreien, Jule; ich weiß das ohne dich.«

Es war seine ältere Schwester, die nach ihres Mannes Tode mit der Kirchschen Rührigkeit eine Speckhökerei betrieb. »Warum sollte ich nicht schreien?« rief sie wiederum, »mir kann's recht sein, wenn sie es alle hören! Du bist ein Geizhals, Hans Adam; aber du hast einen scharfen Kopf, und den können die regierenden Herren nicht gebrauchen, wenn er nicht zufällig auf ihren eignen Schultern sitzt; da paßt ihnen so eine blonde Semmel besser, wenn sie denn doch einmal an uns Mittelbürgern nicht vorbei können.«

»Du erzählst mir ganz was Neues!« sagte der Bruder ärgerlich.

»Ja, ja, Hans Adam, du bist auch mir zu klug, sonst säßest du nicht so halb umsonst in unserem elterlichen Hause!«

Die brave Frau konnte es noch immer nicht verwinden, daß von einem Kauflustigen ihrem Bruder einst ein höherer Preis geboten war, als wofür er das Haus in der Nachlaßteilung übernommen hatte. Aber Hans Kirch war diesen Vorwurf schon gewohnt, er achtete nicht mehr darauf, zum mindesten schien es für ihn in diesem Augenblicke nur ein Spornstich, um sich von dem erhaltenen Schlage plötzlich wieder aufzurichten. Äußerlich zwar ließ er den Kopf hängen, als sähe er etwas vor sich auf dem Straßenpflaster; seine Gedanken aber waren schon rastlos tätig, eine neue Bahn nach seinem Ziele hinzuschaufeln: das war ihm klar, es mußte noch mehr erworben und – noch mehr erspart werden; dem Druck des Silbers mußte bei wiederkehrender Gelegenheit auch diese Pforte noch sich öffnen; und sollte es für ihn selbst nicht mehr gelingen, für seinen Heinz, bei dessen besserer Schulbildung und stattlicherem Wesen würde es damit schon durchzubringen sein, sobald er seine Seemannsjahre nach Gebrauch als Kapitän beschlossen hätte.

Mit einer raschen Bewegung hob Hans Adam seinen Kopf empor. »Weißt du, Jule«, – er tat wie beiläufig diese Frage – »ob dein Nachbar Schmüser seinen großen Speicher noch verkaufen will?«

Frau Jule, die mit ihrer letzten Äußerung ihn zu einer ganz andern Antwort hatte reizen wollen und so lange schon darauf gewartet hatte, meinte ärgerlich, da tue er am besten, selbst darum zu fragen.

»Ja, ja; da hast du recht.« Er nickte kurz und hatte schon ein paar Schritte der Straße zu getan, in der Fritz Schmüser wohnte, als die Schwester, unachtend des Jungen, der seitwärts unter seinen Schinken stöhnte, ihn noch einmal festzuhalten suchte; so wohlfeil sollte er denn doch nicht davonkommen. »Hans Adam!« rief sie; »wart noch einen Augenblick! Dein Heinz . . .«

Hans Adam stand bei diesem Namen plötzlich still. »Was willst du, Jule?« frug er hastig. »Was soll das mit meinem Heinz?«

»Nicht viel, Hans Adam; aber du weißt wohl nicht, was

20

dein gewitzter Junge noch am letzten Abend hier getrieben hat?«

»Nun?« stieß er hervor, als sie eine Pause machte, um erst die Wirkung dieses Eingangs abzuwarten; »sag's nur gleich auf einmal, Jule; ein Loblied sitzt doch nicht dahinter!«

»Je nachdem, Hans Adam, je nachdem! Bei der alten Tante war zum Adesagen freilich nicht viel Zeit; aber warum sollte er die schmucke Wieb, die kleine Matrosendirne, nicht von neun bis elf spazierenfahren? Es möchte wohl ein kalt Vergnügen gewesen sein da draußen auf dem Sund; aber wir Alten wissen's ja wohl noch, die Jugend hat allezeit ihr eigen Feuer bei sich.«

Hans Adam zitterte, seine Oberlippe zog sich auf und legte seine vollen Zähne bloß. »Schwatz nicht!« sagte er. »Sprich lieber, woher weißt du das?«

»Woher?« Frau Jule schlug ein fröhliches Gelächter auf – »das weiß die ganze Stadt, am besten Christian Jensen, in dessen Boot die Lustfahrt vor sich ging! Aber du bist ein Hitzkopf, Hans Adam, bei dem man sich leicht üblen Bescheid holen kann; und wer weiß denn auch, ob dir die schmucke Schwiegertochter recht ist? Im übrigen« – und sie faßte den Bruder an seinem Rockkragen und zog ihn dicht zu sich heran – »für die neue Verwandtschaft ist's doch so am besten, daß du nicht auf den Ratsherrnstuhl hinaufgekommen bist.«

Als sie solcherweise ihre Worte glücklich angebracht hatte, trat sie zurück. »Komm, Peter, vorwärts!« rief sie dem Jungen zu, und bald waren beide in einer der vom Markte auslaufenden Gassen verschwunden.

Hans Kirch stand noch wie angedonnert auf derselben Stelle. Nach einer Weile setzte er sich mechanisch in Bewegung und ging der Gasse zu, worin Fritz Schmüsers Speicher lag; dann aber kehrte er plötzlich wieder um. Bald darauf saß er zu Hause an seinem Pult und schrieb mit fliegender Feder einen Brief an seinen Sohn, in welchem in

21

verstärktem Maße sich der jähe Zorn ergoß, dessen Ausbruch an jenem letzten Abend durch die Dazwischenkunft der Mutter war verhindert worden.

Monate waren vergangen; die Plätze, von denen aus Heinz nach Abrede hätte schreiben sollen, mußten längst passiert sein, aber Heinz schrieb nicht; dann kamen Nachrichten von dem Schiffe, aber kein Brief von ihm. Hans Kirch ließ sich das so sehr nicht anfechten: »Er wird schon kommen«, sagte er zu sich selber; »er weiß gar wohl, was hier zu Haus für ihn zu holen ist.« Und somit, nachdem er den Schmüserschen Speicher um billigen Preis erworben hatte, arbeitete er rüstig an der Ausbreitung seines Handels und ließ sich keine Müh' verdrießen. Freilich, wenn er von den dadurch veranlaßten Reisen, teils nach den Hafenstädten des Inlandes, einmal sogar mit seinem Schoner nach England, wieder heimkehrte, »Brief von Heinz?« war jedesmal die erste hastige Frage an seine Frau, und immer war ein trauriges Kopfschütteln die einzige Antwort, die er darauf erhielt.

Die Sorge, der auch er allmählich sich nicht hatte erwehren können, wurde zerstreut, als die Zeitungen die Rückkehr der »Hammonia« meldeten. Hans Kirch ging unruhig in Haus und Hof umher, und Frau und Tochter hörten ihn oft heftig vor sich hin reden; denn der Junge mußte jetzt ja selber kommen, und er hatte sich vorgesetzt, ihm scharf den Kopf zu waschen. Aber eine Woche verging, die zweite ging auch bald zu Ende, und Heinz war nicht gekommen. Auf eingezogene Erkundigung erfuhr man endlich, er habe auf der Rückfahrt nach Abkommen mit dem Kapitän eine neue Heuer angenommen; wohin, war nicht zu ermitteln. »Er will mir trotzen!« dachte Hans Adam. »Sehen wir, wer's am längsten aushält von uns beiden!« – Die Mutter, welche nichts von jenem Briefe ihres Mannes wußte, ging in kummervollem Grübeln und konnte ihren Jungen nicht begreifen; wagte sie es einmal, ihren

Mann nach Heinz zu fragen, so blieb er entweder ganz die Antwort schuldig oder hieß sie, ihm mit dem Jungen ein für allemal nicht mehr zu kommen.

In einem zwar unterschied er sich von der gemeinen Art der Männer: er bürdete der armen Mutter nicht die Schuld an diesen Übelständen auf; im übrigen aber war mit Hans Adam jetzt kein leichter Hausverkehr.

Sommer und Herbst gingen hin, und je weiter die Zeit verrann, desto fester wurzelte der Groll in seinem Herzen; der Name seines Sohnes wurde im eignen Hause nicht mehr ausgesprochen, und auch draußen scheute man sich, nach Heinz zu fragen.

Schon wurde es wieder Frühling, als er eines Morgens von seiner Haustür aus den Herrn Pastor mit der Pfeife am Zaune seines Vorgartens stehen sah. Hans Kirch hatte Geschäfte weiter oben in der Straße und wollte mit stummem Hutrücken vorbeipassieren; aber der Nachbar Pastor rief mit aller Würde pfarramtlicher Überlegenheit ganz laut zu ihm hinüber: »Nun, Herr Kirch, noch immer keine Nachricht von dem Heinz?«

Hans Adam fuhr zusammen, aber er blieb stehen, die Frage war ihm lange nicht geboten worden. »Reden wir von was anderem, wenn's gefällt, Herr Pastor!« sagte er kurz und hastig.

Allein der Pastor fand sich zur Befolgung dieser Bitte nicht veranlaßt. »Mein lieber Herr Kirch, es ist nun fast das zweite Jahr herum; Sie sollten sich doch einmal wieder um den Sohn bekümmern!«

»Ich dächte, Herr Pastor, nach dem vierten Gebote wär' das umgekehrt!«

Der Pastor tat die Pfeife aus dem Munde: »Aber nicht nach dem Gebote, in welchem nach des Herren Wort die andern all enthalten sind, und was wäre Euch näher als Euer eigen Fleisch und Blut!«

»Weiß nicht, Ehrwürden«, sagte Hans Kirch, »ich halte mich ans vierte.«

Es war etwas in seiner Stimme, das es dem Pastor rätlich machte, nicht mehr in diesem Tone fortzufahren. »Nun, nun«, sagte er begütigend, »er wird ja schon wiederkehren, und wenn er kommt, er ist ja von Ihrer Art, Herr Nachbar, so wird es nicht mit leeren Händen sein!«

Etwas von dem Schmunzeln, das sich bei dieser letzten Rede auf des Pastors Antlitz zeigte, war doch auch auf das des anderen übergegangen, und während sich der erstere mit einer grüßenden Handbewegung nach seinem Hause zurückwandte, trabte Hans Kirch munterer als seit lange die Straße hinauf nach seinem großen Speicher.

Es war am Tage danach, als der alte Postbote dieselbe Straße hinabschritt. Er ging rasch und hielt einen dicken Brief in der Hand, den er schon im Vorwege aus seiner Ledertasche hervorgeholt zu haben schien; aber ebenso rasch schritt, lebhaft auf ihn einredend, ein etwa sechzehnjähriges blondes Mädchen an seiner Seite. »Von einem guten Bekannten, sagst du? Nein, narre mich nicht länger, alter Marten! Sag's doch, von wem ist er denn?«

»Ei, du junger Dummbart«, rief der Alte, indem er mit dem Briefe ihr vor den Augen gaukelte, »kann ich das wissen? Ich weiß nur, an wen ich ihn zu bringen habe.«

»An wen, an wen denn, Marten?«

Er stand einen Augenblick und hielt die Schriftseite des Briefes ihr entgegen.

Die geöffneten Mädchenlippen versandten einen Laut, der nicht zu einem Wort gedieh.

»Von Heinz!« kam es dann schüchtern hintennach, und wie eine helle Lohe brannte die Freude auf dem jungen Antlitz.

Der Alte sah sie freundlich an. »Von Heinz?« wiederholte er schelmisch. »Ei, Wiebchen, mit den Augen ist das nicht darauf zu lesen!«

Sie sagte nichts; aber als er jetzt in der Richtung nach dem Kirchschen Hause zuschritt, lief sie noch immer nebenher.

»Nun?« rief er, »du denkst wohl, daß ich auch für dich noch einen in der Tasche hätte?«

Da blieb sie plötzlich stehen, und während sie traurig ihr Köpfchen schüttelte, ging der Bote mit dem dicken Briefe fort.

Als er die Kirchsche Wohnung betrat, kam eben die Hausmutter mit einem dampfenden Schüsselchen aus der Küche; sie wollte damit in das Oberhaus, wo im Giebelstübchen die kleine Lina an den Masern lag. Aber Marten rief sie an: »Frau Kirch! Frau Kirch! Was geben Sie für diesen Brief?«

Und schon hatte sie die an ihren Mann gerichtete Adresse gelesen und die Schrift erkannt. »Heinz!« rief auch sie, »oh, von Heinz!« und wie ein Jubel brach es aus dieser stillen Brust. Da kam von oben her die Kinderstimme: »Mutter! Mutter!«

»Gleich, gleich, mein Kind!« Und nach einem dankbaren Nicken gegen den Boten flog sie die Treppen hinauf. »O Lina, Lina! Von Heinz, ein Brief von unserm Heinz!«

Im Wohnzimmer unten saß Hans Kirch an seinem Pulte, zwei aufgeschlagene Handelsbücher vor sich, er war mit seinem Verlustkonto beschäftigt, das sich diesmal ungewöhnlich groß erwiesen hatte. Verdrießlich hörte er das laute Reden draußen, das ihn in seiner Rechnung störte; als der Postbote hereintrat, fuhr er ihn an: »Was treibt Er denn für Lärmen draußen mit der Frau?«

Statt einer Antwort überreichte Marten ihm den Brief.

Fast grollend betrachtete er die Aufschrift mit seinen scharfen Augen, die noch immer der Brille nicht bedurften. »Von Heinz«, brummte er, nachdem er alle Stempel aufmerksam besichtigt hatte, »Zeit wär's denn auch einmal!«

Vergebens wartete der alte Marten, auch aus des Vaters Augen einen Freudenblitz zu sehen; nur ein Zittern der Hand – wie er zu seinem Trost bemerkte – konnte dieser nicht bewältigen, als er jetzt nach einer Schere langte, um den Brief zu öffnen. Und schon hatte er sie angesetzt, als

Marten seinen Arm berührte: »Herr Kirch, ich darf wohl noch um dreißig Schilling bitten!«

– »Wofür?« – er warf die Schere hin – »ich bin der Post nichts schuldig!«

»Herr, Sie sehen ja wohl, der Brief ist nicht frankiert.«

Er hatte es nicht gesehen; Hans Adam biß die Zähne aufeinander: dreißig Schillinge; warum denn auch nicht die noch zum Verlust geschrieben! Aber – die Bagatelle, die war's ja nicht; nein – was dahinterstand! Was hatte doch der Pastor neulich hingeredet? Er würde nicht mit leeren Händen kommen! – Nicht mit leeren Händen! – Hans Adam lachte grimmig in sich hinein. – Nicht mal das Porto hatte er gehabt! Und der, der sollte im Magistrat den Sitz erobern, der für ihn, den Vater, sich zu hoch erwiesen hatte!

Hans Kirch saß stumm und starr an seinem Pulte; nur im Gehirne tobten ihm die Gedanken. Sein Schiff, sein Speicher, alles, was er in so vielen Jahren schwer erworben hatte, stieg vor ihm auf und addierte wie von selber die stattlichen Summen seiner Arbeit. Und das, das alles sollte er diesem... Er dachte den Satz nicht mehr zu Ende; sein Kopf brannte, es brauste ihm vor den Ohren. »Lump!« schrie er plötzlich, »so kommst du nicht in deines Vaters Haus!«

Der Brief war dem erschrockenen Boten vor die Füße geschleudert. »Nimm«, schrie er, »ich kauf ihn nicht; der ist für mich zu teuer!« Und Hans Kirch griff zur Feder und blätterte in seinen Kontobüchern.

Der gutmütige Alte hatte den Brief aufgehoben und versuchte bescheiden noch einige Überredung; aber der Hausherr trieb ihn fort, und er war nur froh, die Straße zu erreichen, ohne daß er der Mutter zum zweiten Mal begegnet wäre.

Als er seinen Weg nach dem Südende der Stadt fortsetzte, kam Wieb eben von dort zurück; sie hatte in einer Brennerei, welche hier das letzte Haus bildete, eine Bestellung ausgerichtet. Ihre Mutter war nach dem plötzlichen Tode »ihres Mannes zur See« in aller Form Rechtens die Frau »ihres Mannes auf dem Lande« geworden und hatte mit diesem eine Matrosenschenke am Hafenplatz errichtet. Viel Gutes wurde von der neuen Wirtschaft nicht geredet; aber wenn an Herbstabenden die über der Haustür brennende rote Lampe ihren Schein zu den Schiffen hinabwarf, so saß es da drinnen in der Schenkstube bald Kopf an Kopf, und der Brenner draußen am Stadtende hatte dort gute Kundschaft.

Als Wieb sich dem alten Postboten näherte, bemerkte sie sogleich, daß er jetzt recht mürrisch vor sich hin sah; und dann – er hatte ja den Brief von Heinz noch immer in der Hand. »Marten!« rief sie – sie hätte es nicht lassen können –, »der Brief, hast du ihn noch? War denn sein Vater nicht zu Hause?«

Marten machte ein grimmiges Gesicht. »Nein, Kind, sein Vater war wohl nicht zu Hause; der alte Hans Kirch war da; aber für den war der Brief zu teuer.«

Die blauen Mädchenaugen blickten ihn erschrocken an. »Zu teuer, Marten?«

– »Ja, ja; was meinst du, unter dreißig Schillingen war er nicht zu haben.«

Nach diesen Worten steckte Marten den Brief in seine Ledertasche und trat mit einem andern, den er gleichzeitig hervorgezogen hatte, in das nächste Haus.

Wieb blieb auf der Gasse stehen. Einen Augenblick noch sah sie auf die Tür, die sich hinter dem alten Mann geschlossen hatte; dann, als käme ihr plötzlich ein Gedanke, griff sie in ihre Tasche und klimperte darin, als wie mit kleiner Silbermünze. Ja, Wieb hatte wirklich Geld in ihrer Tasche; sie zählte es sogar, und es war eine ganze Handvoll, die sie schon am Vormittage hinter dem Schenktisch eingenommen hatte. Zwar, es gehörte nicht ihr, das wußte sie recht wohl; aber was kümmerte sie das, und mochte ihre Mutter sie doch immer dafür schlagen! »Marten«, sagte sie

27

hastig, als dieser jetzt wieder aus dem Hause trat, und streckte eine Handvoll kleiner Münze ihm entgegen, »da ist das Geld, Marten; gib mir den Brief!«

Marten sah sie voll Verwunderung an.

»Gib ihn doch!« drängte sie. »Hier sind ja deine dreißig Schillinge!« Und als der Alte den Kopf schüttelte, faßte sie mit der freien Hand an seine Tasche: »Oh, bitte, bitte, lieber Marten, ich will ihn ja nur einmal zusammen mit seiner Mutter lesen.«

»Kind«, sagte er, indem er ihre Hand ergriff und ihr freundlich in die angstvollen Augen blickte, »wenn's nach mir ginge, so wollten wir den Handel machen; aber selbst der Postmeister darf dir keinen Brief verkaufen.« Er wandte sich von ihr ab und schritt auf seinem Botenwege weiter.

Aber sie lief ihm nach, sie hing sich an seinen Arm, ihr einfältiger Mund hatte die holdesten Bitt- und Schmeichelworte für den alten Marten und ihr Kopf die allerdümmsten Einfälle; nur leihen sollte er ihr zum mindesten den Brief; er sollte ihn ja noch heute abend wieder haben.

Der alte Marten geriet in große Bedrängnis mit seinem weichen Herzen; aber ihm blieb zuletzt nichts übrig, er mußte das Kind gewaltsam von sich stoßen.

Da blieb sie zurück; mit der Hand fuhr sie an die Stirn unter ihr goldblondes Haar, als ob sie sich besinnen müsse; dann ließ sie das Geld in ihre Tasche fallen und ging langsam dem Hafenplatze zu. Wer den Weg entgegenkam, sah ihr verwundert nach; denn sie hatte die Hände auf die Brust gepreßt und schluchzte überlaut.

Seitdem waren funfzehn Jahre hingegangen. Die kleine Stadt erschien fast unverändert; nur daß für einen jungen Kaufherrn aus den alten Familien am Markt ein neues Haus erbaut war, daß Telegraphendrähte durch die Gassen liefen und auf dem Posthausschilde jetzt mit goldenen Buchstaben »Kaiserliche Reichspost« zu lesen war; wie immer rollte die See ihre Wogen an den Strand, und wenn der Nordwest vom Ostnordost gejagt wurde, so spülte das Hochwasser an die Mauern der Brennerei, die auch jetzt noch in der roten Laterne ihre beste Kundschaft hatte; aber das Ende der Eisenbahn lag noch manche Meile landwärts hinter dem Hügelzuge, sogar auf dem Bürgermeisterstuhle saß trotz der neuen Segnungen noch im guten alten Stile ein studierter Mann, und der Magistrat behauptete sein altes Ansehen, wenngleich die Senatoren jetzt in »Stadträte« und die Deputierten in »Stadtverordnete« verwandelt waren; die Abschaffung der Bürgerglocke als eines alten Zopfes war in der Stadtverordneten-Versammlung von einem jungen Mitgliede zwar in Vorschlag gebracht worden, aber zwei alte Herren hatten ihr das Wort geredet: die Glocke hatte sie in ihrer Jugend vor manchem dummen Streich nach Haus getrieben; weshalb sollte jetzt das junge Volk und das Gesinde nicht in gleicher Zucht gehalten werden? Und nach wie vor, wenn es zehn vom Turm geschlagen hatte, bimmelte die kleine Glocke hinterdrein und schreckte die Pärchen auseinander, welche auf dem Markt am Brunnen schwatzten.

Nicht so unverändert war das Kirchsche Haus geblieben. Heinz war nicht wieder heimgekommen; er war verschollen; es fehlte nur, daß er auch noch gerichtlich für tot erklärt worden wäre; von den jüngeren Leuten wußte mancher kaum, daß es hier jemals einen Sohn des alten Kirch gegeben habe. Damals freilich, als der alte Marten den Vorfall mit dem Briefe bei seinen Gängen mit herumgetragen hatte, war von Vater und Sohn genug geredet worden; und nicht nur von diesen, auch von der Mutter, von der man niemals redete, hatte man erzählt, daß sie derzeit, als es endlich auch ihr von draußen zugetragen worden, zum ersten Mal sich gegen ihren Mann erhoben habe. »Hans! Hans!«, so hatte sie ihn angesprochen, ohne der Magd zu achten, die an der Küchentür gelauscht hatte; »das ohne mich zu tun war nicht dein Recht! Nun können wir nur beten, daß der Brief nicht zu dem Schreiber wiederkehre; doch Gott wird ja so schwere Schuld nicht auf dich laden.« Und Hans Adam, während ihre Augen voll und tränenlos ihn angesehen, hatte hierauf nichts erwidert, nicht ein Sterbenswörtlein; sie aber hatte nicht nur gebetet; überallhin, wenn auch stets vergebens, hatte sie nach ihrem Sohne forschen lassen; die Kosten, die dadurch verursacht wurden, entnahm sie ohne Scheu den kleineren Kassen, welche sie verwaltete; und Hans Adam, obgleich er bald des innewurde, hatte sie still gewähren lassen. Er selbst tat nichts dergleichen; er sagte es sich beharrlich vor, der Sohn, ob brieflich oder in Person, müsse anders oder niemals wieder an die Tür des Elternhauses klopfen.

Und der Sohn hatte niemals wieder angeklopft. Hans Adams Haar war nur um etwas rascher grau geworden; der Mutter aber hatte endlich das stumme Leid die Brust zernagt, und als die Tochter aufgewachsen war, brach sie zusammen. Nur eins war stark in ihr geblieben, die Zuversicht, daß ihr Heinz einst wiederkehren werde; doch auch die trug sie im stillen. Erst da ihr Leben sich rasch zu Ende neigte, nach einem heftigen Anfall ihrer Schwäche, trat es einmal über ihre Lippen. Es war ein frostheller Weihnachtsmorgen, als sie, von der Tochter gestützt, mühsam die Treppe nach der oben belegenen Schlafkammer emporstieg. Eben, als sie auf halbem Wege, tief aufatmend und wie hilflos um sich blickend, gegen das Geländer lehnte, brach die Wintersonne durch die Scheiben über der Haustür und erleuchtete mit ihrem blassen Schein den dunkeln Flur. Da wandte die kranke Frau den Kopf zu ihrer Tochter. »Lina«, sagte sie geheimnisvoll, und ihre matten Augen leuchteten plötzlich in beängstigender Verklärung, »ich weiß es, ich werde ihn noch wiedersehen! Er kommt einmal so, wenn wir es gar nicht denken!«

»Meinst du, Mutter?« frug die Tochter fast erschrocken.

»Mein Kind, ich meine nicht; ich weiß es ganz gewiß!«

Dann hatte sie ihr lächelnd zugenickt; und bald lag sie

zwischen den weißen Linnen ihres Bettes, welche in wenigen Tagen ihren toten Leib umhüllen sollten.

In dieser letzten Zeit hatte Hans Kirch seine Frau fast keinen Augenblick verlassen; der Bursche, der ihm sonst im Geschäfte nur zur Hand ging, war schier verwirrt geworden über die ihn plötzlich treffende Selbstverantwortlichkeit; aber auch jetzt wurde der Name des Sohnes zwischen den beiden Eltern nicht genannt; nur da die schon erlöschenden Augen der Sterbenden weit geöffnet und wie suchend in die leere Kammer blickten, hatte Hans Kirch, als ob er ein Versprechen gebe, ihre Hand ergriffen und gedrückt; dann hatten ihre Augen sich zur letzten Lebensruhe zugetan.

Aber wo war, was trieb Heinz Kirch in der Stunde, als seine Mutter starb?

Ein paar Jahre weiter, da war der spitze Giebel des Kirchschen Hauses abgebrochen und statt dessen ein volles Stockwerk auf das Erdgeschoß gesetzt worden; und bald hausete eine junge Wirtschaft in den neuen Zimmern des Oberbaues; denn die Tochter hatte den Sohn eines wohlhabenden Bürgers aus der Nachbarstadt geheiratet, der dann in das Geschäft ihres Vaters eingetreten war. Hans Kirch begnügte sich mit dem Räumen des alten Unterbaues; die Schreibstube neben der Haustür bildete zugleich sein Wohnzimmer. Dahinter, nach dem Hofe hinaus, lag die Schlafkammer; so saß er ohne viel Treppensteigen mitten im Geschäft und konnte trotz des anrückenden Greisenalters und seines jungen Partners die Fäden noch in seinen Händen halten. Anders stand es mit der zweiten Seite seines Wesens; schon mehrmals war ein Wechsel in den Magistratspersonen eingetreten, aber Hans Kirch hatte keinen Finger darum gerührt; auch, selbst wenn er darauf angesprochen worden, kein Für oder Wider über die neuen Wahlen aus seinem Munde gehen lassen.

Dagegen schlenderte er jetzt oft, die Hände auf dem Rücken, bald am Hafen, bald in den Bürgerpark, während er sonst auf alle Spaziergänger nur mit Verachtung herabgesehen hatte. Bei anbrechender Dämmerung konnte man ihn auch wohl draußen über der Bucht auf dem hohen Ufer sitzen sehen; er blickte dann in die offene See hinaus und schien keinen der wenigen, die vorübergingen, zu bemerken. Traf es sich, daß aus dem Abendrot ein Schiff hervorbrach und mit vollen Segeln auf ihn zuzukommen schien, dann nahm er seine Mütze ab und strich mit der andern Hand sich zitternd über seinen grauen Kopf. – Aber nein, es geschahen ja keine Wunder mehr; weshalb sollte denn auch Heinz auf jenem Schiffe sein? – Und Hans Kirch schüttelte sich und trat fast zornig seinen Heimweg an.

Der ganze Ehrgeiz des Hauses schien jedenfalls, wenn auch in anderer Form, jetzt von dem Tochtermann vertreten zu werden; Herr Christian Martens hatte nicht geruht, bis die Familie unter den Mitgliedern der Harmoniegesellschaft figurierte, von der bekannt war, daß nur angesehenere Bürger zugelassen wurden. Der junge Ehemann war, wovon der Schwiegervater sich zeitig und gründlich überzeugt hatte, ein treuer Arbeiter und keineswegs ein Verschwender; aber – für einen feinen Mann gelten, mit den Honoratioren einen vertraulichen Händedruck wechseln, etwa noch eine schwergoldene Kette auf brauner Sammetweste, das mußte er daneben haben. Hans Kirch zwar hatte anfangs sich gesträubt; als ihm jedoch in einem stillen Nebenstübchen eine solide Partie »Sechsundsechzig« mit ein paar alten seebefahrenen Herren eröffnet wurde, ging auch er mit seinen Kindern in die Harmonie.

So war die Zeit verflossen, als an einem sonnigen Vormittage im September Hans Kirch vor seiner Haustür stand; mit seinem krummen Rücken, seinem hängenden Kopfe und wie gewöhnlich beide Hände in den Taschen. Er war eben von seinem Speicher heimgekommen; aber die Neugier hatte ihn wieder hinausgetrieben, denn durchs Fenster hatte er links hin auf dem Markte, wo sonst nur Hühner und Kinder liefen, einen großen Haufen erwachsener Menschen, Männer und Weiber, und offenbar in lebhafter Unterhaltung miteinander wahrgenommen; er hielt die Hand ans Ohr, um etwas zu erhorchen; aber sie standen ihm doch zu fern. Da löste sich ein starkes, aber anscheinend hochbetagtes Frauenzimmer aus der Menge; sie mochte halb erblindet sein, denn sie fühlte mit einem Krückstock vor sich hin; gleichwohl kam sie bald rasch genug gegen das Kirchsche Haus daher gewandert. »Jule!« brummte Hans Adam. »Was will Jule?«

Seitdem der Bruder ihr vor einigen Jahren ein größeres Darlehen zu einem Einkauf abgeschlagen hatte, waren Wort und Gruß nur selten zwischen ihnen gewechselt worden; aber jetzt stand sie vor ihm; schon von weitem hatte sie ihm mit ihrer Krücke zugewinkt. Im ersten Antrieb hatte er sich umwenden und in sein Haus zurückgehen wollen; aber er blieb doch. »Was willst du, Jule?« frug er. »Was verakkordieren die da auf dem Markt?«

»Was die verakkodieren, Hans? Ja, leihst du mir jetzt die hundert Taler, wenn ich dir's erzähle?«

Er wandte sich jetzt wirklich, um ins Haus zu treten.

»Nun, bleib nur!« rief sie. »Du sollst's umsonst zu wissen kriegen; dein Heinz ist wieder da!«

Der Alte zuckte zusammen. »Wo? Was?« stieß er hervor und fuhr mit dem Kopf nach allen Seiten. Die Speckhökerin sah mit Vergnügen, wie seine Hände in den weiten Taschen schlotterten.

»Wo?« wiederholte sie und schlug den Bruder auf den krummen Rücken. »Komm zu dir, Hans! Hier ist er noch nicht; aber in Hamburg, beim Schlafbaas in der Johannisstraße!«

Hans Kirch stöhnte. »Weibergewäsch!« murmelte er. »Siebzehn Jahre fort; der kommt nicht wieder – der kommt nicht wieder.«

Aber die Schwester ließ ihn nicht los. »Kein Weibergewäsch, Hans! Der Fritze Reimers, der mit ihm in Schlafstelle liegt, hat's nach Haus geschrieben!«

»Ja, Jule, der Fritze Reimers hat schon mehr gelogen!«

Die Schwester schlug die Arme unter ihrem vollen Busen umeinander. »Zitterst du schon wieder für deinen Geldsack?« rief sie höhnend. »Ei nun, für dreißig Reichsgulden haben sie unsern Herrn Christus verraten, so konntest du dein Fleisch und Blut auch wohl um dreißig Schillinge verstoßen. Aber jetzt kannst du ihn alle Tage wieder haben! Ratsherr freilich wird er nun wohl nicht mehr werden; du mußt ihn nun schon nehmen, wie du ihn dir selbst gemacht hast!«

Aber die Faust des Bruders packte ihren Arm; seine Lippen hatten sich zurückgezogen und zeigten das noch immer starke, vollzählige Gebiß. »Nero! Nero!« schrie er mit heiserer Stimme in die offene Haustür, während sogleich das Aufrichten des großen Haushundes drinnen hörbar wurde. »Weib, verdammtes, soll ich dich mit Hunden von der Türe hetzen!«

Frau Jules sittliche Entrüstung mochte indessen nicht so tief gegangen sein; hatte sie doch selbst vor einem halben Jahre ihre einzige Tochter fast mit Gewalt an einen reichen Trunkenbold verheiratet, um von seinen Kapitalien in ihr Geschäft zu bringen; es hatte sie nur gereizt, ihrem Bruder, wie sie später meinte, für die hundert Taler auch einmal etwas auf den Stock zu tun. Und so war sie denn schon dabei, ihm wieder gute Worte zu geben, als vom Markte her ein älterer Mann zu den Geschwistern trat. Es war der Krämer von der Ecke gegenüber. »Kommt, Nachbar«, sagte dieser, indem er Hans Adams Hand faßte, »wir wollen in Ihr Zimmer gehen; das gehört nicht auf die Straße!«

Frau Jule nickte ein paarmal mit ihrem dicken Kopfe. »Das meine ich auch, Herr Rickerts«, rief sie, indem sie sich mit ihrem Krückstocke nach der Straße hinunterfühlte; »erzählen Sie's ihm besser; seiner Schwester hat er es nicht glauben wollen! Aber, Hans, wenn's dir an Reisegeld nach Hamburg fehlen sollte?«

Sie bekam keine Antwort; Herr Rickerts trat mit dem

Bruder schon in dessen Zimmer. »Sie wissen es also, Nachbar!« sagte er; »es hat seine Richtigkeit; ich habe den Brief von Fritze Reimers selbst gelesen.«

Hans Kirch hatte sich in seinen Lehnstuhl gesetzt und starrte, mit den Händen auf den Knien, vor sich hin. »Von Fritze Reimers?« frug er dann. »Aber Fritze Reimers ist ein Windsack, ein rechter Weißfisch!«

»Das freilich, Nachbar, und er hat auch diesmal seine eigne Schande nach Haus geschrieben. Beim Schlafbaas in der Johannisstraße haben sie abends in der Schenkstube beisammengesessen, deutsche Seeleute, aber aus allen Meeren, Fritze Reimers und noch zwei andre unsrer Jungens mit dazwischen. Nun haben sie geredet über woher und wohin; zuletzt wo ein jeder von ihnen denn zuerst die Wand beschrien habe. Als an den Reimers dann die Reihe gekommen ist, da hat er – Sie kennen's ja wohl, Nachbar – das dumme Lied gesungen, worin sie den großen Fisch an unserm Rathaus in einen elenden Bütt verwandelt haben; kaum aber ist das Wort herausgewesen, so hat vom andern Ende des Tisches einer gerufen: ›Das ist kein Bütt, das ist der Schwanz von einem Butzkopf, und der ist doppelt so lang als Arm und Bein bei dir zusammen!‹

Der Mann, der das gesprochen hat, ist vielleicht um zehn Jahre älter gewesen als unsere Jungens, die da mit gesessen, und hat sich John Smidt genannt.

Fritze Reimers aber hat nicht geantwortet, sondern weiter fortgesungen, wie es in dem Liede heißt: ›Und sie handeln, sagt er, da mit Macht, sagt er; hab'n zwei Böte, sagt er, und 'ne Jacht!‹«

»Der Schnösel!« rief Hans Kirch; »und sein Vater hat bis an seinen Tod auf meinem Schoner gefahren!«

»Ja, ja, Nachbar; der John Smidt hat auch auf den Tisch geschlagen. ›Pfui für den Vogel, der sein eigen Nest beschmutzt!‹«

»Recht so!« sagte Hans Kirch; »er hätte ihn nur auf seinen dünnen Schädel schlagen sollen!«

»Das tat er nicht; aber als der Reimers ihm zugerufen, was er dabei denn mitzureden habe, da –«

Hans Kirch hatte des andern Arm gefaßt. »Da?« wiederholte er.

»Ja, Nachbar« – und des Erzählers Stimme wurde leiser – »da hat John Smidt gesagt, er heiße eigentlich Heinz Kirch, und ob er denn auch nun noch etwas von ihm kaufen wolle. – Sie wissen es ja, Nachbar, unsre Jungens geben sich da drüben manchmal andre Namen, Smidt oder Mayer, oder wie es eben kommen mag, zumal wenn's mit dem Heuerwechsel nicht so ganz in Ordnung ist. Und dann, ich bin ja erst seit sechzehn Jahren hier; aber nach Hörensagen, es muß Ihrem Heinz schon ähnlich sehen, das!«

Hans Kirch nickte. Es wurde ganz still im Zimmer, nur der Perpendikel der Wanduhr tickte; dem alten Schiffer war, als fühle er eine erkaltende Hand, die den Druck der seinigen erwarte.

Der Krämer brach zuerst das Schweigen. »Wann wollen Sie reisen, Nachbar?« frug er.

»Heute nachmittag«, sagte Hans Kirch und suchte sich so grade wie möglich aufzurichten.

– »Sie werden gut tun, sich reichlich mit Gelde zu versehen; denn die Kleidung Ihres Sohnes soll just nicht im besten Stande sein.«

Hans Kirch zuckte. »Ja, ja; noch heute nachmittag.«

Dies Gespräch hatte eine Zuhörerin gehabt; die junge Frau, welche zu ihrem Vater wollte, hatte vor der halb offenen Tür des Bruders Namen gehört und war aufhorchend stehengeblieben. Jetzt flog sie, ohne einzutreten, die Treppe wieder hinauf nach ihrem Wohnzimmer, wo eben ihr Mann, am Fenster sitzend, sich zu besonderer Ergötzung eine Havanna aus dem Sonntagskistchen angezündet hatte. »Heinz!« rief sie jubelnd ihm entgegen, wie vorzeiten ihre Mutter es gerufen hatte, »Nachricht von Heinz! Er lebt, er wird bald bei uns sein!« Und mit überstürzenden Worten erzählte sie, was sie unten im Flur erlauscht hatte. Plötzlich aber hielt sie inne und sah auf ihren Mann, der nachdenklich die Rauchwölkchen vor sich hin blies.

»Christian!« rief sie und kniete vor ihm hin; »mein einziger Bruder! Freust du dich denn nicht?«

Der junge Mann legte die Hand auf ihren Kopf: »Verzeih mir, Lina; es kam so unerwartet; dein Bruder ist für mich noch gar nicht dagewesen; es wird ja nun so vieles anders werden.« Und behutsam und verständig, wie es sich für einen wohldenkenden Mann geziemt, begann er dann ihr darzulegen, wie durch diese nicht mehr vermutete Heimkehr die Grundlagen ihrer künftigen Existenz beschränkt, ja vielleicht erschüttert würden. Daß seinerseits die Verschollenheit des Haussohnes, wenn auch ihm selbst kaum eingestanden, wenigstens den zweiten Grund zum Werben um Hans Adams Tochter abgegeben habe, das ließ er freilich nicht zu Worte kommen, so aufdringlich es auch jetzt vor seiner Seele stand.

Frau Lina hatte aufmerksam zugehört. Da aber ihr Mann jetzt schwieg, schüttelte sie nur lächelnd ihren Kopf: »Du sollst ihn nur erst kennenlernen; oh, Heinz war niemals eigennützig.«

Er sah sie herzlich an. »Gewiß, Lina; wir müssen uns darein zu finden wissen; um desto besser, wenn er wiederkehrt, wie du ihn einst gekannt hast.«

Die junge Frau schlug den Arm um ihres Mannes Nacken: »Oh, du bist gut, Christian! Gewiß, ihr werdet Freunde werden!«

Dann ging sie hinaus; in die Schlafkammer, in die beste Stube, an den Herd; aber ihre Augen blickten nicht mehr so froh, es war auf ihre Freude doch ein Reif gefallen. Nicht, daß die Bedenken ihres Mannes auch ihr Herz bedrängten; nein, aber daß so etwas überhaupt nur sein könne; sie wußte selber kaum, weshalb ihr alles jetzt so öde schien.

Einige Tage später war Frau Lina beschäftigt, in dem Oberbau die Kammer für den Bruder zu bereiten; aber auch heute war ihr die Brust nicht freier. Der Brief, worin der Vater seine und des Sohnes Ankunft gemeldet hatte, enthielt kein Wort von einem frohen Wiedersehen zwischen beiden; wohl aber ergab der weitere Inhalt, daß der Wiedergefundene sich anfangs unter seinem angenommenen Namen vor dem Vater zu verbergen gesucht habe und diesem wohl nur widerstrebend in die Heimat folgen werde.

Als dann an dem bezeichneten Sonntagabend das junge Ehepaar zu dem vor dem Hause haltenden Wagen hinausgetreten war, sahen sie bei dem Lichtschein, der aus dem offenen Flur fiel, einen Mann herabsteigen, dessen wetterhartes Antlitz mit dem rötlichen Vollbart und dem kurzgeschorenen braunen Haupthaar fast einen Vierziger anzudeuten schien; eine Narbe, die über Stirn und Auge lief, mochte indessen dazu beitragen, ihn älter erscheinen zu lassen, als er wirklich war. Nach ihm kletterte langsam Hans Kirch vom Wagen. »Nun, Heinz«, sagte er, nacheinander auf die Genannten hinweisend, »das ist deine Schwester Lina und das ihr Mann Christian Martens; ihr müßt euch zu vertragen suchen.«

Ebenso nacheinander streckte diesen jetzt Heinz die Hand entgegen und schüttelte die ihre kurz mit einem trockenen »Very well!« Er tat dies mit einer unbeholfenen Verlegenheit; mochte die Art seiner Heimkehr ihn bedrükken, oder fühlte er eine Zurückhaltung in der Begrüßung der Geschwister; denn freilich, sie hatten von dem Wiederkehrenden sich ein anderes Bild gemacht.

Nachdem alle in das Haus getreten waren, geleitete Frau Lina ihren Bruder die Treppe hinauf nach seiner Kammer. Es war nicht mehr dieselbe, in der er einst als Knabe geschlafen hatte, es war hier oben ja alles neu geworden; aber er schien nicht darauf zu achten. Die junge Frau legte das Reisegepäck, das sie ihm nachgetragen hatte, auf den Fußboden. »Hier ist dein Bett«, sagte sie dann, indem sie die weiße Schutzdecke abnahm und zusammenlegte; »Heinz, mein Bruder, du sollst recht sanft hier schlafen!«

Er hatte den Rock abgeworfen und war mit aufgestreiften Ärmeln an den Waschtisch getreten. Jetzt wandte er rasch den Kopf, und seine braunen blitzenden Augen ruhten in den ihren. »Dank, Schwester«, sagte er. Dann tauchte er den Kopf in die Schale und sprudelte mit dem Wasser umher, wie es wohl Leuten eigen ist, die dergleichen im Freien zu verrichten pflegen. Die Schwester, am Türpfosten lehnend, sah dem schweigend zu; ihre Frauenaugen musterten des Bruders Kleidung, und sie erkannte wohl, daß alles neu geschafft sein mußte; dann blieben ihre Blicke auf den braunen sehnigen Armen des Mannes haften, die noch mehr Narben zeigten als das Antlitz. »Armer Heinz«, sagte sie, zu ihm hinüber nickend, »die müssen schwere Arbeit getan haben!«

Er sah sie wieder an; aber diesmal war es ein wildes Feuer, das aus seinen Augen brach. »Demonio!« rief er, die aufgestreckten Arme schüttelnd; »allerlei Arbeit, Schwester! Aber – basta y basta!« Und er tauchte wieder den Kopf in die Schale und warf das Wasser über sich, als müsse er, Gott weiß was, herunterspülen.

Beim Abendtee, den die Familie zusammen einnahm, wollte eine Unterhaltung nicht recht geraten. »Ihr seid weit umhergekommen, Schwager«, sagte nach einigen vergeblichen Anläufen der junge Ehemann; »Ihr müßt uns viel erzählen.«

»Weit genug«, erwiderte Heinz; aber zum Erzählen kam es nicht; er gab nur kurze allgemeine Antwort.

»Laß ihn, Christian!« mahnte Frau Lina; »er muß erst eine Nacht zu Haus geschlafen haben.« Dann aber, damit es am ersten Abend nicht gar zu stille werde, begann sie selbst die wenigen Erinnerungen aus des Bruders Jugendjahren auszukramen, die sie nach eigenem Erlebnis oder den Erzählungen der Mutter noch bewahrte.

Heinz hörte ruhig zu. »Und dann«, fuhr sie fort, »damals, als du dir den großen Anker mit deinem Namen auf den Arm geätzt hattest! Ich weiß noch, wie ich schrie, als du so verbrannt nach Hause kamst, und wie dann der Physikus geholt wurde. Aber« – und sie stutzte einen Augenblick – »war es denn nicht auf dem linken Unterarm?«

Heinz nickte: »Mag wohl sein; das sind so Jungensstreiche.«

»Aber Heinz – es ist ja nicht mehr da; ich meinte, so was könne nie vergehen!«

»Muß doch wohl, Schwester; sind verteufelte Krankheiten da drüben; man muß schon oft zufrieden sein, wenn sie einem nicht gar die Haut vom Leibe ziehen.«

Hans Kirch hatte nur ein halbes Ohr nach dem, was hier gesprochen wurde. Noch mehr als sonst in sich zusammengesunken, verzehrte er schweigend sein Abendbrot; nur bisweilen warf er von unten auf einen seiner scharfen Blicke auf den Heimgekehrten, als wolle er prüfen, was mit diesem Sohn noch zu beginnen sei.

– – Aber auch für die folgenden Tage blieb dies wortkarge Zusammensein. Heinz erkundigte sich weder nach früheren Bekannten, noch sprach er von dem, was weiter denn mit ihm geschehen solle. Hans Adam frug sich, ob der Sohn das erste Wort von ihm erwarte oder ob er überhaupt nicht an das Morgen denke; »ja, ja«, murmelte er dann und nickte heftig mit seinem grauen Kopfe; »er ist's ja siebzehn Jahre so gewohnt geworden.«

Aber auch heimisch schien Heinz sich nicht zu fühlen. Hatte er kurze Zeit im Zimmer bei der Schwester seine Zigarre geraucht, so trieb es ihn wieder fort; hinab nach dem Hafen, wo er dem oder jenem Schiffer ein paar Worte zurief, oder nach dem großen Speicher, wo er teilnahmlos dem Abladen der Steinkohlen oder andern Arbeiten zusah. Ein paarmal, da er unten im Kontor gesessen, hatte Hans Kirch das eine oder andere der Geschäftsbücher vor ihm aufgeschlagen, damit er von dem gegenwärtigen Stande des Hauses Einsicht nehme; aber er hatte sie jedesmal nach kurzem Hin- und Herblättern wie etwas Fremdes wieder aus der Hand gelegt.

In einem aber schien er, zur Beruhigung des jungen Ehemannes, der Schilderung zu entsprechen, die Frau Lina an jenem Vormittage von ihrem Bruder ihm entworfen hatte: an eine Ausnutzung seiner Sohnesrechte schien der Heimgekehrte nicht zu denken.

Und noch ein zweites war dem Frauenauge nicht entgangen. Wie der Bruder einst mit ihr, der so viel jüngeren Schwester, sich herumgeschleppt, ihr erzählt und mit ihr gespielt hatte, mit ihr und – wie sie von der Mutter wußte – früher auch mit einer anderen, der er bis jetzt mit keinem Worte nachgefragt und von der zu reden sie vermieden hatte, in gleicher Weise ließ er jetzt, wenn er am Nachmittage draußen auf dem Beischlag saß, den kleinen Sohn des Krämers auf seinem Schoß umherklettern und sich Bart und Haar von ihm zerzausen; dann konnte er auch lachen, wie Frau Lina meinte es einst im Garten oder auf jenen Sonntagswanderungen mit der Mutter von ihrem Bruder Heinz gehört zu haben. Schon am zweiten Tage, da sie eben in Hut und Tuch aus der Haustür zu ihm treten wollte, hatte sie ihn so getroffen. Der kleine Bube stand auf seinen Knien und hielt ihn bei der Nase: »Du willst mir was vorlügen, du großer Schiffer!« sagte er und schüttelte derb an ihm herum.

»Nein, nein, Karl, by Jove, es gibt doch Meerfrauen; ich habe sie ja selbst gesehen.«

Der Knabe ließ ihn los. »Wirklich? Kann man die denn heiraten?«

»Oho, Junge! Freilich kann man das! Da drüben in Texas, könntst allerlei da zu sehen bekommen, kannte ich einen, der hatte eine Meerfrau; aber sie mußte immer in einer großen Wassertonne schwimmen, die in seinem Garten stand.«

Die Augen des kleinen Burschen leuchteten; er hatte nur einmal einen jungen Seehund so gesehen, und dafür hatte er einen Schilling zahlen müssen. »Du«, sagte er heimlich und nickte seinem bärtigen Freunde zu; »ich will auch eine Wasserfrau heiraten, wenn ich groß geworden bin!«

Heinz sah nachdenklich den Knaben an. »Tu das nicht, Karl; die Wasserfrauen sind falsch; bleib lieber in deines Vaters Stor und spiel mit deines Nachbarn Katze.«

Die Hand der Schwester legte sich auf seine Schulter: »Du wolltest mit mir zu unserer Mutter Grabe!«

Und Heinz setzte den Knaben zur Erde und ging mit Frau Lina nach dem Kirchhof. Ja, er hatte sich später auch von ihr bereden lassen, den alten Pastor, der jetzt mit einer Magd im großen Pfarrhaus wirtschaftete, und sogar auch Tante Jule zu besuchen, um die der Knabe Heinz sich wenig einst gekümmert hatte.

So war der Sonntagvormittag herangekommen, und die jungen Eheleute rüsteten sich zum gewohnten Kirchgang; auch Heinz hatte sich bereit erklärt. Hans Kirch war am Abend vorher besonders schweigsam gewesen, und die Augen der Tochter, die ihn kannte, waren mehrmals angstvoll über des Vaters Antlitz hingestreift. Jetzt kam es ihr wie eine Beruhigung, als sie ihn vorhin den großen Flurschrank hatte öffnen und wieder schließen hören, aus dem er selber seinen Sonntagsrock hervorzuholen pflegte.

Als aber bald danach die drei Kirchgänger in das untere Zimmer traten, stand Hans Kirch, die Hände auf dem Rücken, in seiner täglichen Kleidung an dem Fenster und blickte auf die leere Gasse; Hut und Sonntagsrock lagen wie unordentlich hingeworfen auf einem Stuhl am Pulte.

»Vater, es ist wohl an der Zeit!« erinnerte Frau Lina schüchtern.

Hans Adam hatte sich umgewandt. »Geht nur!« sagte er trocken, und die Tochter sah, wie seine Lippen zitterten, als sie sich über den starken Zähnen schlossen.

»Wie, du willst nicht mit uns, Vater?«

– »Heute nicht, Lina!«

»Heute nicht, wo Heinz nun wieder bei uns ist?«

»Nein, Lina«, er sprach die Worte leise, aber es war, als müsse es gleich danach hervorbrechen; »ich mag heut nicht allein in unsern Schifferstuhl.«

»Aber, Vater, du tust das ja immer«, sprach Frau Lina zagend; »Christian sitzt ja auch stets unten bei mir.«

– »Ei was, dein Mann, dein Mann!« und ein zorniger Blick schoß unter den buschigen Brauen zu seinem Sohn hinüber, und seine Stimme wurde immer lauter – »dein Mann gehört dahin; aber die alten Matrosen, die mit fünfunddreißig Jahren noch fremde Kapitäne ihres Vaters Schiffe fahren lassen, die längst ganz anderswo noch sitzen sollten, die mag ich nicht unter mir im Kirchstuhl sehen!«

Er schwieg und wandte sich wieder nach dem Fenster, und niemand hatte ihm geantwortet; dann aber legte Heinz das Gesangbuch, das seine Schwester ihm gegeben hatte, auf das Pult. »Wenn's nur das ist, Vater«, sagte er, »der alte Matrose kann zu Hause bleiben; er hat so manchen Sonntag nur den Wind in den Tauen pfeifen hören.«

Aber die Schwester ergriff des Bruders, dann des Vaters Hände. »Heinz! Vater! Laßt das ruhen jetzt! Hört zusammen Gottes Wort; ihr werdet mit guten Gedanken wiederkommen, und dann redet miteinander, was nun weiter werden soll!« Und wirklich, mochte es nun den heftigen Mann beruhigt haben, daß er, zum mindesten vorläufig, sich mit einem Worte Luft geschafft – was sie selber nicht erwartet hatte, sie brachte es dahin, daß beide in die Kirche gingen.

Aber Hans Kirch, während unten, wie ihm nicht entging, sich aller Blicke auf den Heimgekehrten richteten, saß oben unter den andern alten Kapitänen und Reedern und starrte, wie einst, nach der Marmorbüste des alten Kommandeurs; das war auch ein Stadtsjunge gewesen, ein Schulmeistersohn, wie Heinz ein Schulmeistersenkel; wie anders war der heimgekommen!

– – Eine Unterredung zwischen Vater und Sohn fand weder nach dem Kirchgang noch am Nachmittage statt. Am Abend zog Frau Lina den Bruder in ihre Schlafkammer: »Nun, Heinz, hast du mit Vater schon gesprochen?«

Er schüttelte den Kopf: »Was soll ich mit ihm sprechen, Schwester?«

– »Du weißt es wohl, Heinz; er will dich droben in der Kirche bei sich haben. Sag ihm, daß du dein Steuermannsexamen machen willst; warum hast du es nicht längst gesagt?«

Ein verächtliches Lachen verzerrte sein Gesicht: »Ist das eine Gewaltssache mit dem alten Schifferstuhl!« rief er. »Todos diabolos, ich alter Kerl noch auf der Schulbank! Denk wohl, ich habe manche alte Bark auch ohne das gesteuert!«

Sie sah ihn furchtsam an; der Bruder, an den sie sich zu gewöhnen anfing, kam ihr auf einmal fremd, ja unheimlich vor. »Gesteuert?« wiederholte sie leise; »wohin hast du gesteuert, Heinz? Du bist nicht weit gekommen.«

Er blickte eine Weile seitwärts auf den Boden; dann reichte er ihr die Hand. »Mag sein, Schwester«, sagte er ruhig; »aber – ich kann noch nicht wie ihr; muß mich immer erst besinnen, wo ich hinzutreten habe; kennt das nicht, ihr alle nicht, Schwester! Ein halbes Menschenleben – ja rechne, noch mehr als ein halbes Menschenleben kein ehrlich Hausdach überm Kopf; nur wilde See oder wildes Volk oder beides miteinander! Ihr kennt das nicht, sag ich, das Geschrei und das Gefluche, mein eignes mit darunter; ja, ja, Schwester, mein eignes auch, es lärmt mir noch immer in die Ohren; laßt's erst stiller werden, sonst – es geht sonst nicht!«

Die Schwester hing an seinem Halse. »Gewiß, Heinz, gewiß, wir wollen Geduld haben; oh, wie gut, daß du nun bei uns bist!«

Plötzlich, Gott weiß woher, tauchte ein Gerücht auf und wanderte emsig von Tür zu Tür: der Heimgekehrte sei gar nicht Heinz Kirch, es sei der Hasselfritz, ein Knabe aus dem Armenhause, der gleichzeitig mit Heinz zur See gegangen war und gleich diesem seitdem nichts von sich hatte hören lassen. Und jetzt, nachdem es eine kurze Weile darum herumgeschlichen, war es auch in das Kirchsche Haus gedrungen. Frau Lina griff sich mit beiden Händen an die Schläfen; sie hatte durch die Mutter wohl von jenem anderen gehört; wie Heinz hatte er braune Augen und braunes Haar gehabt und war wie dieser ein kluger wilder Bursch gewesen; sogar eine Ähnlichkeit hatte man derzeit zwischen ihnen finden wollen. Wenn alle Freude nun um nichts sein sollte, wenn es nun nicht der Bruder wäre! Eine helle Röte schlug ihr ins Gesicht: sie hatte ja an dieses Menschen Hals gehangen, sie hatte ihn geküßt – Frau Lina vermied es plötzlich, ihn zu berühren; verstohlen aber und desto öfter hafteten ihre Augen auf den rauhen Zügen ihres Gastes, während zugleich ihr innerer Blick sich mühte, unter den Schatten der Vergangenheit das Knabenantlitz ihres Bruders zu erkennen. Als dann auch der junge Ehemann zur Vorsicht mahnte, wußte Frau Lina sich auf einmal zu entsinnen, wie gleichgültig ihr der Bruder neulich an ihrer Mutter Grab erschienen sei; als ob er sich langweile, habe er mit beiden Armen sich über die Eisenstangen der Umfassung gelehnt und dabei seitwärts nach den andern Gräbern hingestarrt; fast als ob, wie bei dem Vaterunser nach der Predigt, nur das Ende abgewartet werden müsse.

Beiden Eheleuten erschien jetzt auch das ganze Gebaren des Bruders noch um vieles ungeschlachter als vordem; dies Sichumherwerfen auf den Stühlen, diese Nichtachtung von Frau Linas sauberen Dielen. Heinz Kirch, das sagten alle, und den Eindruck bewahrte auch Frau Linas eigenes Gedächtnis, war ja ein feiner junger Mensch gewesen. Als beide dann dem Vater ihre Bedenken mitteilten, war es auch dem nichts Neues mehr; aber er hatte geschwiegen und schwieg auch jetzt; nur die Lippen drückte er fester aufeinander. Freilich, als er bald darauf seinen alten Pastor mit der Pfeife am Zaune seines Vorgartens stehen sah, konnte er doch nicht lassen, wie zufällig heranzutreten und so von weitem an ihm herumzuforschen.

»Ja, ja«, meinte der alte Herr, »es war recht schicklich von dem Heinz, daß er seinen Besuch mir gleich am zweiten Tage gönnte.«

»Schuldigkeit, Herr Pastor«, versetzte Kirch; »mag Ihnen aber auch wohl ergangen sein wie mir; es kostet Künste, in diesem Burschen mit dem roten Bart den alten Heinz herauszufinden.«

Der Pastor nickte; sein Gesicht zeigte plötzlich den Ausdruck oratorischer Begeisterung. »Ja, mit dem Barte!« wiederholte er nachdrücklich und fuhr mit der Hand, wie auf der Kanzel, vor sich hin. »Sie sagen es, Herr Nachbar; und wahrlich, seit dieser unzierliche Zierat Mode worden, kann man die Knaben in den Jünglingen nicht wiedererkennen, bevor man sie nicht selber sich bei Namen rufen hörte; das habe ich an meinen Pensionären selbst erfahren! Da war der blonde Dithmarscher, dem Ihr Heinz – er wollte jetzo zwar darauf vergessen haben – einmal den blutigen Denkzettel unter die Nase schrieb; der glich wahrlich einem weißen Hammel, da er von hier fortging; und als er nach Jahren in meine friedliche Kammer so unerwartet eintrat – ein Löwe! Ich versichere Sie, Herr Nachbar, ein richtiger Löwe! Wenn nicht die alten Schafsaugen zum Glück noch standgehalten hätten, ich alter Mann hätte ja den Tod sonst davon haben können!« Der Pastor sog ein paarmal an seiner Pfeife und drückte sich das Sammetkäppchen fester auf den weißen Kopf.

»Nun freilich«, meinte Hans Kirch; denn er fühlte wohl, daß er ein Lieblingsthema wachgerufen habe, und suchte noch einmal wieder anzuknüpfen; »solche Signale wie Ihr Dithmarscher hat mein Heinz nicht aufzuweisen.«

Aber der alte Herr ging wieder seinen eigenen Weg. »Bewahre!« sagte er verächtlich und machte mit der Hand eine Bewegung, als ob er die Schafsaugen weit von sich in die Büsche werfe. »Ein Mann, ein ganzer Mann!« Dann hob er den Zeigefinger und beschrieb schelmisch lächelnd eine Linie über Stirn und Auge: »Auch eine Dekorierung hat er sich erworben; im Gefecht, Herr Nachbar, ich sage im Gefechte; gleich einem alten Studiosus! Zu meiner Zeit – Seeleute und Studenten, das waren die freien Männer, wir standen allzeit beieinander!«

Hans Kirch schüttelte den Kopf. »Sie irren, Ehrwürden; mein Heinz war nur auf Kauffahrteischiffen; im Sturm, ein Holzsplitter, eine stürzende Stenge tun wohl dasselbe schon.«

»Crede experto! Traue dem Sachkundigen!« rief der alte Herr und hob geheimnisvoll das linke Ohrläppchen, hinter welchem die schwachen Spuren einer Narbe sichtbar wurden. »Im Gefecht, Herr Nachbar; oh, wir haben auch pro patria geschlagen.«

Ein Lächeln flog über das Gesicht des alten Seemanns, das für einen Augenblick das starke Gebiß bloßlegte. »Ja, ja, Herr Pastor; freilich, er war kein Hasenfuß, mein Heinz!«

Aber der frohe Stolz, womit diese Worte hervorbrachen, verschwand schon wieder; das Bild seines kühnen Knaben verblich vor dem des Mannes, der jetzt unter seinem Dache hauste.

Hans Kirch nahm kurzen Abschied; er gab es auf, es noch weiter mit der Geschwätzigkeit des Greisenalters aufzunehmen.

– – Am Abend war Ball in der Harmonie. Heinz wollte zu Hause bleiben; er passe nicht dahin; und die jungen Eheleute, die ihm auch nur wie beiläufig davon gesprochen hatten, waren damit einverstanden; denn Heinz, sie mochten darin nicht unrecht haben, war in dieser Gesellschaft für jetzt nicht wohl zu präsentieren. Frau Lina wollte ebenfalls zu Hause bleiben; doch sie mußte dem Drängen ihres Mannes nachgeben, der einen neuen Putz für sie erhandelt hatte. Auch Hans Kirch ging zu seiner Partie Sechsundsechzig; eine innere Unruhe trieb ihn aus dem Hause.

So blieb denn Heinz allein zurück. Als alle fort waren, stand er, die Hände in den Taschen, am Fenster seiner dunklen Schlafkammer, das nach Nordosten auf die See hinausging. Es war unruhiges Wetter, die Wolken jagten vor dem Mond; doch konnte er jenseit des Warders, in dem tieferen Wasser, die weißen Köpfe der Wellen schäumen sehen. Er starrte lange darauf hin; allmählich, als seine Augen sich gewöhnt hatten, bemerkte er auch drüben auf der Insel einen hellen Dunst; von dem Leuchtturm konnte das nicht kommen; aber das große Dorf lag dort, wo, wie er hatte reden hören, heute Jahrmarkt war. Er öffnete das Fenster und lehnte sich hinaus; fast meinte er, durch das Rauschen des Wassers die ferne Tanzmusik zu hören; und als packe es ihn plötzlich, schlug er das Fenster eilig zu und sprang, seine Mütze vom Türhaken reißend, in den Flur hinab. Als er ebenso rasch der Haustür zuging, frug die Magd ihn, ob sie mit dem Abschließen auf ihn warten solle; aber er schüttelte nur den Kopf, während er das Haus verließ.

Kurze Zeit danach, beim Rüsten der Schlafgemächer für die Nacht, betrat die Magd auch die von ihrem Gaste vorhin verlassene Kammer. Sie hatte ihr Lämpchen auf dem Vorplatze gelassen und nur die Wasserflasche rasch hineinsetzen wollen; als aber draußen eben jetzt der Mond sein volles Licht durch den weiten Himmelsraum ergoß, trat sie gleichfalls an das Fenster und blickte auf die wie mit Silberschaum gekrönten Wellen; bald aber waren es nicht mehr diese; ihre jungen, weit reichenden Augen hatten ein Boot erkannt, das von einem einzelnen Manne durch den sprühenden Gischt der Insel zugetrieben wurde.

Wenn Hans Kirch oder die jungen Eheleute in die Harmonie gegangen waren, um dort nähere Aufschlüsse über jenes unheimliche Gerücht zu erhalten, so mußten sie sich getäuscht finden; niemand ließ auch nur ein andeutendes Wort darüber fallen; es war wieder wie kurz zuvor, als ob es niemals einen Heinz Kirch gegeben hätte.

Erst am andern Morgen erfuhren sie, daß dieser am Abend bald nach ihnen fortgegangen und bis zur Stunde noch nicht wieder da sei; die Magd teilte auf Befragen ihre Vermutungen mit, die nicht weit vom Ziele treffen mochten. Als dann endlich kurz vor Mittag der Verschwundene mit stark gerötetem Antlitz heimkehrte, wandte Hans Kirch, den er im Flur traf, ihm den Rücken und ging rasch in seine Stube. Frau Lina, der er auf der Treppe begegnete, sah ihn vorwurfsvoll und fragend an; sie stand einen Augenblick, als ob sie sprechen wolle; aber – wer war dieser Mann? – Sie hatte sich besonnen und ging ihm stumm vorüber.

Nach der schweigend eingenommenen Mittagsmahlzeit hatte Heinz sich oben in der Wohnstube des jungen Paares in die Sofaecke gesetzt. Frau Lina ging ab und zu; er hatte den Kopf gestützt und war eingeschlafen. Als er nach geraumer Zeit erwachte, war die Schwester fort; statt dessen sah er den grauen Kopf des Vaters über sich gebeugt; der Erwachende glaubte es noch zu fühlen, wie die scharfen Augen in seinem Antlitz forschten.

Eine Weile hafteten beider Blicke ineinander; dann richtete der Jüngere sich auf und sagte: »Laßt nur, Vater; ich weiß es schon, Ihr möchtet gern, daß ich der Hasselfritze aus der Armenkate wäre; möcht Euch schon den Gefallen tun, wenn ich mich selbst noch mal zu schaffen hätte.«

Hans Kirch war zurückgetreten: »Wer hat dir das erzählt?« sagte er, »du kannst nicht behaupten, daß ich dergleichen von dir gesagt hätte.«

»Aber Euer Gesicht sagt mir's; und unsre junge Frau, sie zuckt vor meiner Hand, als sollt' sie eine Kröte fassen.

Wußte erst nicht, was da unterwegs sei; aber heut nacht, da drüben, da schrien es beim Tanz die Eulen in die Fenster.«

Hans Kirch erwiderte nichts; der andre aber war aufgestanden und sah auf die Gasse, wo in Stößen der Regen vom Herbstwinde vorbeigetrieben wurde. »Eins aber«, begann er wieder, indem er sich finster zu dem Alten wandte, »mögt Ihr mir noch sagen! Warum damals, da ich noch jung war, habt Ihr das mit dem Brief mir angetan? Warum? Denn ich hätte Euch sonst mein altes Gesicht wohl wieder heimgebracht.«

Hans Kirch fuhr zusammen. An diesen Vorgang hatte seit dem Tode seines Weibes keine Hand gerührt; er selbst hatte ihn tief in sich begraben. Er fuhr mit den Fingern in die Westentasche und biß ein Endchen von der schwarzen Tabaksrolle, die er daraus hervorgeholt hatte. »Einen Brief?« sagte er dann; »mein Sohn Heinz war nicht für das Briefschreiben.«

»Mag sein, Vater; aber einmal – einmal hatte er doch geschrieben; in Rio hatte er den Brief zur Post gegeben, und später, nach langer Zeit – der Teufel hatte wohl sein Spiel dabei – in San Jago, in dem Fiebernest, als die Briefschaften für die Mannschaft ausgeteilt wurden, da hieß es: ›Hier ist auch was für dich.‹ Und als der Sohn vor Freude zitternd seine Hand ausstreckte und mit den Augen nur die Aufschrift des Briefes erst verschlingen wollte, da war's auch wirklich einer, der von Hause kam, und auch eine Handschrift von zu Hause stand darauf; aber – es war doch nur sein eigener Brief, der nach sechs Monaten uneröffnet an ihn zurückkam.«

Es sah fast aus, als seien die Augen des Alten feucht geworden; als er aber den trotzigen Blick des Jungen sich gegenüber sah, verschwand das wieder. »Viel Rühmliches mag auch nicht darin gestanden haben!« sagte er grollend.

Da fuhr ein hartes Lachen aus des Jüngeren Munde und gleich darauf ein fremdländischer Fluch, den der Vater nicht verstand. »Da mögt Ihr recht haben, Hans Adam

Kirch; ganz regulär war's just nicht hergegangen; der junge Bursche wär' auch damals gern vor seinem Vater hingefallen; lagen aber tausend Meilen zwischen ihnen; und überdem – das Fieber hatte ihn geschüttelt, und er war erst eben von seinem elenden Lazarettbett aufgestanden! Und später dann – was meint Ihr wohl, Hans Kirch? Wen Vaters Hand verstoßen, der fragt bei der nächsten Heuer nicht, was unterm Deck geladen ist, ob Kaffeesäcke oder schwarze Vögel, die eigentlich aber schwarze Menschen sind; wenn's nur Dublonen gibt; und fragt auch nicht, wo die der Teufel holt, und wo dann wieder neue zu bekommen sind!«

Die Stimme, womit diese Worte gesprochen wurden, klang so wüst und fremd, daß Hans Kirch sich unwillkürlich frug: »Ist das dein Heinz, den der Kantor beim Amensingen immer in die erste Reihe stellte, oder ist es doch der Junge aus der Armenkate, der nur auf deinen Beutel spekuliert?« Er wandte wieder seine Augen prüfend auf des andern Antlitz; die Narbe über Stirn und Auge flammte brandrot. »Wo hast du dir denn das geholt?« sagte er, an seines Pastors Rede denkend. »Bist du mit Piraten im Gefecht gewesen?«

Ein desperates Lachen fuhr aus des Jüngeren Munde. »Piraten?« rief er. »Glaubt nur, Hans Kirch, es sind auch dabei brave Kerle! Aber laßt das; das Gespinst ist gar zu lang, mit wem ich all zusammen war!«

Der Alte sah ihn mit erschrockenen Augen an. »Was sagst du?« frug er so leise, als ob es niemand hören dürfe.

Aber bevor eine Antwort darauf erfolgen konnte, wurden schwerfällige Schritte draußen auf der Treppe laut; die Tür öffnete sich, und von Frau Lina geführt, trat Tante Jule in das Zimmer. Während sie pustend und mit beiden Händen sich auf ihren Krückstock lehnend stehenblieb, war Heinz an ihr vorüber schweigend aus der Tür gegangen.

»Ist er fort?« sagte sie, mit ihrem Stocke hinter ihm herweisend.

»Wer soll fort sein?« frug Hans Kirch und sah die Schwester nicht eben allzu freundlich an.

»Wer? Nun, den du seit vierzehn Tagen hier in Kost genommen.«

– »Was willst du wieder, Jule? Du pflegst mir sonst nicht so ins Haus zu fallen.«

»Ja, ja, Hans«, und sie winkte der jungen Frau, ihr einen Stuhl zu bringen, und setzte sich darauf; »du hast's auch nicht um mich verdient; aber ich bin nicht so, Hans; ich will dir Abbitte tun; ich will bekennen, der Fritze Reimers mag doch wohl gelogen haben, oder wenn nicht er, so doch der andre!«

»Was soll die Rederei?« sagte Hans Kirch, und es klang, als ob er müde wäre.

– »Was es soll? Du sollst dich nicht betrügen lassen! Du meinst, du hast nun deinen Vogel wieder eingefangen; aber sieh nur zu, ob's auch der rechte ist!«

»Kommst du auch mit dem Geschwätz? Warum sollt's denn nicht der rechte sein?« Er sprach das unwirsch, aber doch, als ob es zu hören ihn verlange.

Frau Jule hatte sich in Positur gesetzt. »Warum, Hans? Als er am Mittwochnachmittage mit der Lina bei mir saß – wir waren schon bei der dritten Tasse Kaffee, und noch nicht einmal hatte er ›Tante‹ zu mir gesagt! – ›Warum‹, frug ich, ›nennst du mich denn gar nicht Tante?‹ – ›Ja, Tante‹, sagte er, ›du hast ja noch allein gesprochen!‹ Und, siehst du, Hans, das war beim ersten Mal denn schon gelogen; denn das soll mir keiner nachsagen; ich lasse jedermann zu Worte kommen! Und als ich ihn dann nahe zu mir zog und mit der Hand und mit meinen elenden Augen auf seinem Gesicht herumfühlte – nun, Hans, die Nase kann doch nicht von Ost nach West gewachsen sein!«

Der Bruder saß mit gesenktem Kopf ihr gegenüber; er hatte nie darauf geachtet, wie seinem Heinz die Nase im Gesicht gestanden hatte. »Aber«, sagte er – denn das Gespräch von vorhin flog ihm durch den Kopf; doch schienen ihm die Worte schwer zu werden – »sein Brief von damals; wir redeten darüber; er hat ihn in San Jago selbst zurückerhalten!«

Die dicke Frau lachte, daß der Stock ihr aus den Händen fiel. »Die Briefgeschichte, Hans! Ja, die ist seit den vierzehn Tagen reichlich wieder aufgewärmt; davon konnte er für einen Dreiling bei jedem Bettelkinde einen Suppenlöffel voll bekommen! Und er mußte dir doch auch erzählen, weshalb der echte Heinz denn all die Jahre draußen blieb. Laß dich nicht nasführen, Hans! Warum denn hat er nicht mit dir wollen, als du ihn von Hamburg holtest? War's denn so schlimm, wieder einmal an die volle Krippe und ins warme Nest zu kommen? – Ich will's dir sagen; das ist's: er hat sich so geschwind nicht zu dem Schelmenwagstück resolvieren können!«

Hans Adam hatte seinen grauen Kopf erhoben, aber er sprach nicht dazwischen; fast begierig horchte er auf alles, was die Schwester vorbrachte.

»Und dann«, fuhr diese fort, »die Lina hat davon erzählt.« – – Aber plötzlich stand sie auf und fühlte sich mit ihrer Krücke, die Lina ihr dienstfertig aufgehoben hatte, nach dem Fenster hin; von draußen hörte man zwei Männerstimmen in lebhafter Unterhaltung. »O Lina«, sagte Tante Jule; »ich hör's, der eine ist der Justizrat, lauf doch und bitte ihn, ein paar Augenblicke hier heraufzukommen!«

Der Justizrat war der alte Physikus; bei dem früheren Mangel passender Alterstitel hierzulande waren alle älteren Physici Justizräte.

Hans Kirch wußte nicht, was seine Schwester mit diesem vorhatte; aber er wartete geduldig, und bald auch trat der alte Herr mit der jungen Frau ins Zimmer. »Ei, ei«, rief er, »Tante Jule und Herr Kirch beisammen? Wo ist denn nun der Patient?«

»Der da«, sagte Tante Jule und wies auf ihren Bruder; »er hat den Star auf beiden Augen!«

Der Justizrat lachte. »Sie scherzen, liebe Madame; ich wollte, ich hätte selbst nur noch die scharfen Augen unseres Freundes.«

»Mach fort, Jule«, sagte Hans Kirch; »was gehst du lange um den Brei herum!«

Die dicke Frau ließ sich indes nicht stören. »Es ist nur so sinnbildlich, mein Herr Justizrat«, erklärte sie mit Nachdruck. »Aber besinnen Sie sich einmal darauf, wie Sie vor so ein zwanzig Jahren hier auch ins Haus geholt wurden; die Lina, die große Frau jetzt, schrie damals ein Zetermordio durchs Haus; denn ihr Bruder Heinz hatte sich nach Jungensart einen schönen Anker auf den Unterarm geätzt und sich dabei weidlich zugerichtet.«

Hans Kirch fuhr mit seinem Kopf herum; denn die ihm derzeit unbeachtet vorübergegangene Unterhaltung bei der ersten Abendmahlzeit kam ihm plötzlich, und jetzt laut und deutlich, wieder.

Aber der alte Doktor wiegte das Haupt: »Ich besinne mich nicht; ich hatte in meinem Leben so viele Jungen unter Händen.«

»Nun so, mein Herr Justizrat«, sagte Tante Jule; »aber Sie kennen doch dergleichen Jungensstreiche hier bei uns; es fragt sich nur, und das möchten wir von Ihnen wissen, ob denn in zwanzig Jahren solch ein Anker ohne Spur verschwinden könne?«

»In zwanzig Jahren?« erwiderte jetzt der Justizrat ohne Zögern; »ei, das kann gar leicht geschehen!«

Aber Hans Kirch mischte sich ins Gespräch: »Sie denken, wie sie's jetzt machen, Doktor, so mit blauer Tusche; nein, der Junge war damals nach der alten gründlichen Manier ans Werk gegangen; tüchtige Nadelstiche und dann mit Pulver eingebrannt.«

Der alte Arzt rieb sich die Stirn. »Ja, ja; ich entsinne mich auch jetzt. Hm! – Nein, das dürfte wohl unmöglich sein; das geht bis auf die cutis; der alte Hinrich Jakobs läuft noch heut mit seinem Anker.«

Tante Jule nickte beifällig; Frau Lina stand, die Hand an der Stuhllehne, blaß und zitternd neben ihr.

»Aber«, sagte Hans Kirch, und auch bei ihm schlich sich die Stimme nur wie mit Zagen aus der Kehle, »sollte es nicht Krankheiten geben? Da drüben, in den heißen Ländern?«

Der Arzt bedachte sich eine Weile und schüttelte dann sehr bestimmt den Kopf. »Nein, nein; das ist nicht anzunehmen; es müßten denn die Blattern ihm den Arm zerrissen haben.«

Eine Pause entstand, während Frau Jule ihre gestrickten Handschuhe anzog. »Nun, Hans«, sagte sie dann; »ich muß nach Haus; aber du hast nun die Wahl: den Anker oder die Blatternarben! Was hat dein neuer Heinz denn aufzuweisen? Die Lina hat nichts von beiden sehen können; nun sieh du selber zu, wenn deine Augen noch gesund sind!«

– – Bald danach ging Hans Kirch die Straße hinauf nach seinem Speicher; er hatte die Hände über dem Rükken gefaltet, der Kopf hing ihm noch tiefer als gewöhnlich auf die Brust. Auch Frau Lina hatte das Haus verlassen und war dem Vater nachgegangen; als sie in den unteren dämmerhellen Raum des Speichers trat, sah sie ihn in der Mitte desselben stehen, als müsse er sich erst besinnen, weshalb er denn hieher gegangen sei. Bei dem Geräusche des Kornumschaufelns, das von den oberen Böden herabscholl, mochte er den Eintritt der Tochter überhört haben; denn er stieß sie fast zurück, als er sie jetzt so plötzlich vor sich sah: »Du, Lina! Was hast du hier zu suchen?«

Die junge Frau zitterte und wischte sich das Gesicht mit ihrem Tuche. »Nichts, Vater«, sagte sie; »aber Christian ist unten am Hafen, und da litt es mich nicht so allein zu Hause mit ihm – mit dem fremden Menschen! Ich fürchte mich; oh, es ist schrecklich, Vater!«

Hans Kirch hatte während dieser Worte wieder seinen Kopf gesenkt; jetzt hob er wie aus einem Abgrunde seine Augen zu denen seiner Tochter und blickte sie lange und unbeweglich an. »Ja, ja, Lina«, sagte er dann hastig; »Gott Dank, daß es ein Fremder ist!«

Hierauf wandte er sich rasch, und die Tochter hörte, wie er die Treppen zu dem obersten Bodenraum hinaufstieg.

Ein trüber Abend war auf diesen Tag gefolgt; kein Stern war sichtbar; feuchte Dünste lagerten auf der See. Im Hafen war es ungewöhnlich voll von Schiffen, meist Jachten und Schoner; aber auch ein paar Vollschiffe waren dabei und außerdem der Dampfer, welcher wöchentlich hier anzulegen pflegte. Alles lag schon in tiefer Ruhe, und auch auf dem Hafenplatz am Bollwerk entlang schlenderte nur ein einzelner Mann: wie es den Anschein hatte, müßig und ohne eine bestimmte Absicht. Jetzt blieb er vor dem einen der beiden Barkschiffe stehen, auf dessen Deck ein Junge sich noch am Gangspill zu schaffen machte; er rief einen »guten Abend« hinüber und fragte, wie halb gedankenlos, nach Namen und Ladung des Schiffes. Als ersterer genannt wurde, tauchte ein Kopf aus der Kajüte, schien eine Weile den am Ufer Stehenden zu mustern, spie dann weit hinaus ins Wasser und tauchte wieder unter Deck. Schiff und Schiffer waren nicht von hier; der am Ufer schlenderte weiter; vom Warder drüben kam dann und wann ein Vogelschrei; von der Insel her drang nur ein schwacher Schein von den Leuchtfeuern durch den Nebel. Als er an die Stelle kam, wo die Häuserreihe näher an das Wasser tritt, schlug von daher ein Gewirr von Stimmen an sein Ohr und veranlaßte ihn, stillzustehen. Von einem der Häuser fiel ein roter Schein in die Nacht hinaus; er erkannte es wohl, wenngleich sein Fuß die Schwelle dort noch nicht überschritten hatte; das Licht kam aus der Laterne der Hafenschenke. Das Haus war nicht wohl beleumdet; nur fremde Matrosen und etwa die Söhne von Setzschiffern verkehrten dort; er hatte das alles schon gehört. – Und jetzt erhob das Lärmen sich von neuem, nur daß auch eine Frauenstimme nun dazwischen kreischte. – Ein finsteres Lachen fuhr über das Antlitz des Mannes; beim Schein der roten Laterne und den wilden Lauten hinter den verhangenen Fenstern mochte allerlei in seiner Erinnerung aufwachen, was nicht gut tut, wenn es wiederkommt. Dennoch schritt er darauf zu, und als er eben von der Stadt her die Bürgerglocke läuten hörte, trat er in die niedrige, aber geräumige Schenkstube.

An einem langen Tische saß eine Anzahl alter und junger Seeleute; ein Teil derselben, zu denen sich der Wirt gesellt zu haben schien, spielte mit beschmutzten Karten; ein Frauenzimmer, über die Jugendblüte hinaus, mit blassem, verwachtem Antlitz, dem ein Zug des Leidens um den noch immer hübschen Mund nicht fehlte, trat mit einer Anzahl dampfender Gläser herein und verteilte sie schweigend an die Gäste. Als sie an den Platz eines Mannes kam, dessen kleine Augen begehrlich aus dem grobknochigen Angesicht hervorspielten, schob sie das Glas mit augenscheinlicher Hast vor ihn hin; aber der Mensch lachte und suchte sie an ihren Röcken festzuhalten: »Nun, Ma'am, habt Ihr Euch noch immer nicht besonnen? Ich bin ein höflicher Mann, versichere Euch! Aber ich kenne die Weibergeographie: Schwarz oder Weiß, ist alles eine Sorte!«

»Laßt mich«, sagte das Weib; »bezahlt Euer Glas und laßt mich gehen!«

Aber der andre war nicht ihrer Meinung; er ergriff sie und zog sie jäh zu sich heran, daß das vor ihm stehende Glas umstürzte und der Inhalt sie beide überströmte. »Sieh nur, schöne Missis!« rief er, ohne darauf zu achten, und winkte mit seinem rothaarigen Kopfe nach einem ihm gegenüber sitzenden Burschen, dessen flachsblondes Haar auf ein bleiches, vom Trunke gedunsenes Antlitz herabfiel; »sieh nur, der Jochum mit seinem greisen Kalbsgesicht hat nichts dagegen einzuwenden! Trink aus, Jochum, ich zahle dir ein neues!«

Der Mensch, zu dem er gesprochen hatte, goß mit blödem Schmunzeln sein Glas auf einen Zug hinunter und schob es dann zu neuem Füllen vor sich hin.

Einen Augenblick ruhten die Hände des Weibes, mit denen sie sich aus der gewaltsamen Umarmung zu lösen versucht hatte; ihre Blicke fielen auf den bleichen Trunkenbold, und es war, als wenn Abscheu und Verachtung sie eine Weile alles andere vergessen ließen.

Aber ihr Peiniger zog sie nur fester an sich: »Siehst du, schöne Frau! Ich dächte doch, der Tausch wäre nicht so übel! Aber, der ist's am Ende gar nicht! Nimm dich in acht, daß ich nicht aus der Schule schwatze!« Und da sie wiederum sich sträubte, nickte er einem hübschen, braunlockigen Jungen zu, der am unteren Ende des Tisches saß. »He, du Gründling«, rief er, »meinst du, ich weiß nicht, wer gestern zwei Stunden nach uns aus der roten Laterne unter Deck gekrochen ist?«

Die hellen Flammen schlugen dem armen Weibe ins Gesicht; sie wehrte sich nicht mehr, sie sah nur hilfesuchend um sich. Aber es rührte sich keine Hand; der junge hübsche Bursche schmunzelte nur und sah vor sich in sein Glas.

Aus einer unbesetzten Ecke des Zimmers hatte bisher der zuletzt erschienene Gast dem allen mit gleichgültigen Augen zugesehen; und wenn er jetzt die Faust erhob und dröhnend vor sich auf die Tischplatte schlug, so schien auch dieses nur mehr wie aus früherer Gewohnheit, bei solchem Anlaß nicht den bloßen Zuschauer abzugeben. »Auch mir ein Glas!« rief er, und es klang fast, als ob er Händel suche.

Drüben war alles von den Sitzen aufgesprungen. »Wer ist das? Der will wohl unser Bowiemesser schmecken? Werft ihn hinaus! Goddam, was will der Kerl?«

»Nur auch ein Glas!« sagte der andre ruhig. »Laßt euch nicht stören! Haben, denk ich, hier wohl alle Platz!«

Die drüben waren endlich doch auch dieser Meinung und blieben an ihrem Tische; aber das Frauenzimmer hatte dabei Gelegenheit gefunden, sich zu befreien, und trat jetzt an den Tisch des neuen Gastes. »Was soll es sein?« frug sie höflich; aber als er ihr Bescheid gab, schien sie es kaum zu hören; er sah verwundert, wie ihre Augen starr und doch wie abwesend auf ihn gerichtet waren und wie sie noch immer vor ihm stehenblieb.

»Kennen Sie mich?« sagte er und warf mit rascher Bewegung seinen Kopf zurück, so daß der Schein der Deckenlampe auf sein Antlitz fiel.

Das Weib tat einen tiefen Atemzug, und die Gläser, die sie in der Hand hielt, schlugen hörbar aneinander: »Verzeihen Sie«, sagte sie ängstlich; »Sie sollen gleich bedient werden.«

Er blickte ihr nach; wie sie durch eine Seitentür hinausging; der Ton der wenigen Worte, welche sie zu ihm gesprochen, war ein so anderer gewesen, als den er vorhin von ihr gehört hatte; langsam hob er den Arm und stützte seinen Kopf darauf; es war, als ob er mit allen Sinnen in eine weite Ferne denke. Es hätte ihm endlich auffallen müssen, daß seine Bestellung noch immer nicht ausgeführt sei; aber er dachte nicht daran. Plötzlich, während am andern Tisch die Karten mit den Würfeln wechselten, erhob er sich. Wäre die Aufmerksamkeit der übrigen Gäste auf ihn statt auf das neue Spiel gerichtet gewesen, er wäre sicher ihrem Hohne nicht entgangen; denn der hohe kräftige Mann zitterte sichtbar, als er jetzt mit auf den Tisch gestemmten Händen dastand.

Aber es war nur für einige Augenblicke; dann verließ er das Zimmer durch dieselbe Tür, durch welche vorhin die Aufwärterin hinausgegangen war. Ein dunkler Gang führte ihn in eine große Küche, welche durch eine an der Wand hängende Lampe nur kaum erhellt wurde. Hastig war er eingetreten; seine raschen Augen durchflogen den vor ihm liegenden wüsten Raum; und dort stand sie, die er suchte; wie unmächtig, die leeren Gläser noch in den zusammengefalteten Händen, lehnte sie gegen die Herdmauer. Einen Augenblick noch, dann trat er zu ihr; »Wieb!« rief er; »Wiebchen, kleines Wiebchen!«

Es war eine rauhe Männerstimme, die diese Worte rief

und jetzt verstummte, als habe sie allen Odem an sie hinge-
geben.

Und doch, über das verblühte Antlitz des Weibes flog es
wie ein Rosenschimmer, und während zugleich die Gläser
klirrend auf den Boden fielen, entstieg ein Aufschrei ihrer
Brust; wer hätte sagen mögen, ob es Leid, ob Freude war.
»Heinz!« rief sie, »Heinz, du bist es; oh, sie sagten, du seist
es nicht.«

Ein finstres Lächeln zuckte um den Mund des Mannes:
»Ja, Wieb; ich wußt's wohl schon vorher; ich hätte nicht
mehr kommen sollen. Auch dich – das alles war ja längst
vorbei – ich wollte dich nicht wiedersehen, nichts von dir
hören, Wieb; ich biß die Zähne aufeinander, wenn dein
Name nur darüber wollte. Aber – gestern abend – es war
wieder einmal Jahrmarkt drüben – wie als Junge hab ich
mir ein Boot gestohlen; ich mußte, es ging nicht anders;
vor jeder Bude, auf allen Tanzböden hab ich dich gesucht;
ich war ein Narr, ich dachte, die alte Möddersch lebe noch;
o süße kleine Wieb, ich dacht' wohl nur an dich; ich wußte
selbst nicht, was ich dachte!« Seine Stimme bebte, seine
Arme streckten sich weit geöffnet ihr entgegen.

Aber sie warf sich nicht hinein; nur ihre Augen blickten
traurig auf ihn hin: »O Heinz!« rief sie; »du bist es! Aber
ich, ich bin's nicht mehr! – Du bist zu spät gekommen,
Heinz!«

Da riß er sie an sich und ließ sie wieder los und streckte
beide Arme hoch empor: »Ja, Wieb, das sind auch nicht
mehr die unschuldigen Hände, womit ich damals dir die
roten Äpfel stahl; by Jove, das schleißt, so siebzehn Jahre
unter diesem Volk!«

Sie war neben dem Herde auf die Knie gesunken:
»Heinz«, murmelte sie, »o Heinz, die alte Zeit!«

Wie verlegen stand er neben ihr; dann aber bückte er
sich und ergriff die eine ihrer Hände, und sie duldete es still.

»Wieb«, sagte er leise, »wir wollen sehen, daß wir uns
wiederfinden, du und ich!«

Sie sagte nichts; aber er fühlte eine Bewegung ihrer Hand, als ob sie schmerzlich in der seinen zucke.

Von der Schenkstube her erscholl ein wüstes Durcheinander; Gläser klirrten, mitunter dröhnte ein Faustschlag. »Kleine Wieb«, flüsterte er wieder, »wollen wir weit von all den bösen Menschen fort?«

Sie hatte den Kopf auf den steinernen Herd sinken lassen und stöhnte schmerzlich. Da wurden schlurfende Schritte in dem Gange hörbar, und als Heinz sich wandte, stand ein Betrunkener in der Tür; es war derselbe Mensch mit dem schlaffen gemeinen Antlitz, den er vorhin unter den andern Schiffern schon bemerkt hatte. Er hielt sich an dem Türpfosten, und seine Augen schienen, ohne zu sehen, in dem dämmerigen Raum umherzustarren. »Wo bleibt der Grog?« stammelte er. »Sechs neue Gläser. Der rote Jakob flucht nach seinem Grog!«

Der Trunkene hatte sich wieder entfernt; sie hörten die Tür der Schenkstube hinter ihm zufallen.

»Wer war das?« frug Heinz.

Wieb erhob sich mühsam. »Mein Mann«, sagte sie; »er fährt als Matrose auf England; ich diene bei meinem Stiefvater hier als Schenkmagd.«

Heinz sagte nichts darauf; aber seine Hand fuhr nach der behaarten Brust, und es war, als ob er gewaltsam etwas von seinem Nacken reiße. »Siehst du«, sagte er tonlos und hielt einen kleinen Ring empor, von dem die Enden einer zerrissenen Schnur herabhingen, »da ist auch noch das Kinderspiel! Wär's Gold gewesen, er wär' so lang wohl nicht bei mir geblieben. Aber auch sonst – ich weiß nicht, war's um dich? Es war wohl nur ein Aberglaube, weil's doch noch das letzte Stück von Hause war.«

Wieb stand ihm gegenüber, und er sah, wie ihre Lippen sich bewegten.

»Was sagst du?« frug er.

Aber sie antwortete nicht; es war nur, als flehten ihre Augen um Erbarmen. Dann wandte sie sich und machte sich daran, wie es ihr befohlen war, den heißen Trank zu mischen. Nur einmal stockte sie in ihrer Arbeit, als ein feiner Metallklang auf dem steinernen Fußboden ihr Ohr getroffen hatte. Aber sie wußte es, sie brauchte nicht erst umzusehen; was sollte er denn jetzt noch mit dem Ringe!

Heinz hatte sich auf einen hölzernen Stuhl gesetzt und sah schweigend zu ihr hinüber; sie hatte das Feuer geschürt, und die Flammen lohten und warfen über beide einen roten Schein. Als sie fortgegangen war, saß er noch da; endlich sprang er auf und trat in den Gang, der nach der Schenkstube führte. »Ein Glas Grog; aber ein festes!« rief er, als Wieb ihm von dort her aus der Tür entgegenkam; dann setzte er sich wieder allein an seinen Tisch. Bald darauf kam Wieb und stellte das Glas vor ihm hin, und noch einmal sah er zu ihr auf; »Wieb, kleines Wiebchen!« murmelte er, als sie fortgegangen war; dann trank er, und als das Glas leer war, rief er nach einem neuen, und als sie es schweigend brachte, ließ er es, ohne aufzusehen, vor sich hinstellen.

Am andern Tische lärmten sie und kümmerten sich nicht mehr um den einsamen Gast; eine Stunde der Nacht schlug nach der andern, ein Glas nach dem andern trank er; nur wie durch einen Nebel sah er mitunter das arme schöne Antlitz des ihm verlorenen Weibes, bis er endlich dennoch nach den andern fortging und dann spät am Vormittag mit wüstem Kopf in seinem Bett erwachte.

In der Kirchschen Familie war es schon kein Geheimnis mehr, in welchem Hause Heinz diesmal seine Nacht verbracht hatte. Das Mittagsmahl war, wie am gestrigen Tage, schweigend eingenommen; jetzt am Nachmittage saß Hans Adam Kirch in seinem Kontor und rechnete. Zwar lag unter den Schiffen im Hafen auch das seine, und die Kohlen, die es von England gebracht hatte, wurden heut gelöscht, wobei Hans Adam niemals sonst zu fehlen pflegte; aber diesmal hatte er seinen Tochtermann geschickt; er hatte

Wichtigeres zu tun: er rechnete, er summierte und subtra-hierte, er wollte wissen, was ihm dieser Sohn, den er sich so unbedacht zurückgeholt hatte, oder – wenn es nicht sein Sohn war – dieser Mensch noch kosten dürfe. Mit rascher Hand tauchte er seine Feder ein und schrieb seine Zahlen nieder; Sohn oder nicht, das stand ihm fest, es mußte jetzt ein Ende haben. Aber freilich – und seine Feder stockte einen Augenblick – um weniges würde er ja schwerlich gehen; und – wenn es dennoch Heinz wäre, den Sohn durfte er mit wenigem nicht gehen heißen. Er hatte sogar daran gedacht, ihm ein für allemal das Pflichtteil seines Erbes auszuzahlen; aber die gerichtliche Quittung, wie war die zu beschaffen? denn sicher mußte es doch gemacht wer-den, damit er nicht noch einmal wiederkomme. Er warf die Feder hin, und der Laut, der an den Zähnen ihm ver-stummte, klang beinahe wie ein Lachen: es war ja aber nicht sein Heinz! Der Justizrat, der verstand es doch; und der alte Hinrich Jakobs trug seinen Anker noch mit seinen achtzig Jahren!

Hans Kirch streckte die Hand nach einer neben ihm lie-genden Ledertasche aus; langsam öffnete er sie und nahm eine Anzahl Kassenscheine von geringem Werte aus dersel-ben. Nachdem er sie vor sich ausgebreitet und dann einen Teil und nach einigem Zögern noch einen Teil davon in die Ledertasche zurückgelegt hatte, steckte er die übrigen in ein bereit gehaltenes Kuvert; er hatte genau die mäßige Summe abgewogen.

Er war nun fertig; aber noch immer saß er da, mit her-abhängendem Unterkiefer, die müßigen Hände an den Tisch geklammert. Plötzlich fuhr er auf, seine grauen Augen öffneten sich weit: »Hans! Hans!« hatte es gerufen; hier im leeren Zimmer, wo, wie er jetzt bemerkte, schon die Dämmerung in allen Winkeln lag. Aber er besann sich; nur seine eigenen Gedanken waren über ihn gekommen; es war nicht jetzt, es war schon viele Jahre her, daß ihn diese Stimme so gerufen hatte. Und dennoch, als ob er widerwil-

lig einem außer sich Gehorsam leiste, öffneten seine Hände
noch einmal die Ledertasche und nahmen zögernd eine
Anzahl großer Kassenscheine aus derselben. Aber mit jedem einzelnen, den Hans Adam jetzt der vorher bemesse-
nen kleinen Summe zugesellte, stieg sein Groll gegen den,
der dafür Heimat und Vaterhaus an ihn verkaufen sollte;
denn was zum Ausbau lang gehegter Lebenspläne hatte
dienen sollen, das mußte er jetzt hinwerfen, nur um die
letzten Trümmer davon wegzuräumen.

– – Als Heinz etwa eine Stunde später, von einem
Gange durch die Stadt zurückkehrend, die Treppe nach
dem Oberhaus hinaufging, trat gleichzeitig Hans Adam
unten aus seiner Zimmertür und folgte ihm so hastig, daß
beide fast miteinander in des Sohnes Kammer traten. Die
Magd, welche oben auf dem Vorplatz arbeitete, ließ bald
beide Hände ruhen; sie wußte es ja wohl, daß zwischen
Sohn und Vater nicht alles in der Ordnung war, und drinnen hinter der geschlossenen Tür schien es jetzt zu einem
heftigen Gespräch zu kommen. – Aber nein, sie hatte sich
getäuscht, es war nur immer die alte Stimme, die sie hörte;
und immer lauter und drohender klang es, obgleich von
der andern Seite keine Antwort darauf erfolgte; aber vergebens strengte sie sich an, von dem Inhalte etwas zu ver-
stehen; sie hörte drinnen den offenen Fensterflügel im
Winde klappern, und ihr war, als würden die noch immer
heftiger hervorbrechenden Worte dort in die dunkle Nacht
hinaus geredet. Dann endlich wurde es still; aber zugleich
sprang die Magd, von der aufgestoßenen Kammertür getroffen, mit einem Schrei zur Seite und sah ihren gefürch-
teten Herrn mit wirrem Haar und wild blickenden Augen
die Treppe hinabstolpern, und hörte, wie die Kontortür
aufgerissen und wieder zugeschlagen wurde.

Bald danach trat auch Heinz aus seiner Kammer; als er
unten im Flur der Schwester begegnete, ergriff er fast gewaltsam ihre beiden Hände und drückte sie so heftig, daß
sie verwundert zu ihm aufblickte; als sie aber zu ihm spre-

chen wollte, war er schon draußen auf der Gasse. Er kam auch nicht zur Abendmahlzeit; aber als die Bürgerglocke läutete, stieg er die Treppe wieder hinauf und ging in seine Kammer.

– – Am andern Morgen in der Frühe stand Heinz vollständig angekleidet droben vor dem offenen Fenster; die scharfe Luft strich über ihn hin, aber es schien ihm wohlzutun; fast mit Andacht schaute er auf alles, was, wie noch im letzten Hauch der Nacht, dort unten vor ihm ausgebreitet lag. Wie bleicher Stahl glänzte die breitere Wasserstraße zwischen dem Warder und der Insel drüben, während auf dem schmaleren Streifen zwischen jenem und dem Festlandsufer schon der bläulichrote Frühschein spielte. Heinz betrachtete das alles; doch nicht lange stand er so; bald trat er an einen Tisch, auf welchem das Kuvert mit den so widerwillig abgezählten Kassenscheinen noch an derselben Stelle lag, wo es Hans Kirch am Abende vorher gelassen hatte.

Ein bitteres Lächeln umflog seinen Mund, während er den Inhalt hervorzog und dann, nachdem er einige der geringeren Scheine an sich genommen hatte, das übrige wieder an seine Stelle brachte. Mit einem Bleistift, den er auf dem Tische fand, notierte er die kleine Summe, welche er herausgenommen hatte, unter der größeren, die auf dem Kuvert verzeichnet stand; dann, als er ihn schon fortgelegt hatte, nahm er noch einmal den Stift und schrieb darunter: »Thanks for the alms and farewell for ever.« Er wußte selbst nicht, warum er das nicht auf deutsch geschrieben hatte.

Leise, um das schlafende Haus nicht zu erwecken, nahm er sein Reisegepäck vom Boden; noch leiser schloß er unten im Flur die Tür zur Straße auf, als er jetzt das Haus verließ.

In einer Nebengasse hielt ein junger Bursche mit einem einspännigen Gefährte; das bestieg er und fuhr damit zur Stadt hinaus. Als sie auf die Höhe des Hügelzuges gelangt waren, von wo aus man diese zum letzten Male erblicken kann, wandte er sich um und schwenkte dreimal seine Mütze. Dann ging's im Trabe in das weite Land hinaus.

Aber einer im Kirchschen Hause war dennoch mit ihm wach gewesen. Hans Kirch hatte schon vor dem Morgengrauen aufrecht in seinem Bett gesessen; mit jedem Schlage der Turmuhr hatte er schärfer hingehorcht, ob nicht ein erstes Regen in dem Oberhause hörbar werde. Nach langem Harren war ihm gewesen, als würde dort ein Fensterflügel aufgestoßen; aber es war wieder still geworden, und die Minuten dehnten sich und wollten nicht vorüber. Sie gingen dennoch; und endlich vernahm er das leise Knarren einer Tür, es kam die Treppe in den Flur hinab, und jetzt – er hörte es deutlich, wie sich der Schlüssel in dem Schloß der Haustür drehte. Er wollte aufspringen; aber nein, er wollte es ja nicht; mit aufgestemmten Armen blieb er sitzen, während nun draußen auf der Straße kräftige Mannestritte laut wurden und nach und nach in unhörbare Ferne sich verloren.

Als das übrige Haus allmählich in Bewegung kam, stand er auf und setzte sich zu seinem Frühstück, das ihm, wie jeden Morgen, im Kontor bereitgestellt war. Dann griff er nach seinem Hute – einen Stock hatte er als alter Schiffer bis jetzt noch nicht gebraucht – und ging, ohne seine Hausgenossen gesehen zu haben, an den Hafen hinab, wo er seinen Schwiegersohn bereits mit der Leitung des Löschens beschäftigt fand. Diesem von den letzten Vorgängen etwas mitzuteilen schien er nicht für nötig zu befinden; aber er sandte ihn nach dem Kohlenschuppen und gab ihm Aufträge in die Stadt, während er selber hier am Platze blieb. Wortkarg und zornig erteilte er seine Befehle; es hielt schwer, ihm heute etwas recht zu machen, und wer ihn ansprach, erhielt meist keine Antwort; aber es geschah auch bald nicht mehr, man kannte ihn ja schon.

Kurz vor Mittag war er wieder in seinem Zimmer. Wie

aus unwillkürlichem Antrieb hatte er hinter sich die Tür verschlossen; aber er saß kaum in seinem Lehnstuhl, als von draußen Frau Linas Stimme dringend Einlaß begehrte. Unwirsch stand er auf und öffnete. »Was willst du?« frug er, als die Tochter zu ihm eingetreten war.

»Schelte mich nicht, Vater«, sagte sie bittend; »aber Heinz ist fort, auch sein Gepäck; oh, er kommt niemals wieder!«

Er wandte den Kopf zur Seite: »Ich weiß das, Lina; darum hättst du dir die Augen nicht dick zu weinen brauchen.«

»Du weißt es, Vater?« wiederholte sie und sah ihn wie versteinert an.

Hans Kirch fuhr zornig auf: »Was stehst du noch? Die Komödie ist vorbei; wir haben gestern miteinander abgerechnet.«

Aber Frau Lina schüttelte nur ernst den Kopf. »Das fand ich oben auf seiner Kammer«, sagte sie und reichte ihm das Kuvert mit den kurzen Abschiedsworten und dem nur kaum verkürzten Inhalt. »O Vater, er war es doch! Er ist es doch gewesen!«

Hans Kirch nahm es; er las auch, was dort geschrieben stand; er wollte ruhig bleiben, aber seine Hände zitterten, daß aus der offenen Hülle die Scheine auf den Fußboden hinabfielen.

Als er sie eben mit Linas Hilfe wieder zusammengerafft hatte, wurde an die Tür gepocht, und ohne die Aufforderung dazu abzuwarten, war eine blasse Frau hereingetreten, deren erregte Augen ängstlich von dem Vater zu der Tochter flohen.

»Wieb!« rief Frau Lina und trat einen Schritt zurück.

Wieb rang nach Atem. »Verzeihung!« murmelte sie. »Ich mußte; Ihr Heinz ist fort; Sie wissen es vielleicht nicht; aber der Fuhrmann sagte es, er wird nicht wiederkommen, niemals!«

»Was geht das dich an!« fiel ihr Hans Kirch ins Wort.

Ein Laut des Schmerzes stieg aus ihrer Brust, daß Linas

Augen unwillkürlich voll Mitleid auf diesem einst so holden Antlitz ruhten. Aber Wieb hatte dadurch wieder Mut gewonnen. »Hören Sie mich!« rief sie. »Aus Barmherzigkeit mit Ihrem eigenen Kinde! Sie meinen, er sei es nicht gewesen; aber ich weiß es, daß es niemand anders war! Das«, und sie zog die Schnur mit dem kleinen Ringe aus ihrer Tasche, »es ist ja einerlei nun, ob ich's sage – das gab ich ihm, da wir noch halbe Kinder waren; denn ich wollte, daß er mich nicht vergesse! Er hat's auch wieder heimgebracht und hat es gestern vor meinen Augen in den Staub geworfen.«

Ein Lachen, das wie Hohn klang, unterbrach sie. Hans Kirch sah sie mit starren Augen an: »Nun, Wieb, wenn's denn dein Heinz gewesen ist, es ist nicht viel geworden aus euch beiden.«

Aber sie achtete nicht darauf, sie hatte sich vor ihm hingeworfen. »Hans Kirch!« rief sie und faßte beide Hände des alten Mannes und schüttelte sie. »Ihr Heinz, hören Sie es nicht? Er geht ins Elend, er kommt niemals wieder! Vielleicht – o Gott, sei barmherzig mit uns allen! Es ist noch Zeit vielleicht!«

Auch Lina hatte sich jetzt neben ihr geworfen; sie scheute es nicht mehr, sich mit dem armen Weibe zu vereinigen. »Vater«, sagte sie und streichelte die eingesunkenen Wangen des harten Mannes, der jetzt dies alles über sich ergehen ließ, »du sollst diesmal nicht allein reisen, ich reise mit dir; er muß ja jetzt in Hamburg sein; oh, ich will nicht ruhen, bis ich ihn gefunden habe, bis wir ihn wieder hier in unsern Armen halten! Dann wollen wir es besser machen, wir wollen Geduld mit ihm haben; oh, wir hatten sie nicht, mein Vater! Und sag nur nicht, daß du nicht mit uns leidest, dein bleiches Angesicht kann doch nicht lügen! Sprich nur ein Wort, Vater, befiel mir, daß ich den Wagen herbestelle, ich will gleich selber laufen, wir haben ja keine Zeit mehr zu verlieren!« Und sie warf den Kopf an ihres Vaters Brust und brach in lautes Schluchzen aus.

Wieb war aufgestanden und hatte sich bescheiden an die Tür gestellt; ihre Augen sahen angstvoll auf die beiden hin.

Aber Hans Kirch saß wie ein totes Bild; sein jahrelang angesammelter Groll ließ ihn nicht los; denn erst jetzt, nach diesem Wiedersehen mit dem Heimgekehrten, war in der grauen Zukunft keine Hoffnung mehr für ihn. »Geht!« sagte er endlich, und seine Stimme klang so hart wie früher; »mag er geheißen haben, wie er will, der diesmal unter meinem Dach geschlafen hat; mein Heinz hat schon vor siebzehn Jahren mich verlassen.«

Für fremde Augen mochte es immerhin den Anschein haben, als ob Hans Kirch auch jetzt noch in gewohnter Weise seinen mancherlei Geschäften nachgehe; in Wirklichkeit aber hatte er das Steuer mehr und mehr in die Hand des jüngeren Teilhabers der Firma übergehen lassen; auch aus dem städtischen Kollegium war er, zur stillen Befriedigung einiger ruheliebenden Mitglieder, seit kurzer Zeit geschieden; es drängte ihn nicht mehr, in den Gang der kleinen Welt, welche sich um ihn her bewegte, einzugreifen.

Seit wieder die ersten scharfen Frühlingslüfte wehten, konnte man ihn oft auf der Bank vor seinem Hause sitzen sehen, trotz seiner jetzt fast weißen Haare als alter Schiffer ohne jede Kopfbedeckung. – Eines Morgens kam ein noch weißerer Mann die Straße hier herab und setzte sich, nachdem er näher getreten war, ohne weiteres an seine Seite. Es war ein früherer Ökonom des Armenhauses, mit dem er als Stadtverordneter einst manches zu verhandeln gehabt hatte; der Mann war später in gleicher Stellung an einen andern Ort gekommen, jetzt aber zurückgekehrt, um hier in seiner Vaterstadt seinen Alterspfennig zu verzehren. Es schien ihn nicht zu stören, daß das Antlitz seines früheren Vorgesetzten ihn keineswegs willkommen hieß; er wollte ja nur plaudern, und er tat es um so reichlicher, je weniger er unterbrochen wurde; und eben jetzt geriet er an einen Stoff, der unerschöpflicher als jeder andere schien.

Hans Kirch hatte Unglück mit den Leuten, die noch wei-
ßer als er selber waren; wo sie von Heinz sprechen sollten,
da sprachen sie von sich selber, und wo sie von allem andern sprechen konnten, da sprachen sie von Heinz. Er
wurde unruhig und suchte mit schroffen Worten abzuweh-
ren; aber der geschwätzige Greis schien nichts davon zu
merken. »Ja, ja; ei du mein lieber Herrgott!« fuhr er fort,
behaglich in seinem Redestrome weiter schwimmend; »der
Hasselfritze und der Heinz, wenn ich an die beiden Jungen
denke, wie sie sich einmal die großen Anker in die Arme
brannten! Ihr Heinz, ich hörte wohl, der mußte vor dem
Doktor liegen; den Hasselfritze aber hab ich selber mit
dem Hasselstock kuriert.«

Er lachte ganz vergnüglich über sein munteres Wort-
spiel; Hans Kirch aber war plötzlich aufgestanden und sah
mit offenem Munde gar grimmig auf ihn herab. »Wenn Er
wieder schwatzen will, Fritz Peters«, sagte er, »so suche Er
sich eine andere Bank; da drüben bei dem jungen Doktor
steht just eine hagelneue!«

Er war ins Haus gegangen und wanderte in seinem Zimmer hin und wider; immer tiefer sank sein Kopf zur Brust
hinab, dann aber erhob er ihn allmählich wieder. Was hatte
er denn eigentlich vorhin erfahren? Daß der Hasselfritze
ebenfalls das Ankerzeichen hätte haben müssen? Was war's
denn weiter? – Welchen Gast er von einem Sonntag bis zum
andern oder ein paar Tage noch länger bei sich beherbergt
hatte, darüber brauchte ihn kein anderer aufzuklären.

Und auch dieser Tag ging vorüber, und die dann kamen,
nahmen ihren gleichmäßigen Verlauf. – Im Oberhause
wurde ein Kind geboren; der Großvater frug, ob es ein
Junge sei; es war ein Mädchen, und er sprach dann nicht
mehr darüber. Aber was hätte es ihm auch geholfen, wenn
es ein künftiger Christian oder günstigen Falles ein Hans
Martens gewesen wäre! Nur die Unruhe, die jetzt oft
nächtens über seinem Kopfe in dem Schlafzimmer des jungen Paares herrschte, störte ihn.

Eines Abends, da es schon Herbst geworden – es jährte sich grade mit der Abreise seines Sohnes –, war Hans Kirch wie gewöhnlich mit dem Schlage zehn in seine nach der Hofseite belegene Schlafkammer getreten. Es war die Zeit der Äquinoktialstürme, und hier hinaus hörte man die ganze Gewalt des Wetters; bald heulte es in den obersten Luftschichten, bald fuhr es herab und tobte gegen die kleinen Fensterscheiben. Hans Kirch hatte seine silberne Taschenuhr hervorgezogen, um sie, wie jeden Abend, aufzuziehen; aber er stand noch immer mit dem Schlüssel in der Hand, hinaushorchend in die wilde Nacht.

Das Balken- und Sparrenwerk des neuen Daches krachte, als ob es aus den Fugen solle; aber er hörte es nicht; seine Gedanken fuhren draußen mit dem Sturm. »Südsüdwest!« murmelte er vor sich hin, während er den Uhrschlüssel in die Tasche steckte und die Uhr unaufgezogen über seinem Bette an den Haken hing. – Wer jetzt auf See war, hatte keine Zeit zum Schlafen; aber er war ja seit lange nicht mehr auf See; er wollte schlafen, wie er es bei manchem Sturm hier schon getan hatte; die Stürme kamen ja allemal im Äquinoktium, er hatte sie so manches Mal gehört.

Aber es mußte heute noch etwas anderes dabei sein; Stunden waren schon vergangen, und noch immer lag er wach in seinen Kissen. Ihm war, als könne er Hunderte von Meilen weit hinaushorchen nach einem klippenvollen Küstenwasser des Mittelländischen Meeres, das er in seiner Jugend als Matrose einst befahren hatte; und als endlich ihm die Augen zugefallen waren, riß er gleich darauf mit Gewalt sich wieder empor; denn ganz deutlich hatte er ein Schiff gesehen, ein Vollschiff mit gebrochenen Masten, das von turmhohen Wellen auf und ab geschleudert wurde. Er suchte sich völlig zu ermuntern, aber wieder drückte es ihm die Augen zu, und wiederum erkannte er das Schiff; deutlich sah er zwischen Bugspriet und Vordersteven die Gallion, eine weiße mächtige Fortuna, bald in der schäumenden Flut versinken, bald wieder stolz emportauchen, als ob sie Schiff und Mannschaft über Wasser halten wolle. Dann plötzlich hörte er einen Krach; er fuhr jäh empor und fand sich aufrecht in seinem Bette sitzend.

Alles um ihn her war still, er hörte nichts; er wollte sich besinnen, ob es nicht eben vorher noch laut gestürmt habe; da überfiel es ihn, als sei er nicht allein in seiner Kammer; er stützte beide Hände auf die Bettkanten und riß weit die Augen auf. Und – da war es, dort in der Ecke stand sein Heinz; das Gesicht sah er nicht, denn der Kopf war gesenkt, und die Haare, die von Wasser trieften, hingen über die Stirn herab; aber er erkannte ihn dennoch – woran, das wußte er nicht und frug er sich auch nicht. Auch von den Kleidern und von den herabhängenden Armen troff das Wasser; es floß immer mehr herab und bildete einen breiten Strom nach seinem Bette zu.

Hans Kirch wollte rufen, aber er saß wie gelähmt mit seinen aufgestemmten Armen; endlich brach ein lauter Schrei aus seiner Brust, und gleich darauf auch hörte er es über sich in der Schlafkammer der jungen Leute poltern, und auch den Sturm hörte er wieder, wie er grimmig an den Pfosten seines Hauses rüttelte.

Als bald danach sein Schwiegersohn mit Licht hereintrat, fand dieser ihn in seinen Kissen zusammengesunken. »Wir hörten Euch schreien«, frug er, »was ist Euch, Vater?«

Der Alte sah starr nach jener Ecke. »Er ist tot«, sagte er, »weit von hier.«

– »Wer ist tot, Vater? Wen meint Ihr? Meint Ihr Eueren Heinz?«

Der Alte nickte. »Das Wasser«, sagte er; »geh da fort, du stehst ja mitten in dem Wasser!«

Der Jüngere fuhr mit dem Lichte gegen den Fußboden: »Hier ist kein Wasser, Vater, Ihr habt nur schwer geträumt.«

»Du bist kein Seemann, Christian; was weißt du davon!« sagte der Alte heftig. »Aber ich weiß es, so kommen unsere Toten.«

»Soll ich Euch Lina schicken, Vater?« frug Christian Martens wieder.

»Nein, nein, sie soll bei ihrem Kinde bleiben; geh nur, laß mich allein!«

Der Schwiegersohn war mit dem Lichte fortgegangen, und Hans Kirch saß im Dunkeln wieder aufrecht in seinem Bette; er streckte zitternd die Arme nach jener Ecke, wo eben noch sein Heinz gestanden hatte; er wollte ihn noch einmal sehen, aber er sah vergebens in undurchdringliche Finsternis.

– – Es ging schon in den Vormittag, als Frau Lina, da sie unten in die Stube trat, das Frühstück ihres Vaters unberührt fand; als sie dann in die Schlafkammer ging, lag er noch in seinem Bette; er konnte nicht aufstehen, denn ein Schlaganfall hatte ihn getroffen, freilich nur an der einen Seite und ohne ihn am Sprechen zu behindern. Er verlangte nach seinem alten Arzte, und die Tochter lief selbst nach dem Hause des Justizrats und stand bald wieder zugleich mit diesem an des Vaters Lager.

Es war nicht gar so schlimm, es würde wohl so vorübergehen, lautete dessen Ausspruch. Aber Hans Kirch hörte kaum darauf; mehr als bei seiner Krankheit waren seine Gedanken bei den Vorgängen der verflossenen Nacht; Heinz hatte sich gemeldet, Heinz war tot, und der Tote hatte alle Rechte, die er noch eben dem Lebenden nicht mehr hatte zugestehen wollen.

Als Frau Lina es ihm ausreden wollte, berief er sich eifrig auf den Justizrat, der ja seit Jahr und Tag in manches Seemannshaus gekommen sei.

Der Justizrat suchte zu beschwichtigen: »Freilich«, fügte er hinzu, »wir Ärzte kennen Zustände, wo die Träume selbst am hellen Werktag das Gehirn verlassen und dem Menschen leibhaftig in die Augen schauen.«

Hans Kirch warf verdrießlich seinen Kopf herum: »Das ist mir zu gelehrt, Doktor; wie war's denn damals mit dem Sohn des alten Rickerts?«

Der Arzt faßte den Puls des Kranken. »Es trifft, es trifft auch nicht«, sagte er bedächtig; »das war der ältere Sohn; der jüngere, der sich auch gemeldet haben sollte, fährt noch heute seines Vaters Schiff.«

Hans Kirch schwieg; er wußte es doch besser als alle andern, was weit von hier in dieser Nacht geschehen war.

Wie der Arzt es vorhergesagt hatte, so geschah es. Nach einigen Wochen konnte der Kranke das Bett und allmählich auch das Zimmer, ja sogar das Haus verlassen; nur bedurfte er dann, gleich seiner Schwester, eines Krückstockes, den er bisher verschmäht hatte. Von seinem früheren Jähzorn schien meist nur eine weinerliche Ungeduld zurückgeblieben; wenn es ihn aber einmal wie vordem überkam, dann brach er hinterher erschöpft zusammen.

Als es Sommer wurde, verlangte er aus der Stadt hinaus, und Frau Lina begleitete ihn mehrmals auf dem hohen Uferwege um die Bucht, von wo er nicht nur die Inseln, sondern ostwärts auch auf das freie Wasser sehen konnte. Da das Ufer an mehreren Stellen tief und steil gegen den Strand hinabfällt, so wagte man ihn hier nicht allein zu lassen und gab ihm zu andern Malen, wenn die Tochter keine Zeit hatte, einen der Arbeiter oder sonst eine andere sichere Person zur Seite.

– – Auf den Sommer war der Herbst gefolgt, und es war um die Zeit, da Heinzens kurze Einkehr in das Elternhaus zum zweiten Mal sich jährte. Hans Kirch saß auf einem sandigen Vorsprunge des steilen Ufers und ließ die Nachmittagssonne seinen weißen Kopf bescheinen, während er die Hände vor sich auf seinen Stock gefaltet hielt und seine Augen über die glatte See hinausstarrten. Neben ihm stand ein Weib, anscheinend in gleicher Teilnahmlosigkeit, welche den Hut des alten Mannes in der herabhängenden Hand hielt. Sie mochte kaum über dreißig Jahre zählen; aber nur ein schärferes Auge hätte in diesem Antlitz die Spuren einer früh zerstörten Anmut finden kön-

74

nen. Sie schien nichts davon zu hören, was der alte Schiffer, ohne sich zu rühren, vor sich hin sprach; es war auch nur ein Flüstern, als ob er es den leeren Lüften anvertraue; allmählich aber wurde es lauter: »Heinz, Heinz!« rief er. »Wo ist Heinz Kirch geblieben?« Dann wieder bewegte er langsam seinen Kopf: »Es ist auch einerlei, denn es kennt ihn keiner mehr.«

Da seufzte das Weib an seiner Seite, daß er sich wandte und zu ihr aufsah. Als sie das blasse Gesicht zu ihm niederbeugte, suchte er ihre Hand zu fassen: »Nein, nein, Wieb, du – du kanntest ihn; dafür« – und er nickte vertraulich zu ihr auf – »bleibst du auch bei mir, solang ich lebe; und auch nachher – ich habe in meinem Testament das festgemacht; es ist nur gut, daß dein Taugenichts von Mann sich totgetrunken.«

Als sie nicht antwortete, wandte er seinen Kopf wieder ab, und seine Augen folgten einer Möwe, die vom Strande über das Wasser hinausflog. »Und dort«, begann er wieder, und seine Stimme klang jetzt ganz munter, während er mit seinem Krückstock nach dem Warder zeigte, »da hat er damals dich herumgefahren? Und dann schalten sie vom Schiff herüber?« – Und als sie schweigend zu ihm herabnickte, lachte er leise vor sich hin. Aber bald verfiel er wieder in sein Selbstgespräch, während seine Augen vor ihm in die große Leere starrten. »Nur in der Ewigkeit, Heinz! Nur in der Ewigkeit!« rief er, in plötzliches Weinen ausbrechend, und streckte zitternd beide Arme nach dem Himmel.

Aber seine laut gesprochenen Worte erhielten diesmal eine Antwort. »Was haben wir Menschen mit der Ewigkeit zu schaffen?« sprach eine heisere Stimme neben ihm. Es war ein herabgekommener Tischler, den sie in der Stadt den »Sozialdemokraten« nannten; er glaubte ein Loch in seinem Christenglauben entdeckt zu haben und pflegte nun nach Art geringer Menschen gegen andere damit zu trotzen.

Mit einer raschen Bewegung, die weit über die Kraft des gebrochenen Mannes hinauszugehen schien, hatte Hans Kirch sich zu dem Sprechenden gewandt, der mit verschränkten Armen stehenblieb. »Du kennst mich wohl nicht, Jürgen Hans?« rief er, während der ganze arme Leib ihm zitterte. »Ich bin Hans Kirch, der seinen Sohn verstoßen hat, zweimal! Hörst du es, Jürgen Hans? Zweimal hab ich meinen Heinz verstoßen, und darum hab ich mit der Ewigkeit zu schaffen!«

Der andere war dicht an ihn herangetreten. »Das tut mir leid, Herr Kirch«, sagte er und wog ihm trocken jedes seiner Worte zu; »die Ewigkeit ist in den Köpfen alter Weiber!«

Ein fieberhafter Blitz fuhr aus den Augen des greisen Mannes. »Hund!« schrie er, und ein Schlag des Krückstocks pfiff jäh am Kopf des anderen vorüber.

Der Tischler sprang zur Seite, dann stieß er ein Hohngelächter aus und schlenderte den Weg zur Stadt hinab.

Aber die Kraft des alten Mannes war erschöpft; der Stock entfiel seiner Hand und rollte vor ihm den Hang hinunter, und er wäre selber nachgestürzt, wenn nicht das Weib sich rasch gebückt und ihn in ihren Armen aufgefangen hätte.

Neben ihm kniend, sanft und unbeweglich, hielt sie das weiße Haupt an ihrer Brust gebettet, denn Hans Kirch war eingeschlafen. – Das Abendrot legte sich über das Meer, ein leichter Wind hatte sich erhoben, und drunten rauschten die Wellen lauter an den Strand. Noch immer beharrte sie in ihrer unbequemen Stellung; erst als schon die Sterne schienen, schlug er die Augen zu ihr auf: »Er ist tot«, sagte er, »ich weiß es jetzt gewiß; aber – in der Ewigkeit, da will ich meinen Heinz schon wiederkennen.«

»Ja«, sagte sie leise, »in der Ewigkeit.«

Vorsichtig, von ihr gestützt, erhob er sich, und als sie seinen Arm um ihren Hals und ihren Arm ihm um die Hüfte gelegt hatte, gingen sie langsam nach der Stadt zurück. Je

76

weiter sie kamen, desto schwerer wurde ihre Last; mitunter mußten sie stillestehn, dann blickte Hans Kirch nach den Sternen, die ihm einst so manche Herbstnacht an Bord seiner flinken Jacht geschienen hatten, und sagte: »Es geht schon wieder«, und sie gingen langsam weiter. Aber nicht nur von den Sternen, auch aus den blauen Augen des armen Weibes leuchtete ein milder Strahl; nicht jener mehr, der einst in einer Frühlingsnacht ein wildes Knabenhaupt an ihre junge Brust gerissen hatte, aber ein Strahl jener allbarmherzigen Frauenliebe, die allen Trost des Lebens in sich schließt.

Noch während der nächsten Jahre, meist an stillen Nachmittagen und wenn die Sonne sich zum Untergange neigte, konnte man Hans Kirch mit seiner steten Begleiterin auf dem Uferwege sehen; zur Zeit des Herbst-Äquinoktiums war er selbst beim Nordoststurm nicht daheim zu halten. Dann hat man ihn auf dem Friedhof seiner Vaterstadt zur Seite seiner stillen Frau begraben.

Das von ihm begründete Geschäft liegt in den besten Händen; man spricht schon von dem »reichen« Christian Martens, und Hans Adams Tochtermanne wird der Stadtrat nicht entgehen; auch ein Erbe ist längst geboren und läuft schon mit dem Ranzen in die Rektorschule; – wo aber ist Heinz Kirch geblieben?

NACHWORT

Das Verhältnis von Vater und Sohn ist von jeher ein Problem von besonderer Anziehungskraft gewesen. Wie schön und für beide Teile segensreich es sein kann, so bitter und scharf werden gerade in diesem Falle oft Konflikte empfunden, wenn hier etwa die Lebensanschauungen zweier aufeinanderfolgender Generationen feindlich zusammenstoßen, wie wir das z. B. in der Jugend Friedrichs des Großen und Goethes beobachten können, oder wenn sich zwei entgegengesetzte Charaktere aneinander reiben wie in Goethes *Hermann und Dorothea*. Aber auch ähnliche Eigenschaften bei Vater und Sohn können zum Zerwürfnis führen, und das ist der Fall bei Storms *Hans und Heinz Kirch*.

Wie kommt Theodor Storm zu diesem Problem? Er war doch ein »passionierter Vater«, suchte seine acht Kinder mit Milde und ganz ohne Schläge zu erziehen und betonte immer das eigene Recht der Kinder. Und doch entspringt auch der *Kirch* eigenem Erleben des Dichters. Auch er hat den Konflikt zwischen Vater und Sohn kennenlernen müssen. Sein befähigter ältester Sohn Hans, der ihm besonders lieb war, verfiel als Student dem Trunk und machte dem Vater 15 Jahre lang die schwersten Sorgen. Es kamen Zeiten, wo der Vater dem Sohne das Haus verbot, er schrieb ihm nicht mehr, und Hans richtete seine Briefe an die Stiefmutter. So begreift es sich, daß in diesem Dichter der Boden bereitet war für die Aufnahme und Gestaltung von Stoffen, die den Konflikt zwischen Vater und Sohn behandeln.

Seit Frühling 1881 war Hans Arzt in Frammersbach in Bayern und schrieb regelmäßig nach Hause; die jahrelang getragene schwere Last schien von der Seele des Vaters genommen. Das gab ihm die innere Freiheit zur dichterischen Gestaltung des Problems, und gerade in diesem Jahre stieß er auf den geeigneten Stoff. Vom September bis in den Oktober hinein war er Gast im Pastorate seines Schwiegersohns in Heiligenhafen an der Ostsee. Dort hörte er die Geschichte von dem Schiffer Brandt, der einen lange erwarteten Brief seines fernen Sohnes nicht annimmt, weil er nicht freigemacht ist, und dann dadurch gestraft wird, daß er im Zweifel bleibt, ob der später endlich Heimgekehrte wirklich sein Sohn ist. Trotz der äußeren Unähnlichkeit mit seinem eigenen Erleben ist die Gestaltung dieses Stoffes für den Dichter ein »innerer Befreiungsakt« geworden. Die Arbeit hat ihn vom Oktober 1881 bis Ende Februar 1882 beschäftigt.

Im Juni 1880 hatte Storm an Erich Schmidt geschrieben: »Jedenfalls ist mein künstlerisches Bekenntnis, daß eine aufs Tragische gestaltete Novelle, wenn sie ist, wie sie sein soll, so gut wie die Tragödie erschüttern und nicht rühren soll.« Diese Wirkung hat er im *Kirch* erreicht; und so hören wir gerechten Künstlerstolz aus der Äußerung des Dichters über diese Novelle in einem Briefe an Gottfried Keller: »Eine gewisse Genugtuung ist mir, daß man hierbei als Wirkung eine kräftige, tragische Erschütterung zugegeben hat ... Wenn Sie übrigens sagen, daß Sie die harten Köpfe, die ihre Söhne quälen, nicht lieben, so meine ich doch, daß ein solcher in der Menschennatur liegender Prinzipalkonflikt der Dichtung nicht vorbehalten bleiben darf; nur muß man der harten Kraft ... des Vaters auch etwas Derartiges in dem Sohn entgegenstellen ... Übrigens habe ich den Vater als Hauptperson im Auge gehabt; er sündigt und er büßt.«

Walther Herrmann

ball perched at the far end of the stadium. Then it cut straight back to Dunk, squirming in the Oldheim blitzer's grasp.

'It seems Gr'Nash down there shares your passion for a good fight,' said Bob, 'and your skill!'

The crowd erupted in laughter, and the sound drove Gr'Nash even madder than before. The ogre swung at Dunk again, but the Hackers' star thrower managed to angle himself out of the way once more.

Dunk wondered where the rest of his team could be. They wouldn't just leave him up here forever, would they? M'Grash K'Thragsh – the Hackers' own ogre – was Dunk's best friend. Spinne Schönheit shared his bed. Edgar – the treeman they'd picked up in Albion last season – was as solid as his trunk. And Dunk had played alongside Cavre and Reyes for two years now.

Of course, the other players had only been on the team since the start of the tournament. Few of them had set boots on a Blood Bowl field before, and none of them had ever faced down an opposing team of eleven angry ogres.

Dunk barely knew these new players at all. If it weren't for the fact that their names were stencilled across the backs of their green and gold armour, he didn't think he'd have been able to pick them out from each other in the game. Still, they were on his team, and he expected them to come to his aid.

A glance at the Jumboball – which piped the Cabalvision broadcast to the fans in the stadium via the most advanced mass communications magic of the day – showed Dunk that the other Oldheim Ogres had formed a wall of armour-plated flesh between Dunk and his team-mates. He knew that the wall couldn't stand forever. Sooner or later his friends would get around it. M'Grash would just plough right through it. But it would take time, something he didn't have.

Gr'Nash raised the busted bench up for another swing, and the snotling on the end broke free and went sailing off into the stands. The fans there batted the poor creature into the air again, bopping it back and forth like a beach ball, the pathetic beast squeaking like a living chew toy with every blow.

'It's always great to see the fans working together to entertain themselves,' Bob said. 'That just might be our Bloodweiser Beer play of the day.'

'I don't know about that, but keep your attention on that end zone,' Jim said. 'It looks like Hoffnung has a great, early shot at being named the game's Most Violated Player.'

Seemingly to prove the point, Gr'Nash lowered his arm and slammed Dunk headfirst into the Astrogranite below. Stars flashed before Dunk's eyes, and his head felt like the muscles in his neck had turned to rubber.

'I thought the MVP went to the 'Most Violent Player,' sad Bob.

'It's a double-edged acronym,' said Jim, 'and here's Gr'Nash to stake his claim for the other side of the award.'

Stunned, his arms flailing about, Dunk swung his head around to his left. He saw a flash of blue and smelled fresh-cut lumber. Then everything went black.

THE NEXT THING Dunk knew, he was lying flat on his back. This didn't seem so unusual, what with the savage blow to the head he'd just taken, but he couldn't see or hear a thing. He started to panic, then realised his eyes were closed, which at least explained why he was blind.

His eyes felt like they might have been glued shut, but he finally managed to peel them open. He instantly regretted it.

He stared up at the ceiling above him, the light of a number of lanterns flickering across its rough-finished surface. He recognised it as belonging to one of the team locker rooms in Magritta's Killer Stadium, for which the legendary brewing company had bought the naming rights. The holes in the plaster from when M'Grash had leapt with joy after their last victory told him that this was the locker room in which the Hackers had started the day.

'How's your head?' The voice sounded like it had been forced through the chewed end of a halfling's pipe: smoky and distant.

Now that the speaker mentioned it, Dunk realised that his head felt like his brains were beating away at the inside of his skull with spiked warhammers. 'Not good,' he rasped through a mouth coated with an all-too-familiar flavour: dried blood.

The speaker leaned over into Dunk's field of vision. He was an old elf with a bloodstained patch of white fabric slung over his right eye, his lips curled in a disgusted sneer. 'You'll live,' the elf said as he shook his head, his voice dripping with disdain. 'I've seen little halfling girls take punches better than you.'

'There was a board and an ogre involved,' Dunk said. He started to get angry, but the rush of blood to his head made his brain switch over to using steam-powered jackhammers. To placate them, he let out a deep sigh instead of the string of curses he'd been preparing.

Then the elf slapped him in the jaw, and the stars started swirling around his vision again. 'Sit up,' the elf said.

'Take it easy on him,' another voice said, one that Dunk knew as well as any. It belonged to his agent, a tubby halfling by the name of Slick Fullbelly.

'Don't worry,' the elf said as Dunk used his wobbly arms to shove himself halfway up into a sitting position. 'I won't punch your meal ticket here.' The elf fitted a bulging monocle over his good eye and squinted through it at Dunk. 'Looks like the ogres nearly took care of that for you already. If they'd succeeded, maybe a scumbag like you would finally have to go and find some honest work.'

'Like gathering illegal substances to concoct potions designed to get players back on the field?' Slick asked. Dunk saw him flittering around the elf's feet, trying to get the apothecary's attention, but the elf ignored him as if he were nothing more than a fly hunting for carrion. 'Do the Game Wizards know about the little operation you have here, Dr. Pill? Maybe Wolf Sports would be interested in running an exposé.'

The elf removed his monocle and started to rummage through a wooden rack filled with iron flasks. Some of these looked fresh while others rested under thick layers of dust. The elf scratched his chin, and then selected a flask, possibly at random. He turned towards Slick and blew the dust off the bottle and into the agent's face.

As Slick tried to hack the dust from his lungs and rub it from his eyes, the elf pulled a rusty scalpel from a sheath on his belt and worked it around the red wax seal covering the flask's cork. 'Who do you think supplies me with those truly hard-to-find ingredients?'

the elf asked, ignoring Slick once more. 'Do you think ratings go up or down when an injured player manages to hobble back onto the field for a few more plays?'

Dr. Pill stabbed his scalpel into the top of the broken seal and used it to pry the flask's cork free. It came loose with an explosive pop that sent it and the scalpel flying into the ceiling, where they embedded themselves next to one of the holes M'Grash had made.

A green and slimy substance bubbled forth from the flask's open top, spilling down over Dr. Pill's hand, which Dunk now saw was covered with a rubber glove. Where the stuff plopped on the floor, it hissed and sizzled like water on a hot, greased griddle.

'Drink this,' the elf said, shoving the potion at Dunk. The flask smacked him in the face and knocked him back to the table again.

Dunk growled and sat right back up again. The elf grimaced at him, shamefaced. 'My apologies,' he said, pointing at his eye patch with his free hand as he offered up the bubbling flask again. 'No depth perception.'

Dunk crossed his eyes to stare at the flask of frothing gunk, which hung too close to his face, but at least it hadn't smashed into him this time. He felt the sharp scent of it scorch the hair in his nostrils right off.

'How does he know that's not some kind of poison?' Slick squeaked out between coughs.

'Oh, it's a poison, all right,' Dr. Pill said, staring at Dunk with his one good eye, 'arsenic, to be precise. Smell the bitter almonds in it? That's always a dead giveaway.'

'What?'

'But it has an antidote mixed into it, along with some other things, the so-called 'secret ingredients.' This volatile combination can strip the paint off your armour, but it'll put your head right too. Otherwise, it's weeks in the sickhouse. You'll miss not only this game but the rest of the tournament too.'

From somewhere above, Dunk heard a low, muffled roar. The plaster shook loose from the ceiling, and the cork and scalpel came tumbling down, barely missing Slick's feet as they stabbed juddering into the floor. The agent leapt back in dismay.

Dunk reached out with an unsteady hand and snatched the potion from the leering elf's hands. Before his other arm could give out and send him collapsing back on the table, he tipped the flask back, opened up his throat, and swallowed its noxious contents in one determined gulp.

Slick looked up at Dunk as if the thrower had promised him another beer, and Dr. Pill glared at him, his good eye seeming as dead as the other. Dunk felt the potion swirl its way down into his belly where it began its work. Warmth spread out from his stomach to his head, fingers, and toes until he felt like he wanted to jump into a sauna to cool off. Sweat poured off his skin, streaming down from his hairline and into his eyes. His eyeballs started to burn from the inside, and his teeth felt like glowing coals in his mouth.

'Water,' Dunk rasped. 'Please.'

'Here,' Dr. Pill said. He handed Dunk a wide funnel attached to a long, rubber hose that wound its way under the table on which the rack of flasks rested.

Dunk squinted into the funnel, unsure what to do with it. Would it fill with water for him to drink? Should he hold it over his head and let a cascade of water shower him? He needed something to drink so badly that he thought of sticking his face into the funnel and sucking on it until the water came out.

Then his stomach turned on him hard, flipping and flopping like a fish on a dry dock, gasping for water, drowning in air. Dunk's eyes flew open, as wide as the zeroes on a scoreboard.

'What's happening?' Slick asked. 'Son, are you all right?' The halfling turned on the elf, 'I swear to every bastard god that ever sinned I'll turn you over to our own team's ogre if he dies. Dunk's like a brother to M'Grash. He'll take it hard – and he'll take it out on–'

Dunk interrupted Slick's tirade of threats by unleashing the contents of his stomach into the funnel. It started with a savage roar, travelled through the gush of a flooding river, and trickled off into a sickly whimper punctuated with a hack and a spit.

'Nuffle's leathery balls!' Slick said as he rushed to Dunk's side. 'What have you done to him? Son? Son!'

Dunk wiped his mouth on the back of his sleeve and sat up, ready to be knocked over by the tiny force of the halfling's breath. Instead, as he shook his head, he realised it felt fine. The throbbing that had been there was gone, his brains having dropped their excavating tools and called it a day.

'I'm good,' he said, bounding off the apothecary's table, 'better than ever, maybe. I feel great!'

Slick squinted up at Dunk suspiciously. 'When we brought you in here, son, you were half-dead. I thought we'd have to go with a closed coffin at the funeral. How's this quack manage–'

'It's customary to thank those who save your life,' Dr. Pill said, 'although I'm accustomed to not receiving such pleasantries from primitives.'

Dunk smirked at the apothecary. He wanted to be angry at the man and his sour attitude, but he felt too damn fine to be bothered with such things. 'Thank you,' he said sincerely.

'Just doing my job,' the elf said, the sneer back on his face. 'And at the rates I charge I suspect your employer would prefer it if you ceased joining in this riveting knitting circle here in the locker room with your agent and me and got back out on that pitch to do your job.'

Dunk bounded off the table and cracked his neck back and forth. 'On my way,' he said as he headed for the door.

As he left, he heard Slick ask Dr. Pill a question, trying to curry his favour. As an agent, Slick found it his duty to work every possible angle on Dunk's behalf, and being able to call on someone who could heal an injured player like that might come in handy.

'That's an amazing contraption you have there to catch your patients' illnesses. Does it just vent into the sewers?'

The elf snorted. 'Do I just throw it away? Of course not. Do you have any idea how much those materials cost? I find they can last for three or four applications at least.'

Dunk raced out through the tunnel that led to the Hackers' dugout, certain he didn't want to hear any more.

CHAPTER TWO

When Dunk emerged into the dugout, he saw Pegleg glaring out at the open field beyond. The former pirate had his good leg planted on the top step and his wooden prosthetic stabbed right into the Astrogranite that edged the dugout. He braced his fleshy hand against the dugout's roof, designed to keep out bad weather and 'gifts' hurled by furious fans. His hook scratched at the wide-brimmed, yellow tricorn hat that already bore a score of holes from such abuse.

'Reporting for duty, coach!' Dunk said as he strode past the benchwarmers that lined the back of the dugout, supposedly the safest place in the entire stadium. A couple of them glared at Dunk with jealous eyes, but the others trembled as he walked by, fearful not of him, but of anyone who made sudden movements.

'Thank Nuffle you're here, Hoffnung,' Pegleg said. 'Dr. Pill's magic never fails.'

Dunk rubbed his head again, amazed that it didn't still feel like an axe through the kindling of his skull. 'It was worth whatever you paid him.'

Pegleg spat on the field. 'I'm glad you feel that way. I'm deducting his fee from your pay.'

'What?' Dunk goggled at the captain. The man hadn't fallen too far from his piratical roots, it seemed.

'It's the least you can do,' Pegleg said. 'In the grand scheme of things, I'll end up paying more for it than you.'

'How's that?' Dunk asked. As he spoke, he watched the ball sail downfield with something that looked like a long branch jammed atop one of the spikes.

Pegleg growled. 'We're going to have to teach that treeman of ours how to hold the damned ball.'

Dunk pointed down to where Spinne had caught the ball and pulled off the branch to use as a club against the pair of ogres trying to capture her. Even encased in her helmet and armour, Dunk could see how beautiful she was. She moved with a dancer's grace, but struck with the trained savagery of a born warrior.

Dunk smiled, glad that the two of them were finally on the same team for once. Dating Spinne, back when she'd been with the Reikland Reavers, had been trouble for them both. The fact that his brother Dirk played for the Reavers too and had once shared Spinne's bed hadn't made it any easier.

'Do you think maybe Edgar planned that?' Dunk asked. 'It looks like it's working.'

'Edgar's brains are composed of wood, Mr. Hoffnung. What do you think?'

Somewhere on the field, a whistle blew. A russet-coated minotaur dressed in a black and white striped shirt charged out on to the field and scooped up a yellow penalty flag.

'Ooh!' Bob's voice said over the PA. 'That's going to be "illegal use of a weapon on the field" against Schönheit. Bool's going to kick her out of the game for that!'

'Amazing!' Jim said. 'You hardly ever see that kind of solid, fair officiating in a game of Blood Bowl, and clearly the fans don't like it.'

A rousing howl went up from the stands, punctuated with hisses and boos.

'If anyone can take that kind of abuse, though, it's a player like Rhett Bool. It's too bad he chose to play for Nurgle's Nits during this tournament.'

'Too true, Bob! I think Nits' management must have blown its whole stake on his salary, considering the rest of the team was made of up Chaos-tainted halflings. Where do they find these players?'

'I don't know, Jim, but they're going to have to keep looking if they want to try it again. They may have won their first game against the Darkside Cowboys, but Bool was the only player to survive!'

'It didn't help that he trampled half of his own team's starting line on that first-half kick-off runback!'

Dunk scowled. 'I though you paid off the referee,' he said to Pegleg. Dunk didn't like the idea of distracting the ref's eyes with a stack of shiny gold coins, but he knew it was an established and respected part of the game.

'Oldheim paid him more – and he kept our own booty too!' The ex-pirate turned on Dunk. 'Get out there if you like and tell him how wrong he is to do that.'

Dunk stared up at the minotaur as he charged into the stands and gored an unfortunate section of fans that had come to cheer on the red-uniformed Ogres. He swallowed hard.

'Would you give him his money back for Dr. Pill's treatment?' Slick asked as he emerged from the tunnel in the back of the dugout.

Pegleg shook his head, 'Only if he could get me out of my part of the bargain with that blackguard as well.'

'What did you promise him, coach?' Dunk asked.

Pegleg spat on the ground. 'A guest appearance on his bloody Cabalvision show.'

'The one where he heals people in front of a live audience?' Slick asked. 'I thought that was fictitious.'

Dunk gazed up at Pegleg. 'Hand or foot?' he asked.

'Neither!' The coach snarled, stabbing his hook at Dunk.

A roar erupting from the crowd told Dunk something was up. 'What happened?' he asked, unable to hear the announcers over the hullabaloo.

'The Ogres scored,' Slick shouted. He could project his voice well from his tiny frame. 'That evens up the score at two touchdowns apiece.'

Dunk frowned. 'They didn't stop the game for the penalty.'

'You've been playing this game for two years now,' Pegleg said. 'Haven't you ever seen a bloody penalty called?'

'Sure,' Dunk said. 'There was that game against the Chaos All-Stars last year. They called penalties against both me and M'Grash, but then that Jumboball came crashing down.'

'Yes,' Slick nodded, 'and you were called for excessive celebration after your first touchdown.'

'But I was unconscious for that.'

'Ah, yes,' Slick said, stroking his chin. 'Well what about when you got booted from the game for killing Schlitz 'Malty' Likker?'

'That was during halftime, and Zauberer had ensorcelled him to be possessed by the spirit of Khorne. It wasn't in the middle of the game.'

'Actually, since it was halftime, it was exactly the middle of the game.'

'You know what I mean. The game wasn't going on at the time.'

'Well, the game's stopped now, Mr. Hoffnung,' Pegleg said in a voice laced with menace. 'If you'd care to join it instead of taking this sweet jaunt down memory lane, I'd surely appreciate it.'

Dunk blushed with embarrassment, 'Sure thing, coach. Whatever you say.'

Pegleg flashed a gold-toothed grin at the thrower. 'Good lad. Now get out there to take Spinne's place, and try not to get yourself spanked like a wee child this time!'

Dunk nodded, then grabbed his spare helmet from the rack in the back of the dugout and trotted out onto the field. As he reached the sideline, he met Spinne coming off. She stopped for a moment and butted her helmeted head against his. Grinning at him through their faceguards, she blew him a kiss and said, 'Make them pay.'

Dunk grinned when she turned to smack him on his butt, and he hustled out onto the field. The crowd roared as he raced to the end the Hackers were protecting. He raised his hand to acknowledge them, and the noise grew so loud he could barely hear.

When Dunk had first decided to become a Blood Bowl player, the adulation of the fans was the last thing on his mind. As a washed-up dragonslayer – more of a never-was than a has-been – he'd just wanted to put his past behind him and try something new, something entirely different. Taking up a career on the gridiron seemed like just the thing.

He'd resisted the notion at first. After all, his family had disowned his brother Dirk when he'd gone off to join the Reavers. In response, Dirk had even changed his last name from Hoffnung to Heldmann.

Of course, the disgrace and dissolution of the Hoffnung family had been what had spurred Dunk to take up dragonslaying in the first place. He still felt responsible for what had happened in those dark days, even though he'd done his best to put them behind him. Living as a Blood Bowl star player made forgetting his old life a whole lot easier.

'Dunkel!' M'Grash shouted, bounding towards the thrower in joy. 'Dunkel okay!'

Dunk had long since learned not to deny the Hackers' ogre his happy moments. He let the huge lug haul him up in his arms and give him a hug that could have crushed a bear. Once Dunk was back on his feet, he felt thankful he'd been wearing his armour. The ogre had cracked his ribs more than once in the past.

Edgar came up and ran a branch along the back of Dunk's helmet too. 'You're a bloody hard nut to crack,' the treeman said with a gentle rap.

'Good to have you back!' Guillermo Reyes called from his position towards the front of their formation. The Estalian lineman's accent always seemed thicker here in his homeland, and he played harder too. Because of how he'd left Altdorf, the capital of the Empire and his home since birth, Dunk envied

Guillermo his hometown hero status, which he never imagined he could enjoy.

Then Rhett Cavre, the legendary blitzer and the Hackers' team captain, trotted up. 'Are you all right, Dunk?' he asked. Despite the chaos surrounding them, the man's demeanour was as soft and solid as ever. True concern for Dunk as a friend, not just a player, showed in his wide, dark eyes. Cavre saw the players on his team as people, not just bodies to fill positions, and for that he'd earned the respect of each and every one of his team-mates.

'Dr. Pill fixed me right up,' Dunk said, nodding.

Cavre winced. 'Did he use one of the dusty bottles or one of the clean ones?'

'Dusty. Why?'

Cavre smiled, his brilliant white teeth shining like a crescent moon against his ebony skin. 'Those haven't been 'recycled' as often.'

Dunk felt his stomach turn again, empty as it was. 'Think we'll have any more trouble with the ref?' he asked, eager to change the subject.

Carve laughed warmly. 'Not after what she threatened to do to him after the game if he made any more calls like that.'

Dunk glanced down the field at the minotaur in the striped shirt. He noticed that Bool moved with a bit of a limp as he trotted the spiked ball out for the Ogres to kick it off.

'She mentioned something about having him for a steak dinner,' Carve said. Then he knocked Dunk on his pauldron. 'Get into position before that ball comes our way.'

Dunk turned and sprinted off to the end of the field, right in front of the end zone, and then turned around to face the Ogres. Their kicker had booted the ball right into the stands twice so far this game, but if it came down anywhere near Dunk, it was his job to catch it. Then, as the team's thrower, he had to hurl it downfield to anyone he could find open.

This sort of play could be risky. If the Ogres intercepted the ball, they could be in the end zone in a matter of seconds. However, it was the best way to move the ball down the field. Trying to run it past the Ogres was almost impossible. With arms as long as Dunk was tall, the creatures just grabbed any of the Hackers that tried to dash past them.

The crowd hushed for a moment, and then started out with a low, collective moan that rose to a roar as the Ogre kicker approached the ball. When he booted it down the field, the fans burst into bloodthirsty screams, sure their desires would soon be sated.

The ball arced high into the air, and for a moment Dunk thought it might go right over his hands and into the stands – maybe even over the top of the stadium and into the streets beyond. Then a freak wind sprang up and blew the ball back towards the field.

As Dunk tracked the ball's progress, he noticed that dark clouds had raced in to block out the sun in the last few minutes. It seemed strange, but he couldn't worry about that at the moment. If he didn't catch the ball and get rid of it as fast as he could, he risked far worse than a few drops of rain on his helmet.

The weather didn't matter anyway. Blood Bowl games never stopped or even paused on account of rain, sleet, snow, frogs, beetles, locusts, ashes, or even fresh flows of volcanic magma. Any team that left the field before a game was over automatically forfeited the match, and with the amount of money on the line, few teams valued their health more than their share of the gold.

The ball sailed right down towards Dunk. He took two steps up, spread his arms and hands into a basket and caught the ball against his chest, just like in practice. He'd learned the hard way not to catch a ball with any unarmoured parts of his body, and he'd had his breastplate reinforced just so he could receive kick-offs like this.

'Hoffnung has the ball, and he's off! He races towards the sideline, trying to find some blockers and hunting for a receiver downfield.' Dunk tried to tune out the PA system when playing, but Bob and Jim's voices were so amplified that it usually proved impossible.

Dunk saw a wall of angry Oldheim Ogres coming his way and knew that he had to get rid of the ball fast if he didn't want to end up right back on Dr. Pill's table. He wasn't sure what would be worse: being left to mend on his own if Pegleg wouldn't pay the fee this time, or having to 'recycle' the potion he'd just used.

He jinked to the left, and then sprinted to the right, angling forward and towards the sideline as he ran. The Hackers linemen forged a wall of their own in front of him, backed by M'Grash and Edgar. Just as the two lines were about to clash, the linemen scattered to the left and right, leaving only the two tallest Hackers standing between Dunk and the onrushing Ogres.

Some of the Ogres chased after the Hackers linemen. The brain of an ogre is smaller than that of a human, but has to motivate far more flesh. This doesn't leave the ogre a great deal of leftover grey matter with which to do things like make simple decisions, taste its food, or develop emotionally beyond the level of a five-year-old human child. When an ogre starts chasing something, it usually keeps after it – unless something else distracts it. Then it chases that instead – until the whistle blows, and sometimes it ignores that too, a lesson Dunk had just learned in the hardest way possible, barring a messy death and sudden resurrection.

Many of the Ogres followed the linemen as they scrambled out of the way, but most of them were running so fast that they couldn't easily change their momentum. Some of them tried and tripped over their own feet, creating obstacles for those behind them to stumble over too. The resultant crash shook the Astrogranite enough that Dunk almost fell as well.

A few of the Ogres ignored the linemen, concentrating on Dunk instead, or perhaps on Dunk and Edgar. The Hacker ogre and treeman charged straight at the four Ogres who hadn't been fooled by the ploy and lowered their armoured shoulders.

Edgar managed to knock one of the Ogres to a standstill. M'Grash – who was large, even for an ogre – managed to shove two of the Oldheim players back on their rumps, but the last Ogre made it through unscathed, and thundered straight at Dunk.

Dunk peered around the oncoming Ogre and spotted Cavre downfield. When the Ogres had charged after the ball, he'd slid through their line and dashed most of the way down the field. Now he leaped up and down, waving his arms, signalling that he might never be more open for a pass for the remainder of his career.

Dunk cocked back his arm to let the ball fly, but even as he did he realised he'd misjudged the last Ogre's determination. The towering creature seemed to have put on a burst of speed once he got past Edgar and M'Grash. Now, with the Ogre's arms raised high and wide over his head, Dunk didn't see how he could get a clear throw off at Cavre.

On the other hand, if he held onto it, he knew the Ogre racing at him would grind him into dust. He pumped the ball once in an effort to fake out the Ogre, and it worked. The Oldheimer left his feet to try to block the pass.

Still, the Ogre was so large, its reach so wide, that Dunk didn't see any daylight around him. Instead of trying to slip between the Ogre's arms, he took one step back, and hurled the ball downfield towards Cavre.

Dunk looked up and saw the Ogre's long arms coming down over him like a tidal wave, and the ball heading right for the creature's outstretched fingers. Not only was he going to get crushed beneath this beast's mighty bulk, his pass would be intercepted too. Considering he'd already woken up from a head injury in the locker room once that day, he didn't see how this game could get any worse.

Then the world disappeared in a flash of blinding light, followed almost instantly by a boom so loud that Dunk thought he might never want to hear anything ever again.

CHAPTER THREE

UNABLE TO SEE past the afterimage still flashing before his eyes, Dunk stumbled and fell flat on his back. As he did, something that felt like a sack of hot sand hit him and then broke apart. Cloying clouds of some dry substance stuck to his sweaty skin and caught in his nose, throat, and lungs. He spun over onto his hand and knees and tried to hack it out of his chest until it all finally came free.

By the time the thunderous clap finally stopped echoing in Dunk's ears, he could wipe the gunk off his face and out of his eyes to try to see just what had happened. He stared up at the Jumboball towering over the end zone behind him, and his jaw dropped.

'Let's see that one more time, Jim!'

The image on the screen showed the Ogre racing towards Dunk, captured in a slow-motion replay. Just as the creature was about to land on Dunk, the image froze.

29

'Right there, Bob. Do you see it?'

'See it,' Bob said. 'If I wasn't wearing my Sun Protection Fetish, I think it might have fried my grave-delicate skin from here. As a vampire, I owe my life to my Copper-tomb SPF 1,000.'

'The bolt of lightning, Bob. It's right there. Advance that forward just a hair.'

The image on the Jumboball moved almost impercep-tibly, and Dunk saw the flash that had only been a tiny spot before stretch into an explosion of light that crossed the massive crystal, stabbing straight through the Ogre as it went.

'See, there's the bolt. Now just a little bit more.'

The image changed again. The bolt was gone, and the Ogre had disappeared too. An Ogre-shaped pile of ash hung in mid-air in its place.

The image moved forward once more, and the pile of ash fell to the Astrogranite. Some of it had already started to blow away as it dropped, but the bulk of it crashed down to the earth.

As he watched this, Dunk realised he had flash-fried ogre all over him. He stood up and screamed.

Then M'Grash dumped an entire keg of Killer Genuine Draft beer on top of him. The force of the falling liquid knocked him to his knees and left him gasping for air. On the other hand, it did exactly what it was supposed to do. It rinsed the remnants of the ogre from his hair, armour, and skin. The hop-scented residue it left behind made Dunk think more than anything that he needed to get himself something pure and clean to drink to wash the taste of ogre ashes out of his mouth.

'I've never seen anything like this,' Jim said over the PA. 'I mean, death, maiming, even dismemberment, but for the game to stop for it is truly strange.'

'Well it's hard to play when you're missing the ball,' Bob said. 'Most times if the ball gets blown up or just flattened the players can at least scoop up the pieces and play with those until the next break in the action. When it just disappears like that, it's hard to see what you might do with it.'

'Gr'Nash, the Ogres' team captain sure showed some initiative, scooping up a handful of those ashes and running them into the end zone.'

'True, although I think Bool made the right call by nullifying the touchdown. After all, it's impossible to tell if any of those ashes came from the ball instead of poor Ch'Brakk.'

'You gotta admire a competitor like that. Even the death of his cousin isn't enough to slow him down for a second.'

'Well, with the clock winding down here, Bob, it looks like this game might end up in a tie.'

'I hate ties. They're like kissing your sister.'

'I told you to stop dating her.'

'Hey, I said I hate kissing her, but she seems to love it. I can't get her to respect the restraining order!'

'Hold it, Jim. Our roving reporter on the field, the lovely Lästiges Weibchen, would like to check in.'

The image on the screen shifted to a beautiful woman with long, auburn hair and black eyes, who smiled out at the viewer like she had always been your best friend. She stood down on the sidelines, somewhere near the ogre's dugout from the look of it. As she spoke, she glanced up behind her from time to time.

'Thanks, Bob! Eyewitnesses here on the field and in the stands claim that this mysterious thunderbolt did not come from the sky, but from right here in the stadium.'

M'Grash helped Dunk to his feet, and then picked him up and shook him like a wet dog, flinging beer and beer-soaked ash everywhere. Just when Dunk had started to wonder if M'Grash might accidentally kill him, the shaking stopped, and Dunk could watch the Jumboball again.

'There he is, Bob!' Lästiges said, her voice ringing out over the PA system, even though the image on the Jumboball was that of a gaunt, middle-aged man in midnight-blue robes. As the camra zoomed in on the man – picking out his wispy white beard, his silver skullcap, and his watery, green eyes – Dunk recognised him instantly.

Lästiges gasped and said 'It's Schlechter Zauberer!'

The crowd echoed the reporter's sharp intake of breath.

'Blood Bowl fans may remember Zauberer's involvement in the death almost two years ago of the mutant minotaur captain of the Chaos All-Stars, Schlitz 'Malty' Likker. Rumour also has it that he was the motivating force behind the tragic Jumboball accident here in Magritta last year that ended in the messy and permanent death of Krader, the troll player who had showed so much promise up until that point. To make matters worse, Zauberer was on the All-Stars' payroll at the time, ostensibly hired to help them, not murder their star players.'

As Dunk watched, Zauberer – who had been standing among a group of passed-out drunks in the nosebleed section of the bleachers, right under the announcers' box – lifted his arms over his head and took off into the air. Dunk wondered for a moment if the fans the wizard had left behind were really sleeping at all or just not moving under their own power forever. Before he could ponder the issue much longer, an idea struck him, and he turned and sprinted off towards the Hackers' dugout.

'As you might remember, Hoffnung and Zauberer have clashed several times before, both on the field and off. Since the wizard is not listed as an official employee or freebooter for either team, I can only guess that Zauberer has decided to take their rivalry to a new, deadlier level.'

When Dunk was only twenty yards or so from the dugout, another lightning bolt came scorching out of the sky to carve a crater in the ground right behind where Dunk had been, proving Lästiges's words right.

'A ball,' Dunk yelled at his team-mates in the dugout. 'Toss me a ball!'

All of the players in the Hackers' dugout just stared at Dunk in some odd mixture of astonishment and fear. Lined up in their green and gold uniforms, the Hackers' three-sword H logo emblazoned across the sides of the helmets they held on their laps, they seemed like little more than children brought together to play a game. Unfortunately, Blood Bowl was a game of life and death.

Spinne stepped out of the dugout and pitched a ball to Dunk underhand. He caught it neatly in his left hand and swapped it to his right. Then he cocked his head back and searched the sky over the stadium for any sign of the wizard who meant to fry him to ashes in moments.

A third bolt of lightning passed close enough to Dunk to stand his hair on end. The clap of thunder that followed deafened him again, but since it passed behind him he could still see. He spun around, looked directly above him, and spotted Zauberer diving closer, cursing in some language Dunk had never heard, a long, silver wand waving in his hand.

Dunk cocked back his arm and threw the football like a bullet at the wizard. Zauberer tried to dodge the spiked missile, but instead he only managed to put his shoulder forward. This caused the tip of the ball to slam into the wizard's right arm rather than his chest.

Zauberer shrieked like a little girl from the pain. Clutching at the ball still embedded in his flesh, he fluttered towards the ground like a wounded duck, clawing desperately at the air with his fingers, but finding no purchase.

Dunk took one long step to the side, and the wizard crashed to the Astrogranite in front of him with a dull thud. Dunk reached down with one hand and pulled Zauberer to his feet. He needed to know what was going on. He hadn't seen the wizard in over a year, and now he'd tried to kill him for no reason Dunk could discern.

Zauberer's head slumped down between his shoulders, and a thin line of bloody drool trickled out of his mouth. He groaned when Dunk lifted him to his feet, but his feet wouldn't bear his weight, and his eyes only opened long enough to roll back into his head before closing again.

Dunk yanked the ball from the wizard's shoulder, planning to use it to jab him back to consciousness. The open wound bled freely, and what little colour the pasty-faced wizard had drained from him, leaving him whiter than the lines painted on the field.

'Speaking of competitors, Jim, what do you think about Hoffnung there? It seems he's found himself a ball!'

Startled, Dunk peered around the field and saw everyone staring at him. For just a moment, no one in the stadium breathed. Then Gr'Nash, the Old-heim Ogre who'd cracked his skull earlier in the game, threw a long, broken, sausage-sized finger in Dunk's direction – it must have come from one of the other Ogres – and bellowed, 'Kill him!'

Dunk dropped Zauberer and heard the wizard's skullcap crack against the Astrogranite. Then he started to race towards the Hackers' dugout.

'That's a damned shame,' Bob's voice said. 'One little assassination attempt by a wizard tossing lightning bolts around like snotlings in a bar fight, and Hoffnung loses his nerve. He had such potential too.'

'Not to mention the fact that we only have a few seconds left in the game. Looks like you'll be puckering up for my baby sister Bertha tonight!'

'Not today, Jim. Since this game is part of the *Spike!* magazine tournament finals, no ties are allowed. We'll go into sudden-death overtime instead.'

'If those Ogres catch Hoffnung, I think I know whose death we'll see first!'

Dunk ignored the commentators and scanned the Hackers' end zone. He saw Cavre racing towards it now, breaking away from the Ogres eager to carry out Gr'Nash's death sentence.

Dunk brought his arm back one more time and tossed the ball high and long into the air. It arced up and then down like the smooth parabola of a rainbow. At the end stood no pot of gold, just Cavre's outstretched, wide open hands.

Cavre pulled the ball in just as time ran out, but Dunk couldn't tell where the catcher's feet were. Had he scored, or had they been too late?

Bool blew the whistle, but Dunk couldn't tell if it was to signal a touchdown or the end of the game – maybe both?

'Touchdown! The Hackers win the game!'

Dunk started to throw his arms up in the air to cheer, but he saw the Oldheim Ogres still racing towards him. Remembering how well Gr'Nash had treated him after the last touchdown he'd scored, Dunk decided to dive into the Hackers' dugout rather than celebrate their victory within arm's reach of the angry ogres.

THAT NIGHT IN the Bad Water – a sports tavern located in the worst part of Magritta, right down next to the wharf – Dunk raised a tankard of Killer Genuine Draft to toast the Hackers and their advancement to the *Spike!* magazine tournament finals. 'Here's to the finest bunch of hard-bitten killers I've ever played alongside!' he said.

The other Hackers – all of them, including Pegleg – roared in approval, as did the assembled crowd of regulars and hangers-on tough enough to work their way into the main room that night. They clanked their mugs together and drank deeply in approval of Dunk's sentiment.

'Another round of Killers, Sparky!' Slick called. 'Put it on the Hackers' tab.'

Pegleg started to protest, but everyone else in the bar shouted him down, including his own players. He raised his hook to slash the throat out of the nearest of those who'd failed to respect him, but Cavre stepped forward to grab him by the wrist and sit him down before anyone could get hurt.

The dwarf bartender raced along the high foot rail behind the bar – which boosted him up high enough so that he could reach out over the bar – towards a fresh keg of beer. A cheer rose up, and at first Dunk thought it was for the beer. Then Spinne elbowed him in the ribs and pointed up at the set of crystal balls hanging over the bar.

Each of the crystal balls showed a sporting event of one kind or another. These ranged from professional snotling tossing (an event favoured in dwarf taverns around the Old World) to dragon wrestling (dragon vs. ogre, dragon vs. troll, dragon vs. dragon, etc.) to witchball (played by scantily clad women straddling flying broomsticks). On the largest crystal ball, the Reikland Reavers faced off against the Darkside Cowboys, a dark elf team with a reputation for cruelty, even among Blood Bowl players.

The Reavers had just scored the go-ahead touchdown as the time wound down in the half. As the Wolf Sports team cut over to the Gods-Damned Blood Bowl Halftime Show – hosted by Barry Hacksaw and No. J. Pimpson – Spinne nuzzled up under Dunk's arm and kissed him on the cheek, a forlorn look on her face.

'Are you okay?' he asked.

A frown marred Spinne's beautiful face. Here in the bar, her strawberry-blonde hair and blue-grey eyes gleamed in the lanterns' light. The set of her jaw showed the strength she had to have to be one of the few female Blood Bowl players, but her eyes had softened tonight for some reason.

'I don't know whether to root for the Reavers or their opposition,' she said with a sigh.

'I know what you mean,' Dunk said, wrapping his arm tighter around her shoulders. 'I want Dirk and his team to win, but if they do we'll have to face them in the finals. That could get... messy.'

'Their starting thrower may be your little brother, but I played on that team just a couple of months back.'

'Are you worried you'll have to play against your old friends? Maybe hurt them?'

Spinne stood up straight and scoffed at Dunk, his arm falling from her. 'Not at all. They're a bunch of jackasses, Dirk included. Why do you think I'm playing for the Hackers?'

'Because Slick forced Pegleg to make you a great offer?' Dunk smiled behind his tankard as he took a long pull from the fresh beer that Sparky had slid in front of him.

'Okay, that was it.' Spinne grinned at him.

'So what's the problem?'

'Well, if we play against the Reavers, I know them backwards and forwards, every strength and every flaw. The downside is they know mine too.'

'Your flaws? That's a short list.'

'You have a list?' Spinne narrowed her eyes at Dunk.

'It's just a metaphor.' He held up his hands in mock surrender.

'Is that something like a dikphor?' She raised an eyebrow at him.

'What's a dikphor?' Dunk asked, regretting the words as they left his mouth.

Spinne leaned in close and whispered in Dunk's ear. 'Play your cards right, and I'll show you later.'

Then Spinne froze in his arms.

'What?' Dunk asked. He held her at arm's length and stared into her eyes, which were focused on something behind him. 'What is it?'

'Look,' she said, jerking her chin at the wall over the bar.

Dunk turned to see Lästiges interviewing Schlechter Zauberer on Wolf Sports' Cabalvision. The wizard lay sitting up bare-chested in a sickhouse bed, fat and slimy leeches hanging from his wounded shoulder, which looked like it had been stitched up with a dirty shoelace. Without his robes, the man seemed skeletal, his papery, white skin stretched thin over his jutting bones. The dark circles under his red-rimmed eyes made him seem like he might soon be hammering on death's door with his silver skullcap.

Lästiges asked the wizard a question, and he started to rant out the answer. With the celebration in the tavern as loud as it was, Dunk couldn't hear a thing. He grabbed M'Grash by the arm and signalled for the ogre to quiet down the crowd.

M'Grash turned to face the people gathered in the bar and put a finger to his lips. Then he shouted out, 'Shhhh! Be quiet! Dunkel wants to hear the evil wizard talk!'

Dunk blushed as all eyes turned to him, but he ignored the attention and focused on the large crystal ball instead. Everyone followed his example without saying another word.

'So you attack in broad daylight because you like the attention?' Lästiges asked.

The camra focused on the clammy-faced Zauberer. 'This is just the start of everything,' he said, a line of drool hanging from his bottom lip as he spoke. 'Soon the world will know my name. Soon emperors will tremble at my feet. The ultimate power will soon be m-mine!'

Lästiges leaned into the camra's view and said, 'Uh-huh. So, just how does your attempt on Dunk Hoffnung's life earlier today fit in with your plans for world domination?'

A sly smile played across Zauberer's purplish lips. He gazed so intently into the camra it seemed he could see everyone watching back at him through their crystal balls.

'I have friends – acquaintances, really – in high places with low intentions. In return for their favours – their infernal influence – they have requested that I bring them the head of one Dunkel Hoffnung, formerly of Altdorf and now part of the Bad Bay Hackers.'

'That doesn't seem to have gone so well for you.'

Zauberer ignored Lästiges's sarcastic tone and kept staring into the camra, his eyes growing wider, and his words more urgent.

'These noble people have authorized me to place a price on Hoffnung's egg-fragile head.'

Dunk heard Lästiges nearly choke at this news. Once she cleared her throat, she asked, 'And how much would this reward of yours be worth?'

Zauberer's eyes focused off-camra, in the reporter's direction, for just a moment, a horrifying leer on his face. Then he looked back into the camra, which zoomed in tight on his red-rimmed, bloodshot, slime-green eyes.

'One million Imperial crowns.'

Everyone in the bar caught their breath at once. No one moved. Dunk's heart froze in his chest. He wanted nothing more than to rewind that moment and shut the crystal ball off before those words went out again.

Then Zauberer threw back his head, exposing his pale gums and his awkward rows of chipped and stained teeth, and he laughed.

Dunk looked to Spinne, then to Slick and the rest of the Hackers. He could see by the looks on their faces that they stood with him.

It took a lot to bribe a Blood Bowl player, but that kind of money was enough to start a whole new team. Still, the Hackers had become Dunk's family over the past two years, and he knew he could trust them to have his back under any circumstances. Even the new players had trained and practised with him long enough for him to rely on them during a game. This could be no more dangerous than that.

Then Dunk saw the rest of the Bad Water's rough and tumble patrons eyeing him, some of them counting up the odds and figuring how much they'd each get by splitting the reward up that many ways. It wouldn't take them long to realise it would be worth chancing a horrible beating at the Hackers' hands.

'Guys,' Dunk said, his voice serious and low as he clutched Spinne's hand, 'I think it's time to go.'

CHAPTER FOUR

THE FIRST OF the bounty hunters – for that's what everyone in the bar had transformed into with the mad wizard's announcement of an impossible reward – launched himself at Dunk with the neck of a broken bottle in his hand. Dunk dodged the drunken man's clumsy slash, and then smashed his nose back into his head with his fist.

Before the first attacker even hit the floor, a pair of other hopefuls charged forward. Dunk knew that he wouldn't be able to get his arms up to defend himself in time, so he gritted his teeth and waited for them to hit him. Instead, Spinne knocked one of them flat with a spinning kick while Guillermo dropped the other in his tracks with a roundhouse that landed square in the man's overflowing gut.

Dunk righted himself from his own swing and saw that the Hackers had to be outnumbered five to one.

While he knew that he and his team-mates still had
the upper hand, he didn't see how this could end well.
The Hackers had to play in the *Spike!* magazine tournament finals in just a few days. If they lost a few
players in a bar brawl, that could throw off their
whole game.

Since the bar's patrons were all after him, the best
thing he could do for everyone, he realised, was disappear. He glanced around for a way out.

The front door was too far away, he knew, and too
many people stood between him and it. To get there,
he'd have to harm and maybe kill at least a half-dozen
of the bounty hunters, if not more.

People blocked his way to the back door too. Plus,
Dunk knew such an escape would be too obvious.
Even if he managed to make it out to the street, he'd
probably find another dozen people there ready and
waiting for him to emerge.

He eyed the nearest window. At the moment, it
seemed like his best bet. If he managed to crash
through it without killing himself, he might be able to
disappear into the maze of alleys and barely standing
shacks that formed Magritta's seaside district.

Then Dunk spotted Sparky standing on top of the
bar and waving like a marooned sailor trying to signal
a passing ship. He'd done everything but set the bar on
fire, and he looked as if that might be next on his list.

Dunk nodded at the dwarf, who pointed at Dunk
and then back down behind the bar. His intent was
clear. If Dunk could make it over there, he'd do what
he could to protect him, which, given the fact he ran
the place, might be a good deal.

Sparky was a great bartender, always friendly and
respectful and ready to drive off anyone who gave the

Hackers any trouble, which was why they always came here to blow off steam after every game. People in the area knew this, and it had started to drive up business for Sparky – even when the team wasn't in town – and Dunk knew he was grateful for it.

Was that enough of a bond for Dunk to stake his life on? At the moment, it seemed it would have to do. Knowing the eyes of every bounty hunter in the house were on him, Dunk stood atop the bar and shook his fist down at them.

'If any of you think you're tough enough to take me on without all your friends around you, then let's have a go!' Dunk bellowed. 'The one who beats me first can have the entire reward!'

The patrons in the bar paused for a second to stare at Dunk and then at each other. Then they started swinging at each other instead.

Dunk knew that the distraction wouldn't last long. As soon as he moved back onto the tavern floor, the bounty hunters would forget their differences and return their attentions to him. So he took one step backward and fell down behind the bar in a crouch, dropping straight out of sight of anyone beyond.

'Quick!' Sparky pressed at Dunk in a stage whisper. With one hand, the dwarf held up a low, wide hatch set in the floor directly under the bar. The index finger on his other hand jabbed straight towards the dark hole under the hatch.

'Where does it lead?' Dunk asked as he scrambled over to the hatch on his hands and knees.

'Anywhere's better than here right now,' Sparky said. 'Once you go, I can break up the fight quick, but you better move. They'll fill the streets looking for you right after.'

'Thanks,' Dunk said, shaking the dwarf's meaty hand.

Sparky grinned at Dunk through his beer-soaked beard. 'Just add in a hefty tip once I send you your bill.'

Dunk dived into the darkness beyond the hatch. It clicked shut behind him, cutting off all light and leaving him in pitch blackness. For a moment, panic gripped him, and he wondered if Sparky had trapped him in here so he could claim the reward for himself.

Dunk told himself that he'd already made the decision to trust Sparky. Now he'd have to explore the results.

He felt around with his hands and discovered he was in a long, low, and narrow passageway. The sides and bottom of it were lined with bricks, and the roof appeared to be the bottom of the tavern's floorboards. There seemed to be only one way to go, and so that's the way he went.

Dunk found out the hard way that the crossbeams under the Bad Water's floorboards cut through the top of the tunnel. After he banged his head the first time, he resolved to move more slowly and carefully.

As he worked his way further along, the dull thumps and muffled bangs that sounded above his head stopped. For a moment, he hoped the fight was over, but he realised he'd probably just moved out from under the tavern's floor. He tried to picture where the tunnel might lead him, but he couldn't. He'd kept clear of the alleys that ran behind the Bad Water, and it came to him that if the passageway had been slowly turning in one way or the other he'd never have been able to tell. There was nothing to do but keep crawling on.

The tunnel might have been comfortable for a dwarf, but Dunk found it claustrophobic after a while. He yearned to be able to stand up or just stretch his arms out to the sides. He doubted he could even turn around in the passageway, even if he wanted to. It was just too tight.

Then something bit him on his thigh. He fell on his shoulder as he spun around in the tight tunnel and grabbed at it, but he couldn't find anything there. He gasped in horror and began shoving himself down the tunnel with his heels, sliding along on his seat.

A muffled laugh echoed through the tunnel, and Dunk knew what had happened. He sat up in the tunnel – it was just tall enough for him to do so without bumping his head – and stuffed his hand into his pocket. There he found his leather purse. He pulled it out and untied it from his belt and then swung it hard, smacking it against the wall.

'Yowch!' a tiny voice said from within the bag, 'Knock it off!'

'You bit me, you little bastard,' Dunk said.

The thing in the purse sniggered. 'Gotta make my own fun.'

'Do it again, Skragger, and I'll smash you flat.'

'Better than being a shrunken head,' Skragger said in his high, tiny voice.

Dunk swung the purse around fast. 'Are you sure about that?'

'Respect me!' Skragger said. 'Had season scoring record once.'

'Before Dirk broke it.' Dunk said. 'You're lucky to even be a shrunken head after what you tried to do to me. If Cavre hadn't worked his magic on you, you'd be just one more dead orc rotting in the ground.'

Dunk considered crushing Skragger's head into paste right there and then, but he couldn't bring himself to do it. If living as a shrunken head in Dunk's purse wasn't punishment enough, what was? Killing the orc would be too good for him.

If Dunk could have figured out a better fate for his old nemesis, he'd have made it happen. He hadn't asked Cavre to make the old orc into a squeaking caricature of his former self, although Dunk had to admit the little guy was a ton of fun to break out at parties. He felt responsible for him now though. He couldn't just give him to someone else.

Or could he? Either way, that wasn't something he could devote any time to ponder now. He tied his purse to his belt again with its leather strings and let it dangle there. Skragger wouldn't be able to bite him while he swayed about in mid-air, and that would do for the moment.

'What's the big idea biting me?' Dunk asked. 'Don't you think I have enough trouble on my hands?

Skragger snorted. 'Get me that reward, buy me new body. Maybe use yours, get me stitched to your neck.'

Dunk smacked the purse hard and started crawling again, trying to shut the old blitzer's snickering out. After a while, Dunk smacked his own head into something again, but not nearly as hard as the first time. He reached out with his hand to see how far down it ran, and he found that the obstacle ran from the top of the tunnel to its bottom and all the way across.

Dunk took a deep breath to steady his nerves, and when he exhaled it sounded like a shout in the closed-off tunnel. He reached out and felt along the wall in front of him until his fingers found a latch.

Letting loose a sigh of relief, he undid the latch and gave the little door in front of him a push.

Dunk saw lanterns flickering in the distance, but the world outside the doorway stood shrouded in shadows. He heard the familiar sound of water lapping up against a reinforced shoreline, and somewhere above him people shouted something he couldn't make out.

He moved out through this hatch and glanced around to get his bearings. The tunnel had brought him out underneath the base of one of the piers that stabbed out of Magritta's wharfside district. Boots tramped along the wooden planks above him, moving in all directions. He heard his name shouted a few times, but never in alarm. He believed, for the moment at least, that he was safe.

'Fancy meeting you here, kid,' said a high-pitched voice that seemed as if it might break into a wicked cackle any second.

Dunk recognised the voice immediately. He'd never heard anyone else talk like that, and he hoped he never would. In fact, he'd have been thrilled if he hadn't been hearing this exact person's voice.

'Gunther the Gobbo!' Dunk said, keeping his voice at a harsh whisper. 'What are you doing here?'

The thought that Sparky had sold him out to the unscrupulous bookie thrummed in Dunk's mind. It made him want to strike out and kill the greasy creature right there and then. He could just let the body fall into the waters of the harbour below, and no one would be the wiser. No one would miss the bookie anyway, least of all his clients.

Gunther crept out from behind a nearby piling, and Dunk realised he was standing on a narrow, wooden walkway that ran directly under the hatch out of which he was leaning. The bookie had the same wild, green eyes, long, wide nose, and horrible, wart-and-lesion covered skin that Dunk remembered. He swept the long wisps of his forelock back onto his balding scalp and grinned at Dunk with his tiny, child's teeth.

'Waiting for you, of course. You're suddenly a lot more popular than you used to be.'

Dunk crawled out of the tunnel and crouched on the walkway, ready to pounce at Gunther in an instant.

'Where are they?' Dunk asked, glancing around.

'Who?' Gunther jumped as if startled, and almost fell off the walkway as he scanned the darkness for whomever Dunk might have expected.

'Your henchmen, your hired muscle, your thugs, your business associates – whatever you're calling them these days. Trot them out and let me kill them.'

Gunther chuckled softly, and Dunk knew he'd seen through his bluff. Despite the fact that he played Blood Bowl for a living, he was no cold-blooded killer. 'I'm no bounty hunter, kid. I'm a businessman.'

Dunk narrowed his eyes at the squat bookie. 'You're alone?'

'Have you ever known me to want to share my profits?'

Dunk scowled at the piggish bookie, and then said, 'How did you know where to find me.'

'Kid.' Gunther looked at Dunk as if he must be shamming being a moron because no one could really be that thick. 'Sparky's a friend of mine. In my line of work, I've had occasion to make use of that secret passage of his myself. I knew you'd be at the Bad Water tonight celebrating your victory, just like you always do. You're a creature of habit.'

The thought that his actions were so predictable disturbed Dunk. If Gunther could figure out where he might end up, then anyone else could too. Due to his time with the Hackers – and that documentary Lästiges made about their voyage to Albion in search of the Far Albion Cup last year – anyone with access to Cabalvision knew what he looked like. With a million-crown reward on his head, how would he be able to live?

'I was just a few doors down from here myself when I saw that halftime report. That's a bad break, kid. You're going to need all the friends you can get.'

Dunk saw where the Gobbo was going. The man had long made a living as an influence peddler. He saw a wealthy player on a popular team in need of his services, and he pounced on it like a snake on a rat.

'I already have all the friends I want,' Dunk said. 'Besides, I thought you'd shut the Black Jerseys down.'

Gunther smiled, and his teeth seemed to glow in the shadows. 'Let's just say I've learned my lesson about keeping a low profile. Who needs such colourful names and complicated plans when it's so much more effective to just help guide the right players in the right directions?'

'Get out of my way,' Dunk said.

Gunther pointed to where the walkway ran off behind Dunk. 'You'd be better off going that way.' His grin grew wider. 'Take my word for it.'

'I owe you nothing,' Dunk said. He turned and padded off away from the bookie as fast as he could without making too much noise.

'It's on the house, kid,' Gunther called after him, far louder than he would have liked. 'I'm already setting up a pool for when you'll get caught. I'll make a killing!'

● CHAPTER FIVE

DUNK SPENT THE next few days in hiding. That night, he rolled a drunken sailor on the edge of the wharf and stole his clothes for a disguise. He smudged his face with grease he found in a barrel at one dark end of the wharf. Then he made his way through the back alleys near Magritta's wharf until he found a pub that rented out a few rooms in the back, mostly by the hour. Then he collapsed until the sun rode high over the city the next day.

Dunk knew that Pegleg would want him to take part in the team's practices, but he didn't see how he could manage it without starting a riot. So he stayed away, exercising in private to keep himself in condition and to force his mind away from concentrating on his troubles. He would deal with Zauberer and his mysterious employers soon, but right now he just needed to concentrate on getting ready for the game.

The morning of the *Spike!* magazine tournament final match, Dunk slunk through Magritta's predawn streets and found his way to the Hackers' inn. He entered the place through the kitchen, blowing past the workers, who thought he was trying to steal a meal. He took the back passages up to Cavre's room and knocked gently on the door.

'Come in,' Cavre said, looking like he was ready to start the day's match already, even though the sun had just risen over the horizon.

'Were you expecting someone?' Dunk asked as he stepped into the room. 'You're already dressed.'

Cavre closed the door behind Dunk and gestured for him to take one of the chairs in the suite's parlour. 'You, of course,' the blitzer said. 'People have been camped out in front of your and Spinne's room for days. Even M'Grash has a contingent of hopefuls who believe you will go to him first. For myself, I chased every one of them off with a long knife, and so the way is clear.'

'Isn't the fact that we're staying here supposed to be a secret anyway?' Dunk asked. Before the big matches, teams often checked into new inns or stayed in remote areas to prevent their upcoming opponents – or opposing fans – from trying to sabotage them before the game even started. The Hackers stayed only with trusted innkeepers renowned for their discretion, and they paid handsomely for the treatment. With as much gold on the line as there was in top-level Blood Bowl tournaments, even a cheapskate like Pegleg considered the cost a wise investment.

Cavre gave Dunk a smile that said the thrower already knew the answer. 'We pay for our privacy in gold, so gold can penetrate it as well. With a million

Imperial crowns at stake, our privacy looks like a used archery target.'

'So I'm not safe here,' Dunk said, glancing at the door.

'You are not safe anywhere, my friend. As long as there's that price on your head, you're fortunate to find any space where you can rest it.' Cavre took a long look at Dunk. 'Take a nap in my bed. I'll have some food brought up later, and when you're ready we'll gather the team to make a try for the stadium together.'

'I'm surprised some of the new players haven't tried to sell me out.' Dunk lay back on the couch, surprised to realise how tired he was.

'Who's to say they didn't?' Cavre said. 'Captain Pegleg has held team meetings every day in which he emphasises loyalty and teamwork. I doubt any of them would move against you directly, but someone might decide that selling information about your whereabouts would be harmless enough.'

'So it's good I kept away,' Dunk said. 'I thought Pegleg would be furious about me missing so much practice time.'

Cavre laughed. 'I never said he was happy. He's spoken to Mr. Fullbelly about docking your pay, but I believe your agent has convinced him that you're acting in the team's best interests.'

'Let's hope he's right,' Dunk said with a yawn. 'Maybe it would be better for the team if I quit.'

This time Cavre didn't laugh a bit. 'Do you think that throwers with your talent and skill can be found on any street corner? Do not fool yourself, Dunk. The Hackers' fortunes have turned around since you joined our team, and the timing is no coincidence.'

'Why, Cavre, that almost sounded like a compliment.' Dunk's eyes closed of their own accord as he spoke.

'Do not become arrogant about it. Those who let such things go to their heads often have their brains dashed out on the field.'

Dunk thought he had a snappy response to that, but before he could utter it he fell fast asleep.

WHEN DUNK WOKE up, he found himself laid out on a bench in the Hackers' locker room, already dressed in his Blood Bowl armour. He opened his eyes to find Slick staring down at him, a self-satisfied grin on his face.

'Welcome back to the land of the living, son. You're just in time to make your mark on Blood Bowl history.'

Dunk tried to sit up right away, but found that his head felt woozy. Spinne jumped over an intervening bench to give him a hand and get him up on his feet. 'Thank you,' he said before sitting back down again. He considered it a personal victory that he hadn't lain down on the bench once more.

'What happened?' he asked as he tried to shake the cobwebs from his head. 'I don't think I've ever slept that hard before.'

'Well,' Spinne said putting an arm around Dunk and kissing him on his unshaven cheek, 'Pegleg figured that we couldn't be seen walking into the stadium with you. It would have caused a riot, and – as much as I'd be happy to defend you to the death – we have a match to play today.'

'So?' Dunk said, still confused.

'So he called in Dr. Pill who slipped you a little something to help keep you asleep.'

Dunk glanced across the room and spotted the elf watching him, nodding approvingly at his own hand-iwork. He flashed Dunk a grin and gave him a big thumbs-up. 'You'll feel fine in no time,' he called over.

The other players in the locker room paused for a moment to give Dunk a cheer, which he waved off with a sheepish grin. 'Thanks, guys,' he said before they each returned to their own pre-game prepara-tions and rituals.

'How did you get me here?' He ran a hand through his hair and realised it was wet.

'Well, we had to pack you away in something that no one would notice us carrying through the streets of Magritta. We couldn't trust anyone else to transport you, especially since you were unconscious, so it had to be something we regularly had with us. If there had been anything out of the ordinary, people after that bounty on your head would have tried to stop us immediately.'

Dunk cracked his neck, working the stiffness from it. He saw M'Grash coming over to greet him, the ogre's regular, goofy grin on his face. Some people mistook it for an evil leer, but Dunk had known M'Grash for far too long to make that mistake. 'So how did you get me here?' Dunk asked again.

'It really was the only way,' Spinne said, looking up at M'Grash.

The ogre put down the keg he was carrying, and then leaned over and laid a heavy hand on Dunk's shoulder. 'Did it for you, Dunkel. My friend, Dunkel!'

The ogre's breath reeked of beer, and lots of it. M'Grash drank regularly and often, but rarely this early in the day and never before a game. If Pegleg had thought it would help make the ogre mean, he'd have forced the alcohol down M'Grash's throat himself. Unfortunately for the coach, beer just made M'Grash sweeter than ever. He was – unlike any other ogre Dunk had ever met – a happy drunk.

Why M'Grash was drunk now, he could only guess. Then he noticed that when M'Grash had set his keg down on the ground it had thumped with a peculiarly hollow noise. It was empty.

Dunk leapt to his feet, aghast. 'You brought me here in that?' He pointed at the keg, the top of which he could now see was missing.

M'Grash grinned and nodded at Dunk so much that Dunk feared the ogre's head might roll off and crush his legs. Spinne winced in sympathy as she put an arm around him. 'It was the only way,' she said, 'and we knew it wouldn't be comfortable for you. We didn't want to have to worry about you getting cramped or scared in the keg, so…'

'So you had our hired quack slip me something to keep me out.' Dunk shook his head in disgust. As he did, he realised the cobweb inside his skull had disappeared. As creepy as the apothecary was, Dunk had to admit the old elf knew his potions.

Spinne held him tight and cocked her head low to peer up into his eyes. 'Are you all right?' she asked. 'They had to fold you in half to get you to fit in the keg. I begged them to stop, but they promised me it wouldn't hurt.'

'Of course he's fine,' Slick offered as he strode up to stand in front of Dunk. 'Look at him. He's the picture of health. Looks like a million crowns – I mean – oh, never mind me. You look great!'

Dunk scowled down at the Halfling, who beamed back up at him, undeterred by his client's attitude.

'You seem pretty happy for an agent whose top client got his last three days' pay docked.'

'Ah,' Slick said, his grin broadening. 'That might have been the sad fate of an ordinary player with an ordinary agent, but there's nothing at all so pedestrian about you and me, son.'

'So you talked him into forgetting about me ditching practice?'

Slick pursed his lips. 'It's more like I made a little wager with him. If we win today, he'll pay you every dime for those lost days – plus we'll get our share of the championship purse!'

'And if we lose?'

Slick glared at Dunk as if he'd been slapped. 'Shut your mouth, son! We're not going to lose this game.'

Dunk raised an eyebrow at Slick, and then knelt down to whisper at him. 'You convinced Pegleg to bet against his own team?'

'He looks at it this way: If we should – through some horrible twist of fate – happen to lose the game, he gets some of his money back. When, instead, we win, he'll be happy to pay the properly owed amount out of the winner's purse.'

Slick gave Dunk a smug smile. 'Don't think of it as a bet. It's more like we offered your employer a money-back guarantee.'

Dunk laughed quietly as he stood up and looked down at his agent. 'Only you could sell that angle, Slick.'

'That's why you pay me to be your agent.'

Dunk just sighed. Then a thought struck him. 'Who won the game the other night?'

'You don't know?' Spinne asked, concerned.

Dunk shook his head. 'I was busy running for my life. I haven't seen a crystal ball or a broadsheet since. So, who are we playing?'

Spinne stared straight into Dunk's eyes. 'The Reikland Reavers,' she said with a twisted smile, 'of course.'

Dunk put his hands over his face, and then pulled them down past his chin. 'Of course.'

'YOU SHOULDN'T BE here,' Dirk Heldmann said as he shook Dunk's hand for the camras. As team captain, Cavre had asked Dunk to accompany him to the centre of the field for the opening coin toss. With Dirk as the Reavers' captain, this would be the only chance for the two brothers to talk before the game began, and Dunk thanked Cavre for the opportunity.

'I'm just here to play Blood Bowl,' Dunk said.

Dirk glared up at Dunk. It often struck Dunk how different the two brothers looked, seeing as how they'd undeniably come from the same two parents. Dunk had a thick build and his hair and eyes were so dark they were almost black. Dirk, on the other hand, was lean and wiry, with white-blond hair and bright blue eyes, and stood at least an inch taller than his older brother. When the pair stood next to each other, people could see the resemblance, but only then.

'You're going to get killed,' Dirk said.

'That's sweet that you're concerned for me, but I know how to handle myself on a Blood Bowl field.'

Dirk grabbed Dunk by the side of his helmet and pulled him close. 'You're not listening to me. You never listen.'

Dunk sighed. They'd had this fight countless times before, and it had long since become old. 'Okay. Speak.'

'The Reavers – the players, at least – have decided that collecting the reward on your head is more important than winning the game. The first chance they get, they're going to kill you, snatch your body, and load you on the fastest boat to Altdorf.'

'You really know how to make a guy feel wanted.'

'Stop being cute.' Dirk sneered down at Dunk. 'You *are* wanted – dead or alive.'

Dunk scowled. 'Hasn't anyone bothered to consider that Zauberer might be lying? What makes anyone think they can take his word on anything? He's a wizard of the blackest kind.'

'With that amount of money possibly on the line, people are willing to take the chance. Besides, Lästiges's sources say its real.'

'I can't believe you're still dating her.'

Dirk rolled his eyes. 'You need to leave here. Now. Before the first play. You're a fine player, Dunk, but even you can't beat ten-to-one odds–'

'Orcs or Eagles,' the referee – Rhett Bool again – grunted as he presented Dunk and the team captains with a commemorative coin cast just for the game.

'Never bet against the Emperor,' Dirk said. 'Eagles!'

The minotaur flipped the coin into the air and let it bounce to a stop on the Astrogranite. 'Eagles!' he announced before he turned to Dirk. 'Kick or receive?'

'Receive.' Dirk glared at Dunk with desperate eyes. 'Don't let them do this to you,' he said. 'Meet me after the game. We can figure this out.'

'North or south end?' Bool asked.

'South,' said Cavre.

Dunk grimaced at his brother, and then reached out and pulled their helmets together for an instant. 'I'm sorry,' he said. 'I can't.'

With that, he turned and trotted down to the south end of the field.

CHAPTER SIX

SOON AFTER EDGAR kicked the ball, Dunk knew Dirk had been right. The ball went sailing right over every one of the Reavers and landed in the stands behind the end zone. The bloodthirsty fans – eager for the game to get started in earnest – tossed the ball back onto the field, but the Reavers ignored it. Instead of going for the ball, they went straight for Dunk.

'Have you ever seen anything like this, Bob?' Jim's voice boomed out over the PA system. 'The Reavers seem to have decided that taking out Hoffnung is more important than playing the game!'

'With a million crowns on the line, can you blame them?' said Bob. 'Maybe they hope to stake their claim in Hoffnung's valuable chest and then go on to destroy the Hackers to put the froth on that blood money.'

'Hoffnung's a contender though. I don't think he'll go down without a fight.'

'Your money's better than mine already, Jim. In the Gobbo's pool, I had him being found floating in the harbour last night!'

Dunk let the commentators' banter fade into the background as he concentrated on the task at hand: staying alive. He raced towards M'Grash, who was already trotting in his direction.

'They want to hurt Dunkel!' M'Grash said, dismay painted on his face. For a moment, Dunk thought the ogre might weep.

'Let's see that doesn't happen, big guy,' Dunk said. 'Give me a ride?'

M'Grash's fear for his friend's life evaporated in an instant. Childlike joy danced in his eyes instead. 'Piggyback?'

'How about on your shoulders?' Dunk said. He scrambled up the ogre's outstretched arms and wrapped his legs around the ogre's tree trunk of a neck.

Just then, the first of the Reavers hit M'Grash in the legs. The lineman speared the ogre in the thigh with the line of spikes that ran along the crest of his helmet.

M'Grash howled in pain. For all his size and strength, Dunk knew that he was a bit of a baby when it came to being hurt.

Most teams respected M'Grash for his superhuman strength and gave him as wide a berth as possible on the field. He spent most of his time chasing them down and breaking them apart like a series of desert-dry wishbones. Sure, he had to take on the big bruisers on the other teams, but he was ready for that. To have a human attack him directly surprised the ogre, and he didn't like it one bit.

M'Grash reached down and plucked the money-mad lineman from his thigh. He hauled the Reaver into the air by his helmet, the strap of which held tight, choking the man as his feet thrashed in the empty air below them.

'You hurt me!' M'Grash bellowed into the front of the man's helmet, raw spittle drenching the terrified lineman's face. 'Me hurt you!'

With that, the ogre swung his arm in a wide arc and pitched the hapless lineman high into the air. The Reaver sailed through the sky over the field and landed in the stands behind the Hackers' dugout. The fans there – at least the ones that weren't crushed – cheered and set to taking their revenge on the Reaver for having the nerve to fall on top of them.

Downfield, Dunk saw that one of the new Hackers, a Brettonian catcher by the name of Singe de Fromage, had scooped up the ball and was making a mad dash for the end zone. A moment later, Rhett Bool blew the whistle and stuck his arms up to signal the Hackers' first touchdown.

Dunk and the rest of the Hackers were too busy battling with the Reavers to pay any attention. Despite the score, which should have stopped the game for a moment, the Reavers refused to end their assault.

M'Grash tried to avoid the Reavers, but there were just too many of them. They grabbed at his legs and ankles, trying to trip him up or drag him down. Dunk watched Spinne tear the helmet off one of the Reavers and start to beat him senseless with it, and Guillermo was in the process of breaking the arm of one of the Reavers' throwers. Still, Dunk knew it wouldn't be enough.

Then he saw Edgar standing in the middle of the field, waving his arms. 'I'm open!' the treeman hollered. 'I'm bloody well open!'

Dunk tapped M'Grash on the top of his bald skull and pointed towards Edgar. The ogre might have had the smarts of a five-year-old, but he understood Blood Bowl well enough to know what Dunk wanted. He plucked his friend off of his neck and pitched him towards Edgar's waiting branches, a dozen yards away.

Dunk flung his arms and legs wide, trying to make himself as large a target as possible for Edgar to catch. As he hung in the air at the apex of the throw, he realised that M'Grash had hurled him a bit long. He was going to land on the treeman's far side.

Edgar spotted this and spun around, stretching his branches out towards the north end of the field. When Dunk flew over his leafy top, he reached out as far as he could and caught the thrower like a baby in a basket.

'Thanks!' Dunk said, amazed not to be lying flat on the Astrogranite with a crushed spine. Then he glanced back around Edgar's trunk. 'Now run!'

The Reavers had happily given up on M'Grash as soon as Dunk left the ogre's hands. M'Grash lumbered after them with a roar, his flying tackle smashing three of them under his bulk. The rest of the Reavers – a half-dozen of them – kept right after Edgar, ignoring their fallen team-mates.

'Just more for the rest of us!' said one of the Reavers – their fastest catcher – as he clawed onto Edgar's back with his spiked gauntlets and began to climb towards where Dunk sat in the treeman's branches.

Then another Reaver reached out and pulled his teammate off Edgar, smashing his helmet into the ground. Dunk cheered as he saw Dirk pounding away at his own teammate.

'I'm *still* the captain of this team!' Dirk said as he picked up the Reaver catcher and bodily flung him at the other Reavers stampeding up behind them.

'That's just the kind of old-school discipline missing on most teams these days,' Bob's voice said, 'I remember back when Griff Oberwald was the Reavers' captain. He'd have never let his players disobey him like that.'

'True enough,' Jim said, 'but with a million crowns at stake, Oberwald would probably have led the charge. What we have here is less a case of needed discipline than blood being thicker than Hater-Aid.

'Really?' Dunk could hear the vampire licking his lips. 'The Hater-Aid I drink comes with blood in it!'

The Reavers chasing Edgar pounded to a halt in front of Dirk, who stood between them and his brother. Dunk grabbed Edgar and pointed for him to turn around so they could see what happened next. Somewhere in the distance, he heard the protesting screams of de Fromage as the fans pulled the celebrating rookie into the stands and started to pass him up and over the stadium's outer wall.

'Stand down,' Dirk snarled at his team-mates. 'The play is over. If we want to win this game–'

'Sod the game,' said one of the Reavers' linemen, a bearded, bear-like man with a belly that probably weighed more than Dirk. 'And if you stand between us and that reward, sod you!'

As the lineman spoke, he stepped up closer to his captain and stabbed his finger at Dirk's face. Dirk reached out and grabbed the finger, and then snapped it, in one, quick motion. The lineman retracted his mangled digit, screaming at it in disbelief.

Dirk lowered his shoulder and charged into the astonished lineman, driving him backward into the other Reavers. 'Game on!' Dirk shouted, and the brawl started up again.

Seeing how his captain had betrayed the team, the Reavers' coach cleared the team's bench, and another four players in their blue-and-white uniforms raced on to the field. Never one to let another coach get an edge on his team, Pegleg did the same.

With Dirk in the middle of the brawl, Dunk refused to keep out of the fight anymore. 'Toss me in there!' he ordered Edgar.

'A bloody 'please' wouldn't hurt,' the treeman grumped.

'Please!' Dunk said. 'Now!'

A moment later, Dunk found himself arcing through the air again. This time, he came down hard in the middle of the action, spiked knee guards first. As he smashed into one Reaver's back, he lashed out with his fist at another and felt a satisfying crunch.

Joining in the brawl felt right to Dunk. He'd been running from his problems for too long. It was time to take his destiny in his own hands and stop letting others fight his battles for him.

Then all other concerns except the fight dropped away, and Dunk gave himself over to punishing the Reavers for their collective attack. Every time he saw a blue-and-white helmet or armour, he punched, tore, and kicked at it until it went away. He couldn't tell for how long he fought – it could have been seconds or hours – but he kept swinging, determined to put an end to this on his own terms or to go down fighting.

'Wow!' said Bob. 'You don't usually see that much violence until the post-game parties!'

'I think it's refreshing,' said Jim. 'Players these days are all about the money. They don't show any passion for the game.'

'I don't think this is about the game anymore.'

'That's my point! If it was, they'd be more concerned about scoring than surviving. Too many of these pansies want to live forever.'

'I don't think that's going to be a concern for most of the Reavers after today. Look! There's only one of them left standing!'

Dunk dropped the Reaver blitzer he'd been beating and spun around to defend himself. He grabbed at the only Reaver he saw on his feet, and smashed his helmet into the other player's.

'It's me, you idiot!' Dirk snarled as he punched Dunk away, his blow knocking his brother's helmet askew.

Dunk ripped his helmet from his head and stared at his brother, huffing and puffing for breath. He nodded his thanks to Dirk wordlessly, but Dirk ignored him.

Dirk turned around slowly, surveying the human wreckage on the Astrogranite. Dunk followed his brother's eyes and saw that only a few of the players on the field could still stand under their own power. A number of them were clearly dead, including, Dunk guessed, whoever owned the better part of an arm lying near midfield.

Players from both teams counted among the dead, and even more of them were injured. M'Grash bled from a half-dozen wounds he didn't seem to feel. Edgar had sap running out of a hole in his trunk.

Guillermo and Spinne were battered and bruised, with their share of minor cuts, but no worse than they would have received in the course of a game. One of the Hacker rookies lay whimpering to one side, cradling a mangled hand.

Now that it appeared the fight had come to an end, a squad of stretcher bearers from the stadium's staff swarmed onto the field. As the orange-uniformed men lifted the dead and wounded onto their litters, some of them glanced at Dunk with a familiar hunger in their eyes. He snarled at the one closest to him, and the man wet himself. As he scurried off the field, the others returned to their jobs, carefully avoiding Dunk's gaze.

A determined Reaver reached out for Dunk's ankle, and Dunk kicked him in the arm for his troubles. He thought about making sure the man had been knocked senseless, but Dirk grabbed him by the shoulder before he could strike again.

'That's enough,' Dirk said. 'He's had enough.'

Dunk shrugged his brother's hand off him. 'If you'd keep your animals on a proper leash–'

'These are good players,' Dirk said, tearing off his own helmet and getting in Dunk's face. 'Who could resist that kind of reward? You think any of us play this game for the exercise?'

'They tried to kill me.'

'Just like they might during any given game.'

Dunk stared straight into his little brother's bright blue eyes. 'You think maybe you can take that reward all for yourself now?' he asked.

All the frustration of having to run and hide over the past few days had boiled over during the fight, and Dunk hadn't stuffed it back in the bottle yet. If Dirk wanted a piece of him, he'd give it to him.

Dirk raised his fists as if he wanted to throttle the life out of Dunk, but before he could make his move, Rhett Bool stepped between them. He had a ball in his hand, and he shoved it into Dunk's hands.

'It's your kick-off,' he said to Dunk. Then he turned to Dirk. 'You need to get back to receive.'

Dunk and Dirk stared at the minotaur as if he'd grown a second head between his horns. He just gazed back at them with his large, bull's eyes, unblinking and silent.

'You can't be serious,' Dunk said. 'Who's left to play?'

'There's six of you still capable,' Bool said. 'And the Reavers still have one player left.'

Dunk felt sick as he looked over at Dirk, who just glared back at him. 'You can't... Forget it. I won't do it.'

The Reavers' coach stormed onto the field. Dunk had never met him before, but Blitz Bombardi's reputation preceded him. He dressed like a businessman, in a suit of the finest silk, under an overlarge bear-fur coat, purportedly made from the skin of a beast he'd killed with his own hands in his youth. He stared out at Dunk for a moment through a pair of black-rimmed spectacles that legend had it were fashioned from the black horn of a chaos daemon. If so, Dunk thought that might explain the way the man's eyes blazed at him.

'What's the problem?' Bombardi asked Dirk. He held his voice steady, almost quiet, but no one could mistake the menace carried in every syllable he uttered. This man expected his players to execute his orders efficiently and without question. He refused to show his irritation, but Dunk could feel it simmering beneath his placid surface.

'No problem, coach,' Dirk said, keeping his eyes locked on Dunk. 'The game's over.'

Bombardi shook his head. 'The game isn't over as long as there is one Reaver standing.'

'You can't be—' Dunk started to speak, but Bombardi snapped his head in the Hacker's direction and cut him off with a glance that Dunk thought could have stopped a starving troll.

Bombardi turned back to Dirk. 'Get down that field and prepare to receive that ball. We are in the final match of this tournament, and we will not forfeit the game under any circumstances.'

'Coach,' Dirk started.

'That's correct. I am the coach. You are the player. You will follow my lead, or you will be fired.'

Dunk watched Dirk struggle with his emotions. Dirk had been part of the Reavers ever since he'd left home. The team had become his new family, and every member of that family had betrayed him today when he'd stood up to them to defend his brother.

'It's okay,' Dunk said. 'We'll forfeit too. We'll call it a draw.'

Bombardi spun on Dunk. 'You can't do that. This is a tournament. The final game. There is a fortune at stake. There will be a winner. It will be the Reavers.'

M'Grash leaned forward and put a gentle hand on Bombardi's back. 'Pegleg always tells me…' He rolled his eyes back for a moment to concentrate, smiled when he found the thought he'd almost lost, and then continued. '"Just 'cause I say it don't make it real."'

Bombardi looked like he might shoot flames out through the lenses of his glasses. Instead, he shrugged off the ogre's hand and glared at Dirk. 'Get in the game, or go home.'

Dirk chewed on his bottom lip for a moment. Then he tossed Bombardi his helmet. 'Screw you and this screwy game,' he said. Then he walked off the field to the boos and hisses of scores of thousands of angry fans.

'Hackers win!' Bob's voice said. 'Hackers win! The Hackers have won the *Spike!* magazine tournament!'

Dunk stared up at the scoreboard and then at his own baffled face as it appeared on the Jumboball. He raised his arm in victory and tried to offer up a smile, but he just couldn't make it happen.

CHAPTER SEVEN

As Dunk, Spinne, and Slick strolled down the hall of the Hackers' 'secret' inn, the halfling seemed like the only one pleased with the day's results.

'It's wonderful, son, wonderful!' Slick said. 'Do you have any idea what the winner's purse for a major tournament like this is? Why, my percentage alone will be enough to keep me solvent for the rest of the year.'

Neither Dunk nor Spinne cared to respond, but this didn't give Slick any pause. He just stabbed his finger into the air and kept talking.

'Just think what this will do for the Hackers' reputation too. We'll have hopeful rookies crawling out of their burrows.' Slick rubbed his chubby, little hands together. 'And they'll all need representation.'

'I'm just happy you were able to find us another room here in the hotel,' Dunk said. 'I thought they were all sold out.'

'They were,' Slick said, grinning. 'But, because you two are my best clients, I decided I would swap rooms with you to give you a break until we leave this town behind.'

'Thanks,' Dunk said, impressed by the halfling's generosity. 'When do you think we'll be leaving?'

'Pegleg doesn't see any reason to stick around here, especially with you having to deal with this bounty nonsense. He wants to be out of here on tomorrow morning's high tide.'

Dunk couldn't wait to be out on the wide-open ocean on the *Sea Chariot*, the Hackers' team ship. The chances that someone would manage to find him out there and try to grab the reward were far less than they were here on land. He'd grown tired of having to glance over his shoulder every moment he was in Magritta. Leaving the town behind would not sadden him a bit.

'Here we are,' Slick said, turning to present the couple to a round door that stood only five feet tall.

Dunk stared at the door for a moment, then at Slick, and then back at the door.

'This is the halfling part of the inn,' Spinne said.

'Exactly!' said Slick. 'Who would think to look for you two here?'

Dunk had to admit that the halfling had a point. He wouldn't have thought to hole up here himself. He turned and gave Spinne a kiss. 'Will you mind if I don't carry you across the threshold?' he asked. 'It would be hard on my knees.'

'As long as you let me sleep in the bed,' she said with a grin. 'I can't imagine there will be room for us both – for sleeping, at least.'

'That's where you're wrong,' Slick said. 'I had the staff move a standard-sized double bed in here for me.

There's enough room on it for a handful of halflings. I think they thought I was some kind of swinger.'

'You think of everything,' Spinne said, laughing as Slick produced a key and used it to open the door.

'After you, my friends,' the halfling said, sweeping his arm wide to usher them into the room.

With no lanterns burning inside the room, Dunk couldn't see a thing. That was his first clue that something was wrong. He reached towards his belt for his sword, but it wasn't there. They'd come to the hotel dressed as monks, and there hadn't been a place for a blade under the hooded robes. He'd insisted on slipping a knife under the costume though, which Slick had razzed him about when they'd slipped out of the robes after leaving the inn's main room behind.

Dunk had felt silly at the time, but now, as the blade's handle filled his hand, he was glad he had it.

'You don't need that,' a gravelly voice said from somewhere in the darkness. Dunk recognised who it belonged to instantly: his old teacher Lehrer.

A match blazed in the far corner of the room, and Dunk saw the old man set the flame to a lamp sitting on a low table next to the low chair in which he crouched. He looked the same as ever, perhaps a bit more careworn. His silver hair had grown out a bit and threatened to fall into his sparkling, grey eyes. His drab clothes stood out in the brightly decorated room, the muddy colours of the cloth clashing with the primary colours that halflings with money seemed to love so much.

'Here to collect the reward?' Dunk asked as he moved into the room, crouching over to make sure he didn't bump his head. He peered left and right, hunting for some sign that Lehrer was not alone. He didn't think the old man would have brought someone else into their business together, but all sorts of strange things had happened to him that week.

Spinne slid into the room behind Dunk, and Slick marched in after her, closing the door behind him. 'Fancy meeting a scumbag like you in a nice place like this,' Spinne said to Lehrer as she moved to check and then cover the curtained windows.

The old man smirked. 'I don't believe I've had the pleasure, Miss Schönheit, although I almost feel I know you from all the news reports I've seen.' He glanced at Dunk. 'The ones from that Weibchen woman are always so deliciously mean.'

'Get out,' Dunk said, pointing the knife at Lehrer. Even though the old man seemed to be unarmed, Dunk knew better. He'd never known his old teacher to go anywhere without at least two weapons on his body – usually more.

'Now, now,' Lehrer said. 'There's no call to be like that. Just consider this a friendly visit from an old fan of yours.'

'You work for the Guterfiends,' Spinne said. 'They destroyed Dunk's family.'

Lehrer threw up his hands in mock surrender. 'I work for the people who occupy the Hoffnung's old estate, just as I worked for the Hoffnungs before that. Hey, a man's got to eat.'

Dunk dug into his purse, fished out Skragger's shrunken head, and tossed it to Lehrer. 'You hired this bugger to kill me – after he'd been brought back as a vampire – once we stopped him from killing us the first time.'

Lehrer caught Skragger's head neatly and spun it around so he could look into the creature's eyes.

'You've seen better days,' he said to the head with a wry grin.

Skragger snapped at Lehrer with his tiny teeth, but the old man just held him by his temples and let his jaw swing wildly through the air.

'Pathetic,' Lehrer said so softly Dunk could barely hear him. He set Skragger's head upside down on the table next to him, pointing its eyes towards the lamp.

Then Lehrer looked back up at Dunk, who still stared at him, waiting for an explanation. 'Yeah, that's all true,' Lehrer said. 'Guilty as charged, although I was just following the Guterfiends' orders.'

'That's not much of an excuse,' Slick said as he sat down in an overstuffed, halfling-sized chair in the far corner of the room from Lehrer. Seeing the halfling in his chair, Dunk realised that Lehrer had to be sitting in a halfling couch, as it was three times as wide as Slick's seat.

'If I hadn't done it, they would have just got someone else to hire Skragger. As it was, I could keep tabs on this bugger and even try to warn Dunk if he got too close to him.'

'Which you never did.'

Lehrer smirked. 'You didn't need my help, kid.'

'And I don't need it now,' Dunk said, jabbing his knife in Lehrer's direction. 'Get out.'

Lehrer grimaced as if trying to suppress his temper. Dunk remembered that look on the man's face all too well. He'd frustrated Lehrer to the point of losing his cool all too often. Eventually, he'd figured out the signs that he was about to trigger such an outburst, and he'd learned how to step back until everything was fine again.

Now, he didn't care.

'You're wrong,' Lehrer said. 'Again.' He blew out a long sigh and narrowed his eyes at Dunk. 'Who do you think put that price on your head?'

Dunk's jaw dropped. 'You?'

'No,' Lehrer said, disgusted. 'Think, kid, if I'd done that, would I have shown up here alone? I'd have just waited for the bounty hunters to bring you to me.'

'So,' Dunk said. 'Who was it then?'

'The Guterfiends,' Slick said from the couch behind Dunk. 'It has to be. They wanted you dead enough to send Skragger after you.'

'Give the little guy a pipe full of weed,' Lehrer said. 'They want your boy here dead in the worst way.'

'Do they really have a million crowns to spend on my death?' Dunk asked. He looked down and noticed the mattress Slick had mentioned, sprawling right there on the floor before him. He sat down on it and laid his knife across his thighs. If there really was someone willing to offer that kind of money to bring him down, how could he stop it?

'They seem to have a bottomless treasury,' Lehrer said. 'How do you think they managed to break up your family business? It wasn't done with mirrors.'

Dunk sat there in silence for a long moment, just staring down at the knife in his hands. This was it, he realised, the shoe he'd been waiting to drop. And now it had.

'Kid,' Lehrer said. 'I'm sorry to have to be the one to break all this to you. You know how the reward is for you dead or alive. Well, that pretty much means dead. If you show up to the old keep still breathing, they'll take care of that quick.'

Dunk let loose a low growl in his throat.

'What about Dirk?' Spinne asked.

Dunk looked up at her, confused.

'What about Dirk?' Spinne asked again, looking straight at Lehrer.

The old man smirked. 'I can see why the Hoffnung boys like you, girl. You're sharp like a knife.'

'What about Dirk?' Dunk asked.

'Once you're dead, they'll come for him.'

Dunk fought the urge to be sick. 'They want to wipe us out, don't they?' he said. 'And they're doing it in order, one at a time. First it was my parents. Now it's me. Then it'll be Dirk too.' He stared at Lehrer. 'What happens once we're all gone?'

'Then the Guterfiends have a free and clear claim to your family's holdings, uncontested by any heirs who might crop up.'

'Is that so important?' Slick asked. 'They already have those things. Why bother with wiping out the Hoffnung line?'

'You don't know these people,' said Lehrer. 'They're thorough. If they think there's even a chance they'll lose what they have, they'll go to any lengths, track down every possibility and eliminate them.'

'Why are you telling me this?' Dunk asked. 'This all smells like some sort of set-up.'

Lehrer sighed. 'Believe it or not, kid, I'm fond of you. I've been with your family since before you were born, and I've watched you grow from a little infant to a superstar.'

'Then why did you help the Guterfiends destroy my family?'

Lehrer cocked his head at Dunk. 'Who told you I did that?'

'Dirk has some pretty hard words for you.'

'He's just jealous. He always thought I favoured you.'

Dunk thought about that for a moment. 'Did you?'

Lehrer smiled. 'By default. You weren't the one who kept stuffing horse dung in my codpiece.'

'Do the Guterfiends know you're here?' Slick asked.

Lehrer grimaced at this question, and Dunk wondered if a squad of trained killers might erupt from the wardrobe now that someone had finally asked the worst sort of question: one which only had bad answers.

'They think I'm here to kill Dunk myself.'

Slick nodded. 'And if they find out you've been trying to warn him away?'

'Let's just say I won't be welcome back in the family keep – and they won't have to pay anyone to kill me.'

'Why's that?' asked Spinne.

Lehrer winked at her. 'There are plenty of folks ready to do that for free.'

'So,' Dunk said. 'You've delivered your warning. Now what? Just what do you expect me to do?'

Lehrer rubbed his chin as he talked to the thrower. 'If you had a lick of sense, you'd hightail it out of the Old World. Maybe go back to Albion. You might be safe there. Or head someplace even farther away: the Dark Lands, the Chaos Wastes.'

'You don't think they'd be able to find me there?'

'Out of sight, out of mind. These days, they see you every few weeks on their crystal ball – more often if that Weibchen woman covers you the way she likes to. If you quit the game, dropped out for a bit, they might forget.'

'Or they might not.'

Lehrer raised his eyebrows at that. 'True enough, kid. I did say they were thorough.'

Dunk sat with his head in his hands. Maybe Lehrer was right. As long as he continued on as a Blood Bowl player, he was a prime target. His constant presence on Cabalvision would drive the Guterfiends nuts, and his high profile would mean that anyone greedy enough to go after their reward would know where to find him.

It would be easier to give all this up, everything he'd worked for the past two years. After all, he'd never had any burning desire to become a Blood Bowl player. If he hadn't run into Slick in Dörfchen, he probably never would have even considered taking up such a career. He'd made plenty of money. He could live on it for the rest of his life. Spinne might even come with him if he asked her to.

'I don't know,' he said, looking at her. 'Would you join me? If I left all this behind, I mean. Would you come with me?'

Spinne furrowed her brow at Dunk and crept over to sit next to him on the mattress lying in the centre of the cosy halfling room. She reached up and took his face in her hands.

'Blood Bowl is my career,' she said. 'For the past five years, it's been my passion and my life. I can't imagine my life without it.'

Dunk's heart fell into his stomach. He let his head hang low. Could he go on without her? If he was a target, then she was in danger too. Bounty hunters rarely cared who got hurt when they chased after their prey. He couldn't stand the thought that she might get hurt because of him.

'All right,' he said. Before he could continue, she pulled up his chin and looked into his eyes.

'But when I try to imagine my life without you,' she said with a wan smile, 'it's even worse.'

Dunk leaned forward and kissed her soft and tender lips. He hoped their embrace would never have to end.

'Oh, for the love of the game,' Lehrer said. 'How trite can you get? Could you two at least get a room?'

Dunk extricated himself from Spinne's arms and raised his eyebrows at the old man, then glanced about at the ceiling, floor, and walls.

'Oh,' Lehrer said. 'Right.'

Dunk put an arm around Spinne and felt her melt into his chest. With her at his side, at least, he knew everything would be okay, no matter if he stayed or left.

'It's okay with me too, son,' Slick said.

Dunk peered over Spinne's reddish hair at the halfling. In the light of the room's single lantern, Slick looked a bit older than Dunk remembered ever seeing him. He and the halfling had started out at arm's length, but they'd quickly come to trust each other, to depend on each other for the truth. They'd formed a deep and abiding friendship based on mutual respect and need for each other's invaluable skills.

To leave Blood Bowl behind would mean leaving Slick behind too, and M'Grash and Guillermo, and Cavre and Edgar, and even Pegleg.

The only thing Dunk could think of to say to Slick was, 'What?'

'If you must know, I've been thinking of retiring myself. After all, what better time to go out than at the top of your game, right? Why hang around until you're a feeble old fool bumming ales from young fools in exchange for tired tales of the glories of your past?'

'What?' Dunk's brain couldn't digest the feast of foolishness Slick was trying to feed it.

'Don't worry yourself about me, son,' Slick said, piling it on. 'I'll be just fine. I've had my eye on a tavern in

Greenfield for a year or so now. I might even help out
with the Grasshuggers a bit while I'm there, just to keep
my hand in, you know.'

Dunk couldn't help it. He started to laugh. At first, he
tried to hide it. Slick had delivered such a serious
speech to him, after all, and he thought he should try
to give the halfling his due. The more he thought about
Slick retiring from being an agent to take up ownership
of some tavern in a halfling backwater, the harder it
became to ignore the humour in it.

When Spinne joined in, Dunk had no way left to
resist. He threw back his head and laughed loud, hard,
and long until tears streamed down his face and he
turned red from lack of breath. Spinne held him tight,
her own jiggling frame spurring him to wilder howls of
humour. Eventually, they collapsed on top of each
other, too worn out for even one more giggle.

'Nuffle's holy balls!' Slick said. 'The least you could
do is wait until I've left the room before you fall about
yourselves in hysterics.'

The thought that Slick might truly be angry with him
struck fear into Dunk, but when he opened his eyes to
take a look he saw the halfling smiling down at him
and shaking his head. 'I take it you're sticking with the
team,' Slick said with a chuckle of his own.

Without thinking another second about it, Dunk
nodded yes. 'It's strange, I know, but this game, this
team, has got into my blood.'

Dunk wiped his face dry and spoke seriously. 'After
my family's fall from grace, I wandered around lost and
alone for a while. I didn't know how to get back the life
I once had, and truthfully I didn't know if I wanted it.'

He put his arms around Spinne once more. 'With
Blood Bowl, I found everything I ever wanted: good

friends, true love, and a purpose in life. What more could I want?'

'You're insane, kid,' Lehrer said. He hadn't laughed with the others. He hadn't even cracked a single smile.

'I may have tumbled backward into this life,' Dunk said, 'but it's my life. I'm not going to let the Guterfiends or anyone else take it away from me without a fight.'

CHAPTER EIGHT

DUNK HEAVED THE last remnants of his breakfast over the gunwale of the *Sea Chariot* as it churned onward through the open seas to the south of Estalia. He'd never cared much for ocean voyages, but he seemed to be getting worse about them as he got older. He knew that once he finally got rid of everything he'd eaten, he'd be fine. It would be a long trip to Barak Varr, and he'd have lost a few pounds by the time they got there, but he'd survive.

Spinne handed Dunk a skin of Hater-Aid. Dunk didn't normally care much for sports drinks, but they seemed to be the only thing he could keep down when onboard. He thanked her for it, taking care not to assault her with the scent of his breath as he did so.

'Dr. Pill says he has something that can settle your stomach,' Spinne said as she rubbed a comforting hand up and down his back.

'Somehow, I don't find that news reassuring,' Dunk said. He looked over his shoulder and saw the skinny elf raise the eyebrow over his white patch at him with an expectant grin. 'I think I'll take my chances with the seasickness. I can't believe we brought him along.'

'After how much good he did for our team in the *Spike!* magazine tournament, Pegleg became his number one fan. He offered him a year's contract after the finals.'

'You're not making me feel any better,' Dunk said, remembering what the apothecary had done to him to get him back on his feet during the game against the Oldheim Ogres.

Slick strode up next to Dunk and leaned next to him on the gunwale, which rose to the top of the halfling's head. 'What luck, eh?' Slick said.

Dunk retched again, and then wiped his mouth on his sodden sleeve. 'I don't feel lucky,' he said.

'Not that, son. I'm talking about the Dungeonbowl. When we destroyed the Reavers – or rather as they self-destructed – I hadn't thought that it would cost the Grey Wizards their chosen team for their upcoming tournament.'

'I thought for sure that Bombardi would just rebuild the team in time for the start of the games,' Spinne said. 'I'm surprised he let the sponsorship get away from him.'

'More likely it was summarily yanked from his clutches,' Slick said. 'The Grey Wizards may have a lot of faith in the Reavers' management, but they like to think their team should have a shot at winning the tournament. It's hard to rebuild a top-ranked team from scratch in less than three months. If Dirk had stuck with Bombardi, they might have had a chance, but to literally lose every decent member of your team…'

'Did we really kill all of the Reavers?' Dunk asked. 'We must have got more carried away than I'd thought.'

Slick shook his head. 'Some of them died at our hands, true, but the fans took care of the rest. They were furious that the Reavers made the best game in the region not get past the first five minutes of play. Seats for a game like that aren't cheap, you know.'

'No one hurt Dirk, did they?'

Slick snorted. 'A few of them tried, but he made quick work of them.'

Spinne leaned over to look at Dunk, who still had his head and arms hung out over the gunwale. 'You still haven't talked to him?'

Dunk shook his head. 'I couldn't find him before we left Magritta. You'd think he was the one with a price on his head. I left a message for him at the Bad Water, though. Sparky said he'd deliver it if he saw him.'

'Good idea,' Spinne said. 'That was always his favourite watering hole in town. If he hasn't left town already, he's sure to end up there.'

Dunk slumped down with his back against the gunwale, sitting next to where Slick stood. 'He told me something else funny too. Sparky, I mean. He said he hated Gunther the Gobbo with a passion.'

'Who doesn't?' asked Slick. 'He's as loved as the plague.'

'But Gunther was waiting for me that night Sparky showed me the secret tunnel out of the Bad Water. He said Sparky was his friend. That's why he knew about the secret tunnel and where it let out.'

'So the Gobbo's a liar now?' Slick said in mock horror. 'Quick, someone get me Lästiges! This is big news!'

'One of Sparky's real friends probably owed Gunther some money,' Spinne said.

'Maybe,' Dunk said. 'It just seems strange. I mean, he was right there waiting for me.'

'I wonder how Lästiges is doing,' Spinne said. 'She and Dirk seemed to be getting fairly serious.'

'You think she'll dump him now that he's quit playing Blood Bowl?'

Spinne shrugged. 'She's always been a glory hound. Dating an ex-player isn't nearly as glamorous as being seen with someone who's still in the game.'

'Yet another good reason for me to stay with the game myself,' Dunk said. He fended off a half-hearted punch in the arm from Spinne. 'Don't you find professional athletes intriguing?' he asked her playfully.

'I spend far too much time with them,' Spinne said. 'They mostly bore me to tears.'

'I guess I'll have to try harder to entertain you,' Dunk said.

'Don't bother,' Spinne said. 'You're the exception that proves the rule.'

Cavre walked across the deck of the ship towards the trio at the gunwale, a wooden bucket swinging in one hand. He moved with the surety of a man who'd spent many an hour on the sea, a broad smile on his face.

'Dunk,' said Cavre. 'The captain would like to see you.'

Dunk's stomach twisted again at the idea of having to chat with Pegleg. They hadn't said much to each other since the victory ceremony and trophy presentation at the end of the *Spike!* magazine tournament.

Dunk had spent all his time avoiding the public eye while his coach had basked in it.

Pegleg had worked a long time to forge a championship team, and he seemed determined to make the most of it. Every time Dunk sat near a crystal ball, it seemed that one reporter or another was interviewing Pegleg about the Hackers and their victory. Some of the questions inevitably centred on Dunk and the price on his head.

'What's it like when your star player has a massive price on his head? Doesn't a million crowns seem a bit excessive?' one goblin asked on ESPNN (the Extraordinary Spellcasters Prognosticated News Network).

Pegleg smiled and said, 'We're very proud of Mr. Hoffnung and his contributions to the Hackers, so we understand why this mysterious malefactor would value him so highly. However, I'd like to question the authenticity of this mad wizard's bounty. It's clear he doesn't have the kind of treasury required to back up such an amazing offer.'

'Are you saying Schlechter Zauberer is a liar?'

'He's clearly insane. Is he a liar if he's mad enough to believe his own ludicrous tales? Let's just say I doubt there's a reward of any kind and leave it at that.'

Pegleg had hammered at the same point over and over, on every show that would have him: CNN (Corpse-Necromancer News), CBS (Crystal Ball Service), NBC (Nymphomantic Bardic Casters), ABC (Auguristic Bestial Clairvoyants), and even Albion's ITV (Itinerant Telepathic Visionaries). The most incredible spot had been on the 'Impaired and Unbalanced' Cox News, which aired live the night before the Hackers set out from the port city of Luccini on the southwest side of the Tilean Peninsula.

'Don't you think that this Dunk Hoffnung placed the reward on his own head as a means of distracting the people of the Empire from noticing the fact that no one in power in Altdorf has any clothes?' asked anchorman Dill O'Really.

'Are you saying nudity is now in fashion in Altdorf?' Pegleg said with a leer.

'By avoiding my question, you're tacitly acknowledging Hoffnung's part in the vast daemon-winged conspiracy that operates politics in the Old World these days.'

'Nothing of the sort, Mr. O'Really, such accusations sound like they might have come only from the mind of a madman like Mr. Zauberer himself.'

The interview had gone sour when O'Really consulted an unfurled scroll on his desk. Then he glanced over his spectacles at Pegleg and asked, 'Are you aware of Dunk's family history?'

'Tryouts for the Bad Bay Hackers don't involve taking a detailed biography of prospective players. I just care whether or not they can play the game.'

'According to this report published three years ago in the Altdorf Augur, the Hoffnung family was part of a vast scandal involving organised crime, mutant skaven, and the blackest sort of magic.'

'I don't judge a man by the members of his family.'

'Well, maybe you should. It seems that the Hoffnungs were all run out of town with torches and pitchforks after your friend Dunk got in a fight at a party celebrating his engagement to Lady Helgreta Brecher.'

Pegleg looked like a halfling caught in a battle train's headlights. 'Of Brecher International Conglomerated Holdings?'

'Exactly!'

'Well, Blood Bowl teams are filled with killers and worse. That's what we pay them for, after all. I don't see how a simple brawl would be any of my concern.'

O'Really held a painting up for Pegleg to see. 'This is an artist's rendition of what happened that night. Do you see all the daemons flying around, tearing and rending flesh?'

'That's appalling, Mr. O'Really. I didn't know that B.I.C.H. employed daemonic help at their galas.'

A smug grin festered on the commentator's face. 'Those daemons you see came to help your Dunk kill a man, Helgreta's older brother Kügel.'

'Well,' Pegleg said with an uneasy smile. 'At least he got the job done right.'

'So you condone the use of daemonic forces in disputes? Can we expect to see you employ such resources in your next game?'

'Only in the finals.'

O'Really didn't laugh.

'Can't the captain come out here to talk to me?' Dunk asked. 'I'm busy communing with the open sea air.'

Cavre shook his head. 'You know it doesn't work like that.' He handed Dunk the bucket he carried. 'Try not to make too much of a mess. His mood is worse than usual.'

Dunk rolled his eyes as the next wave caught the ship's bow. 'How much worse can it get?'

'That's the kind of question a wise man never asks.'

Dunk got to his feet, clutching the bucket before him in both hands. He nodded his goodbyes to Spinne, Slick, and Cavre before heading to the captain's cabin. 'If I'm not back in ten minutes, dive overboard and save yourselves,' he called back.

Dunk knocked on the captain's door and heard the man call, 'Enter!' Then he slipped inside the cabin and shut the door tight behind him.

Dunk had been on many other ships, but he'd never seen a captain's cabin like Pegleg's. The windows and portholes had all been painted black and covered over with thick, red curtains, which made the place as dark as a cave. Scrolls, furled and unfurled, filled every nook and cranny of the room that didn't have a bit of furniture crammed into it or a framed picture hung on it. These featured scouting reports on all of the teams the Hackers might have to play, including rosters, health reports, playbooks, and even the kinds of dirty tricks each team had historically favoured or was known to have in production.

A massive crystal ball sat perched on a low table in one corner of the room. A scene from the *Spike!* magazine tournament finals played within it, sending a ghostly light flickering around the room. The only other light came from an oil lamp that hung from the ceiling over the red velvet couch on which Pegleg sat hunched over the low, wide table before him. Papers of all sorts covered the table, held in place by the *Spike!* magazine trophy, a mithril spike held in a mailed and spiked fist thrust upward in victory.

'Sit, Mr. Hoffnung,' Pegleg said, gesturing towards a chair across the table from him.

Dunk did as he was told. He folded his hands atop the bucket in his lap and waited for his coach to speak. When, after several minutes, it didn't seem like that would ever happen, Dunk opened his mouth and said, 'I want to thank you for sticking up for me, for telling everyone that the reward was a hoax. I think it–'

'Daemons, Mr. Hoffnung?' Pegleg used his hook to push back his yellow tricorn hat. He had worn so many holes in it that it was in tatters.

'I can explain.'

'There are many things I can abide in a player, Mr. Hoffnung, but even I have to draw the line at consorting with daemons. If that's how you intend to conduct yourself, I'll speak with Slick about selling your contract to the Chaos All-Stars.'

Dunk perched on the edge of his seat. He thought that maybe Pegleg would be upset with him, but he hadn't expected to be traded away – especially not to the Chaos All-Stars. That was a team with a reputation for forcing players to stick to the letter of its contract by unspeakable means.

'But, coach, I didn't consort with daemons. Don't tell me you're going to take O'Really's word for it.'

Pegleg leaned back in his couch and brushed his long, dark curls from his shoulders. 'Of course not, Mr. Hoffnung, if I had, you'd have already found yourself on your way to meet with your new employers. Why do you think I called you in here?'

Dunk looked down at his bucket. 'Some kind of cruel torture for having to answer questions about the reward on me while you'd rather have been crowing about our victory?'

Pegleg allowed himself a thin smile. 'Perhaps under happier circumstances. As it is, I need you to explain yourself.'

Dunk closed his eyes and felt the motion of the ocean in his stomach. He'd hoped that he'd put that part of his life far behind him, but he knew better. As the price the Guterfiends had put on his head illustrated, you carried every bit of your history with you wherever you went.

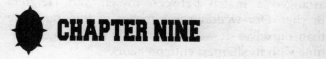

CHAPTER NINE

'I DON'T REALLY know what happened,' Dunk said. When Pegleg scoffed at this, Dunk raised his eyes and continued. 'Okay, I know what happened to me, but I'm still not sure why.

'You've been to Altdorf, so you've probably heard of the Hoffnungs. We were one of the wealthiest and oldest families in the city. I can trace my ancestors straight back to the place's earliest days.

'Over the centuries, our influence waxed and waned. In my grandfather's day, we hit one of our low points and had to sell almost everything. He hanged himself in disgrace when my father was just twenty years old.

'From the family's point of view, that was one of the best things that could have happened to us. My father and grandfather had often butted heads. Grandfather stuck hard and fast to the old ways, while my father advocated moving into new businesses and investing what little money we had aggressively while we still had it. With Grandfather gone, the reins of the business fell into Father's hands, and he made the most of it.

'By the time I was born, the Hoffnung fortune had been revived and the family had become a vital part of Imperial culture once more. Father proved to be an excellent businessman and a cunning student of Imperial politics.

'When I came of age as a young man, my father arranged a match between myself and Helgreta Brecher. Our wedding was meant to join far more than ourselves. It would marry the city's largest fortune with its sharpest entrepreneurs.'

'Didn't you have any say in this?'

Dunk snorted softly. 'Not much, but I didn't much care either. Helgreta was pretty enough – a sweet young lady, really – and I was willing to do whatever Father asked of me. He impressed upon me how important this merger of our two families would be, and I was ready to play along.

'It all seemed to be going well until the night of our official engagement party, which the Brechers held in their family keep, right in the heart of Altdorf. Although we'd been betrothed to each other for years, the party signalled that we would be married within the year.'

Dunk stopped speaking for a moment, his eyes focused on something far beyond the confines of Pegleg's sealed cabin. 'She was so beautiful that night. She gave me a scarf of the finest silk as a symbol of our impending union.' He raised a hand to his neck where he had worn it.

'Towards the end of the night, Helgreta's brother Kügel accosted me. He'd had a great deal to drink, so

I tried to give him his space. He pursued me though, accusing me and my family of worming their way into his family over nothing but gold.'

'Wasn't there a bit of truth in that?'

'Of course. We all knew it. These sorts of marriages happen all the time in Imperial society, and if Helgreta and I didn't have any problem with it, I didn't see what Kügel had to get angry about. And I told him so.

'He didn't take that well at all. He went and found a ceremonial sword hanging in the front hall of their estate, and he came back to the ballroom with it. Everyone stopped and stared at him. The band's instruments froze in their hands.

'The guards – who worked for the Brechers, of course – stayed right where they were. They weren't about to stop the heir to the Brecher fortune from doing whatever he wanted. Nüsse Brecher, the patriarch of the clan, stood up and told Kügel to sit down before he made more of a fool of himself, but Kügel attacked me instead.

'As a rising nobleman, I hadn't been in too many real fights, but I'd been trained in the arts of war since my childhood. Kügel had spent his days writing poetry and swilling wine. When he came at me with the sword, I snatched it from his hand, shoved him away and then held the blade to his neck.

'Now, keep in mind that this is the brother of my fiancée. Although he'd attacked me in his own home, I could see that he was drunk and upset. I had no desire to humiliate him further, much less hurt him.

'Then the most amazing and horrible thing happened. A trio of armoured daemons wielding burning whips and swords smashed in through the skylights over the ballroom and brought the massive chandelier hanging there crashing down to the floor. It crushed several people to death.'

Dunk glanced back at Pegleg and saw that the man was holding his breath.

'They stood eight feet tall on their cloven hooves, not counting the tops of their large, leathery wings. They bore crimson tattoos on their charcoal-coloured skin, which glowed like burning embers in a hot breeze. Their eyes were black, polished marbles, like those of a shark. Long horns thrust from the fronts of their skulls, curling back on themselves again and again. They stank of sulphur, and it hurt to stand in the heat of their presence.'

'How terrible,' Pegleg said. He'd inched away from Dunk as the story unfolded, and now he sat curled up in the far corner of his velvet couch.

'The worst part was how they claimed to know me. One of them pointed his burning sword at me and said, "Do not fear, Dunkel Hoffnung. We will protect you."

'With that, the others used their blades to slice Kügel into bite-sized portions. He was dead before he could scream about it. I blinked, and the floor in front of me was filled with wet pieces of Kügel.

'Helgreta screamed. A lot of people screamed, actually. I think I screamed. Then everyone ran.

'With one daemon standing in front of me, I didn't see a clear path from the hall, so I hacked at it with the sword I'd taken from Kügel. I stabbed the creature clean through the heart, and it howled in pain and then disappeared in an explosion of hot ash.

'I couldn't see a thing. Then someone knocked the blade from me, and two sets of hands grabbed me by my arms and hauled me into the air.

'When I emerged through the shattered windows and into the night sky above, I saw the remaining daemons had me. They laughed as I screamed at them in protest. A few moments later, they deposited me just inside the gates of my own family's keep. Then they flew off into the night, and I never saw them again.'

'By Nuffle's sacred rulebook,' Pegleg said. 'That's an amazing story, Mr. Hoffnung. Is any of it true?'

Dunk stared at the ex-pirate. For a moment, he considered throwing something at him, perhaps the bucket in his hands. Then he realised that telling the story had distracted him so much that his body had forgotten to keep being seasick. He felt fine.

'Every word of it, Coach,' Dunk said.

Pegleg shook his head. 'I'm so sorry to hear that, Mr. Hoffnung.'

Dunk didn't know what to say. He couldn't read the captain at all, even as the man unfolded himself from the corner of the couch.

'Do you believe me?' Dunk asked.

Pegleg arched his eyebrows at Dunk. 'I take it no one in Altdorf did.'

Dunk shook his head. 'My parents did. My father knew what was coming though and started packing to leave right away. My mother just sat there in shock. She couldn't understand what had happened and how it would affect us all.

'When the mob showed up on our doorstep – led by a platoon of Imperial soldiers – she went to open the door. I'd been helping my father pack, and we'd lost track of her.'

Dunk closed his eyes. He didn't think he could go on. He'd got this far through the story that he'd never told anyone since he'd left Altdorf – not Slick, not

Spinne, not even Dirk, who'd left the Hoffnung home a year before the incident. He had to finish it.

'The mob tore my mother apart. We had no idea what she'd done until we heard her screams. By then, it was already too late.

'Father showed me a secret passage out of the estate. It opened up near a public stable, and he purchased us a pair of horses there.

'"They'll be looking for two men riding together," he said. "Best if we split up for now. Meet me at the summer estate near Marienburg when you can."

'That was the last I saw of him. The city's gates were locked at night, so I hid in the alley behind the Skinned Cat until dawn. Well after midnight, a drunken sot stumbled into the alley to look for a place to sleep. I paid him to trade clothes with me and keep his mouth shut, which he did as soon as he passed out again.

'As dawn broke over the city, I mounted up again and rode for the northern gates. I heard some people in the street gossiping about the daemonic attack, but no one recognised me. Once I left the city behind, I rode hard until Altdorf – my birthplace, the only real home I'd ever known – disappeared in the distance.'

'Did you ever see your father again?'

Dunk shook his head. 'I went to the summer estate, but word of the incident at the Brecher keep travelled fast. I couldn't stay there long. I rode into Marienburg in disguise and took work as a warehouse guard there, down near the wharf.

'Every day I had a break, I rode back out to the estate to hunt for a sign of my father. One day when I got there, I found a host of people using the place. Some of them I recognised as our servants.

'I rode into the place, hoping to find my father taking some sun in the gardens, this whole nightmare over. When the servants spotted me, they turned white as sheets. One of them raced into the house, shouting for help.

'"What is it?" I asked the ones still left. "Where is my father?"

'Lehrer emerged from the estate then and strode out to talk with me. "Your father is not here," he said.

'"Fine," I said. "I'm glad you came ahead to prepare the place for him. It's a terrible mess."

'"Your father is dead," he said. Just like that. I nearly fell off my horse.

'"Our new employers – the Guterfiends – are here," he said. "If they find you, they will kill you. You must leave. Now."

'When I tried to protest, Lehrer grabbed the reins of my horse and turned it around. Then he slapped it on its hindquarters and sent it – and me – galloping off.

'"Don't come back – for your own good!" he shouted after me.'

Dunk sat there in silence for a moment, watching Pegleg's impassive face. 'Do you have anything in here to drink?' Dunk asked. 'An afternoon of vomiting and talking dries a man out.'

CHAPTER TEN

PEGLEG RETRIEVED A bottle of wine and a pair of glasses from a cabinet near the still-glowing crystal ball. He removed the cork with the tip of his hook, decanted the wine into the glasses and handed one of them to Dunk. Then he raised his glass in his good hand for a toast.

'To living with our daemons,' Pegleg said. He took a large mouthful of the wine and swirled it around his tongue before swallowing it. 'And to grinding the bastards into bloody paste.'

'Here, here.'

Dunk drank deeply of the wine, and then shoved his glass forward to be topped up. Pegleg obliged him, and then re-corked the bottle with his hook.

'So,' Dunk said, 'do you believe me?'

Pegleg arched an eyebrow at Dunk. 'Why wouldn't I, Mr. Hoffnung? Have you shown yourself to be less than trustworthy in the more than two years you've been with my team?'

Dunk waited for his answer.

'I am haunted by daemons of my own, Mr. Hoffnung, and I don't mean the metaphorical kind. I've seen the kind of creatures you describe. In fact, I once worked for them as their slave.'

Dunk's eyes opened wide.

'Given your own experiences, do you find this so hard to believe?' Pegleg stroked the back of his hook with his good hand as he spoke.

Dunk shook his head, and then nodded. 'Yes – I mean, no. I don't doubt that someone who travels as much as you do has encountered daemons before, but I would never have guessed they'd enslaved you.'

Pegleg swirled his red wine in his glass and took another sip. 'I wasn't always a coach, you know – or a pirate, for that matter. In fact, I was never much of a pirate.

'I used to be a fisherman, like my father before me and his father before him, back as far as we knew. My family lived on the south shore of the Sea of Claws, in a little town so small that no one had ever bothered to give it a name. Those who knew where it was lived there, and few others cared about it at all.

'Now, of course, it's not there at all. Nothing more than the burnt skeletons of a few buildings standing along that distant stretch of shore.'

'What happened to it?'

Pegleg gave Dunk a thin smile. 'Mr. Hoffnung, will you allow me to tell my own story at my own pace, to make my own decisions about how to present the facts as I saw them?'

Dunk flushed red and nodded his apology.

Pegleg stared into the wine sloshing about in his glass for a moment before he continued. 'I was little more than a boy, but I'd served on my father's boat from the moment I could tie a sheepshank. We'd taken in a good haul that day and were sailing home with the harvest of our nets when I saw the smoke rising from our little seaside hamlet.

'At first, we didn't know what to do. If someone had destroyed the town already, there seemed little profit in racing in to add our souls to the pyre. On the other hand, if any were still alive, we knew we could not abandon them there. Soon enough, we decided to drop anchor a hundred yards out and swim in, hoping we could slip in unnoticed.

'When we reached the beach, the sun hung low in the west. My father and I slipped forward into the nearby forest and then circled around to the back of the hamlet. We entered the settlement near our home, where we'd left my mother and sister that morning.

'As we crept closer, we heard screams coming from the house. Before I could stop him, my father dashed from the safety of the leafy cover and charged into the house, holding his filleting knife before him like a cutlass. I followed straight after him, my own knife out and at the ready.

The shingles on our house caught fire just before we entered the place. Smoke filled the main room to the rafters, but we forged our way into it anyway, following the sounds of my sister's screams. Coughing on the smoke, we reached my parents' bedroom and thrust open the door.

'I will not describe the scene we found therein. I can see every detail of it whenever I close my eyes.

The mercy of sleep never takes me far from it, and I cannot escape it in my waking hours.

'My mother was already dead, and my sister followed soon after. The daemons we found in that room with them – crimson skinned monsters with snakes for eyes and limbs – smashed consciousness from us.

'My father and I awoke in chains in the lower hold of a massive ship I later discovered was called *Seas of Hate*. We lay huddled there for I know not how long, recovering from our wounds. There were others in there with us – some from our hamlet but many from parts unknown. Not all of us were human, but we were all imprisoned together.

'From time to time, someone would lower a bucket of boiling gruel or filthy water into the hold, and we would squabble over it. We had to eat the food with our bare fingers while it was still scalding hot or it would have disappeared before we could even have taken a bite.

'Sometimes they would come for us. A noose of barbed wire snaked through the hatch above and ensnared some hapless soul and hauled him up and out of our lives. Then the hatch slammed shut again, leaving us in the darkness once more.

'They caught my father first, perhaps a few days after we were captured. Maybe weeks. I thought I might never see him again, but I refused to weep before my fellow prisoners. Instead, I began to plan my escape.

'I had lost everything that had ever meant anything to me – all but my life. I intended to hold on to that with everything I had, and I swore to myself I'd kill whoever I must to keep myself alive.

'When they finally came for me, I went willingly. I actually grabbed the noose and held it with my hands, letting them pull me up by my wrists rather than my neck.

'The same sorts of daemons I'd seen in my family's home set me down on a bench, shackled my left hand to an oar, and put the oar in my hands. They used the whip on my back straight away to impress their will upon me, but they didn't need it. I knew what they expected of me, and I planned to deliver it without pause or complaint – at least until I saw my chance to escape.

'As I set to building up the blisters that would turn to calluses on my hands, I peered around. There were at least two dozen rows of oars working to move that hateful ship through the water, with three men – or creatures – dedicated to each oar.

'At least two of us would row at a time, with the third sometimes lying collapsed at our side, sleeping from sheer exhaustion. We were never all allowed to rest all at once, and if our reptilian masters wished for more speed, we would all set to our oars with respite for none.

'A pair of daemons licked their long lashes out over the oarsmen, one to the fore and one aft, while a third kept beat on an ogre's skin stretched over the mouth of a deep kettle drum.

'I spotted my father rowing three rows ahead of me and on the other side of the aisle. I tried to speak to him once, and I had my back laid open for my troubles. But I knew that he'd seen me, and for the moment that was enough.

'After countless weeks under those conditions, I still hadn't seen my chance to make my break. A few others had tried it, and they had been struck down before they reached the gunwale. The snakeheads on the daemons' limbs bore terrible venom. A single bite was enough to kill a man within minutes, leaving him a shaking, frothing wreck, bleeding out through his liquefied eyes.

'Some of the captives sought that 'blessed bite,' as they called it, their chance for final release from that horrific life. The daemons were sparing in their use of it, if only because they didn't want to lose too many of their slaves in one go.

'My father's strength eventually gave out. One day, he slumped over his oar and did not move. When the overseers lashed his skin, he did not cry out in pain or even flinch. One of the daemons ran him through with a spear to make sure he was dead. Then they drew up his body and tossed him overboard to feed the school of sharks that many of the prisoners claimed constantly followed in our wake.

'I knew then that I could not stand another moment. As night fell, I spied a nearby shoreline through my oar's hole, and I set to work on my chains in the darkness. I knew I could not remove them, but in the madness of my grief an option came to me that I had not considered before.

'If I could not break my chains, then I would leave behind that which they held.'

The captain held up his hook and watched it shine in the lamplight, a sad but proud expression on his face. Horror ran through Dunk's gut as he gaped at his coach.

'You took off your own hand?' Dunk asked. 'With what?'

Pegleg laughed bitterly, exposing his teeth. The ones up front were made of gold, and they seemed as sharp as razors now in his mouth.

Despite the cabin's warmth, Dunk shivered.

'Once I was free,' Pegleg said, 'I charged for the gunwale. As I cleared it, I felt something sharp sink deep into my ankle. I reached back with my hand to grab the snakehead I found there, and I pulled it and its daemonic owner after me into the briny deep.

'The tales of the sharks proved to be no legend. Once I fought my way back towards the surface, I could see a dozen fins circling in the lantern light that the daemons on the ship shone out at us, laughing at their sport.

'Knowing the wound on my arm would draw the sharks to me, I swam hard for the shore. I could barely see it in the darkness, just a strip of grey caught between the dark of the sky and the sea, but I knew it had to be there, so I pulled myself towards it.

'As I went, I could feel the daemon's venom working its way into the wound from its bite, numbing my nerves as it crawled upwards from my ankle. I didn't know what would kill me first: the sharks, the poison, or the daemon pursuing me through the waves.

'The daemon struck out at me again, its snake-arm tagging me on the same foot as before. Having found purchase in my flesh, it tried to pull me back towards it. Before it could bring me within reach of its other limbs, something pulled it back down into the water, and its grip on my ankle was gone.

'The creature emerged a moment later, screeching and howling in a way I'd never known. I could smell blood in the water, which began to churn beneath the daemon, just before it was hauled down one last time.

'I put my back to the scene and swam for my life. As I went, I could feel my poisoned leg starting to grow cold. Despite this, I kept swimming as fast as my limbs would carry me.

'The first time I felt the shark, it hit me in the side, just with a glancing blow. The massive beast seemed to have decided that the feeding frenzy going on behind me was too much trouble – or that human flesh tasted better than the daemonic variety.

'Perhaps the shark was a daemon itself, or maybe it had just been living in the wake of daemons for too long. Either way, something had gifted it with a sharp malignance I'd not seen in any animal before or since. It didn't just want to eat me; it wanted me to know who was doing it.

'The beast hit me again, this time in my leg. As it came around for a third pass, I saw its entire head emerge from the water, and it looked me straight in the face with its dead-black eyes. I was only yards from the shore, and yet I knew I would never make it – and so did that thing.

'I watched the shark as it circled me and came in for the kill. As it did, I curled my legs under me. When it struck, I kicked out with my poisoned leg and jammed it as far into the bastard's gullet as it would go.

'The damn thing nearly choked on the limb. As it chewed on my flesh, I thrashed about, trying to kick out its brains from its insides.

'Soon enough, I felt myself become a great deal lighter. While the beast gnawed on my limb, I set to dragging myself through the last bit of surf and onto that sacred shore.

'A wave came along and carried my bloodied carcass all the way to the sand. I hit the ground hard, and it almost knocked me senseless. For a moment, I feared the riptide would sweep me back out to sea, but I managed to find purchase in the waterlogged sand for long enough to hold out.

'I hauled myself out on to that shore and bound my wounds with torn strips of my tattered clothing. I thought for sure I'd die during the night, but my will to live was too strong. I made it through to the dawn.

'Some fishermen found me then and carried me back to their village. Their wives tended to me there, nursing me back to health, although I would never be whole again.'

Pegleg tapped the end of his wooden leg on the floor, as if for luck, and gazed down at his missing parts. When the captain raised his eyes again, Dunk realised he must be staring at his coach in horror, and he looked away.

Pegleg sat there in silence, his story apparently done. Dunk couldn't stand the quiet and had to speak.

'And from there you went on to coach the Hackers? What about you being a pirate? Is that all just a sham?'

The coach smiled, wider this time, and picked up the bottle of wine to fill their glasses again, emptying it. 'My Blood Bowl career is a tale for another time, Mr. Hoffnung. I think we've bared enough of our souls for one day. As for me being a pirate, I often find it's easier to let people believe what they like – especially if it can be turned to your advantage.'

Dunk nodded and got up to leave. 'Now I understand your fear of water,' he said. 'Don't get me wrong. You're one of the bravest men I know. I don't think you'd ever get me on a boat again if I'd gone through that.' He glanced around the sealed-up cabin. 'Even like this.'

'Yes,' Pegleg said. 'I'm not one to let my limitations limit me any more than they must. Dr. Pill has been working with me on that detail as well. He seems to think I'm ready to try a short stroll on the main deck. I think I'll take his advice.'

Pegleg rose to his feet. He seemed a bit unsteady, but whether that was from the sea, the wine, or his nerves, Dunk could not tell.

'Could you get the door for me, Mr. Hoffnung?' Pegleg said as he limped towards the thrower.

'Aye, captain,' Dunk said. He unlatched the door, pulled it open and held it wide for the man.

Pegleg nodded his thanks and then stumped his way on through, out into the crisp, night air of the open sea. Dunk waited for a moment, seeing the captain's cabin empty for the first time since he'd known the man. Then he left as well, shutting the door behind him.

CHAPTER ELEVEN

'Dunkel? Who are the bad guys?' M'Grash asked for the third time.

'The Dwarf Giants,' Dunk said, just as he had each time. He knew that pre-game stress often destroyed what small powers of concentration the ogre had, and there was little use in getting steamed about it. If anything, it kept his own mind off his fears.

'Dunkel? Who are the good guys?'

Dunk smiled. 'The Hackers. The guys in green and gold, just like you.'

'Not enough!'

'True,' Dunk nodded. 'Normally we'd play with the full team in the Barak Varr Bowl, but remember the 75th anniversary game two years back? We beat the Champions of Death?'

M'Grash grinned, and not for the first time Dunk gave thanks that this was not his foe, but his friend.

'That tournament had gone so well that they decided to keep using the original rules for Dungeon-bowl. There's only six players on a side, and we move about using magical teleportation pads.'

'Dunkel? How those work?'

Dunk grinned. 'You just step on them and – poof! – You're gone.'

'Gone?' M'Grash clutched Dunk in fear.

'Gone somewhere else, big guy. The wizards of the Colleges of Magic set up for the game in the dungeon. The dwarfs built it for them.'

That seemed to calm the ogre's nerves a bit.

'Dunkel?'

'Yes?'

'Who are the good guys?'

Dunk put his face in his hands.

Spinne jumped in to help out. 'It's okay, M'Grash. There's you, me, Dunk, Edgar, Guillermo, and Cavre. That's all six. That's all we get for this game.'

M'Grash smiled at Spinne. It had taken him a while to realise she was with the Hackers and not a 'bad girl' any-more, but once he had he'd taken a real shine to her.

'Spinne? Are others dead?' Tears welled in the ogre's eyes. He could dismember a troll without blinking, but the thought that his friends might be killed some-times put him into hysterics.

'No. They're right behind you.'

M'Grash turned and saw the other five Hackers, Peg-leg, Dr. Pill, and Slick looking up at him from a sitting area on the far side of the locker room. He gave them a nervous, little wave, and they all waved back with the same level of enthusiasm.

'What about him?' M'Grash asked, pointing at Dunk's neck. Before the game, Dunk had taken Skragger's shrunken head and hung it around his neck on an iron chain. He'd paid a handsome coin to make sure that the necklace's mounting would keep Skragger from biting him in the neck. The last thing he needed was for the black orc to take a gouge out of his throat. A steely ball gag forced between Skragger's tiny fangs provided another layer of insurance against that.

'Slick thought I needed something to make me seem more fearsome on the field. I thought this would do the trick,' Dunk said. 'He doesn't count as a player – or much of anything else.' The thrower turned the tiny head around to look at its face, and its wide, white eyes glared at him from its wrinkled, black eye sockets. Skragger growled something at him, but the gag muffled it.

'Are you ready?' Dunk asked the ogre as he dropped Skragger's head back into place on his chest. 'The game's about to start.'

'Dunkel?'

'Yes?' Dunk shouted, finally pushed far enough to show his frustration with his massive friend.

'Why so tense?'

Dunk closed his eyes. Before he could say anything, he heard the sound of a piercing whistle over the PA system, and the game was on.

Cavre led the way, dashing on to the glowing circle on the floor in front of him. Once he disappeared, Edgar charged after him, followed by Guillermo and Spinne.

'Go, M'Grash!' Dunk said, shoving the ogre from behind.

'Don't have to shout,' M'Grash said as he crept towards the teleportation pad. He put his big toe on it like he was testing the water in a dark and chilly pool, and then he disappeared.

Dunk chased right after the ogre. When he popped into the dungeon, he ran right into M'Grash's back.

'I move,' M'Grash said, jumping out of Dunk's way and heading for the sole exit from the room.

Dunk picked himself up off the floor, which had been painted with the Hackers' logo and name, with gold letters on a green background. The letters seemed to have been done in real gold leaf, which Dunk knew fitted with the level of dedication the dwarfs had to the game.

Drawing the lot to face the Dwarf Giants – the most popular of the dwarf Blood Bowl teams – in the opening round of the Dungeonbowl tournament had put the fear of the gods into the Hackers. Pegleg had taken to walking about the practice area, muttering and grumbling, since he'd heard the news, and it had put a scare into all of the players.

The rookies were glad to not have to play, it seemed. Once when Guillermo had bruised his knee during practice, one of the more promising new recruits had burst into tears. Fortunately, Dr. Pill had been able to make the lineman as good as new in no time.

Having played in the tournament two years ago, Dunk knew exactly what the Hackers were in for, and that had terrified him even more. The dwarfs were renowned for using strange – sometimes crazed – devices in their games. They'd come up with a new dungeon this year, just for this event, and knowledge of its arrangement had been kept protected like a state secret.

Of course, everyone suspected the Dwarf Giants were in on the new layout. Lästiges had even aired an investigative report on it for Wolf Sports. Blaque and Whyte, the two Game Wizards that seemed to have been assigned to her, led her around the labyrinthine halls and tunnels of Barak Varr to show her viewers that any such suspicions were unfounded.

In one segment, unchaperoned by the GWs, Lästiges had interviewed a dwarf by the name of Dimlet. They'd met in a secluded booth in the House of Booze, a legendary watering hole in the dwarf city. The dwarf had a white stripe that ran right through his black hair and beard, making him look something like a walking skunk, and his seedy clothes and weasely demeanour only added to the impression.

'Yeah,' the dwarf said, 'it's all a sham, isn't it? The good lords of Barak Varr would never do anything to help out their own boys for a game as vital as this now, would they? Never happen in a million years, right?'

Lästiges leaned in close to the dwarf for a moment, and then leaned right back, her eyes watering from his scent. 'Are you saying,' she said through her coughs, 'that the Dwarf Giants were given the plans for the new Dungeonbowl dungeon?'

'Do you know that dwarfs is all related? We breed like rabbits, and the orcs is the only things keeping us in line. Every one of us is someone's brother or sister or someone else's cousin. You think it's easy to keep secrets in a family, do you? Even one the size of that?'

'But do you have any proof that this is so?'

Dimlet scoffed, and then one of his eyes rolled back into his head. The other stayed riveted on Lästiges. 'What's "proof"? What's good enough? If I said I'd seen this happen, would it matter? If I had a letter from the Council of Barak Varr to the Dwarf Giants, would that help? If I could show you a meeting of these blackguards on a Daemonic Visual Display, would that be good enough for you?'

Lästiges's eyes shone with lust for the big scoop she scented, or maybe from Dimlet's stench. 'I think our viewers would find such evidence compelling,' she said.

'I can have those things forged for you in a day,' Dimlet said. 'Less if you can double the standard rate.'

The interview had ended there, but the debate had continued. Was Dimlet some kind of crook, or had the Dwarf Giants sent him to Lästiges to throw her off their track?

In the end, Dunk decided it didn't matter. There were some things about the game he could control, and this wasn't one of them. He ran through the door, chasing after M'Grash.

'All the players are in the dungeon now, Jim, but we still don't have a ball. Where do you think they're hiding it?'

'Well, Bob, if you hadn't made a pre-game snack of that young dwarf you found passed out on Bugman's XXXXXX, you'd be conscious enough to remember that the ball's hidden in one of the six chests scattered throughout the dungeon.'

'Does that mean there are six balls?'

'Just one ball, Bob; if the players open a chest that doesn't have a ball in it, it explodes! What more fun could you ask for from a game?'

'Gee, that sounds dangerous, Jim. Has anyone warned the players?'

'Go back to sleep, Bob.'

The next room featured a river of lava that cut across it, disappearing underneath the walls at both ends. A high bridge went over it, and Dunk saw M'Grash just coming off the other end of it and trying to decide which of the two facing doors he should go through.

'Stay here, M'Grash!' Dunk called as he topped the bridge himself. The last time the Hackers had played Dungeonbowl, the Champions of Death had put a few of the players right in the Hackers' own end zone, and getting past them had been horrible. 'You're on defence. If you see a dwarf come through here, stop him. If he has the ball, take it.'

M'Grash nodded at everything Dunk said, but Dunk knew that didn't mean he had understood all of it. M'Grash could only remember an order or two at a time. Anything more complicated risked him losing track of it all.

'Scratch that!' Dunk said. 'Just stay here and knock down any dwarf you see!'

M'Grash grinned at that and gave Dunk a big thumbs-up.

Dunk glanced around and saw something glowing up at him out of the lava below. Shielding his eyes against the heat, he picked out the edges of a teleportation pad right there in the molten rock. To get to it, he'd have to leap off the bridge. He reasoned that the wizards who designed this place would only ask someone to take a risk like that if there was a correspondingly worthwhile payoff.

On the other hand, some of those wizards had a wicked sense of humour.

'Can't win the game without taking some chances,' Dunk muttered, repeating the words that Pegleg and Cavre had tried to hammer into the Hackers over the past few months. They hadn't played any official games since the *Spike!* magazine tournament, and the coach had worried about the players getting rusty. He hadn't wanted to risk any injuries before the Dungeonbowl tournament, but that didn't mean he couldn't browbeat the players into being mentally tough – although that seemed to have backfired with M'Grash.

Dunk vaulted over the bridge's low railing. The heat from the magma nearly flash-roasted him as he neared it, but before his feet even touched the teleportation pad he found himself somewhere else.

After the blazing light from the lava, it took Dunk a moment to adjust to the darkness around him. When his eyes finally cleared, he clamped them shut again. Then he peeled them open slowly.

Dunk looked down first and saw the teleportation pad through which he'd passed. It took up the entirety of a slab of rock that seemed to be floating in midair, four torches ringing it around its base. Pitch blackness yawned below it.

Looking up, Dunk saw the same thing: nothing. The light from the pad and the torches never reached the ceiling – if there was one.

The only thing Dunk could see was a series of stones just like the one he was on, stretching ahead and behind him like a string of steppingstones. A yard or two separated each of them. Had it not been for the torches ringing them, Dunk didn't know if he'd have been able to pick them out of the darkness.

In the distance in either direction, Dunk spotted a portal leading out of the room. It seemed to hover in midair, like a doorway cut from the fabric of night.

'Look, Bob! Hoffnung's found the Bottomless Pit Room. What luck for the Hackers! As first on the scene, he'll have first shot at that chest hovering below him. Amazing!

'Bob?

'Bob?'

Dunk laid down on the rock hovering beneath him and peered over the edge. There, only a couple of yards below him, hung another rock. This one had no torches around it, which is why he'd missed it the first time he'd glanced down. It did, however, carry a small, wooden chest.

'Oh, and look! Here comes Helmut Krakker, the Giants' new captain. Sure was a shame what happened to his predecessor – Gurni Rockrider – during the *Spike!* magazine tournament, eh? I've never seen just a beard left behind like that before. Usually there's at least some part of the chin attached to it!'

Dunk glanced up just in time to see a dwarf in navy and gold armour leap from the doorway to the first of the floating rocks in the string. If the thrower didn't move fast, the dwarf would be on him in seconds.

Dunk lowered himself over the edge of the floating rock he was on. His boots dangled just a foot over the chest below. It would be a good drop for a dwarf, but Dunk didn't hesitate to let go. He landed squarely on the chest and then slid off it to the rock below.

Dungeonbowl chests were never locked, Dunk knew that, but he hesitated for a moment. There was a good chance the chest would explode, and if that happened he'd be lucky if the blast was the only thing that hurt him. If he got knocked off the rock, there was no telling what might happen to him.

Then Dunk noticed a handle sticking out of each side of the chest. He got down on his knees and grabbed the one on the left. As he did, he heard Krakker land on the rock next to the one above him.

Dunk drew a deep breath, held it, and then opened the chest.

It exploded in his face.

Dunk couldn't see, hear, or feel anything for a moment – nothing but the pain and shock of the explosion. Once his head started to clear, he discovered the handle of the chest still in his hand, and he smiled. When he looked down at the handle, though, he saw nothing attached to it but his fingers. Then he noticed how windy it seemed to be. That, coupled with the fact that he didn't see anything below him, told him he was in deep trouble.

He screamed.

CHAPTER TWELVE

Dunk knew he was dead. Any second now, the unseen ground below him would rush up and crush him into paste...

...Any second now.

His voice became hoarse from all the screaming, and he stopped to clear it.

Any second...

Something popped into view below him: a series of lit spots stretched like a string of pearls across the darkness. As he approached them, he realised that they looked just like the set of rocks he'd just fallen from.

The pearls grew into rocks, and Dunk wondered just how deep this bottomless pit was. If he could fall so far and then come upon another set of stepping stones like the last... It seemed impossible.

Dunk zoomed up to the rocks, and then past them. As he did, he saw someone moving along the stepping stones far to his left: a dwarf in navy and gold armour.

A suspicion popped into Dunk's head, and when he zipped past the remains of an exploded chest on a rock hovering just below the line the others made, he knew what had happened.

'Help!' he yelled. 'Heeelllppp!'

It did him no good.

'Hey, Bob! Bob? Ah, never mind,' said Jim's voice.

'Well, folks, it looks like Hoffnung has finally twigged to what's happened to him. While a bottomless pit is impossible, of course, the Colleges of Magic built the largest simulation of such a tired old cliché that I've ever seen. They set up a wide matrix of overlapping teleportation pads at the bottom of this massive chasm. Their pairs are set up on the ceiling of the chasm, upside down. When a victim – I mean, player! – gets within a few inches of the bottom of the chasm, he teleports to the ceiling before he hits the floor, and thus he never stops falling.

'That's my favourite kind of trap: clever *and* cruel!'

If Dunk hadn't been so terrified, he might have been able to admire the inspiration and craftsmanship that had gone into torturing him so effectively. It seemed like a lot of trouble to go to just to remove a player from a game, but Dunk had long ago learned never to underestimate the public's hunger for its sports stars to find new ways to be destroyed. He could almost hear the audience cheering now.

Dunk had no idea how he could get himself out of this. Even if he managed to get one of the

Hackers to help him – he knew the Giants would just laugh at him – what could they do? If they tried to catch him, the impact would probably kill them both. Even M'Grash wouldn't be able to rescue him from falling what seemed to have already totalled up to a couple hundred feet.

The line of rocks appeared in front of Dunk again, signifying that he'd been teleported back up to the vast chamber's ceiling. He noticed that his stomach flipped every time that happened, and he seemed to hover for a moment just before he started falling again. That meant, he thought, that the teleportation killed his downward momentum. When he reappeared at the ceiling, it was like he'd just been dropped from that height for the first time. Otherwise, he'd have kept accelerating downward until he passed out.

At first, Dunk didn't know if this meant anything to him, either for good or bad. This time, when he zipped past the stepping stones, the glow from the teleportation pad that covered the rock in the centre of the line gave him an idea.

If he could somehow angle himself towards that rock and hit the teleportation pad, it might safely teleport him someplace else. If it killed his downward momentum, like the other teleportations seemed to, he'd land gently on the ground wherever he happened to end up.

Of course, if he was wrong, he'd wind up as a large red splash in that same spot.

Coming up with the idea was one thing. Putting the plan into action was something else entirely. Dunk stuck out his arms and tried flapping them like a bird.

'Look, folks! The pressure seems to have caused Hoffnung to crack. He thinks he's playing for the Eagles!'

Dunk snarled at the joke, but he couldn't let it distract him. He didn't know how many times the teleportation pads would keep working for him. It was possible that they'd all shut off once someone won the game, and unless one of the Grey Wizards saw fit to save a member of the team that had just lost the tournament for them, he'd be doomed.

As Dunk neared the bottom of the chasm, he readied himself. The moment his stomach flipped, he reached up and swatted his arms above him. His hands slapped into the ceiling, and propelled him backward, towards the rock with the teleportation pad.

'Dunkel!' M'Grash said as he barged into the room. 'Save Dunkel!'

'No!' Dunk said. If M'Grash tried to grab him, they'd both be hurt, maybe killed. 'Go get the ball! Leave me!'

The ogre didn't seem to hear a word Dunk said. He charged forward, leaping from one stepping-stone to the next. As he went, Dunk saw the rocks sag and bounce in midair. The sorcery that kept the stones hovering in space seemed barely strong enough to hold M'Grash.

Dunk knew that this would be his last clear shot at the teleportation pad. After this pass, M'Grash would officially be too close for comfort. He angled towards the rock, putting his hands in an arc over his head like the cliff divers he'd once seen leaping into the ocean from insane heights on the southern shores of Tilea.

'Save Dunkel!' M'Grash shouted as he sprinted towards his friend.

'No, M'Grash!' Dunk said. 'No!'

M'Grash dived for Dunk just as he hit the teleportation pad. Dunk tried to roll away from him at the last moment and only succeeded in turning his back on the ogre. Then he felt his body slam into the ogre's arms, and everything disappeared in a flash.

Dunk and M'Grash popped into another place. Dunk looked about, and at first glance he knew that they hadn't died and ended up in some kind of afterlife – at least not any of which he'd ever heard. Every surface of the room had a mirror polish, and it seemed there were lots of them.

'Dunkel not dead!' M'Grash said as Dunk pulled himself off the ogre. 'Huzzah!'

Dunk smiled down at his friend. Despite the fact that the ogre had almost ended up getting them both killed, Dunk couldn't get mad at someone who'd tried to save his life. Then he remembered what he'd told the ogre when they'd split up.

'Why aren't you back in the room with the river of lava?' Dunk asked. 'Didn't I tell you to stay there?'

M'Grash's face fell as he nodded at his friend. 'Then Dunkel said, 'Help!' I heard Dunkel. Dunkel says, 'Help!' very loud.'

Dunk slapped himself on his forehead as M'Grash got to his feet. 'You're right,' he said to M'Grash. 'I need to be more careful about what I ask for.'

'Mama tells me that too,' said M'Grash. As the ogre spoke, his voice trailed off to nothing. 'Who are they?' he asked.

Dunk looked around them and saw what had confused M'Grash. The room had been set up as a chamber of mirrors. There didn't seem to be many things in it beyond the mirrors, other than Dunk and M'Grash – and an unopened chest. However, the reflections they saw made it seem like there might be a dozen of each of those things, and that made it nearly impossible to tell which image might be real.

'They look like friends,' M'Grash said, although he seemed unsure of his judgement.

Dunk stepped forward and put his foot out at a chest. His toes struck a mirror instead. He moved back a step and then spat at the mirror. His saliva ran down its slick surface, marking it. As he looked around, he saw the mark on another nearby image, so he could rule that one out as real too.

'M'Grash?' Dunk pointed at where he'd spat on the mirror. 'Think you could do that to every other mirror in this place?'

'Dunkel want me to spit on people?'

'No. Don't spit on us.'

'Dunkel just did. Look!' The ogre pointed to where Dunk's spit ran down his own face.

'That's just…' Dunk arched an eyebrow at M'Grash. 'Never mind. Can you just spit at the chests – and hurry.' Dunk thought he heard someone coming. Instead of the stomping feet of a human or dwarf, it sounded something like the stamp of metal-booted halflings, distant now, but coming closer.

M'Grash hocked up something evil from deep inside his chest and then began to spew it about in all directions. Not wishing to depend on the ogre's sense of what constituted a 'chest' – Dunk had a chest of his own on the front of his upper body, after all – he worked hard to stay behind the ogre, where the creature's spit could not reach.

That's when one of the Dwarf Giants rolled in – literally. The dwarf player sat in the saddle of a monstrous steam-driven machine fronted by a steel-spiked cylinder of stone that stood almost as tall as Dunk.

'Uh-oh,' said Jim's voice. 'It looks like Zam Boney has found a dwarf death-roller, and he's not afraid to use it!'

Dunk and M'Grash stared at the machine as Boney forced it through the doorway and onto the mirrored floor. The glassy material there cracked and crumbled as the death-roller moved across it, shattering it into countless thousands of pieces. The dwarf riding the machine shouted something – a threat, no doubt – but Dunk couldn't hear it over the engine's noise. Then the thing came straight at them, picking up speed as it went.

'Run!' Dunk said, turning and grabbing M'Grash's hand, and hauling the ogre along behind him.

'Devices like the death-roller are strictly against the rules, of course,' Jim's voice said, 'but who cares when they're so much fun! Besides which, what are the chances of the referee stumbling into the right room to spot it – especially when two of the Giants are busy drowning him in the merdwarf room!'

As the two Hackers took off across the room, Dunk felt grateful that M'Grash had managed to mark as many surfaces as he had, no matter how disgusting the method. Otherwise, he knew, they'd have bounced into one mirrored wall after another until the death-roller had crushed them under its tremendous, spiked mass.

'Dunkel!' M'Grash shouted.

Dunk glanced back over his shoulder and saw that the death-roller was almost on them. Boney cackled so loudly that Dunk could hear him, even over the roar of his accelerating machine as it bore down on him and M'Grash.

The ogre grabbed Dunk and thrust him to one side as he dived for the other at the last instant. Boney seemed to have a hard time deciding which of the Hackers to go after, perhaps hoping to take them both out at the same time. Instead, he missed them both, but only by bare inches.

As Dunk scrambled to his feet, he watched Boney race past and then put the death-roller into a controlled slide that ended with the machine swivelled around and pointing back in his direction. The Giant pointed at M'Grash and held up an index finger. Then he pointed to Dunk and held up two fingers, indicating the human would go down last.

Dunk held up his middle finger in response, and then howled in dismay as the machine took off after M'Grash. Despite its size, the death-roller moved so fast that Dunk knew he could never catch it on foot, not in a straight-up race. He needed something to even the odds.

He scanned the area around him, hoping to spy something – anything – that could help. Then his eyes fell on what he'd been looking for before: a small chest.

Dunk dashed over and picked up the chest. At that moment, he was less interested in how it could help the Hackers win the game than he was in how he might use it to stop Boney dead.

'Hey, you sawed-off, half-pint, runt of a litter of dwarf-orcs!' Dunk shouted at Boney. As the Giant turned to look at the thrower over his shoulder, Dunk raised the chest over his head and waved it about like a red flag in front of a bull.

Boney reached over and hauled on a lever as he wrenched the steering wheel to the left. This sent the machine into a hard spin that nearly threw the dwarf from his seat, but it put the death-roller on a path towards Dunk, still moving at top speed.

Dunk glanced left and right, and discovered he'd found the chest in a mirrored cul-de-sac. There was nowhere for him to go. When Boney realised the thrower's predicament, he tossed back his head and loosed a loud cackle that rang out over the engine's noise.

'Well, folks, it looks like the Hackers better put in their order for a Dunk Hoffnung-sized coffin,' Jim's voice said. 'Boney has the thrower dead to rights, and he seemed like he had such promise too.'

Dunk thrust the chest up over his head and then hurled it straight into the death-roller's path. It bounced once, and then landed squarely in front of the machine's spiked roller.

When Boney saw Dunk start to throw the chest at him, the dwarf knew what the Hacker meant to do, and he hauled back on the death-roller's brakes and yanked the wheel to the right. The thing's forward momentum was too much for it to stop that quickly, though, and the machine skidded right into the chest.

Dunk held his breath and waited for the explosion. Instead, all he heard was a loud crunching noise, followed by a muffled pop.

The death-roller smashed into one of the cul-de-sac's walls, and Boney catapulted out of his seat and crunched into the wall right after it, leaving a wet, red streak on the mirrored surface as he slid down it. Dunk raced forward and spotted the remnants of the chest poking out underneath the machine's rear wheels. The death-roller had reduced it to little more than splinters, but Dunk spied a few shiny spikes sticking up out of the wreckage.

The Hacker scrambled underneath the death-roller and snatched the flattened football out from beneath it. The heat from the boiler that drove the machine's steam engine threatened to bake the skin from the back of his arm, but he gritted his teeth and ignored the pain. As he pulled the pancake of a ball free from the wreckage, he heard a high-pitched whistle start to shriek from the steam engine.

A rivet shot out of the engine's casing and zinged over Dunk's head like a bullet from a sling. A fine spray of scalding water and steam followed it, and the pitch of the whistling rose to an ear-splitting crescendo.

Dunk tucked the flat ball under his arm and sprinted away from the machine. He didn't get ten feet before he ran past M'Grash. As he did, he grabbed the ogre's hand and tugged the big guy after him, shouting, 'Run!'

Just then, the steam engine exploded. The shockwave knocked M'Grash and Dunk flying across the room, skidding along the floor's silvery surface to come to a crashing halt in a pile against the far wall.

'M'Grash?' Dunk asked as he mentally took inventory of his body parts. Although a bit squished, everything seemed to be there.

The ogre nodded. 'Dunkel alive!' he shouted with glee.

'Hey, buddy,' Dunk said. 'Are you all right?'

The ogre nodded again.

'Then can you get off me so I can breathe?'

M'Grash leapt off his friend and helped him to his feet. 'Sorry, Dunkel,' he said, blushing.

'It's all right.' Dunk plucked the flat ball up from the ground and held it up for M'Grash to see. 'It was worth it.'

CHAPTER THIRTEEN

'THE HACKERS HAVE the ball!' Jim's voice said. 'The Hackers have the ball. Now all they need to do is get it back to their end zone to score. Remember, folks, in Dungeonbowl, the first to score wins the game!'

Dunk cursed the camras scattered throughout the dungeon. If he'd been thinking, he might have tried to hide the ball from them – and everyone else – a bit longer. Sure, Jim would have eventually figured out that if the chest hadn't exploded then it must have had a ball in it, but as an ogre Jim wasn't the sharpest knife in the corpse.

'Let's get to the end zone,' Dunk said to M'Grash. 'How did you get in here?'

The ogre pointed to the door through which he'd come.

'Then lead the way, big guy,' Dunk said with a grin.

M'Grash lumbered forward like a galloping elephant, and Dunk paced after him, stuffing the flat ball underneath his breastplate to keep it safe. In the confines of the dungeon's passages, M'Grash's head and pauldrons scraped the ceiling and walls. Unlike the other players, the ogre rarely wore a helmet. They were hard to find in his size, and his skull was harder than any helmet could be.

The hall ended in a wall of water. It stretched from floor to ceiling, and it splashed as M'Grash thrust his right arm through it.

'Hold breath, Dunkel,' the ogre said. Dunk did as he'd been told, and M'Grash scooped him up and charged into the water.

Dunk opened his eyes in the water, which was as clear as that in a nobleman's pool. He wondered for a moment if it was all just an illusion, and he thought about testing it by trying to breathe. Then he saw the corpse of a dwarf dressed in a Giant's uniform float by, and he decided against it.

Dunk couldn't tell where they were going, but M'Grash seemed to know. He moved without hesitation, pushing himself and Dunk through the water on his powerful legs.

In Dunk's limited experience, ogres weren't much good at thinking, but if you gave them a clear task – like 'let's get to the end zone' – they put everything they had into completing it. M'Grash set to his job like a starving dog to a fresh steak. Dunk had no doubt they would get through the water in record time.

As the doorway on the opposite side of the room came wavering through the rippling water, Dunk spotted something large and grey coming towards them like a rocket. The face full of huge, vicious teeth told Dunk that this was the largest shark Dunk had ever seen. It looked like the thing might have been able to swallow him alive, and he had no doubt it would tear M'Grash's flesh to tatters with its trap-like maw.

Dunk tapped M'Grash on the shoulder and pointed towards the shark. The ogre shouted out in fear, losing most of the air he'd held in his lungs. A warm, yellow cloud formed around the ogre's waist, but thankfully M'Grash kept moving forward and left it far behind.

Before the shark could strike at them, something thick and brown charged into the water through the doorway and met the prehistoric monster head on. The shark snapped at it with its massive jaws, but Edgar's trunk was too wide around for the creature's teeth to find purchase on it, and his bark protected him from the deepest scratches.

Dunk and M'Grash burst out of the standing wall of water and into the room beyond, the ogre hacking and gasping for air. While Dunk's lungs held far less than M'Grash's, the thrower hadn't panicked when the shark had appeared, and he was the better off for it.

'Hold it right there,' Dunk said after helping pound the water out of M'Grash's lungs. 'I think I spotted something back there.'

Dunk stuck his head back into the water and opened his eyes. He was right. There, just off to the left of the doorway, a wooden chest rested among a stand of seaweed. If M'Grash hadn't made such a wake behind him, shoving aside the weeds as he went, Dunk doubted he'd ever have seen it.

Dunk peered around and saw that Edgar had shoved one of his branches straight down the shark's gullet and was flinging the hapless creature all around, as if his own arm was just a shark from his elbow down. Since Edgar didn't need to breathe in the way that the other players did, the water posed no threat to him. This meant he could tackle the shark with an aplomb any other player had to envy.

Seeing no other threats, Dunk shoved his way into the wall of water and plucked the chest from the weeds. Then he turned and hauled it back into the airy room where he'd left M'Grash.

When Dunk broke through the water, a horrible roar assaulted his ears. He blinked the water out of his eyes and saw a Dwarf Giant standing across the torch-lit room. Unlike the other Giants, this one wore a large pack on his back and dark goggles over his eyes. His black beard, which bristled like a chimney brush, had been cropped short, and he carried a torch in his hand, from which ran a hose that attached to the bottom of the tank.

'Nuffle's smoky joe!' Jim's voice said. 'Weber 'Toasty' Grilmore has caught up with Hoffnung and K'Thragsh. Let's see how they handle him and his legendary flamethrower!'

The dwarf pointed the torch at Dunk – who now noticed that the end of it hissed at him – and said, in a voice that came from lungs that seemed to breathe through a burning pipe, 'Give me that chest. You have until three.'

Dunk hesitated.

'Three!' the dwarf yelled as he pulled a lever on the bottom of his torch. Fire leapt from the tip of the torch like a hungry dragon, reaching for Dunk and the chest in his hands.

The heat singed Dunk's skin and hair. If he hadn't already been soaking wet, he might have gone up in flames right there. Being waterlogged gave him an extra moment to live, and he used it to do the only thing that came to mind: he shoved himself back into the watery room.

The fires that had been starting to smoulder on Dunk went out immediately as the cool waters enveloped him. He glanced backward to see that Edgar had split the shark in half and left the carcass floating in the water. Other, smaller sharks, which Dunk hadn't noticed before, dived into the tendrils of blood as they curled out from their massive cousin and churned the water with their maddened feeding on the fresh-made chum.

Dunk knew he had to stop Edgar from walking into the airy room. He didn't want to face a flamethrower himself, but it turned him pale to think about what such a weapon would do against a treeman like Edgar, waterlogged or not. Being underwater, he could not speak and would somehow have to signal his warning, and perhaps some kind of plan.

Before Dunk could attempt this, M'Grash came splashing in from the room beyond, his skin ablaze, the water turning to steam as it smothered the fires on the ogre. Edgar caught M'Grash before the ogre could float to the ground, but when the treeman turned the blitzer over, Dunk saw that the ogre's face was already turning blue. In his haste to get away from the flames, M'Grash must not have taken a breath before leaping into the water. If Dunk didn't do something soon, his humongous friend would die.

Dunk sprinted out of the water and into the room, where he found Grilmore working a pump handle that came out over his shoulder from the tank on his back.

'Back for more, eh?' the dwarf growled. 'I'll be right with you.'

'Don't!' Dunk said. 'If you want this so badly, you can have it.' With that, he tossed the chest high in the air. It bounced once, and then rolled to a stop under Grilmore's raised boot.

'Wise for a beardless one,' Grilmore grunted. 'Now git!'

The flamethrower spat fire at Dunk once more, and he dived backward into the water behind him to avoid it. Once safe in the cool liquid, he glanced back and saw M'Grash grasping at his throat, strangling on a lack of air. The ogre only had seconds left.

Dunk pressed his nose up to the edge of the water and peered through it into the room beyond. There he watched as Grilmore leaned over and opened up the chest.

The first explosion smacked into the dwarf and sent him flying backward. He landed on his tank, hard, and it sprang a leak, but Grilmore was as tough a dwarf as they came. The blast only stunned him, and he shook it off before he'd even stopped rolling.

Dunk cursed his luck. All the dwarf had to do now was camp out there in the room and wait. In scant seconds, M'Grash would have to charge back into the room for a breath, and Grilmore would flash-fry him that same instant.

But it seemed as if the dwarf was a bit more stunned than he had let on. As Grilmore pushed himself to his feet, he used the hand that held his torch on a tube. It touched the black, viscous fluid leaking from the tank and raced along it until it hit the reservoir.

The second explosion filled the room with raging fire. The shockwave smacked into the water and drove Dunk flipping backward and deeper into it. The water actually receded from the doorway from the force of the blast. When it rebounded back, it overwhelmed the magic keeping the water from plunging through the portal, and it surged through and into the room beyond.

The coursing water dragged Dunk, Edgar, and M'Grash into the room where Grilmore had just been. There was nothing left of him, from what Dunk saw, but a few shreds of his armour attached to the flamethrower's burst-open tank.

The flood carried the three Hackers through that room and into the next. There, Dunk spied Spinne, who had been facing off against a white-bearded dwarf racing along on a steam-powered bicycle. She had managed to grab onto a torch sconce as the waters raged through the room in a flash flood, but the dwarf hadn't been so lucky. The wall of water had knocked the bike flat, and since he was strapped to it, the dwarf had been sucked under the swirling mess.

'The river of lava is next!' Spinne said. 'Then the end zone!'

'Thanks!' Dunk said as the water dragged him past her. 'I love you!'

'Isn't that just too damn cute, folks?' Jim's voice said. 'It just makes you want to gag yourself with a snotling's toes.'

Dunk cursed at the announcer as the new-made river dragged him from the room. Before he could even complete his sentence, he found himself in the room with the lava river – or at least in the room where it had been.

When the water hit the lava, it transformed into steam that curled into the air and filled the room until it was thicker than any fog. It might have been hot enough to parboil anyone nearby when it first hit, but by the time Dunk and the others got there, the lava was submerged three feet below the water line.

The water carried Dunk straight over the river – which still glowed through the cracks forming in the dark crust of cooler rock that had formed on the lava's surface – and deposited him on the other side. When he regained his feet, he turned back to see M'Grash and Edgar stuck on the river's other side. Being heavier than Dunk, they would have scraped the skin right off that river of lava and maybe been burned to death. Edgar had figured this out and managed to catch himself in the hallway leading into the room, and he had caught M'Grash too before the ogre went sailing past or through him.

Dunk waved at the others, and then dashed towards the end zone, just on the other side of the portal ahead of him. Before he could reach the room, another dwarf stepped out into the now-receding waters and stood his ground in front of the doorway.

'Give me the ball,' the dwarf snarled at Dunk. He had no strange weapon in his hands, he sat astride no vicious vehicle, but he didn't need any of these things to exude danger.

The dwarf stood taller than any dwarf Dunk had ever seen – and nearly as wide. He wore his beard in a forked braid, and his head had been shaved, leaving behind only a high-crested, bright orange fan of hair straight down the centre. He bore tattoos on nearly every inch of his body, and he wore no armour, only leather straps fitted with spikes, wound around his arms, chest, knees, and fists.

Dunk yelped, and threw his arms wide to show that his hands were empty.

'Where is it, manling?' the dwarf asked, stalking closer to the thrower.

Dunk stepped to one side and pointed back at Edgar and M'Grash standing on the other side of the river of lava. They'd already started for the stone bridge that arced high over the river, and they would be there in seconds.

The dwarf raced off to take on the others, and Dunk didn't care to lay odds against him, despite the fact he faced an ogre and a treeman together. Something in Dunk rebelled at leaving his friends to face such a foe on their own, but he had a job to do as part of the same team on which they played.

Dunk spun on his heel and dashed into the room where the Hackers' end zone sprawled. Once there, he reached under his breastplate and pulled out the flattened football. He held it up to the camra standing in the corner, and smiled for the viewers at home.

'Hoffnung scores a touchdown!' Jim's voice said. 'Wake up, Bob, you ancient sot! You just missed one hell of a game! The Hackers win!'

CHAPTER FOURTEEN

THAT NIGHT, DUNK settled into a cosy corner of the House of Booze with Spinne, Slick, and M'Grash. The place hadn't changed much since they'd been there two years ago, although Spinne hadn't been with them then. She'd just survived a cave-in during a Dungeonbowl game, which had killed four of her team-mates.

Dunk had later learned that M'Grash had been responsible for that cave-in, something he didn't think he'd ever share with Spinne. He glanced at the two of them chatting happily with each other over their drinks, and decided that perhaps it was for the best.

Dunk had visited a number of taverns in Barak Varr – the dwarfs took great pride in their drink and sampled and shared it often – but the House of Booze was still his favourite. He like Ye Olde Trip to Araby – the oldest tavern in the dwarf kingdoms – too, but he and Dirk had been banned from it two years ago when they'd torn the place apart in a brotherly brawl.

The carved stone ceilings of the House of Booze arched higher than those of a cathedral, and Dunk realised that the place served as a church in a sense. The patrons who came here worshipped no gods, but good friends, food, and drink – and not necessarily in that order. From the clouds of smoke that collected under some of the highest arches, Dunk knew that some of the people were here for a good pipe instead.

The best thing about the place was the way it welcomed people of all stripes. The private booth at which the four sat stood open at one end, but each of the benches on the other three sides could be adjusted to different heights. Slick sat up high on one wing, Dunk and Spinne sat at a standard height in the back, and M'Grash sat down low on the other wing. None of them had to hunch over or stand on a stool, and they could enjoy their fare and each other in comfort and peace.

Dunk raised his stein of Torin Oakencask's Deep Shaft, a black brew concocted in the farthest depths of the dwarf lands. Rumour had it that the brewmeisters used actual ore in the drink's production. Dunk didn't know if that was what made it thick enough to stand a knife in, but he liked it.

'To the Hackers,' he said. 'And to victory.'

The others all joined in, clanking their steins together. Here, even M'Grash had a stein of his own, instead of his usual barrel with the top torn free. It was so large that Slick could have bathed in it – and later in the night might have been tempted to try.

'Winning,' M'Grash said. 'It beats losing.' The skin on his arms and face had already started to heal over. Dr. Pill had given him something to help the process along and to take care of the pain, and it seemed to have worked. M'Grash had been nothing but smiles all night. Nothing fazed him for a moment. Even when he'd tripped over that group of orcs on the way in, he'd just kept walking, not even noticing that he'd crushed one under his heel.

'I like that,' Slick said. 'I think I'll have that put on a T-shirt with your face on it. I'll give you ten percent.'

'Deal,' M'Grash said. He grinned so hard the skin on his face split again, but he didn't seem to notice.

'Shouldn't he have had his agent negotiate that for him?' Spinne asked the halfling.

'Of course!' Slick nodded to Spinne and Dunk, and then turned back to M'Grash. 'As your duly appointed representative in all matters financial, I urge you to take the T-shirt deal, M'Grash. It's a good bargain for you, and I can vouch for the licensee's honour and integrity personally.'

M'Grash furrowed his brow and then looked at Dunk for advice. The thrower smiled gamely and nodded. The ogre reached out to shake hands with Slick, a grin on his face. 'Deal!' he said as the halfling's hand and forearm disappeared in his fist.

'Isn't that a conflict of interest?' Spinne asked. 'I'd like my agent to be more independent than that.'

Slick put on a look of mock dismay. 'Sweetheart,' he said, 'first, you're talking about agents. Honesty and agency are not synonymous.

'Second, what could be more honest? I proposed and executed the deal here in the presence of my client and gave both him and his good friends the chance to comment and even intercede. How many other agents do you think bother going to that kind of trouble?

'Most agents would just set up the T-shirt deal with an old pal and never let their client know who they were really negotiating with. Not so with Slogo Full-belly! I'm as above board as an agent can get.'

Spinne squinted her eyes and frowned at Slick, but Dunk and M'Grash laughed along with the halfling. After a moment, she joined in with them as well.

Dunk took a pull from his stein. As he savoured the rich, bitter flavour, he smiled. Here he had the three people who mattered most to him in his life – except Dirk, of course, who seemed to have cut himself out of Dunk's life. Despite that, Dunk felt happy, and he wanted that feeling to last.

Then someone pushed a tall stool up to the far side of the table. Stuck in the back of the booth, Dunk couldn't see who it was that meant to join them. He heard whoever it was climbing the ladder built into the back of the seat.

When the newcomer's head cleared the table, Dunk dropped his beer. Fortunately, this happened often enough in the House of Booze that the dwarfs had designed the steins to right themselves if possible, and this one did, letting only the barest dribble of the Deep Shaft spill over its edge.

The man who sat in the stool across the table from Dunk looked older, but no wiser. His clothes looked as if he'd been sleeping in a nest of hungry rats, and he smelled something like that too. Somewhere along the line, his nose had been broken, and it had healed poorly, leaving it with a downward bend. His hair might have been greyer – a great deal more white showed in his scraggly beard – but Dunk couldn't be sure of its colour under the layer of filth the man wore with a comfort borne of long companionship.

'Hello, Dunkel,' the man said, his voice a bit rougher too. 'How have you been?'

Dunk didn't say a word. He couldn't. His tongue refused to work. All he could do was sit and stare at this ghost from his past come back to haunt his present.

Spinne and Slick stared at Dunk for a moment, waiting for him to say something, anything. M'Grash, ever oblivious, took a long draught from his beer and then waved at the man.

'Hi,' the ogre said. Then he pointed at himself. 'M'Grash!'

The man wiped his hand on his soiled tunic. Realising that it wasn't any cleaner, he reached out and performed the same task with a napkin instead, leaving a grimy residue on the cloth. Then he stuck out his hand to M'Grash.

'I've seen you play,' the man said as he shook the ogre's hand. 'You're very good.'

'Since when did you ever watch Blood Bowl?' Dunk asked. The question blurted out of him without him even thinking to ask it, and now it lay there between them.

The man recovered his hand from M'Grash and gave Dunk an easy smile. 'Since you and your brother started playing it. I never saw much use in it before that myself. It's not the stage or the opera, but I've come to appreciate it at its own level for what it is.'

'Which is?'

'An alternative to war, of course.' The man waved down a waiter and said, 'Bring a bottle of your finest Montfort, and I'd like to see a menu too, please.'

Dunk slumped back in his seat, stunned.

'I'm Spinne,' the catcher said. 'I don't think I caught your name.'

'There's not much you don't catch, miss,' the man said. 'I've seen you play too. I'll consider it a compliment to have got anything past you.'

'You haven't yet,' Spinne said, wearing a smile that barely covered a bulldog's snarl. 'I'd like to know who you are.'

The man shook a finger at the woman. 'I like that. I really do; sharp, direct, and unafraid of confrontation. Unusual in a woman, especially in these parts, but I find it unnervingly attractive. I see what Dunk finds exciting about you. You'll go far, miss.' He put out his hands in a wide shrug. 'Hey, you already have.'

Spinne's smile closed, and she turned to Dunk. 'Perhaps you could identify our dinner guest for us.'

The man raised his eyebrows and shrugged at Dunk. 'That's your call, Dunkel. We have a lot of catching up to do. Whether you care to share that with your friends is up to you.'

Dunk shook his head at the man. He didn't know how he felt about this yet, but it surprised him how easily the man could still push his buttons.

'Spinne, Slick, M'Grash,' Dunk said looking at each of them in turn and then at the man again. 'I'd like you to meet Lügner Hoffnung, my father.'

Spinne gasped. M'Grash stared back and forth at Dunk and Lügner, confused as ever. Slick reached across the table as best he could and offered his hand, which Lügner took.

'A pleasure, sir,' the halfling said. 'I've often wondered who could have had a hand in raising such a fine boy as you have in your son here.'

Lügner flashed a grin, which grew wider as his drink appeared. 'I'm afraid you'll have to blame most of Dunk's upbringing on his blessed mother, gods rest her soul.'

'Oh, you're just being modest.'

'No,' Dunk said, staring at his father through sunken eyes. 'He's not.'

Lügner looked abashed. 'Come now, Dunkel,' he said. 'Is that any way to speak to your father?'

'How would I know?' Dunk asked. 'I haven't seen you for over three years. We never did have much to say to each other.'

Lügner nodded as he glanced down the menu. 'All too true, I'm afraid,' he said. 'All too true.' Then he turned to the dwarf waiter who stood ready to take his order. 'I'll have the steak Bordeleaux, medium rare, light on the blue cheese, but heavy on the onions.'

'Excellent choice, sir,' the waiter said before gliding off towards the kitchen on a set of tall, metal stilts.

'What are you doing here?' Dunk asked. 'I thought you were dead.'

'You thought wrong,' Lügner said with a devilish grin, 'but you can take comfort in knowing you weren't the only one. I wanted the world to think I was dead. Life, I find, is much easier that way.'

'What are you doing here?' Dunk repeated. He didn't bother to ask his father if he knew about the Guterfiends and Lehrer and all the rest. He knew he did.

Lügner took a long draw from his stein and smacked his lips in satisfaction. 'Well, I usually prefer to leave business for after the meal. I find it aids in the digestion to put such things off until then. But I can tell from your demeanour that you're anxious to get started. Where would you like me to begin?'

'How about with the angry mob killing my mother and sister, and running us out of town?'

Lügner's smile faded. 'Yes. You would want to know about that, wouldn't you?'

'What happened to you?' Dunk asked. 'I went to the summer house. I checked in there for you every day for weeks. Then Lehrer ran me off the property because someone else had taken it.'

'The Guterfiends,' Lügner said with a grim nod. 'I'd heard they'd ended up with the place, but I hadn't guessed they'd take ownership so soon.

'I thought you were *dead*,' Dunk said, his voice cracking on the last word. He grimaced to hold his emotions in check.

'I can see why,' Lügner said. 'I wanted everyone to think I was dead. Even you.'

'Why?'

Lügner snorted at himself. 'Face it, Dunkel. You were better off without me. I'd never done anything but put you and the rest of my family in constant danger just by living with me. You saw what that did to your mother and sister. I didn't want to have that happen to you too.'

'So you did it for my own good?' Dunk asked. 'You just wandered away and let me think you were dead and gone for three years out of your concern for my wellbeing?'

Lügner winced. 'Well, that was what I thought would be a pleasant side-effect of my central reason, which was to escape the people who wanted me dead.'

'It looks like that worked well,' said Slick. Dunk shot him a murderous look, and the halfling sat back in his seat again.

'Why did the Guterfiends want you dead?'

Lügner let a wry smile play on his lips. 'They didn't, really. They didn't even know me. Oh, sure, they knew of me, and they wanted me out of their way, but it wasn't anything personal.'

'Not personal?' Dunk couldn't believe his ears. 'They killed your wife and daughter, ran you off your estate, took everything you owned, and 'forced' you to arrange for everyone to think you were dead.'

'No, Dunkel,' Lügner said. 'You're jumping to conclusions. You've got it all wrong. The Guterfiends didn't care about me or anyone else who lived in our keep. They just happened to work for the same people. Once we were out, they were in. It was that bloodless and simple – at least to them.'

Dunk stared at his father. 'Then who did all that to us?'

'Khorne,' Lügner said.

Dunk felt Spinne recoil next to him.

'You mean 'Khorne' as in 'Khorne's Killers'?' Slick asked, his eyes wide in disbelief.

'Yes.'

'Khorne, the Blood God?'

'Yes.'

'Khorne, one of the Lords of Chaos?'

'Yes!'

Conversation around the table ground to a halt, and Lügner tried to use a smile to mask his irritation. Soon enough, the dull roar of others talking nearby resumed.

'Why?' Dunk asked. 'What would Khorne want with us?'

'Besides the fact that the Hoffnungs were one of the oldest and most influential families in the Empire?'

'There are other families with the same credentials.'

'True,' said Lügner, 'but none of them were in such rotten shape as ours was when I took over the family business.'

Dunk narrowed his eyes at his father and tried to understand where he was heading.

Seeing that Dunk wasn't about to hold up his end of the conversation with anything but prompts, both verbal and otherwise, Lügner continued to speak.

'Your grandfather was a great man: a patron of the arts, a good friend, and kind to all who knew him. Someone who put the 'gentle' in 'gentleman' and the 'noble' in 'nobleman.' But he was a horrible business-man.

'In the twenty-five years my father was in charge of the Hoffnung family holdings, he managed to piss away hundreds of thousands of crowns – maybe even enough to pay for the price that's on your head.'

Dunk winced at that.

'You see, that's why I'm here. I wanted to tell you that the Guterfiends are the ones backing this Zauberer fellow's mad claims. You've done a fine job debunking the man and making him look like the lunatic he is, but he made too big a splash.

'Even if you no longer have every joker with a sword in his closet coming after you for the reward, the profes-sionals – the killers who really know what they're doing – are going to figure it out. They're going to go to that crackpot, and he'll tell them who's offering the money, and then they'll go after you harder than ever. And the worst part is that you won't even be expecting it.

'Or at least you wouldn't, if not for me.'

Dunk smiled finally. 'I already knew.'

It was Lügner's turn to be surprised. 'Really? How? Did you track it down through Zauberer yourself?

Smart boy! I always told your mother you'd get over that head wound.'

'No, I heard it from – Wait! What head wound?'

Lügner grimaced. 'Um, the one you got as a child when you were dropped.'

'Who dropped me?' Dunk asked. 'You?'

Lügner nodded, his cheeks turning pink. 'You were just a few months old, and Lehrer had tossed me a skin full of wine. I just – well, I wasn't used to carrying a child around quite yet.'

Dunk slapped a hand over his eyes. 'You dropped your infant son in favour of a wineskin.'

Lügner nodded, a pathetic look on his face. 'It was some really good wine.'

Dunk put his head down on the table and wrapped his hands over it. For some reason, it seemed to be throbbing.

'So who told you the Guterfiends were behind the reward money?' Lügner asked, clearly hoping to change the subject.

'Lehrer,' Dunk mumbled.

'Who?'

'Lehrer,' Dunk said, raising his head. 'He tracked me down in Magritta to let me know.'

'Lehrer?' Lügner's voice was barely more than a whisper. 'He's still around?'

'He's been with the Guterfiends ever since we left the keep. They came in and hired our whole staff on the spot, it seems.'

'He's been with them far longer than that. He started up with them soon after I signed on with Khorne.'

Dunk blinked. 'You did what?'

CHAPTER FIFTEEN

LÜGNER SCOWLED AT Dunk. 'Don't you dare judge me, Dunkel. The house was floundering. Your grandfather had not only lost everything we had, he'd also run up a horrendous debt. The people who held those markers were ready to take everything we had and then hang our skins from our flagpoles to make their point.'

'You made a deal with one of the Ruinous Powers, and you didn't think that would come back to bite you?' Dunk stared at his father, stunned. He'd known his father had done some pretty horrible things in the course of building the family business back up over the years, but he'd had no idea that it had involved pacts with the forces of darkness.

'Of course I did!' Lügner scowled. 'I knew the deal would go sour eventually – I did – but eventually can be an awfully long time. It got me through your entire childhood. Yours and Dirk's.'

'But it killed Mother and Kirta. Does that seem like a fair trade?'

'That's not fair, Dunkel. You know I would have done anything to save Greta and your sister from that mob. They came on so quick...

'As it was, I was thrilled to be able to save your life at least. That day was the first time I felt glad that Dirk had left home.'

Dunk just gaped at Lügner. The horror of the notion that his father had tied his family fortunes to the whims of the Blood God staggered him.

'You thought you could cheat him, didn't you?' Slick said.

Dunk stared at the halfling, and then back at his father, who was squirming in his seat.

'Go on,' Slick said. 'Admit it. I know what it's like. Someone presents you with a deal you just can't bring yourself to refuse, even though you know you should. You go back and forth on it, but eventually you convince yourself that there's a loophole in it somewhere, some way for you to wriggle out of your end of the bargain – at least if something in the deal goes sour, which it will, especially for something that's supposed to last forever.

'So you make the deal, and you regret it every day after that, knowing that some day the executioner's axe will drop, and you have to be ready to try to dodge it at any second.

'I understand all this. I'm an old wheeler and dealer myself. Sometimes the temptation seems too great. I've seen it break many a desperate man in my time, but you just have to resist.

'It's no way to live.'

Lügner nodded along with Slick, and said, 'It's an even worse way to die. Do you know what part of the deal was? Eternal damnation. Khorne owns my soul. When I die, it becomes his plaything for the rest of time.'

'I take it back,' Slick said. 'You're an idiot.'

'Hey,' Lügner said, becoming indignant, 'I didn't think souls were real back then, and if I did have one I wasn't doing a damned thing with it. I was young. I was naïve. I was–'

'An idiot,' M'Grash said, shaking his head in pity.

Lügner sighed. 'I can't win. Even the ogre thinks I'm an idiot.'

'What did you promise them?' Dunk asked.

Lügner waved his son off. 'You don't want to know,' he said. 'It's not important.'

'As unimportant as your soul?' Dunk felt his anger at his father rising again.

Lügner closed his eyes for a moment. When he opened them again, Dunk could see that he'd been beaten. Given the look of his hair, skin, and clothes, he'd been that way since he'd left Altdorf three years ago. Dunk guessed that the man had lapsed into his old, enthusiastic ways only because of the encounter with him. Now that he'd had the wind taken from his sails, he'd reverted to the worn, tired, old man he'd become.

'I can't say.'

'Can't or won't?'

'It comes to the same thing.' Lügner hung his head low and spoke so softly that he could barely be heard.

'Tell me!' Dunk roared, slamming his fists onto the table.

Once again, all nearby conversation froze. It started up again a moment later, but Dunk knew that his table had just about worn out its welcome. The managers of the House of Booze traded upon their willingness to leave their patrons alone, but that included keeping them from upsetting each other.

Lügner raised his sunken, red-rimmed eyes. Dunk could smell the man's fear.

'My bloodline,' Lügner said in a soft, horrified breath. 'I – I sold you all.'

Dunk's heart froze in his chest. He didn't want to believe what his father had just said, but at the same time he knew that it was true.

'Forgive me, Dunkel,' Lügner whispered.

Dunk bit his lower lip so hard he tasted blood in his mouth. He gripped the edge of the table in front of him so tight he could hear his knuckles crack. Then he shoved out hard and flipped the table over in front of him.

Lügner's chair tipped over hard, but the old man managed to scramble out of the way, squeaking clear before the table's heavy top could crash into him. Dunk leapt down after the table before anyone could stop him. He landed crouched on the table's upper edge and stared down at his father like a vengeful god come from the mountaintop to smite down the most offensive of heretics.

'Forgive you?' Dunk said. 'You're lucky I don't tear out your heart and send you straight off to Khorne here and now!'

Lügner cried out in horror and threw his arms up over his head and face for protection. He whimpered in a soft voice, 'I did it all for you.'

The pathetic display triggered something in Dunk's head. One moment he wanted nothing more than to rip the man's life from him in large, bloody chunks; the next, he couldn't stand the thought of laying his hands on the man, for fear that some of that creature's weaknesses might rub off on him. Then Dunk remembered that this was his father and that it might already be too late.

'Isn't that Dunk Hoffnung?' a lady dwarf asked from the other side of the tavern's main hall.

Dunk knew he shouldn't have been able to hear the dwarf's question. Any other time he'd been in the House of Booze, the general background noise would have drowned it out. Now, it rang out in the silence that seemed to have smothered every other conversation to death.

'Get out of here,' Dunk said to his father as the man squirmed away from him along the tavern's cold, stone floor. 'If I ever see you again, you're dead.'

'So, Dunk,' Lästiges said through the crack in the door, her floating golden camra arcing over her shoulder to get the best shot of the thrower's reaction. 'Tell our viewers just how long you've been worshiping at the altar of the Blood God?'

'Don't do this to me,' Dunk said, trying to rub the sleep from his eyes. 'Not now.'

'So you're not denying reports of you threatening a harmless old man in the House of Booze last night and threatening to sacrifice him to Khorne?'

Dunk slapped both of his hands over his face. Of course, that's what it must have looked like to an outsider, and plenty of them had seen him come within inches of killing his father. He wondered how many of them had tried to sell the story to Wolf Sports, especially considering that no one outside of his friends had moved more than a finger to try to stop him from carrying out his threats.

'Leave him alone,' Spinne called from inside the room. 'He had a rough night.'

'I'm just happy to hear your voice, Spinne,' Lästiges said. 'After the old man got away from Dunk last night, some of the witnesses wondered if he might be desperate enough to try to sacrifice you instead.'

Dunk arched an eyebrow at the reporter. They had spent a lot of time together the previous year. She'd come along on the Hackers' trip to Albion and made a documentary based on how they'd found and captured the original Far Albion Cup.

'Your concern is touching,' he said. 'Now go away.' With that, he shut the door in her face.

'Dunk,' Lästiges said. 'Dunk! You know this story is going to be airing on every major Cabalvision network by the end of the day. I'm giving you a chance to head off the negative publicity and tell your side of the story!'

'Let her in,' Spinne said as she tossed on a fresh shirt and skirt.

'Are you nuts?'

Spinne shrugged. 'She's got a point. Besides, do you think she's going to go away?'

'Not without an exclusive,' Lästiges said through the door.

Dunk sighed and pulled the door open, holding it wide and gesturing for the reporter to enter.

'Thank you,' she said as she strolled past him, her camra hovering around her shoulders, its eye taking in everything at once. She gave Spinne a little wave and then curled up on the couch near the room's bay window, through which the morning sun streamed. Dunk could hear the calls of sea birds riding the gentle breeze across the bay, which stretched out towards the horizon beyond.

'So,' Lästiges said, 'what can you tell me about this man you assaulted? Crazed fan? Jilted lover? Evangelist for Khorne?'

'None of the above,' Dunk said, rubbing his unshaven chin. 'I'll talk to you about it if you like, but you have to turn that camra off.'

Lästiges frowned. 'But what if you say something interesting for once?'

'That's a chance you're just going to have to take.'

Lästiges peered up at him from the couch for a moment before making her decision. 'All right,' she said. At her signal, the camra dropped from the air to land neatly in her hand. She polished it on her sleeve and then stuffed it into a pocket on her Wolf Sports jacket.

Satisfied for the moment, Dunk looked down into Lästiges's deep brown eyes. 'It was my father,' he said.

'Lügner Hoffnung?' The colour drained from Lästiges's face. 'I thought he was dead.'

'No one could have been more surprised than me,' Dunk said. 'I hadn't seen him since the night we were run out of Altdorf.'

'What – what's he doing here?' The news of Lügner's return had shattered the woman's concentration.

'He came back to warn me about who's behind the price on my head.'

Lästiges shook her head. 'But how can you believe a word he says? He's one of the most evil people to ever walk the planet.'

'That's a bit harsh, I think,' said Dunk.

'Do you know what he did to my family?' the woman asked, her eyes welling up with tears of rage and frustration as she spoke. 'Do you know why I ended up taking a job as a Blood Bowl reporter? He

ruined us – entirely! The only way I could deal with
that was to know that at least he was dead.'

Lästiges's eyes shone as she looked at Dunk's
impassive face. 'And now you tell me he's alive?
What do I do with that?'

Dunk shook his head. He knew his father had
done some horrible things with the family business, but up until now he hadn't realised just how
bad they might have been. For the first time, he
truly felt sorry for Lästiges.

'How's Dirk?' he asked. He knew his brother
would want to know about their father, but he had
no way to reach him. He'd be able to commiserate
with the lady reporter at least.

'I – I don't know,' Lästiges said, pouting out her
red lower lip. 'I've been dreading you asking me
that. I haven't seen him since he quit the Reavers.'

Dunk frowned. Dirk and Lästiges had been dating
for a while and becoming a serious couple. If he
had cut off all ties with her as well, it couldn't be
good. He could understand Dirk being mad at him,
but staying away from Lästiges didn't make sense.

'So why did you attack him?' Lästiges asked, her
reporter's instincts kicking in. 'Your father, I mean.
I would think you'd be thrilled to see him.'

Dunk snorted at that. 'I'd love to tell you, but
only as a friend and as the woman dating my
brother.'

'Have you done something to be ashamed of?'
Lästiges asked. Dunk could tell she smelled blood.
If she had to spill that of a few innocents to take her
revenge on Lügner, he didn't doubt she would.

But Dunk and Dirk weren't just innocents to her,
were they? Dunk had come to know and grudgingly

respect Lästiges over the past couple of years, and Dirk had shared more with her than just her bed.

'Do you think I can trust her?' Dunk asked Spinne.

The catcher mulled it over for a moment. 'I think you have to.'

'This has to be off the record,' he said, turning to the reporter.

'Of course,' Lästiges said, leaning forward to catch his every word.

'When the family business was bad, before Dirk and I were even born, my father made a deal with Khorne. He sold the Blood God his soul and the souls of all his heirs.'

The reporter's face went white, and she sat back in the couch, horrified. 'Are you… He told you this?'

Dunk nodded.

'Then what happened?'

'We got rich,' Dunk said, confused by the question.

'Sure, and then you got run out of town. Why?'

Dunk stopped. 'I don't know,' he said, mystified. 'I never asked.'

'You didn't *ask?*'

'My head was still ringing from the "I sold your soul to Khorne" thing.'

Lästiges nodded as she stared out of the window. 'Amazing,' she muttered. 'I should have known.'

'You need to find Dirk.'

'What's that?' she asked, raising her eyebrows at Dunk.

'You need to find my brother and tell him about this. He needs to know.'

'Then what?' Lästiges asked. She felt most comfortable when asking questions. It put her back on familiar ground.

'Then find us, and we'll figure out what we need to do about this.'

'Why did your father come forth now?' Lästiges asked. 'He's been missing for years.'

'The Guterfiends are the ones who put up the reward for my head. He wanted me to know – and know why they want me dead.'

'Zauberer!' Lästiges said. 'I almost forgot. That's the reason I'm here!'

'You didn't come just to ask me awkward questions about that encounter in the House of Booze?'

She dismissed him with a wave of her hand. 'That was just for fun. This is serious.' She reached into her pocket and pulled out her camra. With a little toss, it rose into the air under its own power and hovered near her shoulder again.

'I said, no camra.'

Lästiges gave him an irritated smile. 'I'm not going to record anything. I need to show you something.'

The reporter snapped her fingers twice, and the eye-hole on the front of the camra grew wider. Then a ray of light stabbed out of the hole, shining on a blank wall at one end of the couch.

Dunk blinked his eyes, and stared at the brightly lit spot on the wall. There he saw an image of Schlechter Zauberer frozen in a sneer. It looked like a painting that the light had somehow revealed, as if it had always been there, just waiting for the camra to point it out.

'These Daemonic Lidless Projectors are incredible,' Lästiges said, 'and they just keep getting smaller every year.'

'A DLP?' Spinne asked. 'You can make a moving image without a crystal ball with one of those.'

'Give the girl a clean shirt,' Lästiges said. 'These things are great for playback. It used to be I couldn't see what I'd recorded until I got back to the studio.'

'So what's on the marquee tonight?' Dunk asked.

Lästiges reached out and touched something on the floating camra, and the image on the wall sprang to life. It showed Zauberer slinking down a dark hallway.

'Wolf Sports got this footage from the camras we had set up at the Orcidas Stadium in the Badlands.'

'Isn't that where the Gouged Eye play?' Dunk asked.

Spinne nodded. 'They beat us – the Reavers – in the finals for the Chaos Cup last year.'

'Funny you should mention that,' said Lästiges. 'Watch.'

In the image, Zauberer snaked his way down the hallway until he reached a room in which a couple dozen orcs lay scattered about. From the sounds – which also emitted from the camra – they were all sleeping off a great deal of drink.

'Yesterday, the Gouged Eye beat the Marauders in their annual grudge match. They play it during the Dungeonbowl tournament every year that neither team is invited to the main event.'

'So they play every year,' said Spinne.

'Without fail,' said Lästiges. 'When the Gouged Eye wins, they have a massive party to celebrate. Most of them survive it. Not this year though.'

Zauberer tiptoed through the orcs towards an oak table in the centre of the room. On it sat a large trophy – the Chaos Cup itself, Dunk realised – fashioned from what looked like the skull of a many-horned daemon squatting atop a pile of tiny skulls with equally vicious fangs. As the wizard approached, an eye appeared in one of the daemon-skull's sockets and rolled around to focus on the intruder.

Zauberer froze and said something to the trophy. It opened its toothy maw and began to laugh. The wizard tried to shush it, but it only laughed louder and louder until the orcs nearest to it started to wake up.

Zauberer dashed forward and plucked the cup from its stand. He clutched it to his chest, and the thing bit through his clothes and flesh. His blood ran red on its ivory-bleached bones. He screamed.

The nearest orc – Dunk recognised him as Da Fridge, the Gouged Eye team's best blocker – leapt up and grabbed the wailing wizard. The massive monster stretched up to his full height and held Zauberer out at arm's length, his feet flailing a full yard off of the floor.

Then Da Fridge burst into flames.

The orc dropped Zauberer, who landed nimbly on his feet. The other orcs around him leapt to their feet. Some of them had woken when Da Fridge had started laughing at the wizard, and his screams had jolted even the most intoxicated of them from their sleep.

Da Fridge tried to run, but he only made it a few feet before a blast of ebony lightning lanced out from the cup and ran him through. He collapsed at Zauberer's feet without another sound.

Some of the orcs charged the wizard. Others tried to escape, scurrying in every direction.

Zauberer cackled in evil mirth. With each laugh, another ebon bolt shot out of the Chaos Cup, skewering another screaming orc. Within seconds, the wizard stood alone in the room, surrounded by nothing more than the corpses of charred orcs.

Zauberer stalked around the room like a victorious conqueror surveying a smoking battlefield. No one else moved.

Then the wizard spotted the security camra that had been recording the entire event. He strutted up to it, a wicked smile splitting his face. He held the Chaos Cup up before the device, and the thing's eye swivelled about and focused through it as if it could see right through the camra's lens to Lästiges, Spinne, and Dunk.

Dunk reached out and held Spinne's hand as she stifled a gasp. Lästiges sat unmoved, solid as a rock. She'd witnessed this scene at least once already. It wasn't until he glanced at her chin that he saw that she was shaking.

'Tell the world,' Zauberer said. 'The power I have sought for so long is finally mine.

'Tell everyone you meet. Soon they will all worship me as their emperor-god.

'For anyone else, if Dunk Hoffnung is hurt before I get my hands on him – if anyone even scratches his armour – I'll destroy you and everyone you hold dear.

'And be sure to tell Hoffnung this for me when you see him: Dunk, my old friend, you're next.'

CHAPTER SIXTEEN

'BYUFELL TRIEHUGGER HAS the ball!' Bob's voice said. 'The Elfheim Eagles are on a roll!'

Dunk swore under his breath. This game hadn't gone well at all.

When the Hackers had first lined up against their all-elf opponents, Dunk had thought that the wizards who had sponsored the Eagles must have owed their coach some kind of favour. He hadn't had a lot of experience with elves, but these didn't look like any Blood Bowl players he'd ever seen.

Each of the Eagles was physically perfect with stunning good looks. That they enhanced their appearance with make-up and designer orange-and-purple armour had surprised Dunk. Apparently helmets were out this year, although Dunk couldn't say if this was a fashion decision or that the elf players just refused to mess up their perfectly coiffed hair.

All of this made Dunk think that the Eagles were a team composed merely of poseurs who had showed up simply to display how good an elf could look on the field. He expected that the rough-and-tumble Hackers would tear them apart before they had to break a sweat – something he suspected the Eagles themselves would have refused to do for any reason short of torture.

He'd been sorely mistaken.

The immortal elves had a different kind of strategy than Dunk was used to. Instead of focusing on raw power, or even the elegant use of skill, they excelled at the use of rotten tricks that were technically within the rules. Apparently Nuffle had never written anything in his sacred rulebook about using a herbicide in the middle of a game, for instance, despite the fact that it had sent Edgar into an itching fit that made it impossible for him to do anything during the rest game.

The Eagles had made good use of the dungeon's terrain too. They had drawn M'Grash into the room with the bottomless pit and then knocked him off one of the string of floating rocks. The poor ogre had been falling for over ten minutes now, wailing in terror at the top of his lungs the entire time.

Cavre had been the most successful in dealing with the elves, but he'd had a chest explode on him. While he was stunned, the Eagles had stuffed him into the chest and bound it tight with something Dunk could only guess was an elf's excuse for a jockstrap.

That left Spinne, Guillermo, and Dunk as the only Hackers still in the game. Outnumbered two to one, they were bound to have a hard time of it. The most frustrating part for Dunk was the fact that he'd not even been able to tackle anyone yet. The Eagles had studiously avoided having any contact with him. Whenever he entered a room, they left.

'What's going on?' he'd asked Guillermo. 'Why won't they come after us?'

The Estalian had used the back of his arm to wipe some blood from his eyes. 'I think you mean, why don't they come after you?'

Dunk realised the lineman was right. Word of Zauberer's capture of the Chaos Cup and his subsequent threat against anyone who might hurt Dunk had saturated the Cabalvision networks almost immediately after Dunk had seen it himself. In the middle of talk shows like Bloodcentre, player after player had gone white at the thought of being forced to play against Dunk while the sorcerer's edict against harming the Hacker stayed in effect.

Not so for Lassolegs Gladhandriel, the Eagles' captain. 'As you know, we always play strictly by the rules,' he'd said. 'We do not fear that we might hurt Mr. Hoffnung accidentally.'

Of course, that left a lot of room for things the Eagles might try to do to Dunk on purpose. So far, just isolating Dunk had worked well. Unless he or his team-mates found the ball, the Eagles had no need to get anywhere near him.

Now that the ball had been found, Dunk hoped to turn the tables. He gave up trying to figure out how to rescue M'Grash without getting killed in the process, and bounded across the floating rocks in seconds. When he reached the room with the mirrored walls, he closed his eyes and felt his way through the place, taking care to listen hard for any attackers approaching him while he was blind.

Once through the mirrored room, Dunk found a teleportation pad in the hallway beyond. He didn't know where it would take him, but since he needed to get ahead of the ball carrier fast, he jumped on it and hoped for the best.

He popped into a room filled with rabid, three-headed, seven-tailed cats that smelled of carrion and looked as if they'd been starved half to madness. He moved off the glowing circle, and then jumped back onto it again. It blinked him away.

Dunk landed in another golden circle, and promptly skidded off it, out of control. The floor in this high-ceilinged chamber was a smooth sheet of ice, and his boots could find no purchase on it.

As Dunk slid, he started to pick up speed. The room seemed to go on forever. As he stared around, he realised he wasn't in a room at all. The teleportation pad had transported him to the top of a snowy mountain peak, and it had been engineered to send him slipping along its face at top speed.

Although he had managed to maintain his footing, he could do little to change his course. Peering ahead, he saw the land in front of him disappear into thin air. Then he knew where he was. He'd seen the place from a distance as they'd sailed in to Barak Varr. The dwarfs called it Khalakazam, which had no equivalent in the Imperial tongue. The best that one of the bartenders at the House of Booze had been able to come up with was, 'Mount You-Must-Be-Joking.'

'They call it that because of the steep drop-off on its front face,' the bartender had said. 'If you happen to slip off it, it's nearly a mile down before you hit anything else. They say you'd probably pass out and die long before that happened, but me, I think they just say that. More likely you flounder there screaming in the air every damned second until you smash into the rocks below. I hear most people bounce near twenty feet in the air after an impact like that.'

Dunk and Spinne had paid their tab and gone to find another bar after that.

'Oh, no! Hoffnung's found his way on to Mount No-Freaking-Way!' Jim's voice said from somewhere off to the left. 'He's doomed for sure.'

'If that's true, I'd hate to be the dwarfs who built that death trap – or the wizards who commissioned it,' said Bob. 'I can't imagine that watching this happen on live Cabalvision – *only* here on Wolf Sports! – will make a certain wizard very happy. I can only guess where he'd begin to take his revenge.'

Dunk threw himself down on the ice and tried to grab on with his entire body, but no part of him could find purchase. He clutched at the ice with his hands, hugged it with his body, and kicked at it with his feet, but it ignored his every attempt to cling on. He wound up on his rump, stomping the heels of his cleated boots into the ice zipping past underneath him, but he couldn't even manage to slow himself down.

Dunk looked up and saw a trio of birds circling overhead, carrion eaters waiting for their next meal, no doubt. He turned over on his belly and tried to ram the spikes on the various parts of his armour into the ice too, but the slick surface proved impenetrable. Nothing worked.

Then the ice disappeared, and he found himself sailing out into open space, nothing beneath him but a mile of crisp, cold air. He looked down and saw how the wall of the mountain curved away from the precipitous edge. About a quarter of the way down, the snow and ice gave way to bare rock. Near the bottom – still far away, but already rising fast – the rock plunged into a lush and fertile valley. Down there, Dunk could see tiny white dots moving about, and he realised they were cattle.

An eagle's cry split the open air, cutting through the sound of the wind rushing through Dunk's ears. He tried to look behind him to see what might have made the noise, but he only succeeded in sending his body into an uncontrolled spin.

It took Dunk a full ten seconds to re-stabilise himself. Once he did, he was too dizzy to understand anything he could see. Then a great fluttering of wings surrounded him, and he found himself clinging to a feathered tree trunk.

Dunk peered around the side of the trunk and saw a giant eagle's head staring back at him over its shoulder. 'Relax,' the creature said. 'I'll have you back on the ground in no time. You didn't think they'd just execute you like that, did you?'

Dunk decided that this would be the perfect time to pass out. The last words he heard were, 'By the way, you lost.'

'IS IT TRUE?' DUNK woke up with the words on his lips. He was in his room in the Hackers' official inn again, in bed, alone, but not as alone as he'd hoped.

'Yes,' said Dr. Pill, who leered at Dunk as he stood up from where he'd been sitting on the couch at the other end of the large room.

Dunk stared at the apothecary. 'What happened?'

'You slid off the tallest cliff in the world. A giant eagle rescued you. Your team lost.'

Dunk groaned.

'Really, what chance did Spinne and Guillermo have all by themselves? As it was, they tried so hard that I had to put stitches into both of them.'

'Stitches? Is Spinne all right?'

'She's fine,' Dr. Pill said with a bemused grin. A few minor slashes on her upper right bicep. She'll be back at full capacity in no time.'

'What about the others?'

'Cavre bruised himself trying to get out of that chest. He took some splinters when he succeeded, but it was already too late.

'I got to Edgar in time to save most of his bark. You might see him wearing a long sheet like a toga for the next few weeks, but don't comment on it. It makes him self-conscious.

'Once the game ended, M'Grash finally figured out that he should grab on to something. He nearly pulled one of the floating rocks out of its spot when he hit it. Nothing but minor bruises for him, though. He's tougher than a bag of rocks and nearly as smart.'

'And Guillermo?'

'Took six stabs from elf armour spikes and nearly bled to death, but I got to him in time. He'll be fine soon enough.

'Now, how do you feel?'

'Dunk ran his hands over his body, taking inventory as he went. 'I feel fine,' he finally said. 'Nothing damaged but my ego.'

Dr. Pill nodded. 'I'm afraid I don't have a potion powerful enough to help with that.'

The door to the room opened, and Spinne and Slick came in. 'Dunk!' Spinne said as she dashed over to the bed and took him in her arms. She held him for a long time without saying a word. Then she sat back and caressed his face as she spoke.

'Thank Nuffle I couldn't watch you falling off that cliff while it happened,' she said. 'I think my heart would have stopped dead.'

'Mine almost did,' said Dunk. 'I'm just glad those eagles were there.'

'I've already filed a protest with the Colleges of Magic's Dungeonbowl Steering Committee,' Slick said. 'They shouldn't be able to do something like that to a professional player like you. Sure, it makes for great Cabalvision, but it's hardly fair, is it?'

'I didn't realise Blood Bowl had to be fair,' said Dr. Pill.

'Life's not fair,' Slick said. 'We play games to make it better. We can't just abandon that whenever the mood suits us.'

'So will anything come of your complaint?' Dunk asked.

'Not a chance,' said Slick, 'nothing directly, at least. It might make us look less pathetic to sympathetic members of the Grey Wizards' sponsoring team, though, and that might mean getting invited back next year.'

'I don't know,' Dunk said, shivering as images from sliding down the mountain flashed through his head. 'I could give it a miss, I think.'

'Bollocks!' Slick said. 'Now, son, that's no way for a champion to talk.'

'Champions win games,' Spinne said, holding Dunk's hand. He could see the stitches on her upper arm. They looked clean and well matched, healing already. 'We lost.'

'But you'll all live to play another day,' Dr. Pill said.

'That's more than most teams can manage, especially in Dungeonbowl. That's how I lost my last job. I was working for the Moot Mighties when they lost every single player in just one game against the New Albion Patriots.'

'Don't the Mighties have a total loss at least three times a year?' asked Slick.

'This one was worse. Their coach and manager were killed too, along with about half the fans in the stands.'

'The Patriots did that?' Dunk asked.

Dr. Pill shook his head. 'It was Free Spiked Ball Day for the first five hundred fans. It all went downhill from there.'

Dunk winced. Then he looked to Slick. 'What's the plan from here?' he asked. 'Do we stick around for the final round of the tournament?'

'No, son, we're heading home. Back to Bad Bay as soon as you and the others are fit to travel.' He looked to Dr. Pill.

'We can leave with the next tide,' the apothecary said.

'Any truth to the vicious rumour going around that we'll see Pegleg at the wheel of the *Sea Chariot* as we pull out into the bay?' Spinne asked.

'As many truths as you care to seek,' Dr. Pill said with a mysterious grin.

'Can you translate that for the less enlightened?' Slick asked.

'Yes.'

'Yes, you can translate or – oh, never mind!'

'I am hopeful that Captain Haken has overcome his irrational fear of water,' Dr. Pill said. 'However, I must caution that the relief he experiences from this may cause him to experience an overwhelming sense of confidence that may not be entirely grounded in reality. We should take great care to keep watch over him to ensure that he does not overextend himself and expose the entire ship to danger.'

Slick glared at the apothecary. 'Just in time for a long ocean voyage.'

'Come on, Slick. We've made this same trip many times before,' Dunk said. 'What could go wrong?'

● CHAPTER SEVENTEEN

'JOLLY ROGER OFF the port bow!'

Dunk shaded his eyes to peer up at Guillermo in the crow's nest, tipping back and forth high above the *Sea Chariot*'s main deck. The lineman's arm stabbed off to the left of the ship's nose. Dunk brought his head down in that direction and saw what Guillermo had spotted first from his higher vantage point: a ship sailing towards them from the horizon, a black flag flapping from its mast.

Dunk couldn't make out the flag's design, but if Guillermo – who had a spyglass up there with him – said it bore a skull and crossbones, Dunk believed him.

Dunk climbed up to the bridge where Pegleg stood, squinting through his own spyglass at the oncoming ship. Cavre, who had the wheel, craned his neck to look back at the captain, waiting for his orders.

'Are those really pirates, coach?' Dunk asked.

'Aye, they are, Mr. Hoffnung,' Pegleg said. Try as he might, Dunk couldn't read the man's tone. Instead of fear, it bore something else. Anticipation?

'Orders, captain?' Cavre asked.

'Steady as she goes, Mr. Cavre.'

'But captain, she'll catch us for sure at this rate.' Dunk checked the other horizon and saw that they weren't far from Estalia's western coast. A wide, sandy beach beckoned from that direction, and Dunk pointed towards it. 'If we hurry, we can reach dry land before they catch us. Then we might have a chance.'

Pegleg brought down his spyglass, collapsed it, and stuffed it into one of the pockets of his long, green, velvet coat. He adjusted his bright yellow tricorn hat, which seemed to be mostly made of holes now. 'I'm aware of where the shoreline is, Mr. Hoffnung. Steady as she goes.'

With that, Pegleg limped off the bridge and disappeared into his cabin. Dunk stared after him, hardly noticing when Slick and Spinne climbed onto the bridge next to him.

'What's happening, son?' Slick asked.

'I don't know,' Dunk said. He looked to Cavre, whose face carried a world of worry. 'Shouldn't we do something? That ship looks like it could eat the *Sea Chariot* alive.'

'The captain knows what he's doing,' Cavre said.

'Are you sure about that?' Spinne asked. 'This is the first time any of us have seen him outside of his cabin anywhere but at dock or on dry land.'

'Dr. Pill's treatment seems to have been effective, wouldn't you say?'

Slick frowned. 'Are we certain that the treatment doesn't have any side-effects like, perhaps, insanity?'

Cavre kept silent, his mouth a thin, grim line.

As the pirate ship grew closer, Dunk could make out some of its details. It was huge, twice the size of the *Sea Chariot*, and it had a row of oars sticking out from either side. These were held up from the water at the moment, but Dunk could see how they could be put into service at a moment's notice.

When Dunk got a good look at the ship's mast-head, his stomach shrank into a tiny knot. It had been carved to resemble a bloody daemon with snakes for limbs and eyes. Dunk squinted at the crimson lettering just under that, running parallel with the rail. It read *'Seas of Hate.'*

'We have to get out of here,' Dunk said to Cavre. 'We have to outrun them or we're all doomed.'

'I have my orders.'

Dunk grabbed the wheel, testing Cavre's grip on it. 'You can't follow those orders. The captain's gone mad.'

'Do you hear that?' Slick asked, a hand cupped to his ear, which he'd cocked in the direction of the pirate ship. 'It sounds like hissing.'

'Look,' Spinne said to Cavre, 'I understand your loyalty to Pegleg. He's our captain and our coach, but now is the time to question those orders. Forcing himself out of the cabin has clearly unbalanced him. We need to turn tail and see if we can outrace that ship.'

Cavre gave hard looks to all three of the others in turn. Then his shoulders slumped and he nodded gently. 'All right,' he said. 'What do you propose we do? No one knows this ship better than Captain Haken. We need him and his support.'

'We'll have to live without it,' Spinne said.

This talk of mutiny made Dunk uncomfortable, but he couldn't see any other way around it. Unlike the others – except perhaps the now-haggard Cavre – he knew what hungered for them on that ship and what would happen to those who were captured. To risk meeting such daemons seemed to be insane.

'Belay that, Mr. Cavre!' The captain came stalking out of his cabin, shoving a wheeled rack of cannonballs before him. 'Mad or not, I have a plan. We'll never outrun that ship. Once you see the *Seas of Hate*, your fate is sealed. Your only chance is to fight.'

'With what?' Dunk called down at the ex-pirate. 'We may be a great Blood Bowl team, but half us of don't know how to handle a sword and even fewer have ever fought on a moving ship.'

Pegleg doffed his tricorn hat, exposing his long, black curls to the sun. With a wink and a grin, he waved the hat at the rack of cannonballs squatting next to him. 'Why, with these, of course! You don't think I'd jeopardise the safety of my team without a plan, do you?'

Spinne gaped at the man. 'You did this on purpose?'

Pegleg grinned. 'Suffice it to say, Miss Schönheit, that I knew that there was a significant chance that this particular ship full of daemonic pirates might take a stab at procuring for themselves the substantial reward placed on Mr. Hoffnung's head.'

Dunk's eyes popped wide open. 'How's that? I thought that's why we sailed out of Barak Varr under cover of night. You had us under strict orders not to tell anyone our schedule, our route, or our destination. How could they have found us?'

'They are daemons, Mr. Hoffnung. I suppose it's not beyond them to use magic.'

Slick peered down at the captain from over the bridge's railing. 'But they didn't, did they?'

Dunk stared at his agent, not understanding what the halfling meant to imply.

'No, of course not,' Pegleg said. 'They didn't have to. I *told* them.'

Spinne gasped.

'Don't be so shocked,' Pegleg said. 'I did what I had to do to get those devils right where I want them.' He rubbed his chin, bemused. 'I'll admit that I didn't expect to see them until we were closer to Bad Bay, but no matter. I'm as happy to send them into the briny deep here as anywhere.'

'Dr. Pill told you to do this,' Dunk said. 'Didn't he?'

'All part of the solution to my hydrophobia. In order to surmount your fears you must confront them, after all.'

'Or inflict them on others at least,' said Slick.

The hissing from the other ship grew louder. Dunk peered out at it again and saw that the masthead had come to life. It looked as if someone had taken one of the snake-daemons Dunk could now see gathering on the foredeck, grown it to the size of M'Grash, and then lashed it to the ship's prow. The long snake-arms whipped before it in the wind, reaching out for the *Sea Chariot*.

Dunk had no doubt that when they finally found purchase on the ship's deck the other daemons would use those arms as part of a boarding action.

The Hackers would then find themselves fighting for their lives against a well-armed crew of daemons.

Images of the daemons crashing his engagement party flashed through his head. Dunk felt like he might vomit, but he clamped down on his stomach and went to go find his sword.

'Where do you think you're going, Mr. Hoffnung?' Pegleg reached out with his hook and snagged Dunk by the sleeve as he tried to walk past.

'To get my blade. I'm not going down without a fight.'

Pegleg shook his head. 'That won't be necessary.'

Dunk glanced back at the onrushing *Seas of Hate*. 'I think they might disagree with you.'

Pegleg tapped one of the cannonballs with his hook. They were covered with strange runes arranged in odd patterns. Each of them seemed to have three thick holes bored into one side.

'With these enchanted cannonballs on our side, Mr. Hoffnung, we have the advantage.'

The captain's calm demeanour irritated Dunk. Seeing the creatures that had killed his father and tortured him for so long – badly enough that he'd chewed off his own hand and lost his leg in the escape – how could he be so placid?

'You forgot one thing, coach,' Dunk said, panic creeping into his voice. 'We don't have a cannon on board!'

'Ah,' Pegleg said, holding up his hook, 'but we don't need one.' He glanced up over Dunk's shoulder. 'Ready?' he asked.

'Ready, coach,' said M'Grash.

Dunk turned and gaped at the ogre. M'Grash grinned down at Dunk as he cracked his knuckles.

Did Pegleg think that the ogre could take on an entire ship full of daemons with nothing but his bare hands?

'Fire at will,' Pegleg said. The captain took Dunk by the elbow and steered him to the gunwale facing the *Seas of Hate*, close to the stairs leading up to the bridge and out of M'Grash's way.

The ogre reached down and hefted one of the cannonballs in his hands. Then he stuck his two middle fingers and his thumb into the three holes drilled in the ball of enchanted, cold iron. This left his other two fingers splayed out along the surface of the ball, where they fit perfectly along the symbols engraved there.

'See the formation of the hand, Mr. Hoffnung? Some call a hand held like that a mark of Chaos. It's an integral part of the activation of the ball's magic.'

Dunk just stood there stunned. He couldn't believe what he was seeing.

M'Grash stretched his arms out above him, the cannonball perched in his monstrous mitt. Dunk couldn't recall ever seeing such concentration on the ogre's face. It made him seem more dangerous than ever.

M'Grash took a huge stride forward and swung the ball down and back behind him as he did. The players crouching behind the ogre on the other side of the ship, watching the scene play out, suddenly scattered, fearful that the ball might come back at them.

Then M'Grash took another smooth stride towards the *Seas of Hate*. As he did, he swung his mighty arm forward and released the cannonball.

The massive piece of iron sailed into the air, arcing like a rainbow. As it went, it fizzled and hissed as if angered – no – as if hungry.

The snake-daemons on the *Seas of Hate* all watched the cannonball in unison. They'd been laughing at the ogre and the others in the *Sea Chariot* up until then, contributing to a mad symphony of hisses. Now, they fell silent as they stared at the missile of cold iron coming straight towards them.

The ball landed in the middle of the foredeck. Dunk had expected it to bounce or maybe roll a bit, perhaps to knock some of the daemons into the sea. Instead, it smashed right through the decking, tearing through it as if it were little more than paper.

Dunk wondered for a moment just how far down the ball might go. Where would it stop? Then a geyser of seawater gushed up through the hole it had created.

Pegleg cackled with glee as the snake-daemons scrambled about the deck, looking desperately for some way to seal the hole. Then a second ball crashed down among them. This one caught a snake-daemon square in the back as it fell, and it dragged the creature down into the new hole it made before it could even hiss in protest.

A third ball smashed down a moment later, and the ship's nose started to tilt forward as she took on water. The snake-daemons started leaping over the ship's rail and paddling for the shore. Unfortunately for them, the snakes didn't make particularly good swimmers, and they made poor progress against the outgoing tide.

The monstrous masthead on the *Seas of Hate* let loose a horrendous hiss as it reached for the *Sea Chariot*. The viper's head on one of its arms smashed down in front of Dunk and Pegleg, sinking its fangs into the gunwale's wood. Pegleg pulled Dunk back from the railing and turned him to watch M'Grash's response.

The ogre wrapped his hands around the cannonball this time and stood sideways to the *Seas of Hate*. Then he kicked up his front leg as he brought the ball over his head. He transferred the cannonball into one hand as he thrust his front leg forward. Dunk could see the ball glowing white in an outline around his hand.

M'Grash hurled the cannonball forward with all his might, and it left his hand as if fired from a real cannon. It shot straight towards the living masthead and smashed into its chest. Then it exploded in a blast of noise, heat, and light.

Bits of the snake-daemon masthead went everywhere. Some of them landed on the deck next to Dunk. He kicked one with his foot and saw that it was nothing more than splinters of badly scorched wood.

The rest of the snake-daemons gaped in astonishment at the large hole where their masthead had once been. The only thing left was the one snake arm still attached to the *Sea Chariot*. It held on to where the shoulder had been on the *Seas of Hate*, stretched taut almost to the point of snapping.

The snake-daemons pitched themselves over the side of the ship and swam desperately for the shore. Some of them tried to climb up onto the *Sea Chariot*, but a well-aimed crossbow bolt through the cranium of the first two or three put their ambitions to rest. Dunk glanced back and saw Cavre grin at him from the back railing of the bridge as he loaded his crossbow once more.

Over the hissing of the creatures in the water, Dunk heard a chorus of pathetic wails rise up. At first, he couldn't tell from where they came. Then he figured it out.

'The prisoners!' Dunk grabbed Pegleg by the shoulders. 'The people rowing that ship, they're all chained to it. They'll go down with it!'

Pegleg grimaced. 'They would have all died under those daemons' tender mercies anyhow. It's a small price to pay to rid the seas of the taint of those bastards.'

Dunk cursed. He couldn't just let all those people die. He stared over at the *Sea of Hate*, and then did the only thing he could think of. He leapt upon the masthead's remaining arm.

CHAPTER EIGHTEEN

NOW THAT THE masthead lived no more, the arm had become a plank of well carved wood. With the ship's nose already starting to sink, Dunk could slide down the plank, right to the deck of the *Seas of Hate* – and he did.

Once Dunk reached the ship, he pulled himself up over the gunwale and onto the main deck. There, in the open hold below, he saw a few dozen bruised and battered men straining desperately against their shackles. None had managed to free themselves yet.

'The keys!' Dunk shouted down at the prisoners. 'Where are the keys?'

A few of the slaves stood up and pointed at the rhythm-keeper's drum at the edge of the deck overlooking the hold. Dunk dashed over to it and found a single rusty key hanging from a vicious hook. He snatched it up and dived into the hold below.

Insane with panic, the water already sloshing around their ankles, the men grabbed at Dunk and tried to take the key from him. After he smashed the first few attempts down with his free fist, they held up their iron-cuffed wrists instead and pleaded with him to let them go.

Dunk worked that key into every lock he could find. In, twist, out. In, twist, out. In, twist, out.

A few of the freed muttered their thanks to the thrower, but most scrambled free and dived over the gunwale without a word. Dunk could hardly blame them. The water was rising fast.

Just as Dunk reached the final row of oarsmen, something in the front of the ship gave way, and the sea came rushing into the hold. In, twist, out. In, twist, out. In, twist, out.

Dunk thought he just might make it, but the last prisoner refused to show Dunk his shackles. Instead, he snarled at the thrower and tried to bite him. Dunk considered knocking the man out and then freeing him, but the hold chose that moment to slip beneath the waves.

The water hit Dunk in the back and shoved him up and free. He reached for the shackled madman, but his grip slipped away. As he bobbed on the surface for an instant, he looked down and saw the man struggling with his irons, the air bubbling from his lungs.

Dunk grabbed a good breath and then dived down towards the man. He wasn't going to let this poor soul drown if he could help it. The more people he could rescue from daemons of any kind, the better, and if he had to risk his own life to do it, then so be it.

When Dunk reached the man, his impending death by drowning seemed to have washed his madness away. He presented his shackles and waited for Dunk to work the key into the lock.

Once the man was free, he kicked away towards the surface. Dunk made to follow him, but found that the sleeve of his shirt had caught on the man's irons. Before he could separate himself, one of the last escapee's desperate kicks caught Dunk in the side of the head.

Stunned, Dunk hung there in the water for a moment. As his head started to clear, he heard a loud, horrible creaking noise, and the irons dragged him deeper into the water. The entire ship was going down.

Dunk wanted to curse, but he saved his breath, as he had precious little of it left. He tried to tear himself away from the irons again, but with his feet now dragging along above him he couldn't find the leverage.

The world around Dunk began to spin and close in around the edges, and he felt his consciousness leaving him. Looking up through the water, he saw the sunlight above getting further and further away. Then something huge splashed into the water next to him, knocking the last of the air out of his lungs.

Dunk thought for sure that he was dead. Then he felt his sleeve tear loose from his shirt at the shoulder, and a strong hand yanked him up towards the light.

The next thing Dunk knew he was flat on his back, stretched out on M'Grash's torso, with Spinne shoving on his chest and belly, forcing the water from him. He sat up, coughing and spluttering, choking fresh air back into his lungs. For a moment, he didn't know where he was. Then he saw that M'Grash was lying in the open sea, floating on his back to give Spinne a surface to work on Dunk.

'Thanks,' Dunk croaked, both at M'Grash and Spinne. A cheer went up from the deck of the *Sea Chariot* and from the newly freed men swimming around them in the water.

Spinne pulled Dunk to her and held him tight. Although he'd nearly drowned, she was the one who was shivering.

'You're the bravest, most amazing man I've ever known,' she whispered in his ear. 'And if you ever do something like that again, I'll kill you myself.'

THE REST OF the trip to Bad Bay wasn't nearly so eventful. Pegleg ordered the freed slaves to be brought onto the ship, and the Hackers deposited them safely in Valhallaholic, a resort town founded by the Estalians to cater to the frequent Norscan raiding parties that always seemed to wander a bit off track after spending too much time pillaging. The ex-prisoners treated Dunk like a conquering hero the entire time they were on the ship, and many of them wept for him when they had to leave.

Once the Hackers arrived at Valhallaholic, Pegleg declared an evening of shore leave for them all. They swarmed into the port town, right behind the refugees.

'I need a drink,' Slick said as he, Spinne, and Dunk strolled into the town. M'Grash had stayed behind with Pegleg to guard the ship. Now over his fear of water, Pegleg seemed never to want to leave the *Sea Chariot* again. In fact, he'd threatened to hold practices on the main deck – or at least on a beach right next to the boat so he could call out instructions from the crow's nest during scrimmages.

'I think we all do,' Spinne said, holding Dunk's arm. Ever since she and M'Grash had pulled him from the sinking *Seas of Death*, she'd clung to his side. Dunk knew he'd scared her badly – he'd scared himself – but he didn't see what he could do to make it up to her. Perhaps an evening hanging out in a tavern over a few cold drinks would be the best thing for everyone.

'Wait,' Dunk said, as he scanned the street, looking for a sign of a welcoming inn. 'Is that who I think it is?'

Someone who looked exactly like Gunther the Gobbo had poked his nose out from between two buildings and was peering up and down the street.

'Is that the Gobbo?' Spinne asked, squinting at the figure standing half in the shadows.

'It couldn't be,' said Slick. 'What would he be doing here?'

Then the figure turned towards the trio and spotted them. Even from this far away, Dunk could see Gunther go white. Then he turned and scurried back down the alley from which he'd come.

Dunk took off at a sprint, chasing after the figure. 'Hold it!' he shouted after the Gobbo as he finally reached the mouth of the blind alley. Two doors let out into it. Both of them must have been locked, as Gunther was hanging from the latch of one of them, trying to open it with all of his might.

'Hello, Gunther,' Dunk said as Spinne came pounding into the alley behind him. He could hear Slick's tiny feet padding slowly after her as well.

The clammy-faced bookie let go of the locked door's latch and turned to show Dunk what he probably thought was his best, crooked-toothed grin. 'Hey there, kid. What brings you to this backwater hole?'

Dunk squinted at Gunther. 'Something tells me you already know.'

The greasy bookie laughed nervously. 'No,' he said in false surprise. 'Don't tell me that I somehow stumbled upon the Hackers' new secret training camp.'

Spinne snorted. 'Try again,' she said with a growl.

'Did Pegleg decide to treat the whole team to a holiday here? You really should try the mead and the mulled wine. They're excellent.'

Slick entered the alley, sweating and puffing for breath. 'It is you,' he said, 'you petty little bastard. You sold us out to those pirates.'

'Hey, I don't know what you're talking about,' Gunther said, holding his hands up. His beady eyes darted all over the place, trying to spot some way out of this. 'If a bunch of daemons happen to find you out in the middle of the ocean and attack you, how am I supposed to be responsible for that?'

'Who said they were daemons?' asked Dunk.

Gunther froze. 'It's, um, a figure of speech?' he said weakly.

Dunk and Spinne stalked towards the Gobbo, with Slick bringing up the rear.

'I'll scream,' Gunther said. 'They don't look kindly on killers in this town.'

'How about scum who cut deals with daemons?' asked Dunk. 'We'd be happy to explain everything.'

'If you're lucky, they'll just kill you on the spot,' said Spinne. 'I hear the Norscans like to spit-roast anyone caught trafficking with such creatures.'

'That's a nasty way to die,' Slick said. 'Takes forever, I hear. On a windy day like this, out near the sea, there's no chance that you'll choke on the smoke before the fire reaches you. Your legs will probably burn to a crisp before the fire reaches your vitals.'

'I'll bet they'd hear you screaming in Altdorf,' said Dunk.

'All right!' Gunther said, nearly sobbing, his eyes wide in terror. 'I did it. I did it.' He looked up at them as he started to whimper. 'What are you going to do with me?'

'THAT WAS YOU?' Gunther said to Pegleg as he clapped his warty hand over his pimply forehead. The bookie sat on the deck of the *Sea Chariot*, too stunned to get back on his feet. 'I had no idea.'

'You weren't supposed to.'

'But you were dressed up as a Chaos All-Stars fan, all in leather and spikes – and with a chainsaw in place of your hook!' Gunther gaped at the coach, and Dunk, M'Grash, Spinne, and Slick each took a half step away from the ex-pirate.

'It's called a disguise, Mr. Gobbo. It's not very effective if you can see right through it.'

'But-but-but...' Gunther just couldn't wrap his head around something. 'Why? Why would you sell out your whole team – including yourself – to me?'

'All part of a personal self-improvement project,' Pegleg said with a smile.

'What?'

Dunk shook his head. 'You came here expecting to get some evidence of my death, didn't you?'

'Hey, you can't prove that.'

Dunk leaned over, almost putting his nose in Gunther's face. 'This isn't a court of law. I don't need proof. I know what you did. I just want to know why?'

'He asked me to!' Gunther said, stabbing a fat finger at Pegleg.

'So?'

'He told me that I'd get a share of the reward on your head.' Gunther glared at Pegleg. 'You *lied* to me.'

'And you set up a deal with a boat of daemons to kill a couple of dozen people,' Slick said.

Gunther shut his trap and swallowed hard. 'What are you going to do with me?'

'Nothing,' Pegleg said.

'Nothing?' everyone else in the room said.

The captain grinned. 'Why would we want to do anything to harm the Hackers' newest employee?'

Dunk rubbed his eyes. Everything about this confused him.

'That's right,' Pegleg said, leaning over the Gobbo. 'You work for me now. Secretly and off the books.'

'But I'm a bookie, not a Blood Bowl player! I don't have the ability or the skills. And I bleed easily.'

M'Grash nodded at that. 'He sure does.'

'You're not our latest player,' Pegleg said. 'You're our first scout.'

'No way,' Gunther said. 'Uh-uh. No way, no how, no time.' He folded his arms across his chest as if that settled the matter.

'You act as if you had a choice in the matter,' Pegleg said. 'There's a reason I chose you to act as my go-between with the daemons, you know. After your work with the Black Jerseys went public, you've been in shallow waters. Do you think anyone would do business with you ever again if they knew you'd tried to wipe out an entire Blood Bowl champion-calibre team with the help of your daemon friends?'

'Hey,' Gunther said, 'they got over me fixing games, didn't they?'

'On some level, people admired that. It took smarts, organisation, and a bit of vision to pull that off. Trucking with daemons, that just takes a complete lack of morals or ethics.'

Gunther sighed deeply, and looked Pegleg in the eyes. 'All right,' he said. 'I work for you.'

Dunk stared at the Gobbo and then at Pegleg. 'You planned this from the start, didn't you coach?' he asked.

The ex-pirate just smiled. 'You win games by concocting a plan and then executing it to the letter. We hit this plan perfectly.'

'So we just let him go now?'

Pegleg nodded. 'He's agreed to work for us, but in secret. The less he's seen with us, the better.'

'I'll be leaving right now then,' Gunther said. 'I'll send my reports to you in Bad Bay.'

Dunk reached out and put a hand on Gunther's shoulder. 'I have one last question for you,' he said. 'That night that Zauberer put that price on my head, how did you know where to find me? You're no friend of Sparky's.'

'Did he tell you that? He would. Just because he owes me a little money, he goes and disowns me like that.'

Dunk just glared at the bookie.

'All right,' Gunther said. 'It was Zauberer. He told me where to find you.'

Dunk couldn't believe it. 'Why would he do that?' he asked. 'That was right after he put that price on my head.'

'He said it had something to do with forcing you into the hands of your enemies, forcing you to trust people who would later betray you.' The bookie shot

Pegleg a dirty look. 'I suppose you'd know something about that.'

The ex-pirate smiled down at Gunther. 'Just admit you were well played and move on,' he said.

'So you've been in contact with Zauberer?' Dunk asked.

Gunther started to nod, and then shook his head. 'Oh, no,' he said. 'It's one thing to act as your team scout and pass you information. It's something else entirely to ask me to cross a wizard like that. I won't do it. He'd kill me in a heartbeat.'

'What makes you think we won't?'

Gunther snorted. 'I've seen you play, kid. You don't have that instinct.'

'What about M'Grash?' Dunk asked. The ogre made a good show of cracking his knuckles.

'Don't, kid,' Gunther said, his voice quavering. 'Just don't.'

Dunk frowned. 'I still don't get it though. How did Zauberer know where to find me? And how did he know about the tunnel coming out of the Bad Water?'

'Who knows,' Gunther said with a shrug. 'Wizards work in mysterious ways.'

'You could say the same about Blood Bowl coaches.'

● CHAPTER NINETEEN

WHEN THE HACKERS finally made it back to Bad Bay, tucking into a natural harbour on the Empire's north shore, overlooking the Sea of Claws, they headed straight for the room they shared at the FIB Tavern. Although the place had been named for an obscene variety of Imperial Bastard – a shot at the occasional visitors from Altdorf who sometimes vacationed there – the staff had always treated Dunk like family, and Spinne had come to enjoy the place too. They could have taken a suite in the Hacker Hotel, the poshest place for miles around, but since they spent so little time there Dunk preferred to remain with people he'd come to trust.

The winter snows had come to the place, and the sky had turned its seasonal steel grey. When Dunk and Spinne barged into the tavern, the only thing on his mind was a hot drink and a warm bed that he hoped to not have to get out of for a week. Instead, they found company waiting for them: Dirk and Lästiges.

'You took your damned time getting here,' Dirk said as he gave his brother and then Spinne a hug. 'I thought we might have to send out a search party.'

'We had a bit of a delay near Valhallaholic,' Spinne said. 'Once we got through that, it was smooth sailing.'

'Spending time in a tourist trap while there's a price on your head?' Lästiges said to Dunk. 'That has a certain kind of mad style to it.'

'I thought you debunked that on Cabalvision,' Dunk said.

'To the public, sure, but we all know that what you hear on Cabalvision isn't often even a close cousin to the truth.'

Dunk couldn't help but grin at Dirk as the quartet took a private table in the back corner of the main room, far from anyone else in the place. The people of Bad Bay were used to seeing the Hackers around and had long since become impervious to their fame. They gave the four a wide berth out of respect for them and the kind of money the Hackers brought into town on a regular basis.

'I'm just glad to see you alive and well,' Dunk said to his brother. 'You look good. Not playing Blood Bowl agrees with you.'

'It's just the lack of cuts, bruises, and other injuries,' Dirk said. 'You'd be surprised what that can do for your outlook on life. For the first time in years, I don't hurt every time I move.'

'So,' Spinne said once they'd signalled for a round of beers – Hacker High Life, of course – 'what are you two doing here?'

'It's a crime to want to see my brother?' Dirk asked, taking mock offence.

'Traditionally, it's not been high on your list,' Dunk said with a wry smile.

'Dirk's turned over a new leaf,' Lästiges said. 'Family's important to him these days.'

Dunk frowned as he nodded. 'She told you about Father.'

Dirk nodded too. 'I can't believe the old bastard's still alive. Lästiges told me about your meeting with him in the House of Booze. I've been doing some poking around about him and the Guterfiends since I left the game. It's one hell of a twisted tale.'

'Tell me about it,' said Dunk. As Dirk laughed, Dunk repeated himself. 'No, seriously, tell me about it.'

'All right,' Dirk said, as their drinks arrived. He hoisted his tankard for a toast. 'To the Hoffnung brothers, no matter what their names may be now. May their blood always run thick.'

Dunk grinned. 'You're just trying to put off having to tell me what you know.'

'Not so,' Dirk said. He took a large swing of his beer, leaned forward with his elbow on the table and began to talk in a conspiratorial tone. 'I just want to make sure you're ready to hear it.

'I checked in to what Father told you. It seems like most of it's true.'

'What's not?'

'Well, there seems to be some disagreement among some of the people who were there about how Mother and Kirta died.'

'I always thought the angry mob got them.'

'Sure,' Dirk nodded, 'that theory makes some sense, but I tracked down one person in Altdorf who'd been a part of that mob. He says that Mother and Kirta were already dead when they opened the door.'

Dunk frowned. 'That doesn't make much sense. Who inside the keep would want to kill them? You don't think Father had something to do with it?'

Dirk shrugged. 'It's possible. Maybe he wanted to make a last-second attempt to keep his daemon lords satisfied with his performance. Or maybe he wanted to cheat them of the chance to kill Mother and Kirta and banish their souls to the Realm of Chaos.'

'But he didn't kill me.'

'Maybe he didn't care so much about your soul.'

'It doesn't add up,' Spinne said. 'Why kill them if the mob was about to do that anyhow?'

'Who knows if they would have?' asked Lästiges. 'Maybe they knew something dangerous, something that Dunk wasn't aware of.'

Dunk shook his head. 'I just don't believe it. Father got into trouble with Khorne for refusing him the souls of his children. That included Kirta. If Father loved us enough to squabble with the Blood God over us, I don't think he'd kill any of us the first time things looked bad. You don't defy Khorne without bringing down misery on yourself, after all.' He narrowed his eyes at Dirk. 'What else do you have?'

'I went to Altdorf and spoke with Chiara.'

'The head maid?' Dunk was impressed. Chiara had never cared much for him, but she'd doted on Dirk all his life – up until he'd run away from home. After that point, she'd refused to even speak his name, referring to him as 'that other boy.'

'She wasn't happy to see me at first, but I soon had her eating out of my hand. She didn't want to talk about our family at all when I arrived. 'Better to let the dead stay dead,' she said.

'Eventually she confessed that Father's bargaining with Khorne was an open secret among the keep's senior staff. There's only so much you can do to hide the pentagrams and other things you need to communicate with gods in their far-off realms, after all.

'Some of the staff just ignored it. Lehrer, for instance, never paid it any mind. He only cared that the people who were supposed to dole out his pay actually did. He didn't care how they came up with it in the first place.'

'Ever the practical soul,' Dunk said.

'So what happened?' Spinne asked. Dunk wasn't sure why she felt the need to prod the conversation along, but she clearly wanted to hear everything Dirk had to say – and fast. 'Why did your father turn against Khorne?'

'It seems that his deal with the Blood God stated that Khorne got the souls of his children as well as his own. You can't just sign away someone else's soul though. They have to be given freely. However, Father had promised he could make that happen as part of his own bargain.

'He had until the day one of his children became betrothed.'

Dunk's breath froze in his chest.

'At that point, it seems that the child would be considered to be an adult. After all, if you can pledge yourself forever to a mate, you can certainly do the same for a daemon lord.'

'But Father never mentioned any of this to me,' Dunk said. 'Ever.'

'And what would you have done if he did?' Spinne asked. 'Would you have sold your soul to Khorne to keep your family's fortunes safe?'

Dunk considered this for a moment. 'My first instinct is to say, "No, of course not". However, if it would have saved my mother and sister, I don't know. At the least, I'd have known what was coming our way. I could have helped him fight against it.'

'You'd have been killed as well,' Spinne said, placing her hands on his arm.

'We could have run away and kept everyone safe. Or I could just as easily not got engaged. It was an arranged marriage, for the love of life. Father arranged it himself.'

Dirk frowned. 'Could be he never thought Khorne would try to hold him to the letter of his agreement. Or maybe he thought he could convince Khorne that an alliance with the Brechers would be more valuable than just handing you over. Either way, it seems he meant to protect you from what he was doing.'

Dunk glared at Dirk. 'Did you know what he was doing? I mean, you had all those fights with him, and then you left home without ever telling me why. I thought you two just kept butting heads because you were too alike, but – did you learn something you shouldn't have known?'

'Do you have to ask me that?'

'At this point, I think so. So?'

Dirk screwed up his face for a moment. 'Yes,' he said. 'I stumbled into Father's den once while he was speaking with a daemon.'

'Was it Khorne?' Lästiges asked, suddenly all ears. It seemed Dirk hadn't shared this with anyone else before.

'What did you do?' Dunk asked.

Dirk looked away. 'I – I turned around and left before he could see me. The daemon saw me though. He looked straight at me through the crack in the door that I'd peered through. He caught me with those glowing red eyes, like a fly in amber. For a moment, I couldn't move out of sheer terror that I might send the daemon into a rage. It took everything I had just to shut the door and run away as if I had a horde of daemons on my heels.'

'Did you ever talk with Father about it?'

Dirk shook his head. 'But it came between us anyway. I wanted to demand an explanation from him, but I couldn't conceive of anything he could say that could possibly justify what he was doing – and I hated him for it.

'I finally did say something about it, but not until the night I left the keep for good. I told him not to come after me, or I'd let Mother and the rest of the world know about his sins.'

'He told me he'd had to disown you.'

Dirk smirked. 'It came down to the same thing. Neither of us wanted to have anything to do with each other, and we both got our wish.'

Dunk stared at his younger brother. 'Why didn't you tell me any of this back then?'

'So you could let your guilt over your complicity in Father's plots tear you apart too? No thanks. It was bad enough I had to deal with it. I couldn't drag you into it too.'

Dirk took a long drink of his beer, polishing off the last of what was in his tankard. When he finished, Dunk could still see the hurt hanging in his brother's eyes. Dunk reached across the table and shook Dirk's hand. 'Thanks,' he said. 'I wish you hadn't done it – but thanks.'

'You're welcome,' Dirk said in a dry tone. 'Anyway, according to Chiara, my leaving the keep seemed to be the turning point for Father. I think that's when he realised what he'd be missing if he kept to his deal with Khorne.'

'You think as highly of yourself as ever,' Spinne said.

Dirk ignored her and kept his focus on Dunk. 'That's why when everything went wrong on your wedding day, he was ready for it.'

'Ready?' said Dunk. 'Mother and Kirta were killed, and we had to run for the hills.'

'More ready than he would have been. Honestly, when I heard what had happened that day – weeks after the fact – I was shocked. I thought for sure he'd be better prepared than that. I – well, I thought you were all dead, of course.'

Dirk lowered his head and took a deep breath, then let it out slowly. 'I mourned for you all, but – through that – the one thought I held on to was that if it had happened then at least Father had finally stood up to the daemons and gone back to being his own man.'

Dunk hadn't thought of it that way. He hadn't understood much of what had happened, and he'd blamed himself for it for a long time. He'd thought that he must have done something to bring the wrath of all those daemons down on the night of his engagement party.

Now, although he hated what his father had done, he could respect how he'd refused to sell out his family in the end, no matter what it might cost him. And it had cost him everything he had.

Dunk raised his tankard for a toast, and Dirk joined in. 'Here's to him,' Dunk said. That was enough.

'What about the Guterfiends?' asked Spinne, pulling her hands back to herself. 'Who are they, and how did they end up in your keep?'

'We couldn't find out too much about them,' said Lästiges. 'It seems they were a middle-class family of travelling merchants, supposedly hailing from Nuln, although I couldn't confirm that.

'As for their rise to power, it looks like they were just in the right place at the right time. The day after the Hoffnung keep was nearly burned down, the Guter-fiends were there laying claim to the place. They paid off the right people and secured the deeds to all of the Hoffnung holdings, and they moved in soon after. A few months later, it was like nothing had ever happened, except the name over the gate had changed.

'Of course, they could only purchase these things because everyone in the Empire thought that the Hoff-nungs were all dead, their line extinguished. In such cases, the property goes to the Empire, and the bureaucrats there were only too happy to sell the Hoffnung estate in one large block to the Guterfiends for a monstrous lump sum. If the gold they paid with smelled a bit like brimstone, no one seemed to notice or care.'

'What about Dirk?' Dunk asked. 'He may have changed his last name to Heldmann, but his real identity was an open secret.'

'Father disowned me, remember?' Dirk said. 'It may have come after I'd removed myself from the family, but it meant I had no legal claim to the property as far as Imperial law was concerned.'

'So when I started playing Blood Bowl...'

'The Guterfiends aren't fans of the sport,' Lästiges said, 'but they heard soon enough that you'd come back. They feared you might come forth to claim your inheritance and strip them of everything they'd paid so much for.'

'That's why they put up the money for Zauberer's ludicrous reward,' Spinne said. 'But where would they get that much money?'

'Gold isn't anything to a Lord of Chaos, assuming Khorne's backing the Guterfiends like he did Father,' Dirk said. 'Of course, it's easier to kill those who come to claim the reward than to pay them a million crowns, so I wouldn't count that out either.'

Spinne started to speak, but she choked on her words. Dunk reached out his hands to her, but she pushed them away. 'You need to quit the Hackers,' she said, her voice low and raw. 'You need to leave Blood Bowl behind and get as far away from the Empire as you can.'

Dunk stared at her, trying to understand her distress. 'Hey, now. People try to kill me all the time. It's part of my job.'

'Orcs, elves, ogres, sure,' she said, 'but not people like this. These Guterfiends have real power, and you're a direct threat to that power. They'll do anything they think they must to make sure you're dead.'

Dunk reached out to caress Spinne's flushed cheek, but she pulled away. 'I'll be fine,' he said. 'We can handle this.'

'We can't.' Spinne said. Her chin dropped to her chest. 'I can't.'

Dunk started to ask what she meant, but decided to keep his mouth shut. He knew.

Spinne sat there for a moment, no one saying anything. When she looked back up, her eyes were red and wet. 'We're talking about people who have as much gold as the Emperor. Who have Khorne – the bloody Blood God – backing them.

'We're just people. Sure, we play Blood Bowl in front of hundreds of thousands, and we make a good living at it, but it's just a job. It's not worth death and eternal damnation.'

Dirk stared at Spinne. 'I've known you for years,' he said. 'I've never heard you talk like this. We defy death during every game. What's so different about this?'

Spinne ignored Dirk and Lästiges and gazed into Dunk's eyes instead. 'I never cared much about living before.' Then she frowned and wiped her eyes. 'Besides, we're not talking about my life here. It's Dunk's life and his *soul*. And yours too, damn it. Just because the Empire doesn't see you as an heir to your father – who deserves to burn for all time – doesn't mean Khorne has given up his claim on you.'

Dunk peered into Spinne's eyes. 'I can't walk away from this,' he said.

'Then run!'

'I have to see this through.'

'I know you do,' Spinne said as she stood up to leave, 'but I don't.' She reached down and gave Dunk one last, passionate kiss. Then she walked out the tavern's door.

Just before Spinne shut the door behind her, she turned back and said, 'I can't watch you do this. Tell Pegleg I quit.'

CHAPTER TWENTY

'WELCOME TO SPIKE Stadium here in beautiful down-town Praag for the something-or-other annual Chaos Cup Tournament!' Bob's voice said, ringing out over the snow-covered field. 'We'd tell you how many years it's been, but no one knows. That's Chaos for you!'

'You said it, Bob!' said Jim. 'If you want to see some Chaos around here, look no further than the Hackers. They've lost ten players since their appearance in the Dungeonbowl Tournament – including star standout Spinne Schönheit.'

'Still, they had the guts to accept Da Deff Skwad's invitation to play here in the first round of the Chaos Cup. How many teams would be that stupid? – I mean, desperate? – I mean, brave?'

'Who's the brave team here, Bob? With the edict against harming Hoffnung still hanging over his head, who's going to be crazy enough to try to tackle him?'

The crowd's roar started out low and built to a deafening crescendo as the wall-sized orcs who made up Da Deff Skwad prepared to kick off.

'Well, Jim, I think we're about to find out!'

Dunk rubbed his hands together for warmth, and cursed the cold. To get to Praag from Bad Bay in time for the tournament, the Hackers had been forced to make a mad dash, both by land and by sea. They hadn't had any time to pick up warm underclothes for their armour, and when they got to Praag they found that the other teams had cleaned out what stock there was in the city. The Evil Gits, for instance, had bought ten sets of warm underclothes for each of their players – far more than they needed – and then burned them in the courtyard of their hotel for their first pre-game rally.

'Don't worry about the cold,' Dr. Pill had said to the Hackers in their locker room before the game. 'The cold is your friend. It helps to deaden the pain from all the injuries you're going to sustain. It slows the loss of blood too.'

These thoughts comforted Dunk little as he stamped his feet on the snow-covered Astrogranite, trying to beat some sensation back into his toes. He almost hoped that he would get hurt early in the game. At least then he could spend the rest of the day in the heated confines of the Hackers' locker room.

Dunk looked up into the snow-filled sky, felt the falling flakes melting on his exposed skin, and shivered. Then the ball arced down at him out of the ice-grey, and the game was on.

'Looks like Da Deff Skwad aren't shy at all,' Jim said. 'They kicked the ball straight at Hoffnung!'

'Well,' said Lästiges's voice, 'according to their coach, Yeevil Gutsnatcher, their stated goal is to take out

Hoffnung fast and demoralise the rest of the Hackers. Once they see that Da Deff Skwad's monsters can dismember whoever they like, it may make the surviving Hackers shy of the ball – not to mention their opponents!'

The ball cascaded out of the sky and into Dunk's waiting arms, and he took off running. If a bunch of illiterate orcs wanted to tear him limb from limb, they were going to have to work for it.

Dunk zigged to the left, zagged right, and angled for the sideline. M'Grash and Edgar put up a wall between him and the onrushing orcs, but it wasn't enough. The cold made the treeman sluggish, and a speedy pair of goblins snaked around his trunk to sprint right for the Hackers' thrower.

Dunk cocked back his arm and looked for a catcher downfield. He would have been thrilled to see Spinne waving her arms at him right then, but he hadn't seen her since that night in the FIB Tavern. Most of the rookies had seen her departure as a bad omen, and had left the team soon after.

The new recruits were so green that Edgar took to calling them shoots. Eager as kids on the last day of school, they worked hard, but none of them had the level of skill gained only by being blooded on the Astrogranite. Today, they'd pick up those skills, or die.

But none of them were open.

Then Dunk spotted Cavre breaking free from an orc lineman he'd left clutching a broken nose. Just as the two goblins came at him, Dunk loosed the ball at the blitzer and watched it sail through the air.

He never saw it come down, though, as the goblins hit him hard. They wrapped their arms around his legs and brought him down. One of them sunk his teeth into Dunk's thigh and only became dislodged when Dunk used the other goblin's head to club him away.

Even then, the two creatures kept coming at Dunk. Harming a player who didn't have the ball was a flagrant foul – one that would get the goblins kicked out of the game. But as Pegleg often said, 'It's only a foul if the ref catches it, and if he's been paid to look the other way, that won't happen.'

Still on his back, Dunk couldn't find the leverage he needed to throw the rabid pair of goblins off him. They kept tearing at him with tooth and claw, trying to find the soft parts under his armour or the skin exposed to the bitter-cold air. If the thrower didn't do something to stop them soon, they'd succeed – mortally.

Then the goblins disappeared, and M'Grash stood over Dunk, holding out his hand to help his friend up. 'Dunkel okay?' the ogre asked, concerned. His frown changed to a grin as Dunk leapt to his feet.

'Thanks, big guy,' Dunk said as he scanned the field, searching for where the twinned goblins might have landed. They weren't the kind to give up. He knew they'd be back.

Then black lightning cracked down from the sky, and two smoking holes appeared only yards away. The ashes in them swirled around in the flash-melted snow, forming a boiling, grey paste in which pieces of spiked armour smouldered.

'Wow,' Jim said. 'I haven't seen anything like that since, well, ever!'

'Did you notice how that bolt split into two as it neared the field? You hardly ever see skill like that in a wizard. Most are perfectly happy to use two bolts when one will do, but that's the sign of a true crafts-man, someone who takes real pride in his killings!'

'Let's see that in slow motion!'

Dunk looked up at the Jumboball framed under a gothic arch at the end of the ancient field and watched the two goblins smacking each other a high five before moving to attack him again. As they turned towards him, a single bolt of black energy slipped out of the sky. Then it split into two and arced into the helpless creatures, lancing through them and turning their flesh to ash.

Dunk just stood there on the field, stunned. To think that he had such powerful protection humbled him, and he wondered if Spinne had been right all along. After all, it wouldn't take much for Zauberer to turn such power on him. If that happened, what hope would Dunk have?

Then Dunk noticed a Deff Skwad troll racing down the field at him, dragging a rookie Hacker from each of his legs as it charged for the end zone. Dunk had almost forgotten he was still playing a game. He sprinted towards the troll, angling to get between the creature and the goal line.

When the troll spotted Dunk, it skidded to a halt, sliding several yards on the snow-slick field. The skid sent the troll straight towards Dunk, and the thrower braced himself for the impact from the tackle he planned to throw at the creature. But before he could launch himself at the troll, the creature flipped the ball into the air, straight at Dunk.

Surprised, Dunk did the only thing he could think of. He stood up straight and caught the ball. He snapped his head left and right to see who might be coming at him, but seeing no one he pivoted on one cleated boot and sprinted towards his own end zone.

As Dunk ran down the field, he saw Da Deff Skwad players, not chasing towards him, but scurrying out of his way, terror shining in their eyes. Seconds later, he stood in the end zone, untouched.

'Touchdown Hackers!' Jim announced over the PA system.

Dunk thrust the ball up into the air in triumph, and the crowd went wild. The Hackers fans – a growing contingent at any game these days, all dressed in green and gold jerseys and replicas of Pegleg's perforated, tricorn hat – loved the ease of the score, and even the orc rooters in the crowd had to admire the authority with which Dunk had scored.

'Did you see that?' said Bob. 'Not a finger laid on him. Amazing!'

'Of course no one with any sense of self-preservation wants to get anywhere near him,' said Jim. 'At this point, I don't think his own team-mates would be willing to slap him on the back!'

Dunk just grinned as he trotted back down the field. He might not like having Zauberer's threats hanging over him, but Blood Bowl was an odd game that seemed to change with every match. He'd take touchdowns any way he could get them.

When the Hackers kicked the ball off to Da Deff Skwad, Dunk ran right towards the ball. The orc who had it tossed it away in a hurried pass and then raced off in the other direction. Guillermo intercepted the throw and started to run it back. As he went, Dunk lined up next to him, ready to block anyone who might come their way.

No one did. Every player on Da Deff Skwad kept a respectful distance from Dunk, and Guillermo trotted into the end zone untouched.

'Thanks!' Guillermo said after he tossed the ball into the stands. 'Linemen don't get to score too often.'

'Whatever I can do to help,' Dunk said, holding up his hand for a high five.

Guillermo avoided the extended hand with a sheepish grin. 'Ah!' he said with a grin. 'You almost got me.' With that, he jogged off to get back into his position.

Dunk frowned. Having his foes fear him was wonderful. He wondered if he could get Zauberer to threaten his life on a regular basis. But having his team-mates – his friends – nervous around him made him uncomfortable; he relied on these people to be his support system, and if they couldn't rally around him when he needed them, who could?

Maybe they thought he didn't need them anymore. Maybe they had a point.

In the next play, the Hackers went for a squib kick, knocking the ball only a few yards forward in an effort to get it closer to Dunk's hands. The kicker – another rookie, of course – gave it a bit too much leg, though, and the ball bounced up into the stands.

Losing the ball in the stands was a long-standing tradition in Blood Bowl. The fans loved it, as it made them feel like a bigger part of the game, and the players respected their fervour. More than one over-eager rookie going after the ball had been torn apart by a crazed mob of fans.

In Dunk's first game, for instance, he'd let one of the Reavers knock him into the stands while he celebrated his first touchdown. The fans had body-passed him up to the nosebleed seats and right over the stadium's top edge. Fortunately, a series of awnings had broken his fall, or he might have been killed. Unfortunately, he'd fallen on the stand of a sausage-on-a-stick vendor who'd beat him nine-tenths to death.

When the ball went into the stands, the smart players always waited for it to be kicked back out of the crowd. The game clock kept rolling while the fans had their fun. Blood Bowl had no 'out of bounds' rule. The game only stopped for halftime or for scores.

This time, the fans tossed the ball straight back out at Dunk. As he caught it, they cheered, and he waved back at them with a smile.

Dunk walked all the way down the field and into the end zone. When he got to the goal line, he put the ball down for a moment so he could tie his shoe. One of Da Deff Skwad players reached for it, but the orc snatched his hand back as if burned when Dunk raised his head to glare at him.

When the Hackers set up to kick the ball again, Dunk could sense the crowd starting to get ugly – well, uglier than usual. They'd paid good money to see a brawl of a match, and here they were watching a game in which no player had hit another for minutes. They wanted blood, and someone had denied them that.

'Squib it again,' Pegleg had ordered the kicker. 'We're going to stay on Mr. Hoffnung's free ride for as long as we can.'

The crowd had started booing as soon as the Hackers lined up. That and the rocks, tankards, and other things they started to throw shook up the kicker. He booted the ball just a bit too hard again, and it ended up in the stands.

This time, the crowd refused to give the ball back. Instead, they held onto it, bouncing it back and forth among them like a beach ball.

The crowd roared with delight as they realised that they now controlled the match. They started to chant, and the noise quickly drowned out the general boos. As the volume of the chant grew, Dunk made out the words roaring out over the field.

'Play the game!

'Play the game!

'Play the game!'

'Amazing!' said Jim. 'The fans are refusing to let the game go on until – well, until what?'

'What do you think?' asked Bob. 'There's only one solution to this problem. Hoffnung has to leave the game!'

'Hey, hey, ho, ho, Hoffnung has to go!' the crowd started to chant in agreement.

Dunk flushed red under his helmet. He understood how the fans felt, but he hadn't broken any rules. This was the first time, in fact, that his problems with Zauberer had managed to work out well for him. Still, he trotted over to the Hackers' dugout to talk with Pegleg.

'What in Nuffle's name are you doing, Mr. Hoffnung?' Pegleg asked.

'I just wanted to check in with you, coach,' Dunk said.

'About what?'

Dunk looked up at the crowd. 'The fans, they're pretty mad about all this.'

'Mr. Hoffnung? Do you play for the fans?'

Dunk shook his head.

'I can't hear you.'

'No!' Dunk said.

'Do the fans pay your salary?'

'No.'

'Who does?'

'You do, coach.'

'Right, Mr. Hoffnung. I hired you to win games for me, something I've had cause to regret on some days.' He put his hook on Dunk's shoulder. 'Today is not one of those days.'

'Go home, Hoffnung!

'Go home, Hoffnung!

'Go home, Hoffnung!'

Dunk frowned, upset, but he looked at Pegleg and said, 'Just tell me what you want me to do, coach.'

Pegleg grabbed Dunk by the shoulders, spun him around towards the field, and gave him a push. 'Get in there and win this bloody game!'

As Dunk trotted back into the middle of the field, the crowd's chanting broke down into general boos. He tried to ignore it, but couldn't. The noise made it hard for him to think.

Cavre beckoned Dunk over to where he stood near the sideline in front of the section where the ball bobbed along atop the fans like a bit of flotsam in a rough sea. 'Still in the game?' Cavre asked, leaning in close to Dunk's ear so the thrower could hear him.

Dunk nodded.

'Good,' Cavre pointed up into the stands. 'Now get in there and get that ball.'

Dunk gaped at the team captain, but didn't say a word.

'If a bunch of professional killers like Da Deff Skwad won't come near you, Dunk, I don't think the fans will either.' Cavre patted Dunk on back.

'Are you sure about this?'

'No,' Cavre grinned, 'but there's only one way to find out.'

With a slap on the back of his helmet, Dunk started towards the stands. At first, the crowd kept on jeering the thrower, but when he made it to the restraining wall, the people in the front rows grew silent. He reached up and pulled himself onto the top of the restraining row, and all of the angry fans bundled up in their winter gear turned as white as the snow that had fallen on their furs.

'Boo,' Dunk said.

The fans shoved away from him, parting as if he had the plague or was made of something both unstable and explosive. They pushed each other aside, making room that wasn't there in the sold-out stadium. Then, once he'd passed them, making his way farther up into the stands where the ball was still in play, they closed around him again, forming a bubble of soli-tude around him in a mass of people.

The person who had the ball – a tall skaven with glowing green eyes – held on to it, unwilling to give it up to anyone else. Whether that sprang from arro-gance or paralysing fear, Dunk couldn't tell, but he kept on climbing up towards the creature, taking long steps from one bleacher to another.

When Dunk reached the monstrous rat-man – who'd drooled something chunky onto the ball – the creature put the ball down on the bench beside him and stepped away. Dunk picked up the ball by grab-bing an un-slimed spike, nodded at the creature and said, 'Thanks!'

By the time Dunk made it back down to the Astro-granite, the crowd's booing had grown to a deafening

level. The other Hackers had formed a knot near
where he came out of the stands, and they formed a
cordon that stood ready to escort him to the end zone.
At first, he thought it strange that they offered him
extra protection that he obviously didn't need. Then
he realised that they just wanted to keep close to him
to avoid anyone attacking them instead.

Dunk started towards the end zone, and then
changed his mind and swept out towards the cluster
of Deff Skwad players huddled together by their
dugout. Their coach stood at the edge of their dugout,
snarling and screaming at them. He'd gone so far as to
hurl an axe at them, which had landed in one player's
leg, but they refused to move any closer to Dunk.

When they noticed Dunk coming closer to them,
they panicked. Dunk rushed at them, the other Hackers spreading out behind him like a phalanx of
warriors ready to bring down the ultimate doom. The
troll, who towered over the others, squealed like a little girl and then turned and ran towards Da Deff
Skwad's dugout. The other Deff Skwad players chased
after him as fast as their shorter legs would carry them.

Coach Gutsnatcher railed against his players as they
flooded into his dugout, threatening to disembowel
each and every one of them if they didn't turn and
fight. They ignored him, shoving him aside and tram-
pling each other in a mad race to get down the tunnel
that led to their locker room. After a short commo-
tion, the entire dugout stood empty, except for
Gutsnatcher.

'You!' the black orc said. He towered over Dunk and
reminded him a bit of Skragger – whose head still dangled on the chain around his neck – back when the star
player had been alive. 'You can't do this to my team!'

Dunk grimaced. 'It's not me,' he said, 'blame Zauberer. In the meantime, you might as well chase after your players and see if you can help them find their backbones. This game is over.'

'It's not over until *I* say its over!' Gutsnatcher said.

On the field, a whistle blew. 'That's the game, folks,' Jim said. 'It's over! The Hackers win by forfeit!'

'That's what happens when you can't get any of your players to stay on the field! I haven't seen something like this since the last time the Greenfield Grasshuggers took on the Oldheim Ogres in the opening round of last year's Blood Bowl tournament!'

'Don't knock that game! The Grasshuggers used that to establish themselves as the first halfling team with a survival rate of over fifty percent that year. They've had the best halfling players flocking to their banner because of that – well, that and the pies their manager's mother makes!'

'If this continues, it can only herald the start of a long winning streak for the Hackers,' Bob said. 'The only question is, how long will Hoffnung's luck hold out?'

● CHAPTER TWENTY-ONE

DUNK DIDN'T KNOW how long someone had been pounding on his door. He just wanted them to leave him alone. Pegleg let his players sleep in on game days to get as much rest as they could, and Dunk was determined to take full advantage of that today.

'Go away!' he said, and pulled the extra pillow over his head, sandwiching his ears between the two.

Mornings like this, on the road and alone, he missed Spinne more than ever. He sometimes found it hard to believe that she'd left not only him, but the team as well. As her agent, Slick had tried to talk her out of it, but she'd refused to listen. According to him, she didn't even want Slick to try to sign her with another team.

Dunk knew any team would be lucky to have her. The Reavers, for instance, would probably have knocked themselves out trying to get her back on their team, but she wasn't even willing to talk to them.

'This is your fault, son,' Slick had said, 'and you've cost me a good chunk of my income for it. Fix it.'

'She wanted us both to leave the game. How much of your income would that have cost you? You're just lucky I decided to stick around,' Dunk said, 'and how is this my fault?'

'Take it from me,' said Slick, 'it's always the male's fault. And even if it isn't, the only thing that can fix it is for the male to apologise as if it is.'

Dunk stared at the halfling. 'Is this kind of advice why you're so lucky in love?'

'Don't be unkind, son. It doesn't suit you.'

So when the pounding on the door continued unabated, Dunk buried himself further in his bed. Unless it was Spinne knocking at the door, he didn't want to be bothered, and he knew it wouldn't be her.

'Wake up, lazy bum!' Skragger's head screeched from its spot on the mantel. 'Get damn door!'

Dunk pulled the pillow from under his head and put it on top of the others.

Then the door flew open so hard it slammed into the wall next to it.

Dunk leapt out of bed dressed only in his underwear. His head was still a bit fuzzy with sleep, but he thought he was ready for anything: Slick, Dirk, Pegleg, M'Grash, maybe a horde of angry fans. He held up his fists, ready to fight if he had to.

Two people dressed in black robes emblazoned with the Wolf Sports logo strode into the room, each holding a wand before him: the Game Wizards Blaque and Whyte. The first was a tall, stocky dwarf with soot-black hair and a swarthy, rough-hewn face. The second was a short, thin elf with white-blond hair and a proud, angular face. Despite their differing races, they stood at exactly the same height.

'What?' Dunk asked, confused but still keeping his fists at the ready. 'What do you two want?'

Blaque sniggered. 'That's cute,' he said. 'Can you help out Hoffnung here, Whyte? Perhaps you can enlighten him as to why we're here.'

'Allow me to hazard a guess, Blaque. Could it be because of his performance in his last game, the one against Da Deff Skwad?'

'Yeah, Whyte, I think that could be it. You see, Hoffnung here forced one of the dullest games of Blood Bowl ever upon the public. More specifically, the part of the public paying to see the games in the stadium and over Cabalvision networks like our own sponsors at Wolf Sports.'

The dwarf glared at Dunk. 'You see, that kind of game is a direct threat to the livelihoods of our employers. That means it's a direct threat to our livelihoods as well. We don't take kindly to that, of course, and neither do they.'

'Get out,' Dunk said.

'Are those the kind of manners they teach a man who was once heir to one of the largest fortunes in the Empire? It's a crying shame how politeness seems to have fallen off with the younger generation, isn't it, Whyte?'

'A damned shame,' the elf said. 'Happens all the time in humans, of course. Too short-lived to develop a true appreciation for their elders.'

'Good point, Whyte. Good point.'

Dunk took a step towards the pair of wizards and pointed at the door. 'I said, "Get out."'

Blaque tapped the tip of his wand into his open palm in a way that Dunk could only see as a threat. 'You'd think a player like this – MVP of his last game – would be kinder to GWs like us, given the kind of authority we have over him and his game, wouldn't you?'

Whyte stared at Dunk with ice-white eyes. 'I certainly would.'

Dunk dived for Blaque's wand. The dwarf tried to avoid the thrower, but failed. Dunk snatched one end of the wand and then punched the dwarf in the nose. Dunk felt something crunch, and Blaque let go of the wand.

Dunk spun towards Whyte, the wand in his hand. How could he make something like this work, he wondered? Instead of trying to cast a spell with it, he flipped it in his hand into an overhand grip and stabbed it down at the elf's neck. For some reason, though, his arm caught in mid-stab and refused to come down any farther. Dunk tried to growl in frustration and pull the wand free from where it had become stuck in midair, but he realised that it wasn't the wand that was stuck. It was him.

Blaque stood up from where Dunk's blow had knocked him to the floor. He wiped the blood from his nose and scowled at it. Then he cleaned off his fingers in his mouth. 'Was that really necessary?' he asked.

'I don't see how,' said Whyte.

'I was speaking to Hoffnung,' Blaque snapped. He walked over to the bed and used one of Dunk's pillows to wipe his face clean. The blood stained the pillowcase the red of a bright rose.

'He, um, he can't answer you.'

Blaque shuddered with frustration. 'It was a rhetorical question,' he said. He wiggled his nose. If it was broken, Dunk couldn't tell from its shape. It looked like it had been broken a dozen times before. It seemed to be swelling up around the sides though.

'Your room or mine?' Blaque asked.

'Perhaps the main suite,' said Whyte. 'He might like to watch the game.'

'You're far too kind.'

Blaque grabbed the paralyzed Dunk and threw him over his back. While Dunk stood at least a foot taller than the dwarf, Blaque was built like a boulder, and he hefted the thrower as if he was a small child.

Whyte stood by the door while Blaque toted Dunk out into the hall. As they passed through the doorway, Blaque turned and smacked Dunk's skull against the frame. Then Whyte shut the door behind them, and they strode along the hallway, heading for the back stairs.

'Do you think I should apologise to Hoffnung for that?' Blaque asked as they reached the stairs and headed up to the next floor. 'Tell him I'm sorry for that lump on his noggin?'

'I believe your mother taught you not to lie.'

'Perfectly right.'

As they left the stairwell, Blaque knocked Dunk's head against a doorframe again.

'Clumsy me, eh, Whyte?' Dunk could hear the smile in the dwarf's voice.

'Is that a lie, Blaque?'

'You need to work on your sense of humour, Whyte.'

Whyte strode ahead of Blaque and opened one of the doors that lined the hallway. He held it open for Dunk, as Blaque carried him in, clipping the top of his head once more.

The dwarf chuckled as he brought Dunk over to a couch in the centre of the room and set him down on it. He moved Dunk so he had a good view of a large crystal ball mounted atop an iron stand against one wall.

'He looks a bit awkward like that, doesn't he?' Blaque asked.

Dunk's arms and legs were still bent at the same angles they'd been in when Whyte's spell had frozen him. If not for the pounding pain in his head – which he found far more distracting – he'd have probably thought this uncomfortable.

Whyte waved his wand at Dunk, and the thrower felt his body relax into the couch. Then the two wizards worked together to prop him into a sitting position, slouched low on the couch so they could arrange his head so he could see them instead of the ceiling.

'You bastards,' Dunk said. When he realised he could talk, he tried to stand up again so he could attack the wizards and make them pay for treating him this way. But his body wouldn't work. Everything below his head was dead to him. Not only could he not move it, he couldn't feel it either.

He wondered if this was what it was like to be Skragger.

'Let me go!' Dunk said.

'All in good time,' Blaque said. 'We just wanted to have a private conversation with you without you trying to smash our faces in. I think this fits the bill well, don't you, Whyte?'

'Perfect,' the elf said as he holstered his wand inside his robes.

'What do you want?' Dunk asked. It hadn't occurred to him until now that maybe he should be afraid.

'We just want to talk,' said Blaque, 'about you and your performance in your last game.'

'Wolf Sports named me the MVP.'

Blaque nodded as if that had been an unfortunate mistake. 'True. It was spectacular. We watched the whole thing, didn't we?'

'Every minute,' said Whyte. 'Transfixing.'

'It was an amazing victory,' Blaque said, staring deep into Dunk's eyes. 'But it wasn't great Blood Bowl. Fun to watch the first time, but if that keeps up every game, it'll get – what did you call it, Whyte?'

'Bloody boring.'

'Right. Boring is not good. Boring means people shut down their crystal balls and go do something else instead of watching the game. So, as I said, it's not good for Blood Bowl, for the game itself.'

'Take it up with Zauberer,' Dunk said. 'I can't help it if he wants to kill anyone who tries to harm me.' He glared up at the ceiling and then at Blaque. 'And how come you aren't a pile of ashes yet?'

Blaque smiled. 'That's because your wizard friend and we are on the same side. We both want the same thing, don't we, Whyte?'

'To keep Hoffnung safe.' The elf nodded at Dunk.

Dunk rubbed the sore spots on his head against the pillow the wizards had stuck behind it. 'You're doing a hell of a job of it,' he said.

'You're a Blood Bowl player,' said Blaque. 'A few bruises on that thick skull of yours are nothing. We're out to keep you from dying.'

A chill ran down Dunk's spine, but his paralysed body couldn't shudder along with it. 'How?'

'By keeping you out of the game, of course,' said Blaque. 'Until you work out your issues with Zauberer.'

'I don't have any "issues" with him,' Dunk said. 'He
wants me dead. He just wants to kill me himself. If I
could find him, I'd challenge him right now, but no
one knows where he is.' He narrowed his eyes at
Blaque, and then Whyte. 'Do you?'

Whyte shook his head. Blaque frowned. 'Not yet.
Believe me, we'd like to. Players get threats all the
time, but I've never heard of anyone threatening
everyone else but the player. This Zauberer's a crank,
not much of a wizard as those things go.'

'But he has the Chaos Cup.'

Blaque smiled. 'Exactly. I was worried those knocks
had rattled your brains a bit, but you're as sharp as
ever. He had the Chaos Cup, which somehow gives
him a staggering amount of power. And we can't find
him, either, so we can't stop him, but we can stop
you.'

'Okay,' Dunk said, 'I won't play.'

Blaque snorted. 'Didn't your mother teach you not
to lie, Hoffnung? After how you assaulted me in your
room, we're supposed to take you at your word?

'Whyte, if we let Hoffnung go, what do you suppose
he does first?'

'Runs whining to Pegleg to protect him until the
game starts.'

'And do you suppose he might renege on our deal
and play in the game anyway?'

'Of course, for three reasons: first, Pegleg will force
him to; second, any deal he makes with us at this
point is under duress, and he can't be held to it; and
third, he wants to.'

'Hey!' Dunk said.

'Those all sound like solid reasons to me, Hoffnung.
With any one of those on your side, I don't think we

could trust you. With three, there's no way we can risk it.'

Dunk closed his eyes for a moment, and then opened them again, resigned. 'So what happens now?'

Blaque smirked. 'Now I send Whyte out for a cask of ale and some munchies. We're going to be here for a while.'

'How long?'

Blaque glanced over at the crystal ball in front of Dunk. 'It's still four hours until game time,' he said.

'THIS LATE IN the second half, the Hackers better have a platoon of priests praying for them,' Jim's voice said as the image on the crystal ball showed four of the Champions of Death tackling M'Grash at once.

'That's right,' said Bob. 'Only a miracle could save this game for them now. What a turnaround for the Hackers' fortunes! To go from untouchable to losers in the space of one game!'

'Too true. This loss should knock them right out of tournament, and only yesterday they were the heavy favourites to win! Does anyone else smell the Gobbo's touch here? Gunther?'

'Very funny,' Gunther's voice said. 'Under other circumstances, I might suspect myself too, but I have an airtight alibi. I spent all morning stuck in the stadium with you!'

'I'm convinced!' said Bob, 'but how about all those gamblers who placed money with you on the Hackers? How are they going to take this?'

The image shifted to Gunther, who stood next to Lästiges on the sidelines. 'Fortunately, I'm in the clear there too. With Hoffnung on the team, the Hackers were such clear favourites that I declined to take any bets on the game. See, I lack opportunity *and* motive!'

'True!' said Jim. 'What a difference Hoffnung's absence has made for this team though.'

'Don't forget that Schönheit left just before the tournament too,' said Bob.

'Yes! It's been a hard few weeks for Captain Haken and his merry crew. Can the Hackers do anything to recover from this?'

'Well, Jim,' Lästiges cut in, standing between Gunther and the camra, 'I have an exclusive report that Dirk Heldmann – Dunk Hoffnung's younger brother – has agreed to join the Hackers after the end of the Chaos Cup!'

'Wow!' said Bob. 'That's amazing news. I suspect if Heldmann could have played in this game, the outcome might have been very different.'

'Unfortunately, since he didn't start the tournament with the Hackers, he cannot join in the middle of the competition,' Lästiges said. 'But this should set them up nicely for the Blood Bowl Tournament.'

'Especially if they can manage to turn over whatever rock Hoffnung crawled under!' said Jim.

'Or got stuffed under!' said Bob. 'Even so, if they can recover the body, I'll bet that Coach Tomolandry the Undying would pay a high premium to add Hoffnung to his Champions of Death!'

'I think he coined the necromancer coach motto that says it best, "Blood Bowl players never die. They just end up playing for me!"'

Dunk growled in frustration. 'Can you shut that thing off?'

'Why?' Blaque asked. 'Could it be that you've given up faith in your team? How could that be, Whyte?'

'The Hackers are down by three touchdowns with only a few minutes left, and they've lost four of their players to either lycanthropy or mummy rot.'

'Yeah. A mummy werewolf, or is that a werewolf mummy? Either way, I didn't see that one coming,' Blaque said.

'There was that cloud of blackness that covered the middle of the field just before halftime. That's probably what blocked your view. I think Hugo von Irongrad must have been behind it.'

'The Impaler?' Blaque nodded. 'Seemed like his style. I especially like the way he stuck one of the Hacker linemen on the end of the football after scoring that last touchdown. That's what I call spiking.'

Dunk growled again, louder this time, and Whyte shut off the crystal ball.

'So what happens now?' Dunk asked. 'Are you going to keep me like this forever?'

'I don't see a need for that,' said Blaque. 'Do you, Whyte?'

The elf shook his head. 'The Hackers are out of the tournament. We should be good until the Blood Bowl starts. If Hoffnung decides to play in any games between now and then, Wolf Sports will just refuse to cover them.'

'Why didn't you just do that here?' Dunk asked.

'It's the Chaos Cup,' Blaque said. 'Do you know how much money goes into these tournaments? Do you think those game purses just pop up out of the centre of the field? Most of it comes from Cabalvision fees; money our employer pays to the organisers. They want to recoup some of those costs, and they can't do that if they don't show the games.'

'What happens if I show up for the Blood Bowl?' Dunk asked.

'Gee, you seem a lot smarter than that. Don't you think, Whyte?'

'I do think, but those kinds of questions make me think Hoffnung does not.'

Blaque reached out and patted Dunk on the shoulder. Dunk considered trying to bite the dwarf's hand, but he just wanted to have this all over with. Instead, he glared at the wizards and asked the question that had been burning in his mind for the past six hours.

'How did you find me?'

'See,' Blaque said, waving his finger at Dunk, 'now there's a good question. Can you answer that Whyte?'

'We are the Game Wizards, part of the crew in charge of security for the tournaments. We know every hotel in this city, and we have people happy to talk to us in each of them.'

'And?'

'Everyone in the city wanted us to find Hoffnung and persuade him not to play. For the sake of the game.'

'And?'

'Despite all that, the Hackers' security is surprisingly good. If Zauberer hadn't sent word to us with Hoffnung's location, we might never have found him in time.'

'Zauberer?' Dunk said. 'He told you?'

'Of course,' said Blaque as he got up to leave and motioned for Whyte to follow him. 'He knows your every move. How do you think he keeps track of who's trying to harm you?'

'Where are you going?' Dunk asked. The thought that the two wizards might abandon him, paralysed still, in this room terrified him.

'Our work here is done,' said Blaque. 'The spell on you should wear off in another fifteen minutes or so.'

He rubbed his nose, which showed a good bruise on both sides. 'We'd rather not be here when that happens.'

As the two wizards walked out of the room and locked the door behind them, Dunk hurled curse after curse at them. He wished that he'd studied magic so that he could have put some real hurt behind them. As it was, they were only words.

CHAPTER TWENTY-TWO

'LORD GUTERFIEND WILL see you now, Mr. Hoffnung.'

Dunk stood up and followed Lehrer from the foyer and into the main house. 'Surprised to see me?' he asked as he dogged the older man's footsteps.

'Do you mean me or the Guterfiends?' Lehrer didn't turn back to look at Dunk as he spoke. In fact, he'd studiously avoided meeting Dunk's eyes since the guards at the keep's gate had first presented his old student to him.

'Either. Both.'

'I knew you might try this someday. I had hoped I'd taught you better than to try something like this.'

'Like what? I don't have a weapon on me. I'm here alone.'

'You'd have been an idiot to come any other way.'

'I'll take that as a compliment.' Dunk glanced around the place as they wound through the halls that led to what had been his father's office. Most of the decorations were the same, although the family portraits had been replaced with paintings of a group of people that Dunk presumed were the Guterfiends.

They were a pale, gaunt people with wispy, greyish hair, one and all – even the children – and something burned in their eyes. Whether this was hunger, anger, ambition, something else, or a combination of many things, Dunk could not tell, but the burning looked like it hurt.

'Don't,' said Lehrer. 'You're still an idiot. I tried to warn you away on my own, and you had to come here to push their buttons instead.'

'How do you know what I'm here for?' asked Dunk.

'I know *you*, kid. Better than your parents did, maybe.'

Dunk lunged forward and blocked Lehrer in the back, hurling the older man into a nearby wall. He heard a satisfying thunk as Lehrer's forehead bounced off the plaster.

Lehrer spun around, a knife flashing in his hand. 'Not bad, kid. You surprised me. I didn't think you had it in you.'

'Don't ever compare yourself to my father,' Dunk said. 'He did what he did to help my family. You betrayed him.' He walked forward until the tip of Lehrer's knife pressed against his shirt, right over his heart, daring the man to use the weapon. 'You betrayed us.'

Lehrer pulled his knife away and put it back in its sheath. He glanced up at the sky through a nearby window. 'Still have that wizard looking out for you?'

Dunk flashed a savage grin as Lehrer pushed past him and started down the hall again. They soon reached the main office, and Lehrer stopped and opened the door of polished oak. Dunk preceded him through it and then waited for the man to close the door behind them.

A gaunt man with even less hair than Dunk had seen in the portraits, sat in a tall, leather chair behind the vast mahogany desk that had once belonged to Dunk's father. In Lügner's day, Dunk had almost never seen the top of the desk. Papers, scrolls, and maps of all sorts had always covered it. Today, though, it stood empty but for the hands of the man who sat before him. They were long, thin, and white, with nails that seemed to be sharpened to points.

'Rutger Guterfiend,' Lehrer said, 'may I present Dunk Hoffnung.'

The man behind the desk rose and gave Dunk a stiff bow. 'I wish I could say that this was a pleasure, Mr. Hoffnung.'

Dunk spat on the polished marble floor.

Rutger gasped. 'Is this how you behave as a guest in my house?'

Dunk stepped forward. 'I figure I can spit on anything here I like.'

Rutger narrowed his eyes at Dunk. 'And how do you "figure" that?'

'It's not your house,' Dunk said. 'It's *mine*.'

Rutger's eyes smouldered at Dunk for a moment. Then the man threw back his head and laughed. Dunk had never heard a sound so lacking in humour.

'We will have to agree to disagree,' Rutger said. 'I think you'll find that the Emperor will side with me on this.'

'The Emperor is man enough to admit when he's made a mistake,' Dunk said, 'like selling a man's property out from under him.'

Rutger snorted through his long, bent nose. 'It is not yours, and it never was. It was stripped from your father when his association with daemons was discovered.'

'It should then go to the eldest son,' Dunk said. 'Me. I've never known the Emperor to punish sons for the sins of their fathers.'

'You've been gone a long time.'

'Perhaps the Emperor would be interested to know how you backed Zauberer's pledge of a million crowns for my head. Being accused of dealing with daemons was enough to have my family run out of this place. I suppose it would be enough for you too.'

Rutger screwed his face up at Dunk. 'Your father,' he said softly, 'was a gutless coward. He had the throne itself at his fingertips, and he threw it all away over something as ephemeral and useless as his soul.'

'And those of this family,' Dunk said. 'I suppose you were only too happy to put those of your children on the block.'

Rutger snorted. 'If you knew the things I've done – and had my children do both for and with me – you wouldn't imply such things. You'd shout them from the rooftops. One of my few regrets,' he said with a sneer, 'is that I didn't get to perpetrate some of my favourite atrocities on your family. For cowards, the Hoffnungs are a speedy lot, it seems.'

Dunk launched himself across the desk and wrapped his hands around Rutger's throat. As he did, he felt the tip of Lehrer's knife cut into the back of his neck.

'If you don't put him down in three seconds, I'll cut your throat,' Lehrer said. 'If Zauberer's lightning strikes me now, it'll electrocute you too.'

Dunk felt the pulse of Rutger's pounding heart coursing past the palm of his hand. All it would take would be a firm flick of his wrist and he could snap the man's scrawny neck. Lehrer would kill him and likely be killed in turn. They'd all lie there dead together until someone came to find them, and this would all be over with.

The image had its appeal.

Dunk shoved Rutger away from him. The man staggered back into his chair, clutching his throat and coughing and hacking for breath.

Dunk turned to deal with Lehrer, but the man already stood against the far wall again, his knife in one hand, his arms folded across his chest. Dunk's blood trickled down the knife's blade and into Lehrer's fist.

'State your reason for darkening my door and then be gone!' Rutger said. 'You've wasted enough of my time today.'

Dunk ignored the blood that seeped down his back from the wound on his neck, and walked back around the desk towards the door. The cut was only superficial. He'd sustained worse in almost every kick-off return on a Blood Bowl field.

'Call off Zauberer,' Dunk said.

Rutger stared at Dunk and then laughed. 'If that was in my power, don't you think I'd have done it by now?'

Dunk squinted at the Guterfiend patriarch. 'You sent him after me. You gave him the reward money.'

'I gave him nothing – nothing but a hollow promise, one that he believed and sold to the world with an authority that I could not have mustered myself. Do you really think that if I had a million crowns on hand I would trust them to that madman?'

Dunk grimaced, and then glanced around at the walls and ceiling of the office. 'Look, I don't really care about this place or the fact that you're the filthy, daemon-worshipping bastard who lives in it. Apparently my father was a filthy, daemon-worshipping bastard too, and I've been trying to put all that behind me.

'That's all I want: to put this behind me. Get Zauberer off my back. Rescind that reward. After that, I won't cross the street to piss on this place if it's on fire.'

Rutger leaned forward in his chair. 'If I could somehow manage that, nothing would give me more pleasure, but I'm afraid it's not as easy as calling Zauberer into my office and sacking him. He never was a stable man to begin with. Too many encounters with daemons can drive a man headlong towards madness, and he went charging off that cliff a long time ago.'

'It got worse after he got his hands on the Chaos Cup,' Lehrer said. 'Until then, we had some control over him – especially if we dangled the chance of your death in front of his face. He'd always had this obsession with the Chaos Cup, and we never did know why. The first chance he got to grab it, he did, and we haven't seen him since.'

'The power that the Chaos Cup bestows comes with a price. It saps away the holder's sanity until that price is paid.'

'How long did you hold it for?' asked Dunk. 'Seems like you must have passed it around the table at dinner parties here.'

Rutger ignored him. 'The cup can only be sated with the blood of your worst enemy, the one who has caused you the most pain, the most frustration, the most humiliation.'

A sick feeling grew in Dunk's gut.

Lehrer put a hand on Dunk's shoulder. 'Kid, for Zauberer, I'm afraid that's you.'

Dunk shrugged off his old teacher's hand and stared at Rutger. 'And you don't have any idea where he is?'

'I'd give him up to you if I could. I'd be just as happy to be rid of him as you would, and if the two of you could somehow manage to kill each other… Well, the walls of this keep would ring with a feast the likes of which it has never seen.'

'I wouldn't worry about looking for him, kid,' said Lehrer. 'Now that you're in Altdorf and the Blood Bowl tournament is about to begin, I'd say he'll come looking for you.'

'WHAT A ROUT!' Bob's voice said. 'I haven't seen a massacre this bad since that scheduling accident last year pitted Mother Superior's School for the Blind against the Underworld Creepers!'

'I think those blind kids put up a better fight than the Halfling Titans have against the Hackers today!' said Jim.

'Well, they were the only professional team that would accept a match against the Hackers in the opening round of this year's Blood Bowl tournament. Given the fear that most players have of the Hoffnung Curse, you have to admire the Titans' pluck.'

'They're getting plucked, all right, like chickens! I can almost see the feathers!'

'You're not seeing things, Jim. Those are from the pillows that Berry Butterbeer strapped underneath his armour to help cushion the blows. That last tackle from Edgar knocked the stuffing out of them!'

Dunk loved playing Blood Bowl, but after the walkover that his last game had been – the one against Da Deff Skwad – even he had to admit that this had quickly become dull. The Hackers had scored ten touchdowns in the first half of the game and another in the opening minute of the second.

Over half of the Titans had stayed in the locker room when the ref blew the whistle to start the second half of the game. By Dunk's count, only a few of them had been hurt badly enough to keep them out of the game. Word was that the rest of the slackers had barricaded themselves in their lockers and refused to come out. That left only eight of the little guys to take on the Hackers, who were as fresh as they had been when the game had started.

'Boy, those Titans have taken a real battering today!' said Bob.

'Coincidentally,' said Jim, 'that's just how I like those little morsels: battered and with a side of chips!'

Dunk clapped his hands together as he got ready for the kick-off. At least he'd got to play today, even if it hadn't been much of a game. He wondered how they'd find another team to take them on after this. No truly competitive team would be willing to accept a challenge from them, and this game would likely warn off any of the second or third stringers.

'Enjoying the game?' Dirk asked as he stepped up next to Dunk.

Dunk still couldn't quite wrap his head around seeing his brother in Hacker green and gold. They had been rivals since they were kids. To play on the same team with Dirk just seemed wrong, like it wouldn't be fair to anyone who tried to take them on. This first game against the Titans had driven that home perhaps a bit too hard.

'An auspicious debut for the Brothers Hoffnung,' Dunk said.

'If you consider beating up children before you take their candy auspicious.'

The noise of the crowd rose as Cavre came forward to kick the ball, but the relatively quiet sound spoke volumes about how even the most bloodthirsty fans felt about the game. The ball arced high up into the air and came down like a spear, in a tight, perfect spiral. A Titan stood right underneath it, his arms reaching for it, ready to make a doomed dash towards the end zone.

M'Grash and Edgar raced ahead of Dunk, and he couldn't see what happened next. He expected the halflings to make a valiant attempt to run the ball up the field, just like the last time, and have one of the Hackers pick him up and race into the end zone with him and the ball under his arm – just like last time.

Then the crowd let loose a collective gasp, and everyone on the field stopped – except for Dunk, who still hadn't seen what had happened. Still running, he veered around M'Grash and almost tripped over the halfling on the ground.

Dunk started to reach down for the ball when he realised that it had stabbed right through the halfling, pinning the ball and the Titan to the ground. The gritty little guy lay there trying to pry the ball out of his midsection while his lifeblood spilled out onto the ground around him.

'Oh, no!' Bob's voice said. 'Mofo Waggins, the Titans' long-time captain, looks to be out for the count – and maybe out forever!'

Dunk knelt down next to the Titan and put his hand on the ball to pull it out.

'And where do you think you're going with that?' Waggins asked, clutching the ball to himself. 'That's my damned ball! I earned it with my damned life, and if you try to take it from me I'll ram it down your damned throat and then drag your bloated carcass across the end zone by your damned thumbs!'

Dunk pulled back, surprised by Waggins's vehemence. 'I just meant to–'

'To take the damned ball from me and score another damned touchdown! I know your kind. I've been playing against you for years. I've buried more teammates than you'll ever have.

'You damned biggies always think of us folk as just speed bumps on your way to the end zone. Well it stops here, damn it!'

With a terrible growl, the Titan pried himself up off the Astrogranite, the surface of the fake field crumbling behind him and leaving a large chunk of it still attached to his back where the spiked tip of the ball had gone clean through him. The Hackers huddled around the little guy, admiring his refusal to let his mortal wound bring him low.

'Hey, Mofo,' Dunk said to Waggins, 'do you have any last words? A final request?'

The Titan staggered forward, his face ruddy with pain as he coughed and hacked out his words. Dunk couldn't make them out, so he leaned closer. All the other Hackers gathered around too, straining their ears.

'What was that?' Dunk asked softly.

'Eat. My. Dust.'

'What?' Dunk pulled back, but too late. Before he could shout a warning, a net spun from the finest mithril dropped down over him and the other Hackers. Waggins dodged between M'Grash's legs and out the other side, where he had nothing but daylight between him and the end zone.

'Get him!' Cavre shouted, but he, along with all of the other Hackers, were caught in the fine-spun net.

Dunk snapped his head about and saw the other Titans at the edges of the net, pounding stakes into the ground. Then someone – another Titan, for sure – hit him behind the knees and knocked him off his feet. He tried to stand back up, but found he could only make it to his hands and knees. The netting over the Hackers had been pulled tight enough so that none of them could stand up. Even Edgar and M'Grash had been brought low.

'I can't believe this,' Dunk said. 'That little bastard is about to score a–'

'Touchdown, Titans!' said Jim. 'Mofo Waggins scores!'

'I can't believe it!' Bob said. 'I never thought I'd see such a historic moment as this! Oh, those of you who have seen this will forever have gloating rights over your friends who missed it. To think that we might see the Titans score their first touchdown ever against a human-based team – a *top-ranked* team – like the Hackers. It's just… I'll say it again: unbelievable.'

Dunk buried his face in his hands and wondered if the ref would make the Titans free them before the kick-off. Could he expect to spend the rest of the game in this position, watching the Titans roll in to the end zone for score after score?

Then the net came up off him, the spikes holding its moorings twanging as they popped free from the Astrogranite. Dunk turned on his back to see Edgar standing up, the net now tangled in his upper branches. The treeman leaned over to offer him a branch up.

As Dunk dusted himself off, he glared up into Edgar's glowing green eyes. 'You could have done that any time you liked,' Dunk said.

Edgar smiled down at him. 'Helped you up off the bloody field? Sure thing.'

Dunk narrowed his eyes at the treeman. 'What did they do for you?'

'Well,' Edgar said, 'we tree-men have always had a soft spot in our hardwood for those bloody little buggers, haven't we? It's painful to watch them have such a hard time in a game like this – they're so out-matched – and they had this bloody wonderful plan. I was the only hitch in the bloody thing.'

'So you gave them a pity point?'

Edgar raised his branches towards the mithril net now tangled hopelessly in his upper branches. 'How do you think it looks?' he asked. 'They said I could keep it.'

 **CHAPTER TWENTY-THREE**

'GOOD NEWS, BOYS,' Slick said as he hoisted himself up onto a chair at Dunk and Dirk's table at the Skinned Cat. 'Based on our record, our chances of winning, and our thorough thrashing of the Titans, we've made it to the final round!'

'Who are the poor victims this time? The Association for the Revolution of Self-Euthanasia?' Dirk asked as he sipped at his Bugman's XXXXXX. He'd already had a couple of draughts of the potent ale and was riding high in his cups.

'No. We tried to get them in the opening round, but those ARSEs complained that we wouldn't kill them with the dignity they deserved. The Galadrieth Gladiators apparently dispatched them in an appropriate manner though.'

'So? Don't keep me in suspense.'

'It's the Bright Crusaders!'

'Wait,' Dunk said. 'That isn't some band of flower-tending fairies, is it? This massacring the helpless bit gets old fast.'

'Spoken like someone who's never been helpless,' said Slick as he gratefully accepted a pint of Potter's Field Lager from the waitress, a woman who looked like she might have played on the line for the Vynheim Valkyries several generations back. 'Thanks, love,' he said as he tossed her a stiff tip.

'No, son,' Slick said, smacking his lips once he'd had a sip of his beer. 'The Bright Crusaders is a human team that includes some of the best players in the league.'

'How come I've never heard of them?'

'Because, you pay attention to the part of Bloodcentre where they rattle off the scores for the top-ranked teams; the Bright Crusaders, beloved as they are among the fans, hardly ever win.'

Dunk frowned. 'I don't get it. If they're that good, why don't they win any games?'

Dirk gave Dunk his 'you're *so* naïve' grin and said, 'Because they're too good.'

'How can you be *too* good,' Dunk asked. None of this made sense to him yet.

'Because,' said Slick, 'they don't cheat.'

Dunk's jaw dropped. 'They don't? Not at all? I thought that was part of the game.'

'To those of us who love and play the game well, the way Nuffle meant it, cheating is an integral part of the game. Why, between two well-matched teams, sometimes cheating is the only way for one team to win!'

'Do the Bright Crusaders *ever* win?'

Dirk snickered. 'What team do you think gives teams like the Titans hope?'

'The Bright Crusaders,' Dunk said softly. 'This doesn't sound fair.'

'Who said anything about fair, son?' asked Slick. 'I thought we were talking about Blood Bowl.'

'Maybe I can help you change the subject.'

Dirk turned as white as a sheet, staring at someone over Dunk's shoulder. Slick grabbed his pint and sat it in his lap, ready to dive under the table with it should it be required. Dunk turned around, already aware of who was there.

'Hello, Father,' he said. 'Won't you join us?'

'For Nuffle's sake,' said Dirk, 'they'll let anyone into this place these days.'

Dirk glanced around. All sorts of tough and seedy types filled the tavern. At one table, a pair of minotaurs butted heads over a fresh steak that had just been brought to them, rare. At another, a flock of naked fairies frolicked in a bowl of mead large enough to serve them as a swimming pool. Over by the bar, a man in a cowled robe sold some eager young adventurers a map to a hidden dungeon. Behind the bar, a troll in a bloodstained apron sliced off one of his fingers to pay a bar bet and then watched as a new one grew to replace the old.

'Give me one good reason,' Dirk started, snarling at Lügner as he rose from his seat. Then the drink spinning in his head sat him back down again before he could fall to the floor. 'Aw, never mind.'

Lügner sat down in the empty chair between Dunk and Dirk, opposite Slick, and signalled for another round. 'Make mine a Bloodweiser Dry,' he said.

'Dear Nuffle,' said Slick. 'It's true. Only someone who deals with daemons could drink that pale-spirited excuse for a drink. Have some water instead; at least that's an honest drink.'

'Then it would burn his lips off,' Dirk said.

Lügner put a hand on Dirk's arm. 'It's good to see you too, Dirk.' The younger son stared at the fingers on his forearm, but he left them there.

'All right,' Dunk said. 'I'll ask. What in the Chaos Wastes are you doing here?'

'Excellent question, Dunkel,' Lügner said. 'Direct and to the point.'

When Lügner reached for Dunk's arm, Dunk pulled it away. 'Quit glad-handing me and answer the question.'

Lügner turned serious. 'I came here to see you both and to apologise to you.'

'Apologise?' Dirk said, getting half out of his chair. 'You think that's going to get you off the hook here? We're talking dealing with daemons, getting our mother and sister slaughtered at the hands of an angry mob, and making our lives a living–'

'Sit down,' Dunk said, reaching across the table to push Dirk back into his seat. 'It's bad enough all that's true. Don't announce it to the entire bar. Besides, what harm did any of that do you? You'd already left the keep and declared the rest of us dead to you.' He couldn't keep the bitterness from his voice.

Dirk glared at Dunk, his eyes glassy from the drink, but his fury managing to burn through. 'What harm? I was a kid when I left home – more than a little naïve. I said some stupid things back then, but I never stopped caring about you – any of you.' Dirk looked over at his father, tears brimming in his eyes.

Lügner put an arm around his younger son, and this time Dirk didn't push it away. He just laid his head down on the table and wept into his sleeves. 'I'm sorry, Dirk,' Lügner said. 'I'm so sorry. I'll do anything to help you forgive me.'

'Anything?' asked Dunk.

'Hold on just a minute, Dunkel. I'm having a moment with your brother here. He's finally—'

'Passed out?'

Lügner glared at Dunk, and gave Dirk's shoulders a little shake. 'It's all right, Dirk,' he said. 'It's all right.'

When Dirk didn't respond, Lügner brought his head down nearer to Dirk's face to listen to him breathe. When he didn't hear anything, he grew concerned and put his face closer.

Dirk let loose with a humongous belch right into his father's face. Then he rolled over onto one arm, sprawled across the table and began to snore loudly.

'Damn, damn, and damn,' Lügner said. 'Yet another chance just slipped through my fingers.'

Dunk tried to smother his laughter, but couldn't manage to mask it entirely.

'And you think this is funny?' Lügner asked, turning on Dunk.

'You have to admit,' Slick said, 'the whole burping up your nose thing was fairly hilarious.'

'I didn't think so,' Lügner said, seeming to see the halfling for the first time.

'Well, of course you wouldn't,' said Slick as he started to giggle, a mischievous sparkle in his eye. 'It was your nose. For those of us who maintain noses that have not gathered a snootful of a Bugman's belch, rest assured, it was damned funny.'

Lügner struggled to maintain his anger at Slick, but he failed and broke out into a sheepish smile. 'I suppose it was, wasn't it?'

Dunk took a pull from his bottle of beer, which was filled with Spotted Minotaur. He'd picked up a taste for the mellow brew in Bad Bay, a region filled with the black and white cows that resembled the bull-headed creature on the label. For some reason, it had come to remind him of a place he now thought of as home more than he ever had of Altdorf.

'So,' Lügner said once Dunk put down his bottle, 'you still want to take a shot at me?'

'I've been thinking about it.'

'Here's what I think, Dunkel.' Lügner leaned across the table at Dunk, neatly avoiding the puddle of drool starting to form under Dirk's head. 'If you really wanted to give me the beating I deserve, you'd have done it back in Barak Varr. I know you. You're not violent by nature.'

'Really?' Slick said. 'Have you seen him play?'

Lügner ignored the halfling. 'You might have been able to hurt me in the heat of the moment, but not here, not now after you've had months to think about it. You must know that I never meant you or anyone else in the family any harm.'

'You should try telling that to Mother and Kirta,' Dunk said.

'I would if I could, Dunkel. I miss them as much as anyone. You lost a mother and sister. I lost a wife and daughter, but at least I managed to keep you alive.' He looked down at Dirk and then back at Dunk. 'We still have the three of us. Isn't that worth something?'

Dirk grimaced at his father and shook his head. A part of him still wanted to reach out and twist the man's neck until his head separated from his shoulders. He could hear his mother and sister crying out for retribution, for vengeance, just as he'd heard them every day for nearly four years.

Now he heard other words, too, in his mother's voice: 'He loves you, you know.'

Dunk knew it, but he wasn't sure it mattered one damn bit. Weren't some things unforgivable?

Then he saw Lehrer coming through the bar towards their table.

'What?' Lügner asked, staring at Dunk's face. 'What's the matter?'

Slick started to kick Dirk under the table. When that didn't seem to rouse the man, he moved on to slapping him in the face instead.

'Keep your hands off my son,' Lügner said, blocking the halfling's open hand. 'I won't put up with anyone abusing my–'

Lügner caught sight of Lehrer and his tongue froze. When Lehrer spotted Lügner, he didn't recognise him at first. He smiled at Dunk and Slick as he approached, and then slapped Dirk on the back and grabbed his shoulders as he came up behind him.

Dirk raised his head, his eyes still focused on some place far away. He saw Dunk and Slick and flashed a goofy grin. When his gaze wandered over to his father, he scowled at the man's bloodless face.

'What's wrong with you?' Dirk asked Lügner, his words slurring only a little. He craned his neck around to see who was helping to hold him up, and he saw Lehrer smiling down at him.

Dirk's eyes snapped into focus. He stared at Lehrer for a moment, and then looked back at his father, a wide, mean grin on his face. 'Oh,' Dirk said, 'I'm so glad someone woke me up for this.'

Lehrer shot Dunk a quizzical look. Dunk put a hand towards his father to reintroduce the two old men, but before a single word left his mouth, Lügner stood up and smashed Lehrer in the mouth with a white-knuckled fist.

All conversation in the bar stopped as the patrons turned to see what was going on. No one looked inclined to intervene, instead just craning their necks around towards the two old men. Fights took place in the Skinned Cat all the time. The regulars just wanted a clear view of the action.

'You son of a harpy!' Lügner said as he stood over the fallen Lehrer, pointing down at the man with one hand and waving a fist at him with the other. 'Stand up so I can knock you down again!'

Lehrer glared up at the man as he pushed himself up on to his elbows, and then his eyes went wide and all colour drained from his face. 'Lügner,' he whispered. 'How – how…? You're a ghost.'

Lügner kicked Lehrer in the ribs, and the tavern's patrons cheered. They'd been afraid this bout might end with a single punch, which wouldn't have been nearly enough for them. Most of them hadn't even seen that punch, and they would have hated to miss out on the fight entirely.

'Does that feel like a ghost?' Lügner asked. He followed up the first kick with another to Lehrer's belly. The air rushed out of the servant's lungs. 'Does that?'

Dunk stood and grabbed his father by the arm. 'Stop!' he said. 'You'll kill him.'

'I think that's the point!' the troll behind the bar shouted. The crowd erupted in laughter.

Lehrer pulled himself to his feet and lunged for the door. Before he got two steps, Dirk leapt from his chair and laid a perfect tackle into the man's legs. Slick slid down from his chair and went over to grab Lehrer by the ear and haul him back to the table with Dirk's help.

'See,' Slick said proudly as he and Dirk sat Lehrer down in Slick's chair, 'that boy's a natural at defence.

Even near-dead drunk he can still hit you in the back of the knees. Sheer poetry, I tell you.'

Dunk guided his father to the chair across from Lehrer. Then he and Dirk sat back down in their own seats, between their father and their old teacher. The men flung daggers at each other with their eyes as they smouldered in grim-faced silence.

Most of the other patrons in the tavern went back to conversations or fights-in-the-making of their own. Dirk glared at the others until they looked away.

Slick signalled for another round of drinks. 'We're either going to be here for five seconds or a long while,' he said to Dirk. 'Either way, I'll need a drink.'

'Traitor,' Lügner snarled at Lehrer.

'What did you ever do to deserve my loyalty?' Lehrer asked, his lips curled in an angry sneer as he cradled his injured ribs with his arms.

'Besides pay you handsomely for more than two decades of service?' Lügner rolled his eyes and then snapped them back at Lehrer. 'We were friends once, you and I.'

Lehrer snorted. 'A friend doesn't steal another man's woman.'

Lügner's nostrils flared and his eyes grew so wide that Dunk feared they might pop from his head and roll off the table. 'Steal...? She *chose* me.'

'She was too young.'

'We *all* were. That was thirty years ago.'

Lehrer flinched at that. 'It's still fresh in my mind.'

'I'd be happy to solve that for you – by removing that mind from your skull. You as much as killed her, opening the front gate for that mob.'

'Wait,' Dunk said. 'Are you talking about Mother?'

'Kirta didn't deserve to die like that,' Lügner said, 'and Greta never did you a bit of–'

'She–!' Lehrer bit his tongue and tried again, his voice a harsh whisper this time. 'She was a trollop who played with the hearts of men good and true. She–'

Lehrer doubled up over the table, his eyes watering in pain as he grabbed his privates.

Slick pulled his fist out from under the table and then turned and shrugged at Dirk. 'Does anyone here think he didn't have that coming?'

Dirk gave the halfling a bitter grin, and then grabbed Lehrer by the shoulder and hauled him up so he sat straight again. 'Now,' he said. 'Let's talk about this some more, but this time without the cracks about my mother. Next time, I'll let Dunk have his way with you instead of the halfling.'

Dirk glowered at Lehrer and cracked his knuckles. The barmaid brought their drinks and placed one each in front of everyone but Lehrer.

'What'll you have?' she asked.

'Nothing,' said Lügner. 'He won't be living that long.'

She shrugged and left. As she did, Dirk hoisted his mug by its handle as if to take another drink. Instead, he brought it down on the edge of the table and shattered it, leaving only the handle in his hand, with several jagged shards still sticking out of it.

'That's extra!' the barmaid said. When she saw the look in Dunk's eyes, she gave him a nervous smile. 'I'll put it on your tab.'

Dirk shoved the makeshift weapon into Lehrer's face, stopping bare inches from his eyes. 'Let's try that again.'

Lehrer's shoulders slumped, and the fight left him.

He released a deep sigh. 'I never meant for your mother or sister to get hurt,' he said. 'Your father,' he glared at Lügner, 'he crossed the wrong people. They decided to destroy him that night.'

'But you helped them?' Dunk asked. He still found this hard to believe, although glancing around the table it seemed like he was the only one. 'Why?'

Lehrer squirmed in his chair.

Dirk jabbed the broken mug into the man's cheek. 'Why?'

Lehrer flinched away, but not fast enough. Blood trickled from a small cut on his face. 'It's his fault. He betrayed Khorne. You can't just do that and hope he won't notice. If I hadn't stayed loyal to the Blood God, I would have shared his fate.'

'So you chose Chaos over your old friend,' Slick said to Lehrer. Then to Lügner, he said, 'and you trusted him not to. I don't know which one of you is a poorer judge of character.'

Dunk put his head in his hands. 'What are we going to do with you?' he asked Lehrer.

'Kill him,' said Dirk.

Dunk ignored him. 'We can't let him report back to the Guterfiends. If they find out that Father's alive... Well, you saw how far they'd go to get me, and I'm just the heir to their troubles.'

'Kill him,' said Lügner.

'Just like that?' Dunk asked. 'In cold blood?'

'My blood is boiling,' Lügner said.

'We can't,' Dunk said. 'This is Altdorf, not the wild. They have laws against that sort of thing here.'

'We kill people every game,' Dirk said.

'That's different,' said Dunk. 'Just by getting on the field, they're asking for it. That act alone is considered an assault. Any killings during the game are considered self-defence – at least in places where they care about such things.'

Dirk pulled the broken mug from Lehrer's face. The old teacher looked at him askance.

'Let him run then,' said Dirk. 'We can catch him in hot pursuit.'

Lügner stood up and placed his hands on the table. Then he leaned over and put his chin in Lehrer's face. 'Go ahead,' Lügner said. 'Give me your best shot.'

Lehrer glared up into his old employer's eyes and shook his head. He refused to say a word.

'Come on,' Lügner said. 'You know you want to.' He reached out and took one of Lehrer's hands and placed it around his throat.

'Do it,' Lügner said. 'Kill me.'

Lehrer smirked through trembling lips. 'Your sons will drop me before your body hits the table.'

Lügner nodded. 'And then we'll both be dead, and this entire horrid affair will be over. Don't tell me that holds no appeal for you.'

Lehrer squeezed Lügner's throat with a touch that surprised Dunk with its tenderness. Then the old teacher's hand fell to the table with a thud. 'You may hate yourself. You may think you deserve to die,' Lehrer said. 'But I don't feel that way about myself.'

'You're in the minority then,' Dunk said as he stood and hauled Lehrer up by his elbow.

'Where do you think you're going with him?' Lügner asked, standing up behind the table. Dirk shoved himself away from the table and tried to stand, but fell back in his chair. Slick followed after Dunk.

'Somewhere no one will find him,' Dunk said, 'until I want them to.'

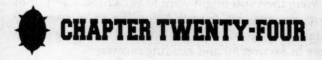

CHAPTER TWENTY-FOUR

'THE BRIGHT CRUSADERS score!' Bob's voice said. 'That puts them in the lead, one to nothing!'

Dunk swore. He hadn't brought his best game to the field today. The meeting between his father and Lehrer had him preoccupied, and he just couldn't seem to keep his mind on the action.

'That so-called Hoffnung Curse hasn't been much help to the Hackers today,' said Jim. 'I don't think Hoffnung has even touched the ball yet!'

'That's one way to avoid a mad sorcerer's wrath!' said Jim. 'Personally, I've found that burying yourself underground for a century or so works fine. You'd be surprised how short the memories of mortals can be.'

'I prefer tearing them limb from limb, myself,' said Jim. 'But as you know, that's just not always possible. Every news organisation in the Empire has been scouring the land, hunting for Zauberer, hoping to

score an exclusive interview with the man, and so far
we've all turned up zilch. It's not hard to see why
Hoffnung might just have to live with the curse – at
least until the wizard comes for him!'

'Tell me, Jim. Do you think it's better to confront
your fate as soon as possible, or to avoid it for as long
as you can?'

Jim laughed. 'I've always thought it best to put off
for now what you can face another day!'

'Well, then you might want to get a head start out of
here, my massive friend. According to our security
camras, I see your mistress's husband stomping up the
aisle in Section 30 and heading our way!'

Dunk trotted back to the Hackers' side of the field to
wait for the kick-off. He stared down the field at the
Bright Crusaders, resplendent in the dazzling sun; the
light reflecting off their suits of armour, which had
been polished to a mirror finish.

At first, Dunk had wondered how the Crusaders
managed to keep their armour so clean given how
hard a game Blood Bowl could be. Then he noticed
that the team's coach – Father E. A. 'the Padre' Matten
– kept substituting the dirty players off the field so
that a team of cheerleaders dressed in black and white
habits could restore the soiled players' shine.

The first time the Crusaders had taken the kick-off,
they had squibbed it into the stands. The fans had
squirted it back out at the Crusaders, and they had driven it all the way down the field and into the end
zone. Every time Dunk had come near the ball, the
Crusader holding it had thrown it away. He hadn't
been able to get within ten yards of the spiked pigskin.

This time, he refused to let the same thing happen
again. When the Crusaders lined up to kick the ball,

he raced forward instead of hanging back. The kicker squibbed it again, but when the ball popped back out of the stands and into the field, Dunk was right there, ready and waiting for it. He leapt up and snagged the ball from the air.

'Hoffnung has the ball!' Bob's voice said. 'Now we'll see how well the Padre's plan stacks up!'

Dunk tucked the ball under his arm and ran for the end zone. He expected the Crusaders to dive out of his way. They might have wanted to play by the rules, but that didn't mean they wanted to be turned to ash on the spot.

When the first Crusader came at Dunk, he almost stopped and let himself get hit. He thought, on first blush, that the Crusader was a man, but the armour had large bumps on the chest, presumably to protect large breasts, and the back fringe of a wimple hung out from under the back of its helmet. The fuzzy moustache on the lady's lip, and the shoulders that many a lineman would kill to have, threw him off.

'Leave it to Sister Mary Mister to break the tacit injunction against harming Hoffnung!' said Lästiges's voice. 'I've been following her career for years, Bob, and she's never been one to let something like a dae-monic curse stand in her righteous way.'

'Repent, sinner!' Sister Mister bellowed as she thundered after Dunk. Her stomping treads shook the Astrogranite beneath her so hard that Dunk wondered if she were somehow half-ogre – or maybe full. 'Hold still, and I will send you directly to Nuffle for judgement!'

Dunk dodged left, and the large lady lurched right past him. Then he saw an open hole and cut right to surge down the field. M'Grash got in front of him to provide blocking and smashed down two linemen who came his way. Unfortunately, those Crusaders tripped M'Grash up as they went down, and Dunk found himself without protection again.

'It looks like only Brother Mother stands between Hoffnung and the goal line now!' said Bob. 'Will Mother martyr himself for the cause?'

To Dunk's mind, there was no question Mother would try to tackle him. Instead, he needed to smack this Crusader down hard and fast. Perhaps then Zauberer wouldn't need to zap him to smithereens.

Brother Mother was the skinniest Blood Bowl player Dunk had ever seen, a young man with a figure that could only be described as girlish. As they grew closer, Dunk marvelled at the man's lips and eyes, which looked as if they'd been abused. The eyes were sunken into dark, shaded holes, and the lips shone redder than fresh blood. It took Dunk a moment to realise that Mother wasn't hurt. The man wore make-up – and lots of it.

Mother stretched his arms wide, and Dunk wondered if he should stiff-arm the weakling out of the way or just spin out of his grasp. Then an image of the last person who'd tackled him filled his mind, and he found that he just couldn't do it. He couldn't let Mother even touch him.

Dunk jinked to the right and then ran to the left, hoping to find daylight. Mother followed his every move, not fooled for even an instant. Seeing that he couldn't get past the Crusader, Dunk looked for an open Hacker, but he couldn't see a single one.

So Dunk did the only thing he could think of. He turned and ran away from the end zone.

'Has Hoffnung turned coward?' Bob's voice asked. 'Are the Hackers' new colours yellow and yellow?'

'I don't think so, Bob,' said Lästiges's voice. 'In his own twisted way, I think Hoffnung is trying to save the Crusaders' lives.'

'On a Blood Bowl field?' Bob said. 'Now *that's* blasphemy!'

Dunk shut all the chatter out and looked for some way, any way, to get rid of the ball. That's when Brother Mother hit him.

The tackle caught Dunk just behind the knees and brought him down clean. As he bounced off the fake stone surface, the ball bounced free from his hands. Not caring what happened to it next, Dunk reached back and grabbed Mother by the helmet.

'You moron!' Dunk said. 'You just killed yourself!'

'Yea, though I sprint through the Darkside Cowboys' Stadium of Darkness, I will fear no evil,' Mother said. 'Nuffle does windsprints by my side. Where there is only one set of footprints on the Astrogranite, that's where he carried me!'

'He should have carried you to the nearest asylum and left you there!'

Mother tried to pull himself from Dunk's grasp, but the thrower kept his death grip on the Crusader's faceguard. Mother kept pushing away anyhow, somehow hoping that the far stronger Hackers would give up before he did.

'Don't you get it?' Dunk asked. 'As soon as you walk away from me, you're dead.'

Mother gave Dunk a serene smile with his ruby-painted lips. 'My faith is my shield and my armour.'

'All the other victims wore armour too,' Dunk said. 'None of them made it to the sidelines.'

'You are faithless,' Mother said. 'Those of us who have accepted Nuffle into our lives as our own personal saviours do not fear death. When this game is over, can I discuss the emptiness in your soul with you? Perhaps I can leave you with some literature?'

'Crusaders score!' Bob's voice said.

'You see,' Mother said. 'It's not too late to join the winning team – at least in spirit.'

'Would you just listen to me?' Dunk asked. 'Pull your head out of your damned sacred rulebook for one minute so I can get through to you?'

'Pull my head out?' Mother said with a satisfied grin. 'That's an excellent idea.'

Before Dunk realised what Mother meant, the Crusader reached up and undid the strap on his helmet. His head slipped free from Dunk's grasp on his faceguard, and the rest of his body followed along right after it.

'No!' Dunk shouted as he fell backward, Mother's helmet still in his hands. 'Come back!'

'There's no reason to go back,' Mother said as he started towards his dugout. 'With Nuffle on your side, you're always on your–'

The crack from a bolt of ebony lightning drowned out Brother Mother's last words.

Tears of utter frustration rolled down Dunk's cheeks as the wind blew Mother's ashes back at him. The Crusader's blackened armour hung there in the air for a moment, held together by little more than memories. Then it came crashing down into a clanging heap.

'Dunkel okay?' M'Grash asked as he trotted up behind Dunk, who sat there on the Astrogranite, hugging his legs to his chest.

Dunk shook his head. 'No, big guy,' he said. 'I'm anything but all right.'

'Okay, Dunkel,' the ogre said. He reached down and scooped Dunk up in his arms like an infant. Looking down at the man cradled against his chest, M'Grash said, 'Dr. Pill make everything all right.'

'I DON'T SEE anything wrong with you,' said Dr. Pill.

'You are the worst quack excuse for a physician I've ever seen,' said Dunk, clutching his back. It felt fine, but he wasn't about to let the apothecary know that.

The gaunt elf with the eye patch scowled at Dunk. 'If I tell Pegleg that you're faking an injury–'

'Then I will tear out your spleen and stuff it down your throat with my bare hands,' Dunk said. 'If I can somehow manage to work my way through the pain.'

Something banged away in a large locker in the corner, one of those custom-made for gigantic players like Edgar or M'Grash. Dunk ignored it.

'What in Nuffle's re-broadcast warning is making that noise?' Dr. Pill asked, scratching his chin.

'It's nothing,' Dunk said. 'Leave it alone.'

'I think it's coming from the ogre's locker.' The apothecary crept towards the locker's red, steel door as if he could sneak up on it.

'He likes to leave livestock in there for an after-game snack.'

Dr. Pill turned to sneer at Dunk in disgust.

'Hey,' Dunk said. 'He gets hungry after a big game. Are you going to be the one to tell him to wait until dinner?'

'Pegleg isn't that much of a savage.'

'He doesn't eat any of it.' Dunk said.

Dr. Pill turned back towards the banging locker. The noises coming from inside it grew louder, faster and more insistent. A sign on the front of it read 'KEYP OWT – DAYNJER!' in M'Grash's crude scrawl.

'However,' Dunk said, 'Pegleg does believe in giving the food a fighting chance. He picks out the meanest, nastiest critters he can to give M'Grash a challenge. Sometimes the vicious little buggers manage to get out and run wild through the place. A few of them even get away.

'Some aren't so easy to deal with though. There was that massive, rabid badger Pegleg stuck in there one time. That bugger killed two rookies and maimed a third before M'Grash finally crushed its skull.'

Dr. Pill looked at Dunk as he reached the locker and cocked his ear so that it almost rested against the metal. 'You're lying,' he said.

'Okay,' Dunk said, 'you got me.'

Dr. Pill hesitated for a moment, his hand on the locker's handle.

'It was a wolverine.'

Dr. Pill scowled. Before Dunk could stop him, he yanked open the locker in one swift move.

For a moment, nothing happened, and Dunk breathed a sigh of relief. Then a bound and gagged Lehrer toppled out of the locker and landed on his face. The prisoner looked up at Dunk and Dr. Pill and let loose a muffled scream.

'Oh, dear,' said Dr. Pill. 'This won't do at all.'

'Hold on a moment,' said Dunk. 'I can explain.'

'I certainly hope so. You and your accomplices have done an awful job of this.' The apothecary stared down at Lehrer with a critical eye.

'That's true. I – What do you mean?' Dunk was confused.

Dr. Pill pointed down at the ropes holding Lehrer's limbs. 'These are tied all wrong. In another hour or so, he'd have been able to wriggle out of them all by himself.'

Dunk blinked. 'Ah,' he said. It was the most intelligent thing he could think of at the moment.

Dr. Pill went over to a black leather case on a nearby bench and unfolded it. His back to Dunk, he rummaged around inside it. First, he snapped on a pair of rubber gloves. Then he grabbed and shook something hard.

'Ropes are such crude devices anyhow,' he said. 'I prefer a proper hog-tying for restraints myself, when pressed to rely on such measures. However...'

The apothecary turned around and displayed a large syringe in his hands. He watched the sharpened tip of its wide-bore needle as he pushed a drop of clear, but pungent fluid through it. 'There are such excellent chemical alternatives that one need hardly ever bother.'

Dr. Pill walked over to Lehrer. Tears ran down the man's face as he whimpered into his gag. 'Hold still,' the apothecary said. 'I'm afraid this is going to hurt a great deal.'

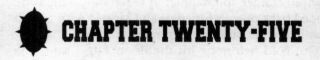

CHAPTER TWENTY-FIVE

'HERE'S TO THE Hackers!' Slick said, raising his tankard in a toast. The others gathered around the table in the Skinned Cat cheered in accord.

'And here's to making the final match of the Blood Bowl Tournament!' said Guillermo. More cheers followed.

'Ah, it's not that big a deal,' Dirk said with a grin.

Dunk put one arm around his brother's neck and ruffled his hair with the other. 'Just because the Reavers do it every year doesn't mean it's not great for us. And you're a *Hacker* now!'

'Go Hackers!' M'Grash crowed. The ogre leaned back and downed the rest of the keg of Killer Genuine Draft he'd been powering through. By Dunk's count, this was the ogre's third.

M'Grash leaned back further and used the heel of his hand to pound the last drops of ale out of the keg. Then he set it back down on his lap and grinned from ear to ear. Had Dunk not been the best of friends with the ogre, he might have fled from the table right then. As it was, a few of the others clutched the backs of their chairs as if they might toss furniture behind them in an attempt to trip up the ogre as they fled.

Then M'Grash unleashed a monstrous belch that shook the tavern's walls. After that, his grin was, if anything larger and happier. It faded only a bit as he tipped back over in his chair and landed with a thud that made the building tremble.

'Out cold before he hit the floor,' Edgar said. The treeman stood next to the table instead of sitting, as his body would not bend in the middle. Fortunately, the main room of the Skinned Cat was tall enough to accommodate him, although his upper branches brushed the ceiling. 'Bloody ogres can't handle their bloody drink for bloody anything.'

'It's just good that you're here, old friend,' Slick said to Edgar.

'Of course it is.' The treeman scowled down at halfling. 'I'm the only one of this bloody pack of tree-swinging mammals that has a bloody prayer of hauling his gargantuan carcass home, ain't I? What in hell did you lot bloody well do before I came along?'

'Mostly we left him where he fell,' said Dunk.

'It is not like we had much choice in the matter,' Guillermo said.

'Oh, who'd dare to not "let a drunk ogre lie"?' asked Slick.

'Do we know who we're playing yet?' Dirk asked. Sometimes Dunk's younger brother surprised him with how seriously he took his job – and the game.

'Right here, Mr. Heldmann,' Pegleg said as he limped into the room, Cavre at his side. He waved a scroll in his good hand and gave it to his team captain to read.

Cavre unfurled the scroll and read its contents silently. Then he spoke. 'The other semi-final game was between the Chaos All-Stars and the Badlands Buccaneers.'

'We know all that. What happened to the broadcast?' Dirk asked. 'We were watching it here on the giant crystal ball when it went black.'

Pegleg nodded. 'Since it was a game that Mr. Hoffnung wasn't involved in, Mr. Zauberer took the chance to destroy every camra in the place.'

'Nuffle's masticated mouth guard,' Slick said. 'Why would he do that?'

'Apparently it was an attempt to get each and every one of the game's sponsors up in arms,' Pegleg said. 'The tournament organisers were nearly crucified in front of the stadium on those nice new lights the Guterfiend family paid to have installed after the post-game riots last year. They made scores of other improvements to the place as well.'

'The Guterfiends?' Dirk and Dunk said together.

Pegleg nodded. 'I know about the troubles your family's had with them, but they did something good with their money there at least.'

Dunk shook his head. 'I don't believe it for a second. The lamps are probably all filled with explosives.'

'Or death rays,' Dirk said, nodding his head.

'Or a bunch of bloody fairies trapped in those bloody, little glass balls and forever forced to shed bloody light on their evil masters' command.'

Everyone craned their necks to stare up at Edgar.

'What?' he said. 'Now don't tell me you lot are a bunch of bloody fairy lovers.'

The others all decided to ignore him.

'So that's all that happened?' asked Dunk. 'Just a bunch of ruined camras?'

'To you, Dunk, those are "just a bunch of ruined camras,"' said Cavre. 'To Ruprect Murdark, that's the loss of hundreds of thousands of crowns in advertising dollars.'

'I have heard that the commercials during the final match can go for a million crowns a minute,' said Guillermo.

'Too true, Mr. Reyes,' said Pegleg. 'Now stretch your imagination if you will and think about what would happen to Wolf Sports if Murdark had to refund all that money because no one ever saw the commercials.'

Everyone fell silent for a moment. Then Edgar started to giggle, a low and hollow sound that tickled the ears. Slick joined in soon after, and then Dirk, Dunk, Guillermo, and even Cavre. The laughter grew from snickers, through guffaws, to full-blown belly laughs. In the end, even Pegleg had cracked a wry smile.

'We don't need to worry about that, though,' Cavre said. 'We just need to play the best we can, no matter who is watching.'

'Well said, Mr. Cavre,' said Pegleg. 'However, I have it on good authority that Murdark is paying a fortune to have every camra in the Emperors Stadium replaced and reinforced so that no magic – however strong – can damage them or interrupt their signals.'

Slick let out a low whistle. 'That'll cost him a small fortune.'

'He'll make it up with the ads, Mr. Fullbelly. Word is that he's getting premium rates for this game. After all, it's a grudge match.'

Dunk frowned. 'A grudge match?' He glanced at the other players, each of whom seemed just as mystified as he – except Cavre, of course, who always seemed to know what the coach was talking about. 'I don't think any of us like the All-Stars, coach, but they're no worse than any other rival team.'

'Oh, really, Mr. Hoffnung?' Pegleg said. 'I would have thought you'd have been able to understand the spin on this game better than anyone.'

Dunk narrowed his eyes at the coach. 'Why?'

'Who is the most renowned team wizard the All-Stars have ever fielded?'

'Didn't Olsen Merlin help them out for a year about fifty seasons back?' asked Slick.

Pegleg moved to backhand the halfling with his hook, but Slick slinked behind Edgar's trunk before the ex-pirate could land the blow. 'You always remind me of a saying, Mr. Fullbelly,' Pegleg growled.

'Which is?'

'Agents aren't necessary, just evil.'

Slick turned red, but managed to say, 'So, Zauberer's back working for the All-Stars, is he?'

Dunk gasped. He'd wondered when the wizard might finally show his hand. Now, during the championship game of the Blood Bowl Tournament, seemed like as good a time as any. Dunk wondered how he could ever defeat Zauberer now that the man had his wormy hands on the Chaos Cup. Any wizard who could incinerate anyone who tried to hurt Dunk could flash-fry him in an instant too. Still, there had to be a way. At least during the game, he might finally have a chance to try to take the wizard out and put an end to the hated Hoffnung Curse.

The nasty snarl on Pegleg's face faded to a simple frown. 'That he is, Mr. Fullbelly.' He gave Dunk a sympathetic look. 'We'll do everything in our power – such as it is – to help you take him out. We can assume that his edict against killing you is only in effect until the game begins. After that, all bets are off.'

'Now who would be so heartless as to say something like that?' said Gunther the Gobbo as he shouldered his way close to the table.

Dunk's eyes grew wide. 'What are you doing here?' he asked as he leaned over and whispered at the bookie. 'I thought we agreed you couldn't be seen with us.'

'Leave now?' Gunther said a bit too loudly. 'But you guys are my favourite team – unless you lose, of course. The odds are already three to one against you.'

'Against us?' Dirk asked. Dunk felt ill.

'Of course. The All-Stars were the heavy favourites beforehand, but when someone leaked their roster for the championship game…' Gunther winked at Dunk. 'Well, now everyone knows you're going to get your ashes handed to you – or to your next of kin, at least!'

'Has he…?' Dunk asked Pegleg.

'He's been quite helpful so far, Mr. Hoffnung.'

'It doesn't hurt that I've made a mint so far at it.'

'How's that?' asked Dirk, ever suspicious of the Gobbo.

'If there's one thing I've learned in this business,' said Gunther, 'it's that you never bet against your team. I've been betting with the Hackers since just after the Dungeonbowl, and it's been easy money.' The Gobbo leered. 'Of course, starting a rumour that Zauberer's been known to miss his targets with those lightning bolts from time to time helped out with putting the odds more in my favour too.' As an aside, he whispered to Dunk. 'Not true. Don't believe it.'

'Should you really be seen in our presence?' Guillermo asked. 'At least out in such a public place?'

Gunther snorted, and then replied with a fake grin pasted on his face. 'Kid, I'm the most notorious odds maker in town. The two teams that'll compete in the Blood Bowl championship game just got announced. If I don't track you guys down and chat with you, *that's* going to look suspicious. So just shut your trap and try to tolerate my company for a few more minutes so we can make this look good.'

'Have you been doing anything to help, other than just lining your pockets?' Dunk asked.

Gunther shook a finger at Dunk. 'See, now that's the kind of question I can respect: full of the suspicion and the derision I've earned. Well done, kid!'

'Have you?'

'It's just that kind of doggedness that's going to lead the Hackers to victory in the championship game. Go Hackers!'

Gunther raised his arm to lead a cheer in which no one else joined. 'Give me an H!'

Silence.

'Go to *hell*,' said Guillermo.

'There's an H! Give me an A!'

Dunk leaned towards the bookie. '*Answer* my question.'

'Hey,' said Gunther. 'I got you that match against the Titans, didn't I?'

The eyes of the Hackers turned towards Pegleg.

'Aye,' the coach said, 'that he did.'

'And how about how I brought Dunk's old flame here tonight, to help him celebrate?'

Dunk's heart went cold. 'You did what?'

'Well,' Gunther said, wincing. 'She's been after me for a while to tell her where you are, but I wouldn't say a word! I absolutely refused to let her know where the Hackers are staying during the tournament. She gave me a few notes to pass on to you, but I refused those too. I didn't want her to bother you. I was protecting you.'

'But now that Dunk's in the championship, you think it's all right to shake him up a bit?' asked Dirk. He'd ended up on the other side of Gunther from Dunk, and the bookie now stood sandwiched between them.

'Well,' Gunther said, 'with Schönheit gone and Zauberer on the loose still, I... Well, I figured...'

'If I'm facing certain death I might as well get this out of the way?' Dunk said.

Gunther grimaced. 'I'd have put it better than that, of course, given a bit more time, but sure, that's the gist of it. Thanks, kid!'

Dunk glanced around the room, peering over the shoulders of his team-mates. 'Where is she?' he asked.

Gunther's face lit up. 'I figured you two lovebirds would want a little privacy, so I arranged for a sheltered booth in the third room back.'

'I left her, Gunther.'

'Is this Helgreta?' Dirk asked. He glared at the Gobbo. 'This is Helgreta Brecher, isn't it?'

Gunther nodded as if his neck had been replaced with a loose spring.

'I thought she tossed you out on your chin,' Dirk said to Dunk.

'That's the official story,' Dunk said. 'That's what the Brechers told everyone. I never saw her after that... incident during our engagement party.'

'So you call fleeing town with an angry mob of daemon-hunters on your tail "leaving her"?'

'She wrote me letters,' Dunk said. 'They found me somehow. She said she wanted me back. No matter what people said about Father, she knew I was innocent. She still wanted to go through with the marriage.'

'Daemons, weddings,' Slick said. 'All the reasons I left my little halfling home in the Moot far behind.'

'And still she wishes to speak with you?' Guillermo asked, astonished.

'Amazes me too,' said Gunther. 'I don't know what you've got in that codpiece, kid, but I'd be careful with it if it inspires that kind of loyalty.'

Dunk fought the urge to smack Gunther across the room. 'Where did you say she is?'

'Back booth, third room back.'

Dunk stood up and noticed that everyone at the table was watching him. 'If I'm not back in five minutes, send a search party for me.'

'If you're not dead within the first minute, you may need longer than that,' said Cavre.

Dunk nodded. 'Make it twenty.'

With that, Dunk turned and walked towards the open doorway in the back of the Skinned Cat's main room. He scooted through the room beyond, in which a number of Bright Crusaders players nursed their wounds and their pride. Dunk didn't know if any of them recognised him – he saw Sister Mister weeping into a trough of ale that M'Grash would have appreciated – but he took comfort in the fact that he could rely on them to stick to the rules and leave him alone off the field.

The second room back felt smaller than the first because of the draperies that could be pulled across the faces of each booth. About half of these had been drawn, and in the others the occupants shot Dunk dirty looks for glancing in their direction. Six people – a goblin, an elf, three orcs, and a dwarf – sat around a table in the middle of the room, playing a low-stakes hand of pogre. Dunk had tried to play the game with M'Grash a few times, but they stopped when Dunk realised the game was designed to start fights.

The door to the third room back stood closed. It took Dunk a while to find it. At first, he thought it was an exit to the place's outdoor privy. Seeing no other option, though, he tried it. The latch rose easily, and the door pushed inward on oiled hinges.

'Hello, Dunkel,' a voice said. 'I've been waiting for you for a long time.'

CHAPTER TWENTY-SIX

DUNK SLIPPED INTO the room, but left the door open behind him. The sounds of the pogre players and of the rooms beyond comforted him somehow. The thought of cutting them off, of leaving him alone in this room with Lady Helgreta Brecher, terrified him.

'Please,' Helgreta said, motioning to the chair next to her at the lone table in the room. 'Have a seat.'

The room was, in fact, a booth all to itself. Two stuffed leather chairs crouched next to a small, circular table made of clean, polished wood, all of which were of exquisite make. The place smelled of fresh cedar – which Dunk saw lined the walls – and an enticing perfume, which he recognised as Helgreta's favourite scent.

Helgreta looked as stunning as ever. Her auburn curls had straightened a bit as she'd let her hair grow out, but her wide, dark eyes issued the same strong invitation to him that they always had. She carried a few more wrinkles around her eyes and mouth, and to Dunk's chagrin they seemed to have been caused by frowning.

A pair of golden goblets sat on the table in front of her, next to an uncorked bottle of wine – an excellent vintage by Dunk's memory. He hadn't bothered to keep track of such things since fleeing from his home four years ago. The cups stood empty, but somehow Dunk caught the scent of spirits from somewhere else.

'You look well,' Dunk said as he took the seat offered to him. He found he could not relax in it. Instead, he perched on its edge, his hands on the table in front of him. 'The years have been kind to you.'

'You flatter me,' Helgreta said with a sly grin. As she spoke, Dunk knew from where the smell of alcohol had come: her breath. She batted her eyes at him, 'But you always did have a way with words.'

Dunk blushed at this and lowered his eyes. 'I must apologise,' he said, 'for not answering your letters. By the time they reached me–'

'No need,' Helgreta said, placing a hand on his. 'Those were trying times. I understand that you needed to take care of yourself then and couldn't possibly have spared time for me.'

'It's not that I didn't–'

'Hush,' Helgreta said, pursing her soft, red lips. 'Let's not insult the memory of what we once had with such words.'

Dunk smiled at her softly. This was going better than he could have hoped. The sense of dread he'd felt since Gunther had announced Helgreta was here slowly sloughed away. 'You're far too kind,' he said.

Helgreta breathed in through her nose, her smile now thin and brittle. 'Adversity builds character, or so they tell me.'

Dunk glanced down at her hand on his. It bore no ring. 'You never married?' he asked. 'I find that hard to believe.'

Helgreta frowned. 'I– Since you insist... After the incident in my family's home, we were tainted with suspicions of dealing with daemons as well. Arranging another marriage for me proved...'

'Difficult?'

'Impossible.' She sighed. 'But I never minded. I'd already given my heart away once. Since it was never returned to me, I didn't have it to bestow on another.'

Dunk felt ill. He glanced at the wine, but his appetite for such things had left him.

'How is your family?' he asked, hoping to change the subject she'd claimed to wish to avoid.

Helgreta smiled pleasantly. 'Well, for the most part. My father still soldiers on, despite the way half of his body was paralysed by a stroke following that horrid, fateful night. Sadly, we lost my mother soon after that. Some say she died of sheer shame.'

'How about your cousins?' Dunk asked. Helgreta had always been close to them, and he had enjoyed carousing with them in more carefree days.

'With the taint that followed us, we were forced to ever more desperate measures to retain our holdings and position. Karl disappeared while leading a caravan over the Grey Mountains to Parravon. Kurt, though, decided to follow in your footsteps.'

'He was chased from his family home by an angry mob?'

The bitter look Helgreta shot Dunk was as far from the smile he'd hoped for as he could imagine.

'He took up Blood Bowl. He said, 'If Dunk and Dirk can do it, then why not me?' Did you know you two set off quite a trend among the disaffected sons and daughters of the Empire's elite? For a while, there was even an all-nobility team called "the Imperial Counts".'

Dunk thought hard on this. 'Whatever happened to them? I don't think I ever heard of them.'

'They became embroiled in a trademark dispute with a team of vampires from the Dark Lands over the "Counts" name. They submitted to binding arbitration over it, and the vampires bound them and bled them dry.'

Dunk gasped. 'Was Kurt on that team?'

'No, sadly,' Helgreta said. 'That would have been far easier for him, I'm sure.'

'What happened to him?' Dunk wasn't sure he wanted to know the answer, but he couldn't keep from asking.

'He started to question his sexuality. Then, while he was at his most vulnerable, he fell in with a team – more a cult, really – called the Bright Crusaders.'

Rivers of ice ran through Dunk's veins. 'You can't be–'

'He became a "brother" in their organisation. He took on the new name "Mother" to show how he'd channelled his maternal urges into helping the team and furthering the cause of good and fair play, both on the field and off. They raised thousands of crowns for poor children through their charity matches alone, and Karl donated all but a small portion of his wages to keeping the homeless off the streets – via a euthanasia program he started before he joined the team.'

'The Association for the Revolution of Self-Euthanasia?'

'You've heard of them?' Helgreta smiled warmly. 'Karl would have been so pleased. I understand they've started a Blood Bowl team of their own. Karl said he often scrimmaged against them and dispatched at least one opponent each game – with the dignity they deserved, of course.'

Dunk put a hand over his mouth.

'Helgreta, I–'

'I know,' she said. 'It was your job to kill him, and I don't begrudge you that. He'd lost so much weight over the past few years, I wouldn't be surprised if you hadn't recognised him at all.'

Dunk nodded. Between that, the armour, and the man's caked-on make-up, he couldn't possibly have known who Brother Mother had once been – or so he told himself. Still, he had to set the record straight.

'I didn't kill him though,' he said. 'I tried to save him. I didn't want for him to tackle me.'

'Oh, you weren't the first player to flee from Karl's embrace,' Helgreta said. 'He scared more than one macho man off the field with his aggressive yet feminine ways.'

Dunk shook his head. 'That's not it. I didn't know who he was, other than another innocent Blood Bowl player.'

Helgreta failed to stifle a giggle. 'Is there any such animal as an "innocent Blood Bowl player"?'

'I just wanted to keep from having Zauberer kill him,' said Dunk.

'Ah, yes,' Helgreta smiled, but Dunk felt no warmth behind it, 'the wizard who's threatening your life. Aren't you getting tired of using that excuse?'

Dunk stared at her. 'What do you mean? It's not imaginary. So far, he's struck down anyone who's managed to tackle me on the field.'

'And yet you keep playing. Why is that?'

'I…' Dunk had wrestled with this question a great deal on his own. 'It's complicated.'

Helgreta picked up the bottle of wine and proceeded to fill the two glasses sitting in front of her and Dunk. 'We have the whole night ahead of us.'

That thought made Dunk shiver, but he decided to take a shot at explaining himself anyhow. When he looked at Helgreta and saw what had happened to her family and her life, he knew she deserved at least that much.

'There are a number of reasons, and they all get mixed together in my head. First, my coach demands that I play. I've signed a contract with him to play. If I don't play, I get fired.'

'You don't think you could find work elsewhere?'

'Sure. Maybe. I don't know if I'd want it. The Hackers are like my family now, especially since Dirk joined the team. I don't think I'd want to play for anyone else.'

'There is a world out there beyond Blood Bowl, you know.' Helgreta sipped from her glass. Her smile pronounced the wine delicious.

'I've been in that world. I was trying my hand at slaying dragons when Slick found me and convinced me to try out for the team. I didn't know much about Blood Bowl back then, and I thought it would have taken a team of wild horses to drag me to a try-out. As it turns out, it took a hungry chimera and a town full of angry citizens to push me into it.'

'Can one get used to being run out of a town?' The way Helgreta asked made Dunk wonder if the wine had gone to her head already.

'I don't think so. The last time was enough to get me to try something new, to put my old life behind me entirely.'

'But that hasn't really worked, has it?' She tossed back the rest of her wine in one, long drink.

Dunk pondered that. 'No. At least not the way I did it. Every day, it seems like my past comes back to haunt me in different ways. First it was Dirk. Then Lehrer and the Guterfiends. Then my father, and now–'

'Your father is alive?'

Dunk nodded. He reached for his wine, but Helgreta grabbed it before he could, and dumped the contents of his cup into hers. 'How could that be?' she asked as she set his empty goblet back in front of him.

'He and I both managed to get out of the keep before the mob came and tore my mother and sister to pieces. I lost track of him after that and figured he was dead. It seems I was wrong.'

Helgreta looked at Dunk through lidded eyes. 'And how do you know this? Have you heard from him?'

'I had a drink with him in this very bar earlier this week.'

Helgreta gasped. She sipped the wine she'd taken from Dunk and curled up in her chair like a contented cat. 'Do you know where he is? I always liked him.'

Dunk shook his head. 'He shows up when he wants to. You know, when I first saw him, I wanted to kill him.'

'What kept you from doing it? You've killed lots of people, haven't you?'

'Not that many.' Dunk frowned. 'This is my father we're talking about. I... Well, if the reason why I keep playing Blood Bowl with a wizard's curse over my head is complicated, then my reasons for not killing my father are right up there with the rest of the great mysteries of the world.

'I wanted to kill him, especially when I found out what he'd done, how he'd been responsible for so much of the misery in my life, for Dirk leaving home, for the deaths of my mother and sister. But he didn't mean any of it. He'd been trying to do right by his family, and somehow it all got messed up.'

'So you think you should judge people by their intentions, not by the results of their actions?'

'I – I suppose that's right. After all, there are so many things that can go wrong with a plan; so many awful, stupid things. It seems harsh to only account for an action's results without considering what the actor meant to happen.'

Helgreta smiled, and then sat up and poured Dunk some more wine. 'You see,' she said, 'it's probably better that we never got married anyway. That's a huge point on which we differ.'

Dunk shrugged. 'After everything you've gone through on account of me and my family, I can understand that.'

Helgreta raised her goblet. 'Here's to putting the past behind us,' she said with a savage grin.

Dunk picked up his own goblet and clinked it against hers. 'And here's to second chances,' he said.

As Dunk brought the goblet to his lips, he knew something was wrong. The scent of the cedar, of Helgreta's overpowering perfume, of his own nervous sweat had all drowned out something else he'd sensed there, something more subtle and more dangerous. He sniffed at the wine, and there it was.

Bitter almonds.

Dunk choked on his own spit and dropped the goblet to the floor. As he hacked and coughed until he was red in the face, Helgreta gazed at him and laughed.

'When I first heard you'd come back to town two years ago, Dunkel, I ignored it. I satisfied myself with watching that championship game you played against the Reavers, and I hoped and prayed that someone would tear your head off in the middle of the match. When that didn't happen, I cried myself into a stupor. By the time I'd recovered, you'd left town once again.

'Last year, when you played the Reavers again, I prayed that a horrible plague would destroy you and everyone you held dear, all your friends from your new life. A new beginning denied to me. My petitions went unanswered again.'

Dunk finally managed to bring the coughing under control. He shoved himself back in his chair and clutched at his throat and stared at Helgreta with wide-open eyes.

'This year, I prayed again. I prayed so hard. When I heard about the reward on your head and then the Hoffnung Curse, I thought my prayers had finally been answered.

'Then you killed Karl, and I knew I had to take matters into my own hands. Like the saying goes, "the gods help those who help themselves".'

Helgreta crept from her chair and stood over Dunk. 'Can you feel the poison working its way through

your veins? Has it reached your lungs? Your brain?'
She reached over and rubbed her hand against his
chest. 'Has it stopped your heart?'

Dunk's hand snaked out and caught Helgreta by
the throat. Then he shoved her back into her chair.
'This charade is over,' he said. 'You're insane.'

'You?' She stared at him, her eyes wide as zeroes on
a scoreboard, her voice rising to a screech. 'Why can't
you ever seem to die?'

Dunk clenched his hands into claws. He wanted to
strike back at Helgreta, to kill her for trying to kill
him, but he couldn't.

'The poison's not affecting you; that liquor I
smelled on your breath when I came in-'

'Was the antidote,' Helgreta said. 'You always were
the clever one.'

'If anyone in the world deserves to kill me,' Dunk
said, 'it's you, but I won't just roll over and die.' He
shook his head in amazement at the lengths to
which this woman had been willing to go to end his
life.

'Who gave you a choice in the matter?' Tears
streamed from Helgreta's dark eyes, forming rivers of
black that streaked down her face from the ebony
smudges of make-up surrounding her eyes. 'No one
asked me!'

'You took your best shot,' Dunk said. 'It didn't work
out. Let it go.'

'Never!' Helgreta launched herself at Dunk and
clawed at him with her long, sharp nails. He caught
her by the wrists and held her away from him at
arm's length. 'Somehow, some way, you will die!'

Dunk shoved the woman back into her chair again.
'Someday,' he said, 'but not today.'

Helgreta shrieked at Dunk in frustration, snatched the bottle from the tabletop and hurled it at him. He ducked beneath it, and it shattered against the wall behind him.

By the time Dunk had stood up again, Helgreta had already dashed out of the door of the tiny room, screaming the entire way. 'He's evil!' she said. 'Evil!'

'No!' Dunk lunged for the door and into the room beyond. There he saw the pogre players standing between him and the door. 'You best leave 'er alone,' one of the orcs said. The rest of them nodded in agreement.

Dunk charged at the group, cutting his way between the elf and the goblin as if they were linemen he'd caught flat-footed on the field. With one move, he grabbed the end of the table closest to him and overturned it, shoving it forward against the orc and the dwarf on the far side of the table. They tried to duck under it, and the table started to roll right over them.

Dunk went with the momentum and somersaulted across the bottom of the flipping table. This put him on its far side, with the table between him and the angry players.

He charged into the next room, and he could see Helgreta's back as she fled past the Hackers' table in the main hall. 'No!' he shouted. 'Stop her!'

The Bright Crusaders had leapt up from the chairs and stools at which they'd been drowning their sorrows. They closed ranks around Dunk, forming a human wall between him and the doorway as they linked their arms together.

'Get out of my way!' he shouted at them. 'Or she's dead!'

'We won't let you kill again, Hoffnung,' Sister Mister said in a voice as rough as an ogre's beard, 'especially not Karl's cousin.'

Dunk stared at the woman in horror – and not just because he could finally get a good look at her without her helmet on. Then he dived straight at her. She rebuffed him with a push of her belly, and he found himself on the floor.

'She attacked me,' Dunk said. 'She's going to die!'

'How dare you threaten that lady?' the dwarf called from the other side of the room. Dunk glanced back and saw that a line of Bright Crusaders had closed that doorway off too.

'Don't worry, Hoffnung. You have nothing to fear from them. We won't allow anyone else to come to harm because of your so-called curse,' Sister Mister said, the menace in her voice unmistakable. 'As a charter member of ARSE, Helgreta has already come to terms with her fate. You can do nothing to stop it – nor to save yourself.'

With that, the circle of Bright Crusaders began to tighten around Dunk. He searched for a way out, a hint of daylight between his attackers, but he could find none. It looked like he was just going to have to kill his way out of the situation. The Crusaders outnumbered him ten to one, though, and had absolutely no fear for their lives. They'd come here to martyr themselves for their cause: his death.

A large hand shot out from behind Sister Mister and grabbed her by the head. With a quick twist of her neck, she fell down to the floor, dead. She bore a wide smile on her face.

M'Grash stuck his head through the door after his arm and said, 'Dunkel okay?'

Somewhere outside the Skinned Cat, thunder rolled across what Dunk knew to be a crystal clear sky. Grim frustration marred Dunk's face as he grimaced at the ogre and said, 'All right, big guy. Let's give these bastards what they want.'

CHAPTER TWENTY-SEVEN

'WELCOME, BLOOD BOWL fans, to the championship pre-game show for this year's Blood Bowl tournament. I'm Jim Johnson!'

'And I'm Bob Bifford! This should be one humdinger of a match, Jim, featuring the Bad Bay Hackers versus the Chaos All-Stars!'

'True enough, Bob! Due to the now infamous Hoffnung Curse the wizard Schlechter Zauberer placed on star Hacker Dunk Hoffnung, the Hackers were heavily favoured going into this game. Let's talk to our able odds-making consultant, the legendary Gunther the Gobbo, to see what happened. Gunther?'

'Thanks, Jim! It's simple. In a nutshell, Zauberer's backing the All-Stars. As long as he has the power of the Chaos Cup behind him, he's the heavy favourite.'

'And what are the chances that the Hackers might be able to find Zauberer and take the Chaos Cup away from him, thereby evening the odds?'

'That of a snotling's snowball in an ogre's pitcher of hot blood.'

'Excellent,' said Bob! 'Now lets check in with our roving reporter Lästiges Weibchen to set up this burgeoning rivalry for us.'

'Thanks, Bob! Traditionally, the Hackers and the All-Stars haven't had much time for each other. Remember, just a few years back, the Hackers weren't considered contenders for the championship games for any of the majors, despite the leadership of Captain Pegleg Haken and of team captain Rhett Cavre, not to mention the brute force of M'Grash K'Thragsh.

'That changed three seasons ago when then-protégée Dunk Hoffnung joined the team. Something about the chemistry of the team gelled strongly around a central group of players that has survived to this day, despite dozens of casualties to the Hackers' roster.

'The modern-day Hackers have faced the All-Stars twice in the past three seasons. The first time was in the Chaos Cup two years back. In that game, Hoffnung killed the All-Stars' team captain Schlitz 'Malty' Likker during a half-time ceremony set to honour former All-Star captain Skragger.'

'Didn't Hoffnung claim at the time that the Blood God had possessed the minotaur with Zauberer's help?' asked Jim.

'He certainly did, and that seems to have been the start of the conflict between Zauberer and Hoffnung. This flared up whenever the two met, but it usually ended up with the humiliation of Zauberer, who sometimes served as the All-Stars' team wizard.

'Still, the All-Stars won that game, as they did in their only match against the Hackers the following year in the *Spike!* magazine tournament. That's the game with the infamous Jumboball incident, when the gigantic display at the end of the field came off its mount and crushed hundreds of fans to death as it rolled onto the field.'

'I remember that,' said Bob, licking his lips. 'I almost couldn't restrain myself from getting down there and helping to, ah, clean up.'

'That game ended with several players dead on both sides, including the All-Stars' new team captain, Macky Maus. In the end, though, the All-Stars prevailed when Coach Haken threw in the towel. With only three players left on the field, he knew the Hackers didn't stand a chance.'

'How many players are still left from the original team that Hoffnung joined just three years ago?' Jim asked.

'Only four: K'Thragsh, Cavre, Reyes, and Hoffnung himself. That's a hard-bitten, battle-tested core, and to that they've added Edgar – a treeman from Albion – and Dirk Heldmann, Hoffnung's younger brother and long-time fixture of the Reikland Reavers. Up until this year, at least.'

'So this is a grudge match to beat all grudges,' said Bob. 'Just the way it should be!'

Pegleg shut off the Cabalvision feed to the crystal ball in the Hackers' locker room. He gazed out at the players sitting on the benches in front of him, staring back, and he let loose a grim sigh.

'I know you've been watching that crap every day since we beat the Bright Crusaders,' Pegleg said. 'I want you to ignore every word of it. All that analysis, all those stats they throw at you, everything, all of it.

'It's all crap. Sophisticated fairy tales they feed to the emotionally stunted excuses for sentient creatures we call fans. The fans need this stuff. They feed on it. They have to have a story woven around the game, some kind of framing device to give the match more purpose than it really has to them.

'Honestly, what does a fan care about Blood Bowl? Even when it comes to a championship game like this? Anyone?'

'Whatever they bet on it,' said Erhaltenes Spiel, one of the more promising rookies the Hackers had seen this year. He'd joined them back in Magritta, so just the fact that he had survived this far spoke volumes about his ability to play the game – or at least to find ways to collect a cheque while warming the bench.

'Exactly right, Mr. Spiel,' said Pegleg. 'Anyone else?'

'Bloody pride,' said Edgar, who stood in the back of the rows of benches, towering over all the other players, even M'Grash, who sat at one end of one of the middle rows, next to Dunk.

'Well put,' Pegleg said with a grin. 'We thank those rabid fans who stake their pride on our success. They wear our jerseys, come to our games and buy the things we endorse. In a real sense, they pay all of our salaries, and I love them for it.'

Pegleg held his hook in the air. 'But the only things they have at stake in this game are money and pride. That Cabalvision crap caters to them and their needs.'

'But coach,' Jammernder Anfäger – another rookie, but with far less promise than Spiel – said, 'don't we have money and pride on the line as well?'

Pegleg smiled. Dunk knew that smile. The ex-pirate reserved it for when some fool walked straight into one of his rhetorical traps. Pegleg lived for straight men like this, the ones who handed him the set-ups for his punch lines, but he showed them no pity. He always made them pay.

'True, Mr. Anfäger. We have even more to lose, in those senses than any but our most rabid fans. Our jobs are on the line, and our professional reputations. That's something to fight for, isn't it?'

Anfäger nodded, pleased with himself for having triggered this portion of the coach's pep talk. Then the ex-pirate lunged forward and brought his hook up under the rookie's chin, pressing there just enough to break the skin, but not to catch the man by his jaw-bone like an unlucky, warm-blooded fish.

'I suppose then that you don't much value your life,' Pegleg said as he glared deep into the rookie's fright-ened eyes.

Anfäger swallowed hard, but didn't move, for which Dunk was thankful. Right here before the game, they wouldn't be able to replace the rookie if he made a stupid decision. Pegleg's glare dared the man to try to escape the hook threatening him, but Anfäger remained frozen.

Pegleg dropped his hook and stepped back to the front of the benches. He gazed out at the players, all staring at him, and wiped the blood on his hook on his bright, white shirt, where it left a crimson trail.

'That's what's really at stake for you, my hearties. Not fame, not fortune, not the way people will remember you. Sure, all those things are there, and more, but they're nothing more than phantoms striv-ing to distract you from the most vital thing you each possess: your very lives.

'This is no idle threat on my part. Only four Hack-ers are still left here from our game against the Chaos

All-Stars last year, and they remember the mayhem from that fateful day all too well.'

Dunk nodded at that, as did M'Grash, Guillermo, and Cavre. He missed the friends he'd lost during that game and since. So many Hackers had died last year – although a good number of them had been the creatures brought to the team by the Far Albion Cup. Those he wouldn't miss at all.

The deaths that surrounded the game – permeated it – didn't bother Dunk most days. He'd come to Blood Bowl from a failed career as a dragonslayer, so this had seemed to be a step up.

Now, though, he had things to live for. He'd reconciled with his brother. He'd found his father. He had more money than he'd ever dreamed of since he'd left the family keep in the hands of an angry mob, and there was Spinne, whom he loved. The only thing keeping them apart, it seemed, was this damned game.

Dunk considered standing up and leaving the team, the stadium, and the game behind there and then. After all, he was sure that Zauberer would kill him shortly after he stepped onto the field. The wizard would only want to wait for the right moment, something that fit his quirky sense of drama.

But Dunk knew he couldn't leave all this behind. He couldn't abandon his friends, his family. He glanced at Dirk, who flashed him a cocky smile. Dunk could see past it to how nervous the man was underneath the façade. He couldn't leave him behind.

And, of course, Pegleg would murder him on the spot if he tried to go now.

'This is kill or be killed,' Pegleg said. 'We have the All-Stars outmatched in every position. We play better ball than them. We can score on them at will.

'But that's not how they win games. They don't care about touchdowns. We could be ahead ten to zilch, but if the game ends under their terms, they won't care.

'All they have to do to win is murder every damned one of you. Once we can't put any players on the field, they win by forfeit, no matter what the score.

'Now, that's not a very big field out there as battle-fields go. There are no forests to hide in, no hills to skulk behind. In short, there's nowhere you can hide.

'The only thing you can do is face up to the bastards the best you can – and kill them before they kill you!'

The Hackers stood up and cheered at the top of their lungs.

'Are you with me?'

'Yes!' the Hackers shouted as one.

'What?'

'*Yes!*'

'I can't hear you!'

'*YES!*'

'Then get on out there and kill! Kill for your fans! Kill for your family! Kill for your team! *Kill for your-selves!*'

'Go! Go! Go!' Cavre took up the chant, and the oth-ers joined in straight away. 'Go! Go! Go!'

Pegleg stamped over to the door to the tunnel that led to the Hackers' dugout and to the field in the cen-tre of the Emperors Stadium, where a hundred thousand fans waited to watch them prove themselves the champions they knew they could be. '*Let's GO!*' he bellowed.

The Hackers' voices devolved into a cacophony of howls that would have sent a tribe of wild wolves flee-ing, their tails between their legs. Then they charged after Cavre as he led them down through that dark tunnel and towards the chances for life and glory that awaited them beyond.

◆ CHAPTER TWENTY-EIGHT

DUNK STOMPED HIS feet and jumped up and down in the dugout as he waited for the game to begin. They'd already introduced the teams and gone through all the pre-game nonsense. All that was left was the coin toss and the kick-off.

Trotting out onto the field to the deafening roar of the crowd had been a rush. After a moment, his ears had adjusted to the noise, and he could hear the people chanting, 'Dunk! Dunk! Dunk!' He'd grinned wide and waved at them and listened to them roar their approval.

No amount of gold could buy a feeling like that.

'Hold still,' Dr. Pill said as he approached Dunk and waved a wand at him that looked like it had been constructed with leather straps and chicken bones.

'What's this?' Dunk asked. 'Some kind of blessing?'

The apothecary shook his head. 'Big game like this, it pays to check everything. The All-Stars like to slip cursed contraband into their foes' kits. I already found a mouth guard that would have turned into a snake.'

Without another word, Dunk stretched out his arms and legs, and let Dr. Pill wave the wand over them. It whined like a stuck snotling as it approached his throat, rising in pitch as it got nearer and then lowering as he moved it away.

'What's this?' Dr. Pill asked, pointing at the shrunken head. The thing twisted on its chain under the apothecary's glare.

'You ever hear of a player named Skragger?'

Dr. Pill nodded. 'Black orc, star player for the All-Stars, set all sorts of records.' He cocked his head at Dunk. 'Killed while attacking you and then came back as a vampire player for the Champions of Death. I heard you ripped his head off in the middle of a game.'

Dunk gestured towards the shrunken head. 'Cavre made it for me.'

'Is it a replica? Some kind of memento?'

Dunk shook his head. 'It's the real thing. Cavre shrunk it.'

Dr. Pill leaned over and peered at the tiny head closely, getting within inches of it, but never touching it. Then he strode over to the other side of the dugout to chat with Cavre. A moment later, the two of them came back to talk with Dunk. Dr. Pill had his black bag with him.

'I'm so sorry, Dunk,' Cavre said.

'How do you get this thing off?' Dr. Pill asked, pointing at the metal ball gag in Skragger's mouth. 'Can you remove it?'

'Sure,' Dunk said. He reached down and released the gag, letting it fall into his hand.

'Sons of witches!' Skragger's head said in its squeaky voice. 'Gonna grow my head, get my body back, and kill every damn one of you!'

'I can see why you had him gagged,' said Cavre.

'Hold still,' Dr. Pill said as he rummaged about in his bag. He produced a small silver vial and uncorked it. Then he tapped a small amount of bright red powder from the vial into the palm of his hand.

'I hear all your records were fakes,' Dr. Pill said to Skragger's head.

'Who said?' Skragger screeched. 'Lies! All lies! Earned every–'

Dr. Pill blew the red dust into the shrunken head's face. Skragger inhaled most of it, and it set him off on a coughing fit.

'How is that possible?' Dunk asked. 'He doesn't have any lungs.'

'You're toting around a talking shrunken head on a chain around your neck, and now you want to debate its physiology with me?' Dr. Pill permitted himself a smirk.

'Whoa!' Skragger said. 'That's good stuff.'

'What's going on?' Dunk asked.

Dr. Pill re-corked his vial and then stuffed it into his bag. As he did, Cavre spoke. 'My most sincere apologies, Dunk. If I'd known this was possible, I never would have allowed it.'

'Known what was possible?'

Cavre pointed at Skragger's head as the thing mumbled on about all the pretty orc cheerleaders in its path. 'That thing,' Cavre said. 'It's telepathic.'

Dunk's eyes flew wide. 'You're kidding.'

'I'm afraid not. It makes sense when you think about it. How could someone as dense as Skragger be such a great Blood Bowl player? Simple. He reads his opponents' minds. He could tell what they were going to do as soon as they thought about it.'

'He knows everything they think?' Horror gripped Dunk's heart.

Cavre shook his head. 'He's a simple orc who can barely construct a sentence. Even if he could read your mind, he probably wouldn't understand most of it – beyond the violence. That he understands, and that's what he's been communicating to Zauberer.'

Dunk felt like he might fall over. He stabbed his finger at the thing hanging on his chest. 'This is how he's been doing it? How Zauberer knows where I am and when I'm in danger?'

Cavre raised his eyebrows and nodded.

Dunk reached for the head. 'I'm going to stomp this thing into tiny pieces.'

'No!' said Dr. Pill. 'I just went to a great deal of trouble to drug that little bugger before Zauberer would be able to notice it. Don't you dare wash my work down the drain.'

Dunk narrowed his eyes at the apothecary. 'What did that stuff do to him?'

'It's a powerful hallucinogenic. It makes him see things that aren't there.'

'And things that are?'

'He can't distinguish between reality and fantasy at the moment. He's also highly suggestible.'

'What exactly does that mean?'

THE HACKERS WON the opening coin toss – handled by the only referee both teams could agree on: Rhett Bool – and elected to receive. Dunk trotted down to one end of the field and waited for the All-Stars to kick the ball.

The more he thought about it, the more he knew that Zauberer would probably wait until the worst moment to attack him. He also knew that the wizard had a traitor's soul. He saw anyone and anything as expendable in the race to achieve his goals. He'd zap Skragger in an instant.

He wanted to kick himself for not figuring out about the connection between Zauberer and the black orc. Zauberer had been such a horrible shot in that game against the Oldheim Ogres back in Magritta. How had he got to be so deadly accurate? He had a tiny little spotter working for him, helping him call down his ebony bolts from the blue.

Dunk rattled Skragger's chain just for fun and heard the head howl in protest. 'Yer gonna die!' he said. 'Zappity-zap-zap!'

Then the crowd started in on the rising shout that told Dunk the ball would be coming his way soon. When it reached its climax, it ended in a massive, unified shout and then shattered into thousands of cheers.

Dunk spotted the ball spinning end over end through the crisp, afternoon air, arcing right towards him. He spread his arms, and it landed right between them and his chest with a satisfying thump. He turned his head to the right and spotted Rotes Hernd, the Hackers' back-up thrower, standing near the sideline, waving her arms at him. Dunk snapped a quick pass to Rotes, who stood behind the protective wall of M'Grash and Edgar, and then sprinted upfield.

The first few All-Stars ignored Dunk and chased after the ball instead. Then Dunk heard a chorus of horrifying barks, and he knew that he'd attracted the attention of Serby 'Dawgy-Dawg-Dawg' Triomphe, the All-Stars' new team captain.

Dunk glanced to his right and saw Serby sprinting after him. The mutant beastman's three canine heads – each with its own black and red helmet, but none with a muzzle – growled in harmony, their eyes blazing red, blue, and green. Drool dripped from each head, slicking down Serby's jersey. Dunk had heard that he had to change jerseys at least four times a game, which close up, didn't seem to be often enough.

'Mine!' the green-eyed head said. 'Mine! Mine! Mine!'

'Catch!' the blue-eyed head said. 'Catch! Catch! Catch!'

'Kill!' the red-eyed head said. 'Kill! Kill! Kill!'

Any one of the heads looked like it could rip one of Dunk's arms clean from its socket. He'd seen just that happen in the scouting report Pegleg had prepared before the game too. Serby had taken hold of a doomed orc blitzer playing for the Underworld Creepers. In one blood-soaked blur, the orc had gone from four limbs to a single arm, which still held on to the ball as Serby's three heads scurried off into the dugout to enjoy their hard-earned snacks.

Dunk's legs pounded against the Astrogranite, propelling him downfield. He gave thanks that Serby's stride wasn't much faster than his, and that the creature's three heads made him top-heavy. When the beastman got too close, Dunk jinked to one side or the other, and Serby's helmets clashed against each other as he tried to follow Dunk's moves.

Dunk knew he couldn't keep this up forever. There was only so much open field around him. Sooner or later, Serby would corner him or get some of the other All-Stars to team up on him, and then Dunk would be doomed.

'Look at Hoffnung run!' Jim's voice said. 'That's one way to walk the Dawgy-Dawg-Dawg!'

'Let's see if Hoffnung has it in him to curb that canine!' said Bob. 'If he can't somehow collar that mutt, he's going to end up having kibble made from his bits!'

Dunk spun away from Serby's snapping jaws once again and sprinted towards the end zone. As he did, he glanced back and saw the ball spinning down out of the sky towards him. He reached out his gauntleted hands and caught the pigskin between them.

The crowd cheered. With Dunk scant yards from the goal line, he had a touchdown in the bag – or so it seemed.

Dunk reached up and pulled Skragger's chain from around his neck. As he did, he turned and stopped, standing a mere yard in front of the end zone. 'I can't believe I'm about to score,' he shouted. 'I can't wait to hear the crowd cheer when I do!'

'Cheer!' Skragger said, his tiny eyes focused on something far away. Froth filled his miniature mouth. 'Make 'em cheer!'

Dunk wrapped the chain around the ball, winding it fast around the spikes. Then he held it up in front of him and waved it at Serby. 'Here, Dawgy-Dawg-Dawg!'

All six of Serby's eyes flashed red at the insult. Their words devolved into nothing more than rabid barking. The beastman charged straight at Dunk with the speed of a runaway mining cart sliding on its way down to hell.

Just as Serby reached him, Dunk said, 'Here it comes.' He gave the ball a little flip into the air and then dived to the side. The ball hung there for a moment, right where he had been. Then Serby crashed into it at full speed and wrapped his arms around it.

'Amazing!' Jim said, the crowd's cheers drowning out his voice. 'Just as Hoffnung was about to score–'

A crack of black lightning cut off the announcer's comments. The noise sent Dunk's ears ringing, and the flash blinded and dazzled him. He smelled something that reminded him of the sausage-on-a-stick vendor just outside the stadium.

He grinned. The plan had worked.

'Nuffle's gnarled nads!' Bob's voice said. 'Triomphe is gone! Blasted to ashes by a freak bolt of lightning that seemed to come from nowhere! Do the Hackers have a wizard on their side who's not listed on their roster?'

'We'd better check the replay on that!' Jim said. 'That colour of bolt has been a trademark of Zauberer's ever since he stole – I mean, apprehended. No that's not right either. He – ah, forget it!'

'What was your point again, Jim?'

'Just this: Since Zauberer *stole* the Chaos Cup, he's been blasting all of Hoffnung's foes with bolts just like that one, with the same dramatic and messy results.'

'Does this mean that Zauberer's somehow switched sides?' Bob asked. 'How could he have killed Triomphe instead of Hoffnung?'

'Hold on a moment. We have a report coming in from our intrepid correspondent on the front lines – I mean, the sidelines. What's up with the All-Stars, Lästiges?'

'Total chaos, Jim!'

'Well, that's nothing new. How about we check in with–'

'Wait, Jim! The All-Stars' dugout is even more chaotic than normal. As usual, their dugout is shrouded in an impenetrable cloud of blackness, but bodies and parts thereof have been appearing from it ever since that bolt passed through Triomphe, hot enough to blast his shadow onto the Astrogranite beneath him.'

'Have you been able to get a word in with the coach?'

'You well know, Bob, that no one has ever interviewed the All-Stars' coach – at least not without either dying or falling into a gibbering heap on the spot. Whoever he is, he likes his privacy and has protected it for decades. Even under such unusual circumstances, it seems that he will maintain that secrecy for now.'

'So, if you can't get into the dugout, and you can't ask anyone any questions, what can you tell us?'

'Not much, I'm afraid. Back to you, Jim!'

'Thank you, Lästiges, for that confuzzling report!'

While the announcers blathered away over the PA system, Dunk shoved himself to his feet and poked around through Triomphe's ashes, helmets, and bits of armour, for the remains of the ball. All he could find were a few blackened spikes, a couple of which had melted into steaming lumps of metal.

Dunk discovered even less of Skragger's shrunken head: nothing at all, not a single trace. Wherever the black orc vampire was now, Dunk hoped it hurt.

Bool whistled the play dead when he came to the same conclusion that Dunk had. There was no ball left to be found. The ref signalled for a fresh ball to be thrown in from the sidelines, and one was.

Cavre conferred with Bool and the newly appointed captain of the All-Stars, a squid-headed woman with ink-black eyes, by the name of Kathula Lustcruft. Dunk trotted over to join with the other Hackers on their side of the field, and the All-Star players congregated together on the other.

'What's going on?' Dunk asked.

'They're trying to figure out what to do about the missing ball,' Dirk said.

'Last time we just had another one thrown in.'

'The Blood Bowl Tournament organisers got an interpretation of Nuffle's Rules that made that illegal,' Rotes said.

'What's their bloody alternative then?' Edgar asked. 'Call it a bloody tie only two bloody minutes into the bloody game?'

Spiel shook his head. 'According to the latest dispatch from the Church of Nuffle, ancient scholars delved deep into the apocrypha and came up with a new rule for what to do if such a thing ever happened again.' The rookie noticed everyone staring at him. 'What? Don't you people read what they send you?'

'Read?' M'Grash said, scratching his head.

'So what's going to happen?' Dunk asked. 'Give us the short version.'

'That was,' Spiel said, scowling. 'It's called a death match. They put two players in the middle of the field, ten yards apart. Everyone else has to be twenty yards back. Then the ref drops the ball between them and runs for his life.'

'Nuffle's jolly jockstrap,' said Guillermo. 'That will be a mess. How do they decide who enters this match of death?'

'That's what I just spent the last minute figuring out, Mr. Reyes,' Cavre said as he trotted over from the conference. He looked over at the ogre. 'Mr. K'Thragsh, you're up!'

CHAPTER TWENTY-NINE

THE ALL-STARS put their largest, meanest player up against M'Grash: a headless, slime-skinned troll by the name of Ichorbod. The green-slick thing carried an All-Star's helmet around under his arm like a mother cradling an infant – a starving, undead infant. It stood as tall as M'Grash, even without a head atop its shoulders, and its mass was at least equal to the ogre's.

As M'Grash lined up in his designated spot, the other creature did the same and let loose with a horrifying bellow that made Dunk wish he'd taken up a safer sport, like daemon baiting. Cavre stood by the ogre, calming him with a pat on the arm and some words shouted into his ear over the roar of the crowd.

'If he has no head, how does he yell like that?' Dunk asked.

'See that helmet under his arm?' Dirk said. 'It's not empty.'

Dunk did a double-take. 'You mean he carries his own head around in that thing? That's insane.'

'Strong words from a man who toted a black orc vampire's head about on a chain around his neck for the past year.'

'Good point.'

Cavre trotted back from the centre of the field, where he'd left M'Grash. He lined up in the centre of the rest of the Hackers, all exactly twenty yards away from the middle of the field. This put him right between Dunk and Dirk.

'Get ready, Hackers!' Cavre shouted. 'As soon as that ball drops, it is live! Grab it and go!'

'What did you tell M'Grash?' Dunk asked.

'To kill the troll. It's not called a Hug Match. Now keep your eyes on that ball. When it squirts out of there, we need to grab it.'

'You think he can follow those directions?'

'Kill. Troll.' Cavre smiled and shrugged. 'It's M'Grash. I don't know.'

Dunk nodded and focused on the new pigskin. He hoped that his stunt with Triomphe had disrupted Zauberer's plans enough that he'd be able to play the rest of the game without interference from the wizard. At the very least, by getting rid of Skragger, he'd removed the bright, red target on his chest.

Bool walked to the centre of the field and held up the new ball. He showed it to the two monstrous players flanking him. A humongous image of it played on the Jumboball looking down on the stadium from the wall behind the northern end zone.

Bool tossed the ball straight up in the air and then galloped out of there as fast as his boots would take him.

Ichorbod ripped the faceguard off his helmet while the ball was still in the air, and then hurled his head straight at M'Grash. Distracted by the ball, the ogre didn't see the head coming at him until it hit him in the face, smashing flat a nose that had been broken countless times before.

As M'Grash howled in pain, a long, pink tongue lashed out of the helmet and wrapped all the way around his throat. Then it pulled tight, constricting around his windpipe as he tried to claw it off with his thick, stubby fingers.

While M'Grash struggled with Ichorbod's head, the troll's body lumbered forward and blindly lashed out at the ogre. Its hands found M'Grash's arm and locked on. Acrid vapours rose from where the troll's flesh touched that of M'Grash, and the ogre howled in pain.

'Get that ball!' Cavre shouted.

The pigskin thudded in the middle of the field and took a bounce towards the Hackers. Dunk lunged forward, closest to it of anyone, but the choice between grabbing the ball and helping his friend tore at him as he went. In the end, he decided to do both.

Dunk plucked up the ball. It felt good in his hand – clean, a good heft, nicely balanced – the perfect weapon.

Dunk cocked back his arm and leapt up at M'Grash, who'd staggered backward towards him and the rest of the Hackers' line. He grabbed the ogre's pauldron and used it to lever himself up high enough that he had a good shot at Ichorbod's head. He brought the ball down hard, and the spike on its tip slammed right through the troll's helmet.

Ichorbod's body shivered and fell back a step as it released its grip on M'Grash's arm, leaving red blisters behind. The creature's head, though, roared around its still-extended tongue. It did not let go.

'Wow, Jim! You have to admire a player who's willing to use the ball like that.'

'You sure do! Too bad it doesn't seem to have done any good. Hoffnung was probably aiming for Ichorbod's brain. Those are darn small things to have to find in a skull the size of a troll's!'

Dunk yanked the ball from the troll's helmet and cocked back his arm to have another go at lobotomising Ichorbod. If he kept at it, he knew he'd strike grey matter soon.

Ichorbod's body slammed into M'Grash, which sent Dunk toppling to the ground. He tucked the ball under his arm and tumbled away. When he rolled to his feet, he saw that two ram-headed beastmen had knocked the troll into the ogre, and then leapt away before the creature's skin could harm them as well.

M'Grash tried to howl in pain, but he couldn't get enough air past Ichorbod's tongue. He marched a few tremendous steps and then fell backward, the troll clutching its toxic skin to him.

'Over here, Dunk!'

The thrower turned and saw Dirk sprinting towards the right sideline and waving an arm at him. No All-Stars had bothered to cover him. When Dunk glanced straight up field, he saw why. They were all coming for him.

Dunk hurled the ball towards Dirk and then turned to run before he even saw if his brother caught it. As he did, he saw M'Grash on the ground between him and the other All-Stars, struggling for his life.

Although it seemed like suicide, Dunk charged forward, lowered his shoulder, and dived into M'Grash's neck, headfirst, using his helmet as a spear. It smacked into Ichorbod's helmet, and something gave way with a wet sound. The head popped free and twirled off towards the onrushing All-Stars.

One of the All-Stars, an orc with a giant crab's arms and pincers, stopped to catch the screaming troll's loose head. The others came at Dunk like an ebony-jerseyed wave.

Dunk braced himself for the impact, but he couldn't have imagined how bad it would be. The two ram-headed All-Stars smashed into him first, sending him flying back and to the ground. Then a man with the body of a bear landed on him, crushing the air from his lungs.

As spots floated before Dunk's eyes, Kathula dived at him, the tentacles that dangled from her face wrapping around his helmet, creeping in underneath it, and gripping at his skin. Unable to move his arms or even cry for help, all he could do was watch in panicked terror as her beak-like mouth appeared from among her tentacles and made its way towards his face, its sucker-surfaced tongue flicking out at him like a slaver's lash.

One side of the tongue slapped wet and warm against Dunk's cheeks and stuck there. Then it started to pull him in towards the black beak, which flexed in anticipation of biting into his flesh. The tip of the tongue flailed free, searching, pressing for a way between Dunk's lips and into his mouth.

Then Kathula's tongue pulled free from Dunk's face, pocking his skin as it left. The rest of her tentacles followed along with her tongue, and then the two ram-headed linemen disappeared as well. Still flat on his back, Dunk saw M'Grash grinning down at him and offering him a hand up.

'Thanks, big guy. I thought the ram-men and noodle-face there were going to make a cheap lunch out of me.'

'S'alright.'

Dunk glanced around and saw his attackers getting up and starting to circle him and M'Grash again. 'Doesn't anyone around here ever play the ball any more?' he asked.

'Touchdown, Hackers!' Jim's voice said. 'What an amazing play. Dirk Heldmann's pass to Rhett Cavre put the ball way down the field, and then Cavre worked his foot magic to break three tackles – and a couple of arms – to get into the end zone!'

'It's that kind of attention to basics – things like scoring points – that has always served the Hackers well. If they can avoid the All-Stars' Total 'Ponent Kill strategy, they should be able to win this game.'

Lästiges chipped in at that point. 'I just finished talking with Dr. Shnahps Magillicutty, the team apothecary for the All-Stars. He says he thinks the team will abandon the TPK tactics now. With Dr. Pill on the Hackers' side, it's likely the team could manage to outlast the All-Stars. If so, the game would come down to points, and with the Hackers already up by a touchdown, the All-Stars have some catching up to do.'

'Good point, Lästiges. It would be great to see a game based upon the classic 'scoring' strategies rather than total annihilation. Call me old-fashioned if you like–'

'You're six hundred years old, Bob!' said Jim. 'Of course you're old-fashioned.'

'Maybe. And maybe I just like yelling, "Touchdown!"'

'Well, you have to admit, it does have a certain ring to it.'

Dunk trotted back to the Hackers' end of the field to line up for the kick-off, a grin on his face. Cavre's score couldn't have come at a better time. For the first time all day, he started to think about more than just surviving the game. If things continued to go this well, they might just win.

'Don't go thinking about victory yet,' Cavre shouted out to the other players as they got into position, almost as if he could read Dunk's mind. The thought made the thrower nervous for a moment. He hadn't suspected that Skragger was telepathic. Could he have missed something with his team's captain too?

'No,' Cavre called over to Dunk. 'You just wear every emotion you have on your face.'

'Remind me not to play pogre with you.'

Cavre held up his arm to signal the others to get ready. Then he charged up to the ball and booted it towards the distant end zone. It arced through the sky and came down in the arms of a lizardman called Tzun Su, who had a bright orange crest that ran along the top of his skull.

The lizardman reminded Dunk a bit of Sseth Skinshucker, who'd played for the All-Stars last year. His career had ended after M'Grash had tossed him into the stands in Magritta. The fans there had skinned the creature alive and made, from later accounts, five sets of quality boots from his scales. Sseth had survived the incident and later claimed one of the pairs of boots for himself as a memento of his playing days.

Dunk hung back to cover the All-Star catchers who raced down the field. As they raced towards him, M'Grash and Edgar led the charge against them. On their way towards the lizardman, they trampled a beetle-headed man – one Kanz Frafka – under their feet as if he were nothing more than a giant cockroach caught unwillingly in a game not of his own design – and then paying the ultimate price.

An eagle-headed creature with wings for arms flapped towards Dunk, his feet almost leaving the ground as he sped along. The thrower threw himself forward to check the catcher, whose uniform read 'Sam,' but the birdman skirted away from Dunk's check and left him clutching air.

Downfield, Edgar put his branches in the lizardman's face, giving him nowhere to throw the ball. As the treeman started to gloat, Tzun Su darted his head forward and spit fire from deep in his gullet.

The flames incinerated some of Edgar's leaves and ignited his smaller branches. The treeman let loose a terrified scream that made Dunk think he might never care to go into a forest alone again. Then he began to dash back and forth across the field, looking for some kind of relief.

Under Cavre's direction, M'Grash slammed into Edgar from behind and knocked him over. As the treeman toppled to the ground, the ogre yelled, 'Timberrrr!' This did nothing for the bug-eyed goblin caught underneath Edgar's bulk as he fell.

The poor creature chattered madly as its legs were crushed. This rose to a fevered pitch as M'Grash began to roll Edgar back and forth on the ground like a rolling pin, trying to put the flames out. By the time he succeeded, the goblin was little more than a nice, flat sheet of reddish paste that had been baked solid by the burning treeman's heat.

'Cookie?' M'Grash asked as he scooped up the hot goblin/baked goodie.

Dunk didn't see what happened next. He saw the ball appear in the air high above the field, and he angled towards Sam to try to intercept the pass.

It wasn't a good throw, but the kind Pegleg liked to call a 'wounded parrot,' and Dunk had the angle on it. All he had to do was jump up a little at the last second, and the ball would be his.

The sound of a massive bird cry from behind him almost sent Dunk diving to the Astrogranite instead. He managed to keep his composure long enough to jump for the ball as he'd planned, but as his fingers reached up, a taloned foot reached down and snagged it as the beating of wings sounded in Dunk's ears.

Dunk looked up and cursed. Sam's wings were more than just for looks. The creature had made it into the air and was now winging back around for a shot at his end zone. Dunk leapt up to try to grab Sam, but his fingers closed only on air. A moment later, the eagleman, having gained enough height, went into a power dive that deposited him and the ball right in the middle of his end zone.

'Touchdown, All-Stars!' Bob said. 'Yep, I never do get tired of that word! Touchdown!'

'That hardly seems fair,' said Jim. 'The birdman there was flying! Blood Bowl isn't one of those sissy games wizards play on the backs of broomsticks. It's down and dirty action! Three yards and a cloud of dust! Ploughing divots out of the Astrogranite! It stays on the ground!'

'Spoken like someone who can't fly!' Bob said.

CHAPTER THIRTY

THE ALL-STARS and the Hackers stymied each other for the rest of the half. Sam kept his flying to a minimum, but only when Rhett Bool wasn't looking his way. During one harrowing play, the eagle-man dived into Edgar's upper branches in an effort to strip the ball from the treeman. He only ended up coming away with some bark, but ever after that Edgar chased the creature around the field, ignoring the ball unless it happened to cross his path.

When the whistle blew and the Hackers trotted back down the tunnel to their locker room, no one said a word. Ever since their early score, the game had been one frustration after another for them, and the Hackers were worn and tired.

'What in Nuffle's nine original divisions is going on out there?' Pegleg demanded as the players sat down on their benches once again. 'These scurvy dogs finally decide to give us a real ball game, and you bilge rats can't be bothered to make them pay for it?'

'We're down to only ten players,' Dirk said as he poured a tankard of water over his head. 'Plus, it turns out the All-Stars aren't all that bad when they actually play.'

'"Not all that bad"?' Pegleg's eyes grew large and showed whites all around. 'These are the Chaos All-Stars we're talking about here! They're nothing *but* bad! We need to go out there and punish them like the evil beasts they are!'

'Coach?' Dunk said. When Pegleg turned his furious eyes on him, he instantly regretted saying a word, but this game was too important for him to back down. 'Are you just going to yell at us, or do you have a plan?'

Pegleg's face turned bright red, and spittle sputtered from his lips. He raised his hook as if looking for something soft and yielding to plunge it into – like a beating heart. Then he managed some small amount of control over himself, just enough to speak. He spat each word out with a precision that said that to do otherwise might cause him to explode.

'What, Mr. Hoffnung, would you have us do?'

'I have some ideas.'

THE HACKERS KICKED the ball off to start the second half. It arced down towards the All-Stars, and Sam the eagleman leapt into the air and snatched it.

Dunk stood right where he was, not making a move, while he watched Cavre, Edgar, and M'Grash stomp down the field after the ball. The rest of the Hackers gathered around him.

Dunk peered over their helmets and saw that the two ram-headed All-Stars had challenged the referee to a head-butting match right after he'd blown the whistle to start the half. As an ex-player himself, Bool managed to gore one of the creatures with his horns before the other laid him flat on his back.

With the ref out of the picture, Sam beat his wings and gained altitude. M'Grash jumped up and made a grab at the eagle-man, but fell short.

'Sam takes the kick-off, and he's got nothing but daylight in front of him!' Bob's voice said. 'The All-Stars seem to have come up with a spectacular plan during halftime. If they keep this up, we can put this game into the record books right now.'

'The All-Stars are turning this into a game of broom-ball!' Jim said. 'I don't like it, and the fans don't either!' A rousing chorus of boos and hisses confirmed the commentator's opinion. 'Drop the airborne routine, All-Stars! We came here to see Blood Bowl!'

Cocky from his clear shot at success, Sam performed a barrel roll, spinning his wings as an insult to Jim and the fans. This put him straight on course for Edgar, who raised his branches up high over his head.

The eagle-man let loose the screech of a predator bird spotting its prey. He dived straight for Edgar, planning to skim the tops of the treeman's branches and prove that literally no one could touch him.

As Sam zoomed in hard and fast, Edgar flung a shimmering something between his arms. It glinted like a spider's web in the clear sunlight.

Sam spied the thing at the last second and tried to pull up, but it was too late. He hurtled straight into the mithril net the Halfling Titans had given to Edgar.

The net engulfed the eagle-man, and the momentum of his sudden stop knocked Edgar to the ground.

The treeman kept his grip on the net and brought it and its occupant down along with him.

The net rolled into a tight ball around Sam as he struggled to break free. He failed to do so before the net slammed into the Astrogranite and knocked him senseless.

'That's one way to ground all flights in and out of Emperor Stadium!' Bob said.

The ball squirted free from the net and took a Hacker bounce. Rotes dashed forward and scooped it up. Standing alone in the middle of the field, she saw the rest of the All-Stars charging at her, and she froze.

'Stick to the plan!' Dunk shouted. 'Throw the ball!'

Rotes broke the hold her terror had on her, spun and hurled the ball back towards the other players, who still stood huddled in the middle of the field. Anfäger reached up and dragged it down into the scrum like a frog snatching and swallowing an errant fly.

'All right,' Dunk said. 'Break!'

The Hackers burst out of the huddle, each in a different direction. They left only one player still standing there, clutching something under his arms.

The All-Stars ignored the other players and went for the stationary one, who seemed to be just standing there with the ball, daring them to try to hurt him. They were happy to oblige.

'I smell something up here, Jim. Do you have any idea who number 18 is for the Hackers? He looks like he's pleading for a quick death!'

'I don't have him listed on my roster. Lästiges?'

'Coach Haken tells me he's a last-minute addition to the roster, a new rookie who's never seen a minute of play!'

'It looks like our man of mystery might *only* see a minute of play!' said Jim. 'Here come the All-Stars!'

Dunk glanced back over his shoulder and saw three of the Chaos players slam into number 18 at once. They knocked him flat on his back and piled on top of him, trying to crush the life from him with the weight of their bodies. A moment later, they leapt to their feet, howling.

'Can you see what's going on down there, Lästiges?'

'It's a huge mess, Bob. Whatever number 18 was holding down there, it wasn't a ball! When the All-Stars hit him, it burst, and the contents of – it looks like a canvas sack – went everywhere. Oh, gods! The smell is awful!'

Dunk grinned as an image of number 18 flashed up on the Jumboball above the end zone before him. Inside the spare set of armour, Lehrer had just been awakened by the horrible scent of the gunk that had coated nearly every part of him. As the old man tried in vain to wipe away the cast-offs of Dr. Pill's overused healing potions, he started to scream.

'Amazing!' Bob said. 'But if that wasn't the real ball in number 18's hands, then where is it?'

'Look!' said Jim. 'Hoffnung's heading for the goal line, and there's only one All-Star who can stop him!'

'Where you goin'?' Ichorbod asked as he stomped between Dunk and the end zone.

Dunk skidded to a halt, nearly sliding into the acid-skinned troll. 'Nowhere special,' the thrower said, putting up his hands to show they were empty. 'I don't have the ball. I'm just decoy number two.'

It took Dunk a moment to remember the troll's voice couldn't have come from the area above his shoulders. He looked straight ahead and saw

Ichorbod's face grinning at him from where his slime-covered body held it right between his outstretched hands.

'Don't care,' Ichorbod said. 'Yer dead.'

Dunk reached out and grabbed the troll's helmet by the edges of the rim that framed the creature's face. 'Don't!' he said, falling to his knees. 'Please! You can't kill me! I have too much to live for. I have five kids back home! I'm – I'm *pregnant!*'

The troll stared out at Dunk, dumbfounded, which wasn't a big mental leap for him. The thrower's outburst had confused it so much it didn't hear the thunderous footsteps approaching over the crowd's raucous cheers.

'Touchdown, Hackers!' Bob's voice said. 'Heldmann strolls into the end zone untouched! I *love* this game!'

Before Ichorbod could turn to see the replay on the Jumboball, M'Grash's spike-cleated boot came rushing at him. At the last second, Dunk snatched his arms back, and M'Grash punted the troll's severed head up and away.

Dunk scrambled backward away from Ichorbod's body, eager to escape its final efforts at senseless violence. As he did, he watched the troll's head soar past the fans in the nosebleed seats and nearly knock a circling gull from the cloudless sky. It arced out over the stadium's upper edge, and was gone.

Ichorbod's body tripped on something and toppled to the Astrogranite. It lay there for a moment, and then started to beat its fists and feet against the ground like a massive, acid-skinned toddler in the middle of a monstrous tantrum.

'Thanks, big guy,' Dunk said to M'Grash as they trotted back to their end of the field for their next kick-off.

'Dunkel safe!' the ogre said with a tusk-filled grin. 'We win!'

'Not yet,' Dunk said. Above them, the scoreboard changed to show the new tally: All-Stars 1, Hackers 2. 'But it's a good start.'

When Dunk got into position, he turned and saw the All-Stars leading Ichorbod's body into the dead centre of the field. As they did, a figure in black robes strode out onto the field, bearing in his arms a massive, fanged skull mounted atop a short stand covered with smaller skulls.

Dunk stared for a moment. He recognised Zauberer, but he couldn't imagine what the wizard could be thinking, walking right onto the field in the middle of the biggest game of the year. Whatever it was, it couldn't be good.

'Stop him!' Dunk said as he dashed ahead. 'We have to stop him!'

Ten of the All-Stars stepped forward between the Hackers and Zauberer. They formed a wall through which the Hackers would have to fight to stop the wizard's plot. Dunk led the charge, launching himself at the crab-armed man who stood closest to him.

Zauberer set the Chaos Cup down on top of Ichorbod's chest and withdrew a pair of black-bladed knives from the sleeves of his robes. As he did, the two ram-headed men leaned over the cup to peer into it. The cup's handles lashed out and snared the beastmen, holding them fast. They bleated in terror and tried to pull free, but they could not manage it before Zauberer ducked in with his blades and slit their throats.

As the lifeblood of the ram-men flowed into the cup's main bowl, the skulls around the base rolled off and began to burrow into Ichorbod's torso with their vicious, sharp teeth. The troll flailed about, trying to keep itself from being devoured alive, but it couldn't seem to shake a single one of the skulls from its flesh. Each of them had found an unbreakable purchase and continued to gnaw at the troll's sinews until long after it had stopped fighting them.

One of the crab-armed man's claws caught Dunk around his left bicep and started to pinch. The thrower shoved down hard and wedged his pauldron into the claw to keep it from clipping his arm in half. Still, the pressure started to bend the armour, and Dunk howled in pain.

Desperate, Dunk began pounding the crab-armed man in the face. Each blow seemed like it should have been enough to knock the All-Star senseless or dead, but the man's mutated arms kept holding on.

Dunk stopped punching the man for a moment and realised that he was unconscious or worse, but his claw had not unclenched. He pulled and yanked at the claw in frustration, but it refused to give. M'Grash reached over and tore the claw from the All-Star's arm, then jammed his fingers into the pincer and pried it loose.

Dunk rubbed his arm as he sprang free. 'Thanks!' he said, staring at the ogre as he looked down at the monstrous crab claw in his hands. 'I owe you a tub of butter!'

Dunk spun around and spotted Zauberer standing over a skeleton, holding the Chaos Cup aloft in his hands. Even as Dunk watched, the troll's flesh started to re-grow on its bones, knitting them together once again. He wondered what had happened to the smaller skulls, since none of them were around the trophy's base, or attacking Ichorbod's torso any longer.

Then he spotted the last of the small skulls emerge from the troll's ribcage with something pulsing between its savage teeth. Defying gravity, it tumbled up the wizard's robes and over the rim of the Chaos Cup.

'We are ready, o mighty Khorne, for your sacred embrace!' Zauberer shouted.

The sky turned to blood, and everyone screamed.

CHAPTER THIRTY-ONE

ONE MOMENT, DUNK stood in Emperor Stadium in Altdorf, in the heart of the Empire, the seat of power and
culture in the Old World. The next, he and everyone
else in the stadium – including the entire building –
were somewhere else.

Dunk didn't know how he knew that it wasn't just
that the sky had changed colour. Perhaps it was the
hot, humid air, or the stench of blood and brimstone,
or the foul taste of ashes in his mouth. Or perhaps it
was the screams of the more than one hundred thousand people in the stadium with him, who all sounded
as if their souls had been ripped from their flesh.

Whatever it was, he knew he was somewhere else,
and he couldn't stop screaming about it either.

In the entire stadium, only Zauberer's voice wasn't
screeching in horror. Instead, the wizard had thrown
back his head and started to laugh.

Dunk thought he'd never heard anything so evil in his entire life. He covered his ears and cringed at the sound.

As he did, he saw Ichorbod's body pull itself to its feet, only it didn't look anything like Ichorbod any more. Its skin had the same wet sheen, but it was crimson coloured now, and it had a head.

Dunk had never seen the face on that head before. He'd heard it described, and he'd known there and then that he preferred to know nothing more about it. He'd tried to do many things to remove those descriptions from his head, but nothing, not sleep, not drink, no oblivion but death could help. And now that face stared down at him and smiled as it opened its mouth and took a deep breath.

Next to the creature's laugh, Zauberer's seemed little worse than the giggles of a happy child.

Khorne. It could only be Khorne.

'By all that's unholy,' Bob's voice said, 'the Blood God has come to life in Ichorbod's corpse!'

'I think that's an illegal substitution,' said Jim, 'but since Bool's cowering under the Hackers' bench, I don't see how he's going to call it!'

The All-Stars gathered around Khorne – or at least his avatar brought to life in Ichorbod's flesh – and fell to their knees before him. The Blood God waved his hand over each of them, and they transformed. Their armour writhed around them, as did their flesh.

One by one, the All-Stars rose once more. Their black armour glistened as if with wet paint, but Dunk knew without touching it that it now seeped ebony-coloured blood. Their skin all mirrored that of Khorne himself, shining red as if their epidermises had been stripped away. Their eyes glowed as if lit from within by the fires of hell.

Beyond the stadium's rim, Dunk saw dark mountains gathered round the place. These towered over the
people, like dead gods forced to bear witness to the
atrocities that would be carried out within. Red-gold
lightning lit the roiling crimson clouds that scudded
overhead as if carried by a hurricane bringing a storm
of blood.

Between the flashes of lightning and the terrified
rolls of thunder that seemed like the moans of a million cursed souls, Dunk realised he could see, high
above the highest seats, a ring of floating lights illu-
minating the stadium with a hellish glow. Dunk
recognised these as the new lamps that had once surrounded the arena in a tremendous circle – the ones
paid for by the Guterfiends.

'What's that Lästiges?'

'I said, according to Hacker apothecary Dr. Pill, it
seems that Schlechter Zauberer has transported the
entirety of Emperors Stadium to the Realm of Chaos,
home of such legendary chaos lords as Nurgle and
Khorne!'

'Stunning!' said Bob. 'Just like we told you before
the game folks, this is one Blood Bowl final you cannot afford to miss!'

'Are we still broadcasting via Cabalvision?' asked
Jim. 'I know I'm an ogre, but that doesn't seem possible!'

'It's all done with the latest in camra magic,' said
Bob. 'Remember that Zauberer destroyed the old camras in the semi-final game that pitted the All-Stars
against the Badlands Buccaneers. Wolf Sports had
them replaced with the finest camras available! These
babies can transmit our Cabalvision feeds across
unlimited distances, even to hell and back it seems!'

Dunk fell back and found himself standing with the other Hackers on the field in an impromptu huddle. Looking around to see his friends by his side helped to calm his pounding heart. He reached out and put his hand on Dirk's shoulder. His brother glanced back at him, and Dunk saw the fear ebb in his eyes. Then he gave Dunk a reckless grin, and the two clasped hands. No matter what they had to face, they'd face it together. Dunk only wished that Spinne could be there too.

Khorne raised his hands and brought them down in a cutting motion. Every scream in the stadium stopped, and an eerie silence reigned over the entire place. Even Bob and Jim had quit their chattering.

'People of Altdorf,' Khorne said. Although the Blood God didn't raise his voice, Dunk could hear him perfectly, and he had no doubt that everyone else in the stadium could as well. In the absence of the deafening screams, Dunk was surprised that everyone couldn't hear the blood rushing through his veins as well.

'My servant Zauberer has completed the ritual that activates the Chaos Cup. My followers placed this with your people centuries ago. It is now carrying out its true purpose.

'My champions will play your champions in this sacred game handed down to you by means of Nuffle and his writings. If your champions win, you and your stadium will return to your home realm.'

Khorne gestured to the ensorcelled All-Stars. 'If my champions win, your realm will become mine.'

'No,' Dunk whispered.

'Wow!' said Bob. 'That's the deal of a lifetime – for Khorne!'

Dunk stepped forward. 'No way!' he said, the words leaping from him before he could pause to consider the creature at which they were directed. 'You can take your deal and shove it!'

The crowd cheered.

'We won't do it,' Dunk said. 'We won't play!'

'It seems that Hoffnung has lost his mind!' said Jim. 'He's refusing to go along with the Blood God's deal!'

Khorne stared down at Dunk with his glowing, unblinking eyes. Dunk wondered if the Blood God would bleed him dry there on the spot. Then Khorne threw back his head and laughed. The sound felt like knives in Dunk's ears.

'If you refuse to play, you will be my guests here in my realm forever,' Khorne said. Then he crossed his arms on his chest and stood as still as a statue.

Pegleg ran out onto the field, with Slick and Dr. Pill trailing in his wake. 'Mr. Hoffnung!' he said. 'When the Blood God says, "play ball," you play ball!'

'Coach,' Dunk said. 'We can't. They'll kill us either way. If we lose, Altdorf and maybe the whole of the Empire – possibly the world – becomes Khorne's. This way, he only gets a stadium full of souls instead of everyone alive.'

'That's a fine theory,' Zauberer said, calling over from where he stood in Khorne's shadow, 'but sooner or later, some of you will crack, and then we will have a game!'

'He has a point,' said Dirk. 'I'd rather play them while we're still fresh. A few days from now, we may be too weak to have any hope.'

'We don't have any hope now!' Dunk said. 'Look around you! Have you seen where we are? Do you see who we have to play? We are doomed!'

Someone wrapped her arms around Dunk from behind. 'No, Dunk,' said Spinne. 'There is always hope.'

Dunk gasped, spun around and took the woman in his arms. 'What are you doing here?' he asked, half thrilled and half terrified. Hugging her tight, he saw his father standing behind her, nodding his support.

'I held out hope,' Spinne said, 'for you. I hoped that if you won this game, you might consider retiring. I wanted to be here to see that happen, to cheer you on, even if you might never have known I was here.'

Dunk gaped at the woman for a moment, and then kissed her tenderly. 'You are the most amazing person I've ever met.'

'Ditto,' Spinne said with a toothsome grin. 'Now what do you say we kick that Blood God's ass?'

'Hey,' said Slick, 'if you're going to rejoin the team, I'd like to renegotiate your contract!'

'Belay that,' said Pegleg. 'We'll renew our old agreement, or I'll toss you into the arms of Khorne as a blood sacrifice before the game begins.'

'We're still short some players, captain,' Cavre said. 'We lost a few in that last drive.'

'Who do we have left?'

'Hoffnung, Heldmann, K'Thragsh, Reyes, Edgar, Spiel, Anfäger, Hernd, now Schönheit, and myself.'

'That's ten,' Pegleg said, scratching yet another hole in his yellow tricorn hat. 'We only need one more for a full team.'

'I'll give it a try if you don't mind,' Lügner said.

'Father!' Dirk and Dunk said at the same time.

'Thanks, my sons, for pointing out that I'm old enough to make these sorts of decisions on my own. I used to be one hell of a brawler back in my day, and

I've had the occasion to put those skills to use over the past few years.'

'Who else would be mad enough to give it a go?' asked Pegleg. He stuck out his hand towards Lügner, who shook it. 'Welcome aboard, sir!'

Slick stuck up a hand to say something about negotiating a salary, but a scowl from Pegleg shut him up.

'All right,' Dunk said. 'That's eleven players, but I still don't like our odds. We're talking about playing against a Chaos Lord. How can we even tackle him? What else can we do to even things up?'

'How are the All-Stars doing?' asked Spinne. 'They were down to nine players before Khorne took over Ichorbod.'

'Is that nine with or without Ichorbod?' asked Guillermo.

'Without.'

'Does that make sense? He never did leave the field – most of him, at least.'

Spinne arched an eyebrow at Guillermo. 'Given that M'Grash kicked his head so hard that it's probably now floating down the Reik, I was comfortable counting him out.'

Guillermo nodded, and then noticed that all the other players were staring at him. He shrugged. 'I just wanted to be sure.'

'They're putting someone into a uniform,' Rotes said. 'It's that man we propped up here at the start of the half.'

'Lehrer?' Dunk said. He peered around the Blood God and saw Kathula and the bear-bodied All-Star stuffing Lehrer into a black suit of armour. As they cinched the straps around him, an evil grin grew on his face.

'It makes sense,' said Lügner with scorn. 'The Guter-fiends have worshipped Khorne for decades, and he was in their pocket.'

Dirk stared at his father in disbelief. 'That's a glass castle you're standing in there.'

'Hey, I gave it up.' Lügner gazed up at Khorne. 'Look what it got me.'

'They're still short a player,' Anfäger said. 'Think we can get them to forfeit?'

Pegleg shook his head. 'They'll find someone they can press into service, have no doubt.' He glanced down at his hook. 'Daemons excel at that sort of thing.'

'Look at this!' said Jim. 'The Game Wizards are coming in to break up this shindig! They'll set things straight!'

'Jim,' Bob said, 'I don't know what it is you've been smoking over there since we ended up in the Realms of Chaos, but you'd better damn well share it!'

'That's not me!' said Jim. 'That's the network's Censer Wizard, who's in charge of keeping our broadcast clean. The smoke is coming out of his ears!'

Dunk spotted Blaque and Whyte running across the field towards them. 'Right!' the dwarf said as they trotted up. 'You didn't have a team wizard. Now you have two.'

Dunk coughed in surprise.

'You can't do that,' Dirk said. 'It violates the GWs' neutrality.'

Blaque glanced over at Khorne, who still stood waiting. 'Can anyone blame us if we ignore a few picky regulations at this point?' he asked Whyte.

'I don't see how,' said the elf.

'Fair enough, then,' said Blaque as he turned to Pegleg. 'We're with you now.'

'We're still going to get slaughtered,' Dunk said. 'We can't play against a Chaos Lord.'

Spinne and Lügner started to protest Dunk's lack of faith, but Pegleg cut them off. 'The young Mr. Hoffnung has a point.'

The ex-pirate pivoted on his wooden leg and strode out towards midfield. He stopped ten yards short of Khorne. 'Ahoy, the Blood God!' he said.

Khorne bowed his head to look down at the man. 'You are ready?'

'The Bad Bay Hackers accept your challenge and will play on your terms – with one exception.'

'Which is?'

'You must sit on the sidelines and not interfere with the game, except as a coach.'

Khorne unfolded his arms and cracked his knuckles. They made a sound like claps of thunder. 'Why?'

'We are but mortals and can barely tolerate your mighty presence. If you are on the field, you cannot play.'

'Plus,' Dr. Pill said, strolling up behind the coach, 'the Chaos Cup's spell requires your champions to beat ours. If you play, you technically cannot be considered a champion. You run the risk of negating the spell and everything you've worked for.'

Khorne stared down at the two men. For a moment, Dunk thought he might smite them dead right there.

Instead, an evil smile played across his face. 'Standard rules. Sudden death,' he said.

'Done,' Pegleg said without hesitation.

A moment later, Ichorbod's body fell away from Khorne as if the Blood God's own form – which then revealed itself – had turned as insubstantial as that of a ghost. It crashed to the ground at an awkward angle, leaving Khorne floating there in the air in all his gory glory.

Khorne slowly settled to the ground. He snapped a salute at the Hackers and then stomped back to the All-Stars' dugout. The ground shook as he walked, and he left wide pools of blood behind in every footstep.

'Wow, folks!' Bob's voice said. 'It looks like we have a game here!'

'And not just any game,' said Jim. 'The only game I've ever been to where the fate of the Empire rests on its outcome!'

'Not to mention all our lives!' Lästiges chipped in.

'Always looking on the dark side, aren't you?' said Bob. 'I've been dead for centuries!'

As Khorne left the field, Zauberer strode up to Ichorbod's headless form. Once there, he removed something from a pocket deep within his robes and waved it over the stump of the creature's neck.

'What's that bastard doing?' asked Dirk.

'I don't know,' Dunk said with a sick feeling in the pit of his stomach, 'but it can't be good.'

Zauberer pulled out a knife with his other hand and sliced open Ichorbod's neck stump. As the blood flowed hot and free from it, he jammed the thing in his hand into the wound. He chanted a few words over it, and then stepped back to admire his work.

One of Ichorbod's legs twitched, then the other. Soon the entire body convulsed to a spastic beat no one else could hear. Then it stopped.

The body pushed itself up on its arms and then climbed to its feet. As it did, Dunk saw a small sphere sticking up out of the centre of the neck. From this distance, he couldn't make out what it was, but he had the awful feeling it was staring right at him.

Then he heard a pitiful squeak, and he knew what Zauberer had done. Despite the stifling heat in this horrible realm, he shivered.

'Can we get a close-up on Ichorbod's neck there?' asked Bob. 'Thanks!'

The image on the Jumboball zoomed in at the top of the troll. Dunk watched it until he could pick out a confirmation of his fears. There, stuck atop the stump of Ichorbod's neck, sat Skragger's shrunken head. The vampiric orc's skull must have gone flying in the blast from the bolt of lightning that had incinerated Triomphe, and Zauberer had used his magic to locate and collect it.

'Dear Nuffle's nasties!' Jim said. 'It's Skragger, the black orc legend and former captain of the Chaos All-Stars! He's back!'

'And looking better – if far stranger – than ever!' Bob said.

Skragger flexed the muscles on his huge, new, acid-skinned body and grinned up at his image on the Jumboball.

'That's right!' Skragger growled with an insane grin. 'And the Hackers are dead!'

CHAPTER THIRTY-TWO

RHETT BOOL LIMPED into the centre of the field. One of his horns had been snapped in half, and the end of it was missing. 'Captains!' he said, his voice carried over the PA system. 'Please meet in the centre of the field for the coin toss!'

Cavre trotted over to the minotaur referee, while Skragger stomped there from the other side of the field. Cavre offered his hand, but Skragger refused to take it and snarled at him instead.

'We are playing by the standard rules, but the game will be sudden death. The first score wins the game.' Bool glanced up at the blood-red, lightning-traced sky. 'Here, the All-Stars are considered the home team. The visiting team calls the coin toss in the air.'

Bool pointed at Cavre. 'Orcs or Eagles?' he said, and flipped the coin into the air.

'Eagles!' Cavre called out.

'Orcs!' said Bool.

The crowd groaned as one.

'Do you wish to kick-off or receive?' Bool asked Skragger.

The creature showed his fangs with a horrible grin. 'Receive.'

'We will take the south end of the field,' Carve said, pointing back to where the Hackers already stood. He glanced at the mountain faces leering down at the game. 'If that means anything here.'

Cavre called the Hackers to him before they scattered to their positions.

'This is bad,' he said, 'but not insurmountable, as they will have the ball first. The good thing is that they will start deep in their own territory. We cannot let them score.

'This is no time to settle old fights. We must take the ball from them as fast as we can. Once we have it, we must put it in the end zone.'

Cavre gazed at each of the Hackers in turn. 'This is no ordinary game, but you are no ordinary players. I am proud to have served as your captain. Now, let's kick some ass!'

'Go Hackers!' the players shouted in response.

The Hackers trotted out to their positions. Dunk showed Lügner where to stand, in a spot just ahead of his own and to one side. While Pegleg had parlayed with Khorne, Lügner had borrowed a suit of armour from a fallen Hacker and donned it with Dirk's help. Spinne had done the same.

'You do this for a living?' Lügner asked, a worried smile on his face. 'I thought I raised you better than that.'

'Mother raised us,' said Dunk.

'Right,' Lügner said. Dunk noticed his hands shaking.

'It's okay, Father,' Dunk said. 'We'll get through this.'

Lügner tried to smile. 'You're a good son, Dunk.'

'Hey,' Dirk said from a few yards away, 'what about me?'

'Your problem,' said Dunk, 'is you're too much of a suck-up.'

Dirk stalked over and pulled both his brother and their father into a quick embrace. 'It's good to be back in business with you two,' he said before jogging back to his position.

Spinne, who had the spot in front of Dunk and opposite Lügner, turned and blew Dunk a kiss through her helmet. 'See you after the game,' she said.

Then Bool blew the whistle, and Cavre signalled for the Hackers to get ready. The crowd watched in silence, too terrified to bother with their long-standing traditions.

Cavre laid into the ball, and it sailed far down the field. He led the charge after it, with the Hackers running in his wake.

The ball tumbled into Skragger's hand, and the blitzer spurred his new body into action. M'Grash headed straight for him, while Edgar hung back a bit, hoping to intercept any pass the All-Star captain might attempt.

Dunk raced along behind his father. He appreciated his father's valiant offer to take the field with his sons, but he knew he didn't have the experience they did. If he got into trouble, Dunk wanted to be able to help him.

Of course, taking the ball and winning the game ranked far more important than Lügner's life. After all, if the Hackers failed to manage those things, far more people than Dunk's father would suffer.

Still, Dunk kept an eye on Lügner anyhow.

M'Grash roared as he slammed into Skragger, and the All-Star captain bellowed in response. The noise echoed throughout the stadium, and the fans screamed, although whether in terror or excitement Dunk could not say.

A sleek skaven raced through the Hackers, hunting for a clear part of the field so he could get open for a pass. Lügner charged at the ratman, whose eyes glowed red, just like those of the rest of the All-Stars.

'While K'Thragsh mixes it up with Skragger near the All-Stars' end zone, Morty Maus makes a break for daylight near the other end of the field,' Bob said. 'Morty is new to the All-Stars this year, having been drafted to fill the shoes of his cousin, Macky, the All-Stars' captain who was killed in a game against the Hackers in last year's *Spike!* magazine Tournament.'

'Amazing! How can you say all that without taking a breath?' Jim asked.

'I don't breathe at all!' the vampire said.

Morty seemed faster than Dunk remembered him. He moved with a surety the rookie hadn't shown earlier in the game, and he showed no signs of exerting himself, despite sprinting up the field at top speed.

Lügner threw himself at the skaven, and Morty stiff-armed him for his trouble. Lügner fell back as if he'd hit a brick wall, and lay there, unmoving.

Dunk knew he was the only player standing between Morty and the end zone. He couldn't stop to check on his father. He had to concentrate on the skaven.

As Dunk closed with Morty, he looked into the skaven's eyes, which glowed red under his helmet.

Right then, Dunk knew that Morty wasn't there any more. Just as Khorne had taken over Ichorbod's frame, a lesser daemon had possessed Morty's body and made him stronger and faster than ever.

At the last instant, Dunk dived under Morty's out-stretched claw and slid along the Astrogranite at the creature, lashing out at him with his feet. The move surprised the skaven, who failed to even attempt to leap over Dunk's legs.

Morty tripped over Dunk at full speed and cart-wheeled into the ground. The impact knocked off his helmet, and Dunk heard the telltale, sickening sound of at least one of the skaven's limbs snapping.

The Hacker thrower rolled to his feet and looked back to where he'd been. His father was already stand-ing up, and staggering towards the next All-Star coming at him.

'Lower your shoulder!' Dunk shouted at him. 'If you stand straight up, they'll just–'

Dunk cut himself off when he spotted the ball arc-ing out over the field at him. Skragger had clearly meant the throw for Morty, but with the skaven down and possibly even out, Dunk had a clear shot at it. He leapt up into the air and felt the ball bend back his fingers and then stick between then.

Dunk hauled the ball down and landed in a crouch. When he did, he saw the bear-bodied All-Star slam into Lügner. Dunk's father either hadn't heard his son's advice or hadn't bothered to heed it. When the All-Star hit him, he'd not only been standing up, but he'd been back-pedalling to get in front of his oppo-nent.

Lügner went flying backward and landed near Dunk's feet.

Dunk wanted to help his father, but he couldn't just hand the ball over to the All-Stars. He scanned downfield and couldn't find a single Hacker open for a pass.

Cavre had become embroiled in a mass pile-up in the centre of the field. He couldn't possibly break free in time.

Spinne had managed to get past the jam in the middle of the field, but Kathula was covering her like a blanket. Dunk didn't even know if Spinne could see through the tentacles the squid-headed woman was waving in her face.

Dunk thought about tucking the ball under his arm and making a run for it. Chances were good he'd get stuck in the middle, just like Cavre, though, and it would mean leaving his father to the tender mercies of the bear-bodied All-Star, and another who'd just broken out of the mess: Lehrer.

The sight of his family's former servant made the decision for Dunk. He cocked his arm back and fired the football off like a bullet. It skated over the heads of the players in the scrum and angled straight for Spinne, but when she reached up for it, it kept on going. It was far too high for her or Kathula to catch. In the end, it disappeared into the stands, where the fans swallowed it behind their bodies.

'It looks like the Hoffnung family reunion is about to be over!' Jim said. 'Bik Dutkus is about to lay a bear-style body slam on the senior Hoffnung's chest.'

'I've seen Dutkus burst open chests with that move before. It's a real heartbreaker!'

Dunk charged forward just as the bear-bodied All-Star raised his arms and leapt from his feet, aiming to land flat atop the stunned Lügner, and put a quick end to his short career. Dunk hit Dutkus right in the ribs as he came down, knocking him clear of his fallen father.

'What a hit!' Bob said. 'The last time I saw someone get knocked around like that was when I had dinner at your house last Friday, Jim!'

'My baby girl's usually much more gentle than that with our guests, I swear!'

As Dunk scrambled to his feet, he noticed where Dutkus had sliced open Lügner's exposed forearm, splattering blood everywhere. Before he had the time to wonder why, Lehrer came at him.

Dunk took his own advice and bent low and came up under his old teacher's attack. He shoved his forearm up under Lehrer's helmet and hit him with everything he had.

Lehrer's helmet went flying off, leaving his head still attached to his shoulders, and the man flipped over onto his back. Dunk piled on top of him, determined to finish him off as fast as he could, before Dutkus could recover and kill Lügner.

'Good hit, kid,' Lehrer said. 'I taught you well.'

Dunk didn't say a thing. He just laid into the man with his fists, smashing his spiked gauntlets into his face. After three solid blows, the fight flushed out of Lehrer, and he went limp.

Dunk grabbed the old man by the top of his breast-plate so he could get in a good, solid hit. Then he cocked back his arm for the killing blow.

Dunk hesitated. He'd wanted to kill Lehrer for months, but faced with the chance to do it with his bare hands, he found it hard to follow through. Killing other players on the field was one thing. It was all part of his job. But to kill the man who'd taught him to fight, who'd raised him as much as his father had – maybe more – gave him pause, no matter how much Lehrer deserved it.

'Go ahead, kid,' Lehrer said. 'I got it coming.'

Dunk realised that the old man hadn't been possessed like the other All-Stars. He'd joined the team after the daemons had taken over the roster – which meant he'd taken up with them of his own free will.

Dunk shook his head. As he did, he spotted Dutkus getting to his feet. If he wanted to kill Lehrer, it had to be right now. Even so, it might take too long and doom Lügner to death at the bear-man's claws.

Dunk let the old man drop to the ground. 'This isn't over,' he said as he charged Dutkus again.

This time, the bear-man stood ready for Dunk. This wasn't some old man who'd never suited up for a game before. Dutkus had played Blood Bowl for years – a lifetime for an All-Stars lineman – and Dunk's last hit had driven him – and the daemon inside him – furious.

Dunk lowered his shoulder and rammed straight into Dutkus's chest. Too late, he realised that this had been exactly what the All-Star had wanted him to do.

Dutkus wrapped his arms around Dunk and managed to keep his feet. With the strength of the daemon possessing him, the bear-man worked Dunk up against him and started to squeeze, forcing the air from his lungs.

Dunk tried to break free, but Dutkus had pulled him from his feet to prevent him from getting any leverage at all. The bear-man's embrace proved impossible to shrug off. The only thing left to do was to head-butt the bear-man, but his helmet kept him too well protected. Dunk's efforts only bounced off Dutkus's faceguard.

For a moment, Dunk hoped that his own breast-plate would protect him from suffocating. If Dutkus couldn't squeeze him any further, he'd get tired eventually, and then Dunk could make his move.

But the breastplate started to give. The middle bent in towards Dunk's sternum, threatening to break his ribs and crush his lungs. Dunk flailed about with his helmet and hands, looking for some opening – anything – but nothing he did had any effect.

Dunk started to black out. Somewhere impossibly far away – maybe in a dream, he thought – he heard Lügner say, 'Let go of my son!'

Then Dutkus let loose a horrible howl right in Dunk's face. The thrower screamed back, both in pain and terror, and then he was free. He staggered backward gasping for breath, and saw his father stabbing the spikes on his gauntlet up under the bear-man's custom-made breastplate, over and over again. Each blow made a hard, meaty sound and produced gouts of blood.

Dutkus reached out and slapped Lügner away with a rough backhand, but instead of following up on the blow, the All-Star fell hard to his knees, keening in pain.

Lügner picked himself up off the ground and looked towards Dunk, worry flaring in his eyes. 'Are you okay?' he asked.

Before Dunk could shout a warning, Lehrer hit Lügner from behind. The two of them went down in a tangle of tired limbs.

'I've never seen anything like this before, Jim! The fans are refusing to give up the ball!'

'Would you want to give it back to a team who would condemn you and the entire world around you to eternal damnation, Bob?'

'That's a delicious idea! I'll have to get back to you on that one!'

'This is for Greta!' Lehrer said as he used a sharp edge on the side of his gauntlet to slice through the chinstrap on Lügner's helmet.

Dunk found that he couldn't shout because he still couldn't breathe. His crushed breastplate pressed so hard on his lungs, that even without Dutkus's help, he'd pass out if he didn't get some relief soon. He clawed at the straps that held his armour together, but they were trapped under the bent metal, and he couldn't quite reach them on his own.

'She was mine!' Lügner said to Lehrer as he held the other man's arm at bay. Lügner's helmet had fallen off, exposing his head. Blood flowed from a half-dozen small cuts on his face and neck.

'She loved me first!' Lehrer said. 'You stole her from me, and because of you, she's dead!'

Lügner shoved his free hand up under Lehrer's face-guard and wrapped his fingers around the man's throat. 'You think you grieve for her more than me? I know it's my fault that mob stormed the castle. There's not a day goes by that the guilt doesn't crush me!'

Lehrer started to laugh, low and strained, as Lügner's choking of him made anything louder impossible. 'You don't understand,' he said, 'but then you never did.

'I let that mob in,' Lehrer said. 'I gave Greta the chance to escape with me, to take Kirta and run away with me to start a new life somewhere else.'

'You–!'

Lehrer spat down into Lügner's face. 'She spurned me – again – because of you. She slapped my face.'

Dunk strained against his armour with all his might, but it just wouldn't give. He fell forward on his knees and started to crawl forward, but he could not get enough air in his lungs to proceed. He collapsed onto his face.

'I killed her,' Lehrer rasped as Lügner's fingers crushed his windpipe. 'I killed them both, and I let the mob in to cover my sins.'

Lügner let go of the hand Lehrer had poised near his own neck and drove both of his hands into the other man's larynx. As he did, Lehrer punched up under his old master's jaw with his spiked gauntlet, piercing the soft flesh there and tearing open his throat.

As Dunk watched, unable to do anything to prevent the horrors before him, a blade slipped between the halves of his breastplate and sliced through the straps holding them together. He ignored the pain that flared in his side as the blade cut through the flesh in his haste. He drew in a large gulp of air and bellowed, 'No!'

CHAPTER THIRTY-THREE

'FORGET THEM,' DIRK said as he hauled Dunk to his feet and helped him shrug off his crushed breastplate. 'It's too late for them, but maybe not for the rest of us.'

Dunk growled in frustration, and turned to see the ball bouncing around in the stands. Skragger had waded in after it, slaughtering helpless fans left and right, causing a general stampede away from him, but every time he got near the ball, the fans would toss it away from him again towards another part of the stadium.

Now some of the other All-Stars, emboldened by Skragger's success, were venturing into the stands too. Eventually, the fans would make a mistake – or one of them would decide to buy his own life with the ball – and the All-Stars would get the pigskin back, unless the Hackers did something fast.

Dunk and Dirk sprinted towards the end zone, where they saw Spinne sparring with Kathula. They looked like they'd been at it for a while. Each of them had lost pieces of armour and bled from a handful of superficial wounds. Kathula's helmet had gone missing, but she made up for it by lashing out harder and faster with the unrestrained tentacles that made up the lower half of her face.

One of the tentacles wrapped around Spinne's bare forearm and started to pull her in towards Kathula's snapping beak. Spinne braced her feet and spun around, swinging Kathula after her by the tentacle attached to the catcher's arm.

The squeals of pain that spouted from Kathula's face only encouraged Spinne, and she began to turn faster and faster, pulling the squid-woman from her feet. The soft tissue of the attached tentacle began to stretch, and this caused the tentacle's grip around Spinne's arm to tighten until it started to cut off the circulation to her hand.

The Hackers' catcher spun faster and faster. She screamed from the pain in her arm as the tentacle stretched thinner and thinner and began to slice into her bare flesh like a length of sharp wire.

'That's one way to dance!' Bob said. 'Looks like Schönheit's the one calling the tune!'

'I think Kathula is regretting extending the invitation now. She looks like she – or her face, rather – might snap at any second!' said Jim.

A moment later, that's exactly what happened. The tentacle around Spinne's arm pulled free from Kathula's face, and the squid-woman went flying towards the stands. She landed against the restraining wall, and the fans in the first row caught her. She screamed again as they pulled her into the bleachers, blood spouting from her face. The people there tore her to pieces with a dozen sets of hands at once, and they kept at her until long after she stopped screaming from the pain.

'What happened to you?' Spinne asked Dunk as she unwrapped the length of tentacle from her arm. It left a deep cut behind, but it had not gone through the muscle to the bone. She glanced at his bare chest. 'I like the new look.'

Dunk wanted to smile at her, but found he couldn't. 'We need to get that ball,' he said. 'Do you think we'll survive if we go into the crowd?'

Spinne nodded. 'The trick is that the All-Stars will then use you as a shield so they can get in too. At least, that's what they've done twice so far, and when the shield fails, they'll kill you if they can. We've lost Anfäger and Hernd that way already. I think I even saw Slick disappear in there.'

Dunk glanced around. M'Grash and Cavre were trying to get into the crowd, but a trio of All-Stars had blocked them. Spiel had climbed into Edgar's upper branches to get away from an orc whose arms seemed to have become axes. Guillermo had made it ten rows up into the stands and was waving and hollering for the fans to throw him the ball. Skragger was working his way towards the Estalian, slaughtering fans as he went.

Up in the stands, Dunk saw a Hacker helmet bouncing along atop the heads and upraised hands of the fans, but there didn't seem to be anything but a jersey beneath it, somehow snagged inside the helmet. It turned his stomach to think whose head might be in it. Oddly, it seemed to be heading for the ball, as if the fans wished to bring the two together.

'We'll have to chance it,' Dunk said. 'I'll distract Skragger. You two get that ball!'

He charged towards the worst part of the devastation, a section of stands cleared out entirely but for a couple of handfuls of dead or dying fans. 'Skragger!' he shouted. 'You damned coward! Come on down here and fight someone your own – fight me, you wuss! I'm looking forward to keeping your tiny head in the bottom of my chamber pot from now on.'

'You!' Skragger said as he turned to see who had insulted him. 'Kill you!'

Dunk stood his ground in the end zone, waiting for the crazed troll-bodied, vampire-headed orc creature to make his way down to him. They were going to end this here, one way or the other, he was sure.

As Dunk braced for Skragger's attack, a bolt of red lightning cracked into the Astrogranite next to him. He turned around just in time to see a pillar of ash that had once been a dark elf in an All-Stars' uniform crumble into a pile of dust.

'That Chaos Cup must have made Zauberer a better shot,' Jim said, 'because without it he doesn't seem like he could hit the backside of an ogre!'

'He can't even do that!' said Bob. 'He's missed K'Thragsh three times already today!'

Dunk spotted Zauberer floating high over the stadium, cursing as he pointed his wand in Dunk's direction again. The thrower stared up at the wizard and wondered just how someone could try to dodge a lightning bolt. As he watched, Zauberer's robes transformed into a writhing sheet of vipers.

'Got 'em!' Blaque shouted from the sidelines near the Hackers' dugout. He turned towards Whyte. 'Do you have something about snakes? Why not just kill the bugger?'

Dunk never heard the reply. As he laughed, watching the snakes strike at the wizard in an effort to keep from falling to their deaths, a shadow fell over him. He had just enough time to glance over and see Skragger coming down at him – and maybe to wonder just how he could possibly survive this.

Acting on instinct instead of conscious thought, Dunk dived forward. Most of Skragger sailed over him, but the creature's boot tagged Dunk on his pauldron and knocked him spinning to the ground.

When Dunk got up, he found Skragger standing over him. 'You're dead!' the creature snarled, spreading its arms wide and gathering Dunk into its fatal embrace.

Contact with Skragger's skin burned Dunk's bare chest, but just barely. At first he fought it, but having gone through that just moments ago with Dutkus, he knew that he was doomed to fail. Instead, he began to claw at Skragger with everything he had.

As Dunk clawed at Skragger with his fingers, he realised that the creature wasn't all there. His fingers passed right through Skragger's flesh, striking bone instead. When Khorne had remade the body, it seemed it had only been an illusion, not real at all. The bits that had burned Dunk's skin a bit were the bare remnants that were left: not much more than a skeletal frame underneath it all.

Confused, but still determined, Dunk kept pulling at Skragger. His efforts became more desperate as the bony Skragger increased the pressure on him, squeezing the breath from him, realising that the skin he thought would burn Dunk wasn't doing a thing. Dunk's digging hands found a set of ribs and started yanking on them, pulling them out and tossing them over his shoulder.

'Crush you dead!' Skragger growled as Dunk continued his grisly work. Once through the ribcage, he stabbed his hand into the creature's chest, hoping to find a vital organ, or maybe to snap Skragger's borrowed spine.

Instead, his fingers struck something hard and gnarled. He felt for purchase, and then it bit him hard, straight to the bone. Dunk pulled his bloody fingers back for a second and then dived back in with both arms. This time the thing inside didn't put up a fight. But the creature it was inside of did.

'No!' Skragger screeched in his high-pitched voice. 'You can't! I won't let you!'

Skragger went from crushing Dunk to his chest to desperately trying to shove him away. He wedged an arm between himself and Dunk and pushed with all his might.

Dunk had found the grips his hands needed, and he refused to let go, no matter what happened. He gritted his teeth and pulled with both his arms, using Skragger's strength to reinforce his own.

'No!' Skragger said, bashing at Dunk with his free arm. The blows smashed into Dunk's helmet and rattled his brains in his skull. Still he held on as best he could. He worked his knees up between himself and Skragger and pulled as hard as he could on the thing in the creature's chest. Soon, he knew either the thing would give out or he would. Soon it would all be over, one way or another.

Then Bob said, 'Touchdown, Hackers!'

'No!' something inside of Skragger screamed. At first, Dunk thought it had come from Skragger's head, but the voice had been far too deep. Then, with one last pull, the thing inside Skragger yanked free from his ribcage, and Dunk went tumbling backward off the beast.

Dunk landed in the end zone, right next to Slick, who stood over him, grinning and holding the ball. The halfling wore a Hacker helmet that fit him like an umbrella, and a Hacker jersey that tumbled past his knees like a dress.

'Good work, son!' Slick said. 'That's an astonishing prize you have there.'

Dunk glanced back to discover what he held in his hands, and he saw the Chaos Cup staring back at him. It screamed at him, its beady, black eyes blazing red fire.

Another, more horrible scream, echoed that of the Chaos Cup. It came from the All-Stars' dugout, still shrouded in blackness. It didn't remain in there. A moment later, Khorne's blood-soaked form burst from the dugout and sailed high into the sky over the stadium.

'The preparation of a thousand years gone to waste!' the Blood God shouted in disgust. 'I was so close! It was almost mine!'

With that, the blazing hot air around the stadium shimmered and gave way to crisp, cool weather. The sky turned clear and blue once more, and the leering mountains disappeared from the distance. The scent of brimstone faded away, and Dunk's mouth tasted not of ash, but of his own tongue again.

The crowd stood up and cheered.

'Hackers win!' Bob said, even happier than when he'd announced the touchdown. 'The world is saved! We all get to live! Hackers win!'

CHAPTER THIRTY-FOUR

'LET'S SEE THAT replay again,' Slick said. The image on the crystal ball leapt backward and showed the halfling standing alone in the stands with the ball in his hands. Then Dirk appeared next to him and lifted him up over his head. With a two-handed throw, Dirk hurled Slick down the field, where Spinne caught him just before his head smacked into the ground.

Dunk listened from the doorway for a moment and smiled. Seeing everyone together like this made all the strange, horrible, and sometimes even wonderful adventures of the past three years seem worthwhile.

'I think that's enough,' Lästiges said. 'You'll wear out my Daemonic Visual Display.'

'I thought you could run a DVD forever?'

Lästiges smiled as she leaned back into Dirk's arms in the plush couch. 'After what we've all been through, I thought you'd know that daemons don't last forever.'

'Show what happens to Skragger instead, then,' Slick said. 'I love seeing justice served.'

'Must we suffer through that again?' Guillermo asked with a shiver, from the other end of the couch. 'It is bad enough we have to watch his tiny head torn from the skeleton time after time, but to see the sad little thing disappear into the stadium's communal bog… I can do without that.'

'Are you getting soft, Mr. Reyes?' Cavre asked with a smile from his overstuffed chair across the way.

'Just on myself,' Guillermo said with a wry smile.

'That bloody bastard had worse than that coming to him,' said Edgar. Here in the private courtyard, he could stretch his branches high into the open sky, which tended to put him in a much better mood than when he was forced indoors just to be near his team-mates, his friends. 'He's just lucky I didn't get my bloody twigs on him, or I'd have crushed him under my roots.'

'He got off easier than that accursed wizard for sure,' Pegleg said. The coach reclined on a divan, his good leg up on the furniture while his wooden one rested, removed, on the floor.

'Still sorry,' M'Grash said with a frown. He sat on the floor, too morose still to permit himself anything more comfortable. 'Didn't know.'

'It's okay, M'Grash,' Spiel said. 'The way you don't like snakes, it's easy to see why you'd want to stomp all those vipers to a bloody paste. It's just unfortunate that Zauberer happened to be underneath them when you did.'

Dunk took this as his cue to stroll back into the room. The best thing he could do for M'Grash would be to help keep his mind off that accidental, but convenient killing.

'Did you get rid of it, Mr. Hoffnung?' Pegleg asked.

Dunk nodded. 'The Champions of Death were pleased to get their trophy, and I was happy to get rid of it.'

'We could have won that game if not for the Game Wizards,' Pegleg said. 'The Chaos Cup should be ours.'

'That's one honour I think I can do without,' Dunk said.

'Besides, captain, we do have the Blood Bowl trophy to help assuage that pain,' said Cavre. 'I can contact Dr. Pill if you need anything stronger.'

'That one-eyed elf gives me the willies,' Spinne said from an overstuffed love seat that bore scorch marks from a wayward torch. 'I'll be happy to not see him for a couple of months.'

'Careful,' said Pegleg. 'Just because we've won the greatest trophy in the land doesn't mean we can rest on our laurels. Now we have a title to defend!'

'Right,' said Dunk, 'but for my part I'm looking forward to a little rest and relaxation.' He raised his head and looked around at the walls of his old family keep. 'Besides, cleaning up this place properly is going to take weeks.'

Dirk grinned at his brother. 'So you got it back in roughly the same condition as when you left it. As I recall, a mob of angry people ran through the place back then too, just like yesterday.'

Dunk nodded. 'It's too bad some of the Guterfiends got away. I suppose with the game being broadcast live it was bound to happen. They just weren't stupid enough to stick around after Khorne's team lost.'

'I don't think they'll be back to Altdorf any time soon,' Lästiges said with a carefree laugh.

'Why were you gone so long?' Spinne asked, motioning for Dunk to sit down next to her.

'I had something else to pick up,' Dunk said as he came over to stand in front of Spinne. He reached into his pocket, knelt down in front of her and gazed into her eyes.

'Blood Bowl has been great to me,' Dunk said. 'When I met Slick for the first time, I was just about ready to give up and let that chimera eat me. I was homeless, penniless, and friendless.

'Playing this game has changed all that.'

He nodded at Pegleg. 'It gave me money.'

He smiled at Dirk. 'It brought my brother back to me.'

He glanced around at the others. 'It made me many of the most loyal and trustworthy friends a man could wish for.'

He stared around at the four walls around them. 'It even restored me to my ancestral home.'

Dunk turned back to Spinne again. She was so beautiful he almost couldn't stand to look at her, but to turn away seemed far worse.

'There's only one thing I'd like to change,' Dunk said, as he presented the ring to Spinne. It had a wide band of gold and a diamond cut into the shape of a football.

'Yes!' Spinne said before Dunk could say another word. Her grin split her face and showed all her pearly teeth. 'I cannot wait to marry you!'

Dunk held her close for a long moment, and then kissed her, and she kissed him back like she wanted it to last forever. When their lips parted, they held each other still, and she wiped away the lone tear that had found its way onto his cheek.

'So, son,' Slick said. 'I hope this doesn't mean you're entertaining any silly notions of retiring from the game and settling down?'

Dunk cocked his head to one side. He heard something coming from outside the keep's walls. 'I don't think so,' he said as he leapt to his feet. 'Follow me.'

Taking Spinne's hand, he strode with her through the keep until they reached the balcony that overlooked the public square outside the small fortress's doors, which still lay smashed open from the night before.

As Dunk and Spinne stepped up to the balcony, the people of Altdorf in the square below erupted in cheers. When Pegleg, Slick, and the rest of the Hackers appeared behind them, the noise rose to a roar.

Dunk turned to kiss Spinne again, a grin on both their faces.

'What's that they're chanting?' she asked.

'Can't you make it out?'

'They may be wonderful fans, but they don't have the best rhythm. Tell me.'

Dunk leaned closer to her. 'Listen,' he said. '"Repeat! Repeat! Repeat!"'

'Oh,' Spinne said with a sly smile as she leaned in to kiss Dunk again. 'Don't mind if I do.'

ABOUT THE AUTHOR

Matt Forbeck has worked full-time in the adventure game industry for over 15 years. He has designed collectible card games, roleplaying games, miniatures games, and board games, and has written short fiction, comic books, and novels. His previous novels include the critically acclaimed *Secret of the Spiritkeeper* for Wizards of the Coast. *Death Match* is his third novel for the Black Library.

A GUIDE TO BLOOD BOWL

Being a volume of instruction for rookies and beginners of
Nuffle's sacred game.

(Translated by Andreas Halle of Middenheim)

NUFFLE'S SACRED NUMBER

Let's start with the basics. To play Blood Bowl you need
two warrior sects each led by a priest. In the more com-
monly used Blood Bowl terminology this means you need
two teams of fearless psychotics (we also call them 'players') led by a coach, who is quite often a hoary old
ex-player more psychotic than all of his players put
together.

   The teams face each other on a ritualised battlefield
known as a pitch or field. The field is marked out in white
chalk lines into several different areas. One line separates the
pitch in two through the middle dividing the field into each
team's 'half'. The line itself is known as the 'line of

scrimmage' and is often the scene of some brutal fighting, especially at the beginning and halfway points of the game. At the back of each team's half of the field is a further dividing line that separates the backfield from the end zone. The end zone is where an opposing team can score a 'touchdown' – more on that later.

Teams generally consist of between twelve to sixteen players. However, as first extolled by Roze–el, Nuffle's sacred number is eleven, which means only a maximum of eleven players from each team may be on the field at the same time. It's worth noting that many teams have tried to break this sacred convention in the past, particularly goblin teams (orcs too, but that's usually because they can't count rather than any malevolent intent), but Nuffle has always seen fit to punish those who do.

TOUCHDOWNS AND ALL THAT MALARKEY

The aim of the game is to carry, throw, kick and generally move an inflated animal bladder coated in leather and – quite often – spikes, across the field into the opposing team's end zone. Of course, the other team is trying to do the same thing. Once the inflated bladder, also known as the ball, has been carried into or caught in the opposing team's end zone, a 'touchdown' has been scored. Traditionally the crowd then goes wild, though the reactions of the fans vary from celebration if it was their team that just scored to anger if their team have conceded. The player who has scored will also have his moment of jubilation and much celebratory hugging with fellow team–mates will ensue, although a bear hug from an Ogre, even if his intention is that of mutual happiness, is best avoided! The team that scores the most touchdowns within the allotted time-frame is deemed the winner.

The game lasts about two hours and is split into two segments unsurprisingly called 'the first half' and 'the second half'. The first half starts after both teams have walked onto the pitch and taken their positions, usually accompanied by much fanfare and cheering from the fans. The team captains meet in the centre of the pitch with the 'ref' (more on him later) to perform the start-of-the-game ritual known as 'the toss'. A coin is flipped in the air and one of the captains will call 'orcs' or 'eagles'. Whoever wins the toss gets the choice of 'kicking' or 'receiving'. Kicking teams will kick the ball to the receiving teams. Once the ball has been kicked the whistle is blown and the first half will begin. The second half begins in much the same way except that the kicking team at the beginning of the first half will now become the receiving team and vice-versa.

Violence is encouraged to gain possession, keep and move the ball, although different races and teams will try different methods and varying degrees of hostility. The fey elves, for instance, will often try pure speed to collect the ball and avoid the other team's players. Orc and Chaos teams will take a more direct route of overpowering the opposing team and trundling down the centre of the field almost daring their opponents to stop them.

Rookies reading this may be confused as to why I haven't mentioned the use of weapons yet. This is because in Blood Bowl Nuffle decreed that one's own body is the only weapon one needs to play the game. Over the years this hasn't stopped teams using this admittedly rather loose wording to maximum effect and is the reason why a player's armour is more likely than not covered in sharp protruding spikes with blades and large knuckle–dusters attached to gauntlets. Other races and teams often 'forget' about this basic principle and just ignore Roze–el's teachings on the matter. Dwarfs and goblins (yes, them again) are the usual suspects, although this is not exclusively their domain. The history of Blood Bowl is littered with the illegal use of weapons and the many devious contraptions brought forward by the dwarfs and goblins, ranging from monstrous machines such as the dwarf death–roller to the no–less–dangerous chainsaw.

THE PSYCHOS... I MEAN PLAYERS

As I've already mentioned, there are many ways to get the ball from one end of the field to the other. Equally, there are as many ways to stop the ball from moving towards a team's end zone. A Blood Bowl player, to an extent, needs to be a jack–of–all–trades – as equally quick on the offensive as well as being able to defend. This doesn't mean that there aren't any specialists in the sport, far from it – a Blood Bowl player needs to specialise in one of the many positions if he wishes to rise above the humble lineman. Let's look at the more common positions:

Blitzers: These highly–skilled players are usually the stars of the game, combining strength and skill with great speed and flexibility. All the most glamorous Blood Bowl players are blitzers, since they are always at the heart of the action and doing very impressive things! Their usual job is to burst a hole through their opponents' lines, and then run with the ball to score. Team captains are usually blitzers, and all of them, without exception, have egos the size of a halfling's appetite.

Throwers: There is more to Blood Bowl than just grabbing the ball and charging full tilt at the other side (though this has worked for most teams at one time or another). If you can get a player on the other side of your opponents' line, why not simply toss the ball to him and cut out all that unnecessary bloodshed? This, of course, is where the special thrower comes in! These guys are usually lightly armoured (preferring to dodge a tackle rather than be flattened by it).

Throwers of certain races have also been known to launch other things than just the ball. For decades now, an accepted tactic of orc, goblin and even halfling teams is to throw their team-mates downfield. This is usually done by the larger members of said teams such as ogres, trolls and in the case of the halflings, treemen. Of course this tactic is not without risk. Whilst the bigger players are strong it doesn't necessarily mean they are accurate. As regular fans know, goblins make a reassuring 'splat' sound as they hit the ground or stadium wall head-first – much to the joy of the crowd! Trolls are notoriously stupid with memory spans that would shame a goldfish. So a goblin or snotling about to be hurtled across the pitch by his trollish team mate will often find itself heading for the troll's gaping maw instead as the monster forgets what he's holding and decides to have a snack!

Catchers: And of course if you are throwing the ball, it would be nice if there was someone at the other end to catch it! This is where the specialist catcher comes in. Lightly armoured for speed, they are adept at dodging around slower opponents and heading for the open field ready for a long pass to arrive. The best catcher of all time is generally reckoned to be the legendary Tarsh Surehands of the otherwise fairly repulsive skaven team, the Skavenblight Scramblers. With his two heads and four arms, the mutant ratman plainly had something of an advantage.

Blockers: If one side is trying to bash its way through the opposing team's lines, you will often see the latter's blockers come into action to stop them. These lumbering giants are often slow and dim-witted, but they have the size and power to stop show-off blitzers from getting any further up the field! Black orcs, ogres and trolls make especially good blockers, but this fact has hampered the chances of teams like the Oldheim Ogres, who, with nothing but blockers and linemen in their team, have great trouble actually scoring a touchdown!

Linemen: While a good deal of attention is paid to the various specialist players, every true Blood Bowl fan would agree that the players who do most of the hard work are the ordinary linemen. These are the guys who get bashed out of the way while trying to stop a hulking great ogre from sacking their thrower, who are pushed out of the way when their flashy blitzer sets his sights on the end zone, or who get beaten and bruised by the linemen of the opposite side while the more gifted players skip about scoring touchdowns. 'Moaning like a lineman' is a common phrase in Blood Bowl circles for a bad complainer, but if it wasn't for the linemen whingeing about their flashier team-mates, the newspapers would often have nothing to fill their sports pages with!

DA REFS

Blood Bowl has often been described, as 'nearly-organised chaos' by its many critics. Blood Bowl's admirers emphatically agree with the critics then again they don't like to play up the 'nearly-organised' bit, in fact some quite happily just describe it as 'chaos'. However, it is widely accepted that you do need someone in charge of the game's proceedings and to enforce the games rules or else it wouldn't be Blood Bowl at all. Again, this point is often lost on some fans who would quite happily just come and spectate/participate in a big fight. In any case, the person and/or creature in charge of a game is known as 'the ref'. The ref, in his traditional kit of zebra furs, has a very difficult job to do. You have to ask yourself what kind of mind accepts this sort of responsibility especially when the general Blood Bowl viewing public rate refs far below tax collectors, traffic wardens and sewer inspectors in their estimation.

Of course some refs revile in the notoriety and are as psychopathic as the players themselves. Max 'Kneecap' Mittleman would never issue a yellow or red card but simply disembowel the offending player. It is also fair to say that most (if not all) refs are not the bastions of honesty and independence they would have you believe. In fact the Referees and Allied Rulekeepers Guild has strict bribery procedures and union established rates. Although teams may not always want to bribe a ref – especially when sheer intimidation can be far cheaper.

THAT'S THE BASICS

Now I've covered the rudimentary points of how to play Blood Bowl it's worth going over some of the basic plays you'll see in most games of one variation or another. Remember, it's not just about the fighting; you have to score at some point as well!

The Cage: Probably the most basic play in the game yet it's the one halfling teams still can't get right. This involves surrounding the ball carrier with bodyguards and then moving the whole possession up field. Once within yards of the team's end zone the ball carrier will explode from his protective cocoon and sprint across the line. Not always good against elf teams who have an annoying knack of dodging into the cage and stealing the ball away, still you should see the crowd's rapture when an elf mis-steps and he's clothes-lined to the floor by a sneering orc.

The Chuck: The second most basic play, although it does require the use of a semi-competent thrower, which rules a large proportion of teams out from the start. Blockers on the 'line of scrimmage' will open a gap for the team's receivers to run through, and once they are in the opposing team's back field the thrower will lob the ball to them. Provided one of the catchers can catch it, all that remains is a short run into the opposing end zone for a touchdown. The survival rate of a lone catcher in the enemy's half is obviously not great so it's important to get as many catchers upfield as possible. The more catchers a team employs, the more chances at least one of them will remain standing to complete the pass.

The Chain: A particular favourite of blitzers everywhere. Players position themselves at different stages upfield. The ball is then quickly passed from player to player in a series of short passes until the blitzer on the end of the chain can wave to the crowd and gallop into the end zone. A broken link in the chain can balls this up (excuse the pun), giving the opposing team an opportunity to intercept the ball.

The Kill-em-all!: Favoured by dwarf teams and those that lack a certain finesse. It works on the principle that if there isn't anyone left in the opposing team, then who's going to stop you from scoring? The receiving team simply hides the ball in its half and proceeds to maul, break and kill the opposition, Chaos teams are particularly good at this. When there is less than a third of the opposing team left, the ball will slowly make its way upfield. The downside is that some teams can get so engrossed in the maiming they simply run out of time to score. Nevertheless it's a fan favourite and is here to stay.

WARHAMMER

DAY OF THE
DAEMON

AARON ROSENBERG

BOOK ONE IN THE AWESOME DAEMON GATES TRILOGY

More Warhammer action from the Black Library

DAY OF THE DAEMON

An extract from book one in the Daemon Gates Trilogy
by Aaron Rosenburg

DIETRICH 'DIETZ' FROEBEL flattened himself against the wall, the rough stone digging into his back through his sweat-soaked shirt and vest. 'If I make it out of here,' he muttered to himself, 'I swear I'll never look at cats the same way again.'

Just past him, an arched doorway broke the wall, and by craning his neck Dietz could see several tall, husky figures prowling down the hall beyond. He had seen beastmen before, of course – mostly when their bodies had been dragged back to Middenheim by bounty hunters and bored guardsmen. He'd even fought a few since enlisting in that madman Alaric's service. When he thought of beastmen he pictured those creatures: animals that walked upright, bestial men with strangely distorted features and scraps of leather and cloth for makeshift clothes. Some had crude armour they'd clearly ripped from their victims and pieced back together. Weapons were the same way, crude or stolen and poorly tended.

Not these, however. The creatures stalking past were

built like men, except for their long lashing tails, but moved with the grace of cats, as well they should. Their bodies were covered in striped orange and black fur, their heads those of tigers, but with more intelligent eyes, their hands tipped with claws, but able to grasp weapons easily. These beastmen were nothing like he'd imagined. Their armour was clearly handmade, little more than tooled leather straps holding flat discs of metal and stone in strategic locations, but handsome and effective. Their weapons were hatchets and short swords, and spears with blades of glittering black stone and hafts of gleaming wood, far finer than Dietz had imagined beastmen capable of creating.

Everything about Ind had come as a surprise. Of course, that made sense. They were several thousand miles from the Empire, after all. If it were all like home, what would be the point in travelling? Some of the surprises, like the lush landscape, were actually pleasant; shame this wasn't one of them.

He ducked back and pressed himself even harder against the wall when one of the beastmen paused and snarled something. Hoping they hadn't heard him – or smelled him – Dietz held his breath. He heard a soft padding sound and knew at least one was approaching. His right hand crept to the long knife at his belt, though he knew he could only take one down before the others jumped him. Just as he was sliding the blade from its sheath he heard a loud, musical clang that echoed through the chamber, shaking the floor and setting his teeth vibrating. At last!

The padding stopped, then resumed again, but moving away, and Dietz slowly let out his breath. A moment later the hall was silent and he risked another glance. They had gone.

He and Alaric had watched the temple for several days before attempting to enter and had quickly seen the pattern. Every day, as the sun hit its height, a gong sounded from the temple's peak. All the beastmen stopped what they were doing and funnelled indoors. Whether it was the mid-day meal or group worship did not matter. The important thing was that all of the beastmen were occupied, which would leave the halls clear. Dietz had wanted to wait until the gong to enter, but Alaric had pointed out the temple's sheer size. 'You'll never get to the centre in time if you wait that long,' he'd explained. 'You'll have to start sooner so the gong can clear the final passages for you.'

And he'd been right, damn him. Dietz was only halfway through the maze of corridors, though the rest of his progress would be quicker without having to duck along side passages. He hated it when Alaric was right. Not that his employer would even notice. And where was he, while Dietz was doing all the hard work? Probably still staring at that tablet by the entrance, he thought.

'FASCINATING!' ALARIC VON Jungfreud brushed some dirt from the flat panel embedded in the temple wall before him and traced the rune he'd revealed. Then he copied it down in his notebook. 'Not an honorific at all. That's definitely a warning of some sort, or an admonition – perhaps a conditional? Coupled with this other mark here...'

His blond head bent over his notebook, Alaric barely registered the gong's vibrations. Nor did it occur to him to wonder where Dietz was, or whether the other man was in any danger. Or to worry about crouching by the temple's entrance, in easy view of anyone approaching or stepping out onto one of the balconies above. All Alaric thought of was the tablet and the words inscribed upon it. Dietz would be fine. He always was.

'SIGMAR'S BEARD!'

Though he kept his voice low, the words still echoed through the small chamber. Dietz had made his way down the corridors, trading stealth for speed now that the gong had cleared the halls of occupants. He had finally reached a door, the only one he had seen – every other portal had been an open archway. This archway held a slab of stone polished to silky smoothness, its glossy black surface providing a perfect reflection of Dietz and the hall behind him. The door had no lock he could find, but from its centre protruded a tiger's head of red marble, a massive ring clutched in its jaws. A sharp tug on the ring and the door had slid open silently. He had stepped quickly inside and the sight beyond was the cause of his sudden outburst.

This was the heart of the temple. It had to be. It was a small chamber, barely twenty feet across, with strange angled corners and walls that curved up to form a vaulted ceiling. A second smaller door stood to one side. The centre of the ceiling was a circle of clear crystal, and the sun shone down, its light flooding the room and spilling across the intricately tiled floor. Dietz saw tigers and lions, and other great cats battling beneath his feet, rending men and horses and each other.

That was not what had stopped him. Nor was it the carved columns at each corner of the room or the inset nooks holding sculptures and vases, or even the tapestries that hung between them. No, the statue facing the door had provoked his outburst. It covered the entire wall and dominated the chamber.

Dietz stepped closer, studying the carving. Much of it was the red marble of the door sculpture, though a paler, brighter red. The dark marbling had been artfully arranged to reproduce tiger stripes across the torso and limbs. The figure towered above him, its uppermost claws almost scraping the skylight. Other arms held a golden sword, a glittering black mace, a strange barbed fan and a black-headed spear. The bottom arms clutched a crimson scroll between them. Gold-set jewels hung from the tufted ears, decorated many of the claws and even pierced various points about the chest. A heavy belt, gold links connecting rubies and diamonds and other stones, hung on the hips. A curving golden spike capped the tail arcing up behind, but it was the face that captured his attention. Carved from a single slab of stone, golden brown with streaks of light where the sun touched it, the face spoke of cruelty and blood lust and a horrible intelligence. It's only a statue, Dietz reassured himself as he gasped for breath, but his heart did not believe that. No, this was She'ar Khawn, the eight-armed tiger-god of Ind, standing before him. And She'ar Khawn was not happy.

The sound of a second, lighter gong rippled through the temple air and shook Dietz from his panic. It was the first of several, and after the fourth there would be one final peal from the larger gong. Then the beastmen would return to their duties and the hall would be swarming with them again. He had to hurry.

Alaric had not known what to expect, so his instructions had been vague. 'Grab something small enough to carry, valuable enough to be worth our time and distinctive enough it could not come from anywhere else,' he had said. Dietz thought about this. The figures in the wall niches were handsome but perhaps not that unique. The tapestries were too large to carry easily. The jewels about the statue might be fused to the stone. He considered the scroll, but could not see its surface well enough to know whether it was real or a clever carving, and what good would a sculpture of a scroll be to him? Then his gaze returned to the tiger-god's face, and Dietz nodded. Since She'ar Khawn was already displeased, he saw no reason to be nice about it.

Pulling his knife, Dietz stepped up close to the statue, resisting a shudder as he passed within the compass of those eight arms. Raising his blade, he applied its tip to the bottom edge of the statue's golden face and exerted pressure, just enough to see how securely the face was held. Much to his surprise he heard a faint pop and a shrill keen, and it slid free. He caught it reflexively as it dropped, surprised by its lack of weight. Turning it over, Dietz realised why. It was not a solid carving so much as a mask, the interior carved away to allow space for a face behind it. Glancing up again, he saw that the statue still had a face the same red marble as the rest. The mask had been laid over it.

As he stepped back, sheathing the knife and sliding the mask into the pack at his back, Dietz noticed the keening had not stopped. In fact it had grown louder, and now it was joined by a strange hiss.

Trusting his instincts, Dietz hurled himself backwards. A sharp breeze tugged at his hair and beard as the hiss intensified, and he felt as much as saw a sheet of silver plummeting from the ceiling. He struck the ground hard, landing on his rear and rolling to his feet as the massive blade dropped from the ceiling and sank into a groove carved along the floor mere inches from the statue, and right where he had been standing.

'Time to go,' he muttered to himself, and turned in time to see the door sliding shut. 'Damn!' He pushed against it, but it did not budge. Beyond it he could hear the pad of feet and the scrape of claws against stone. Glancing around, Dietz saw the second door also sliding shut and dived for it, scraping through just before the heavy stone slab thudded into the doorframe. 'What have we here?' he wondered, glancing around.

This was an even smaller room, though with more traditional squared walls and corners. It had no windows, no elaborate carvings and its floor was the same smooth red granite he had seen elsewhere in the temple. A second door barring the far side of the room was of polished wood rather than stone. Clearly, this was an antechamber of some sort, but for what purpose?

Then Dietz noticed the cages.

They were small, barely the size of his head, and made from tightly fitted wooden slats. He had missed them at first because of their size and because they were all piled in the corners. Scraping sounds, whimpers, clicks and other noises told him they were occupied, as did the smell, which finally hit him. With a shudder, Dietz remembered the scroll in She'ar Khawn's lowest hands and understood. The crimson was old blood from sacrifices. These poor creatures were the victims.

'Sorry I can't help,' he told them as he hurried past to the outer door. Hauling it open, Dietz found himself facing a narrow corridor – and several beastmen charging towards him, faces twisted into snarls, blades at the ready.

A quick glance around confirmed that the antechamber had no other exits. The corridor was empty save the approaching guards, but the antechamber itself–

'Your lucky day,' Dietz said as he grabbed the cages stacked there. 'Freedom and revenge all at once.' He picked them up and hurled them, one at a time, at the charging beastmen.

The cages burst on impact, spilling angry, desperate animals into the hall. They clung to the beastmen, hissing and spitting, biting and clawing. The organised charge collapsed into a desperate attempt to remove these tiny fiends from head and arm, torso and back. In their panic, the beastmen dropped their weapons, reverting to claws and teeth, and Dietz took advantage of the moment. He darted through the frenzied mass, using one beastman's fallen axe to club anyone in his way. Finally, he was through the small throng and back in a larger hallway. Snarls and growls were everywhere, and Dietz knew he could not return the way he had come. Choosing a direction at random, he took off at a run, hoping to avoid any more surprises.

Behind him, unnoticed, the last creature he had spilled from its cage hopped off a fallen beastman, shook itself, and darted after him.

SEVERAL MINUTES AND a few hair-raising encounters later, Dietz burst through an archway onto a small balcony. The beastman he had clubbed lay groaning behind him, and he had eluded the others, so he took the time to glance around. He was facing the jungle, which was a good sign – he had already seen an interior balcony, but had avoided it, knowing it would leave him open to the beastmen's spears. This one was on the temple's exterior, along the west wall, judging from the sun. Peering down, he saw one of the temple doorways some fifty feet beneath him. A familiar figure knelt to one side of the arch, scribbling furiously.

'Alaric!' At Dietz's shout the other man glanced up and waved. 'Time to go!' Dietz added, and then looked around behind him. The beastman had rolled over and was trying to lever itself to its feet. Past him, Dietz saw several more rounding the corner. They would soon be here. The balcony was too high to jump from and the temple's exterior had been planed smooth as glass, but handsome tapestries hung to either side of the archway. He grabbed the one to the left, kicking the beastman in the head as he passed, and hauled the heavy cloth from the wall. Running back to the balcony, Dietz used his knife to slice the tapestry down the middle, eliciting a cry of dismay from Alaric below. Ignoring it, he tied one half around the balcony railing and twisted the other end around his hand. Then he jumped.

The tapestry tore under his weight; a loud rip he knew would bring the other beastmen running. However, it slowed his fall enough so that he dropped the last few feet, landing with a loud grunt, but otherwise unharmed.

'That tapestry was priceless!' Alaric complained, giving him a hand up.

'Then it won't cost anything to replace,' he snapped back, grabbing Alaric's arm and tugging him towards the jungle. 'Come on!'

A pack of beastmen burst from the temple entrance, growling and waving spears and swords, and Alaric nodded. 'Right, I'll have to come back for the tablet.' Then he took off after Dietz, who was already among the first trees.

Behind them, the small creature from the antechamber had reached the balcony. It hopped up onto the tapestry and scrambled down it, sharp claws finding easy purchase in the thick cloth. Leaping the last few feet to the ground, it darted into the jungle after the men, disappearing in the thick undergrowth.

'TAAL'S TEETH!'

Alaric slid to a stop, slamming into Dietz's back as he came upon the taller man suddenly. Only Dietz's outflung arm, grasping tightly to a thick vine, kept them both from falling into the chasm that yawned at their feet. Dietz had almost missed it, too intent upon ducking vines and low branches, and skipping over thick roots to notice the approaching line of grey that slashed across the green around them. Now, however, the wide gap was impossible to miss – the plants ended suddenly and beyond them was empty air, and another jungle-covered cliff beyond that.

'Where did that come from?' demanded Alaric, righting himself and taking two cautious steps back from the edge. 'That wasn't there before.'

Dietz rolled his eyes. 'We didn't come this way before.'

'Oh.' Alaric looked around, and pointed. 'What's that over there?'

Following his finger, Dietz saw something dark curving across the gap. 'Come on.'

As they reached it, they saw it was a bridge, though not much of one. A thick rope was strung across the chasm, with two thinner ropes above and on either side.

'You call that a bridge?' Alaric said in disgust, staring at it. 'I've seen better from orphans living in ditches!'

'Insult it later,' Dietz warned him, shoving the younger man towards it. 'Use it now.'

They both glanced back, hearing the growls and roars growing behind them, and Alaric nodded. Setting one foot upon the thicker rope and clutching the two thinner ones, he walked quickly across – for all his complaints his steps were sure and steady, and he seemed no more inconvenienced than a man on an afternoon stroll. Dietz was right behind him, doing his best not to look down. His attention entirely focussed on the ropes at his hands and feet, and the sounds behind him, he never even noticed as a small figure darted from the jungle and leaped, its front claws latching onto the leather of his pack.

'Shall we?' Alaric asked lightly as Dietz reached the other

side, and was half-turned to the jungle beyond when Dietz shook his head.

'Hang on.' Drawing his knife, Dietz turned back to the bridge and sliced at one of the hand-ropes. The sharp edge of the blade slid off, repelled somehow. Looking more closely, Dietz saw a thick, sticky coating about the ropes, most likely sap. 'Clever,' he admitted.

'Leave it,' Alaric urged him, tugging at his sleeve. 'They're right behind us.'

Dietz shook him off. 'That's why I have to cut the bridge. Otherwise they'll keep chasing us.' With a sigh, he turned and started back onto the bridge. 'Get back among the trees,' he shouted over his shoulder.

As he had hoped, the sap only protected the ropes at either end. Twenty paces back it faded away and his knife sliced easily through the first hand-rope. Unfortunately, a dozen beastmen were already on the bridge and stalking towards him.

'Hurry!' Alaric shouted from the trees and Dietz snarled. What did the fool think he was doing? But he had two ropes left. A quick look at the rapidly approaching beast-men and Dietz made a decision. He stooped, just in time to avoid several spears thrown from the far side, and sliced down with all his strength, his free hand tightly curled around the other hand-rope. With a twang the rope below parted and his feet dropped out from under him. His grip held and Dietz dangled from the third rope. Most of the beastmen had not been that lucky. Their snarls turned to yowls as they plunged into the darkness below. A series of thuds a moment later testified to the chasm's depth and the presence of a solid bottom.

Three beastmen had reacted quickly when the bridge was cut, dropping their weapons and curling their paws around the remaining rope. Now the foremost began creeping towards Dietz, hauling itself hand over hand, its face twisted into a vicious array of teeth and whiskers. Dietz was not waiting around. With his other hand he lashed out again, and the knife slid easily through the last rope just behind him. The taut cord parted with a loud snap, and the remaining beastmen plummeted to their deaths. Dietz almost joined them, his sweaty hand slipping as his weight tugged on the rope, and dropped his knife just in time to grab the rope end with his other hand. The chasm wall was solid stone and his breath whooshed out as he slammed against it, but his grip held. After catching his breath again, Dietz wrapped the rope around his right hand and began hauling himself up with his left.

That was when he heard the chanting.

Looking over his shoulder, he discovered that one of the beastmen had not attempted the bridge. Standing on the far side of the chasm, this one's fur was shot with white, especially around the muzzle. One hand held a glittering black sword and the other bore a long staff of golden stone, several long claws mounted near the top. More claws and stones decorated a chain around the beastman's throat, and others rose like a crest above its head. The beastman continued chanting, strange liquid sounds rolling from its throat, and it gestured with its staff towards Dietz.

Expecting to be struck dead, Dietz was surprised when instead he felt the rope in his hands writhe. As he stared, horrified, the rough brown cord turned a glistening greenish black, its dry surface growing wet and scaly. The end, just beyond Dietz's right hand, narrowed at the tip and split across, revealing a pair of long, dripping fangs and small diamond-shaped yellow eyes just above them. The beastman had transformed the rope into a snake – and its fangs were only inches from Dietz's face.

Dietz knew this was the end. His second knife was in his boot and too far away to reach. His right hand was too tightly wrapped to get loose, and his left was still clutching to keep him from falling. He couldn't duck the snake's attack, not this close. His only hope was to let go and pray he caught on the cliff wall somehow before he struck bottom. He could almost feel Morr hovering nearby.

Even as his left hand was losing its grip, something

darted past Dietz's head from behind. A small furry form lunged down, its tiny mouth wide open, its needle-like teeth latched onto the snake just below the jaws. The newcomer's mouth shut with an audible snap and the snake thrashed in Dietz's hands as its head was torn free and tossed aside. Instantly, it reverted to rope, and Dietz hauled himself the rest of the way up, pausing only to grab a loose rock and hurl it at the beastman on the far side. It snarled and dodged the missile, but backed away and disappeared into the jungle.

Alaric stepped forward and grasped Dietz's free hand once he came into view, helping the older man haul himself onto solid ground. The small creature leaped down at once from Dietz's pack and began rubbing its head and shoulder against Dietz's chin.

'Well, that was exciting,' Alaric murmured. 'Find anything worthwhile?' Dietz handed him the mask and watched his employer's face light up. 'Ah, excellent! Most excellent!' He glanced down at Dietz again. 'Good work, and where the devil did you get that monkey?'

Dietz blinked at the small creature, which stared back at him. 'No idea, but it saved my life,' he admitted. 'It can stay if it wants.' He studied it more closely. 'Maybe the antechamber – lots of small animals there. Monkey? Are you sure?'

The creature was the length of his arm, though much of that looked to be its thick tail, and covered in short tawny fur, with bands of red along its body and darker red at its head and feet, and tail end. It had a long, narrow face with a pointed nose and small round ears. Its eyes were dark and had a look of lively intelligence.

Alaric looked offended. 'Of course I'm sure. That is an Indyan tree-monkey.'

The creature reared back as if offended, and Dietz chuckled despite himself.

'Doesn't look like any monkey I've seen, but you're the expert. We'll need a name for you, little one.' He considered. 'I'll call you Glouste.' He rubbed its head and it pushed against his fingers like a contented cat. 'Well, Glouste, we shouldn't sit here all day. Come on.' Dietz stood up and Glouste skittered up his arm and settled around his neck like a fur collar.

Alaric shook his head and shoved the stone mask into his own pack. 'Yes, well, do not expect me to help you clean up after it!' he insisted as they moved away from the chasm, heading into the jungle to begin the long, dangerous trek back to their boat and eventually to civilisation.

'I'LL BE SPEAKING with your superiors about this!' Alaric shouted over his shoulder as he kicked his horse forward. 'The nerve,' he muttered to Dietz as they cleared the gate and entered Middenheim proper. 'Searching my bags! As if I was a common merchant, or a pedlar! This is the twentieth year of Karl-Franz's reign. You'd think he'd have brought some culture to these people by now!'

Dietz shrugged. He'd been a bit surprised to see so many soldiers at the gate when they'd arrived, including several half-familiar faces, but he couldn't fault them for searching their belongings. These were dangerous times and they were strangers here. Well, at least Alaric was.

As they passed out of the gate's shadow, Dietz glanced around, eager to see how his former home had fared of late. The sights that greeted him, however, made him wish they had chosen a different city to visit. What had happened here? When they had left, Middenheim had been the rock of the Empire, the mighty stone city that no foe could breach. Its homes had stood high and proud, its streets smooth and clean, its people rough but lively.

All that was gone. As they rode Dietz saw rubble everywhere, homes in ruins, buildings shattered. Their horses moved slowly, carefully setting hooves between chunks of stone, rotten foods, old rags, and even bodies. Some of the figures stretched out on the paving stones groaned and twitched, but others lay still; whether in sleep or worse Dietz could not tell. Those people walking past had a hard look about them, a look of despair as if they had seen the pits of Chaos and had not escaped unscathed.

'Madness,' Dietz said softly, eyeing their surroundings. He had heard about the war, of course, and the plague – the sailors had told him during their return voyage, and both he and Alaric had counted themselves lucky to have avoided such events. Clearly they had not escaped its aftermath. He found himself wondering how many of his old friends had survived both illness and combat. He was deliberately not wondering the same about his family.

'Absolutely,' Alaric agreed, but when Dietz glanced over he saw his employer rummaging through a saddlebag, not even noticing the dreariness around them. 'That lout could have destroyed these items easily, with those ham-hands of his!' Alaric exhaled sharply as his hands closed about something wrapped in several silk scarves, and pulled it loose to feel its contours carefully. 'Well, the mask is intact, at least,' he assured Dietz. 'Now, as I was saying earlier, I don't think the symbols are writing exactly. More of a pictogrammatic style, I'd guess, illustrating some significant…'

Dietz tuned out the rest of the lecture. He enjoyed Alaric's company, and liked working for the young noble-turned-explorer, but by Sigmar the boy could talk! Since Dietz didn't care to hear all the details of centuries-old writing, and Alaric could happily talk to himself for hours, the arrangement worked perfectly – Alaric continued to babble on about runes and carvings and ancient languages, and Dietz guided their horses down street after street, leading them through the city and back to Rolf's shop. At least some parts of the city were intact, and he was surprised how happy he was to see the carved wolves' heads still atop the mounting posts and the street lamps that resembled icicles, and the bite- and claw marks traditionally carved above every door, showing that Ulric had set his seal upon it and offered his protection to its occupants. Still, it was not all pleasant. Several times along the way Dietz had to kick loose hands as people grasped their saddles and reins, begging for coins or food or death, and he was finally forced to keep his gaze on the shop signs and street posts so that he would not see yet another starved, maimed wretch hobbling after them, pleading for help.

Rolf's shop looked the same, at least, its thick stone front undamaged and the heavy wooden plaque above, supported by stout chains whose links were shaped into wolves biting their own tails, still well polished. They left their horses at a livery one street over, where the stable hand remembered them and promised them the best stalls, and tossed the saddlebags onto their shoulders. Glouste made a small sound of protest as Dietz's bags rose perilously close to her, but forgave him an instant later and lowered her head against his neck again.

She had been one of the only saving graces during their long voyage back, and Dietz had distracted himself from all that water around them by testing the limits of his new pet's intelligence. He had been pleasantly surprised – though he had never had a pet himself, Dietz had known boys with cats and dogs and even tame rats, and Glouste was smarter than he remembered any of them being. She clearly understood him, at least his tone and simple words, and obeyed commands unless she was feeling unappreciated. One of the sailors, seeing the monkey pretend not to hear Dietz, had chuckled and said 'got yerself quite the little woman there, friend. Mine demands baubles and fine food afore she'll do aught for me – bettin' yers is the same.' Nor had he been wrong – though affectionate and surprisingly protective, Glouste had shown a strong will and a sense of humour, and often resisted Dietz's instructions or obeyed in such a way as to cross his intentions. Alaric she alternately ignored and obstructed, and Dietz couldn't help feeling that his pet still disapproved of the 'monkey' label his employer had given her.

'Hello? Rolf?' Alaric strode through into the shop, sidestepping a variety of carvings and sculptures. No one responded to his hail and so he continued on to the back of the shop. Dietz followed him, Glouste emitting tiny sneezes from her perch around his neck. In the rear wall was a wide doorway that led to Rolf's outdoor workshop, and Alaric pushed his way though the thick leather curtain there. He immediately backed out again, coughing. 'Damned dust!' Pulling a silk handkerchief from one sleeve, he covered his mouth and nose, and stuck his head past the curtain again, blinking furiously to keep his eyes clear of the stone dust that swirled in the cold breeze. 'Rolf, are you out here?'

'Aye, and who's calling now?' a voice replied, and Alaric stepped outside, Dietz right behind him.

The area behind the shop had been fenced off and was littered with blocks of stone in various shapes, sizes, and states of carving. Near the far wall stood a heavy table and a large man leaned over it, chipping flecks of stone from a small block set before him. Rolf was as broad as a dwarf, though he swore no such blood tainted his line, and as tall as Dietz, with massive arms and hands, and thinning red hair tied back in a long braid. That hair looked greyer than Alaric remembered, as did the full beard, but perhaps that was simply the dust. Rolf's eyes, grey as granite and twice as hard, seemed as sharp as ever, and they widened slightly when they finally spied him.

'Alaric!' The husky stonemason laid aside his hammer and chisel and turned, wiping both hands on the heavy leather smock covering his torso. 'And Dietz as well – still with this young rascal, then?'

Dietz smiled and nodded. He had known Rolf for many years, from back when his own father had traded goods with the man, and it had been his recommendation that had first brought Alaric here. 'Can't get rid of him,' he admitted wryly, earning a glance of mock-reproach from his employer.

'Aye, and you've missed the worst of it, to be sure,' Rolf assured them as he clasped their hands in turn. 'First the siege and the war, and then the plague' – he gestured past the fence, where the roofs of the neighbouring buildings could just be seen peeking up. 'It's a wonder there's a city left!'

'We saw,' Dietz admitted, though he knew Alaric had barely noticed. He started to ask another question, but couldn't bring himself to. The stonemason understood.

'Your father's still alive,' he said softly, 'though his sight's utterly gone now. Dagmar still tends to him, poor lass. And Dracht – he lost a leg in the war and a son to the plague, but he's back in the shop now, hopping about with the aid of a stick.'

Dietz nodded, grateful for the news. Both Dagmar and Dracht still alive – that was more than he'd dared hope. Deisen had been lost long ago, as had Dehanna, and Darulf had been killed by a panicking horse only the year before – their father had always claimed he chose their names because he felt 'D' was good luck, but Dietz suspected the man had simply never learnt the alphabet beyond that point. Rolf had not mentioned Darhun, which could only mean he had died as well, though whether from a blade or sickness Dietz did not know. He promised himself he'd visit his two surviving siblings while they were here, and perhaps even look in on their father if he had the time and the stomach for it.

'Now, what have you brought me?' Rolf asked finally, leading them back into the shop and over to his scarred desk, casting an amused glance to where Alaric was hopping excitedly from foot to foot. 'It must be a rare treat for you to dance so.'

'It is, it is,' Alaric assured the larger man, setting the scarf-wrapped bundle down on the desk, safely away from a small carved wolf with impressively sharp claws. 'From Ind itself, my good man, an exquisite find indeed. I believe the markings on it…'

Dietz took the opportunity to wander away – he'd heard enough from Alaric about the mask, so much so that at times he'd regretted finding it. Now he left the two other men to discuss the matter, knowing Rolf would never cheat them beyond the normal craftsman's need for a small profit, and distracted himself by roaming the shop. Rolf was an expert carver, and though he trafficked in building blocks, most of his business was sculpture and fine carving. His work filled the large store, lintels and benches and sculptures leaning against the walls or lined up to create narrow aisles, and Dietz strolled among them, admiring several new additions. He could still hear snippets of the conversation towards the back, enough that he would hear Alaric if the younger man needed his aid or his input.

'Fine work indeed,' Rolf was saying, turning the mask over and stroking one chiselled cheek with a surprisingly delicate touch. 'I've not seen the like of it, to be honest, but the carver was a true master to shape it so thin without shattering the material.' He frowned and held it up so the light from the door shone upon it. 'Not seen this stone before, either.'

'Nor have I,' Alaric admitted. 'Much of the temple was marble, but this – I'd say some form of chalcedony, perhaps, but those bands that catch the light–'

'Aye, they're stunning,' Rolf agreed, tilting the mask again, 'and capture the sense of a cat's stripes beautifully. The problem is, since I canna identify the stone, I canna say its quality. Oh, I can vouch for the craftsmanship, certainly, but not whether this is a valuable stone or some common rock to them, or even stone that's been treated somehow.' He held up a hand to stop Alaric's protests. 'I'm not saying it's worthless – the carving alone makes it a prize for some, but without knowing the stone I canna tell you a fair price for it.'

'Of course, of course,' Alaric murmured, trying to hide his disappointment. He did not do a good job of it – as usual his handsome features reflected his mood all too clearly.

'Not to worry,' Rolf assured him, setting the mask back on the desk. 'I know a few who might be interested. I'll ask around, get a feel for it, and find out what they're willing to pay. Then you tell me if that's enough. If so I'll set up the deal as usual. If not you'll have your mask back and can take it elsewhere. Perhaps someone in one of the coastal towns knows this stone and can find a better buyer.'

Alaric hesitated a moment. He knew Rolf would try his best, but was loath to relinquish the mask at all. Still, they had brought it here from Ind to sell it, and he had already sketched it and its runes for future study.

'Done,' he said finally, and they clasped hands upon it.

'Now that's settled,' Rolf said, folding the scarves back over the mask, 'I've got a few new pieces you might want to see yourself. Came to me from a wandering tinker, a week or two back, and they're not the sorts of thing I normally buy, but I knew they'd draw your interest. Got them back here for safekeeping, not the sort of thing I'd leave lying about.'

Dietz, still half-listening, had just turned down another aisle when Glouste distracted him. She had been glancing at the objects around them, her whiskers quivering with curiosity, and more than once a small squeak had indicated interest in a particular piece. This time, however, the sound was higher, more drawn-out and strangely trilling, and Dietz knew at once it was not pleasure but fear. His pet confirmed this by leaping from his shoulders and darting back down the aisle and out of sight.

'Glouste!' Swearing under his breath, Dietz took off after her, following the brief flashes of red fur he saw far ahead. Fortunately, the doors were all closed and the windows covered in heavy metal grilles, so Glouste could not escape. Even so, it took several minutes before Dietz caught up to her, and then only because she had stopped her mad flight and was cowering within a small stone cabinet.

'There there, little one,' Dietz whispered, scooping her from her hiding place and tucking her into the front of his leather jacket. 'You're safe now.' He stroked her head gently with one finger until her fur stopped puffing and the trilling faded back to her normal purr.

'Now, what had you so frightened?' he wondered out loud, retracing his steps and still petting her. The aisle they'd entered was near the back of the shop, and the piece he had almost reached before Glouste's retreat was actually covered by a large sheet. Whatever it was stood taller than he did, and he could tell from the shape that it was more likely to be a sculpture than a building ornament, with a wide round base and projections above. His own curiosity aroused, Dietz tugged the sheet free. As its folds fell to the ground his face turned as white as the fabric, and it was a second before he could find his voice.

'Alaric!'

'What?' Hearing the panic in his companion's voice, Alaric all but dropped the scroll Rolf had been handing him and ran towards the sound. When he turned the corner and skidded to a halt, he found Dietz standing stock-still, pale as chalk, one hand still clutching the sheet. The other was inside his vest, where Alaric could just hear the frightened squeaks of that infernal tree-monkey. He quickly forgot about Dietz's unruly pet as his eyes registered the object before them, and Alaric took a step back himself.

The sculpture was large, easily seven feet tall, and roughly carved. Indeed, at first glance it looked uncarved, simply a rough block of stone. On second glance the depressions and protrusions began to assume a pattern, to show some semblance of design, and then individual features began to appear. At least, flashes of them did – Dietz felt as if he'd been watching a fast-moving deer through a thick wood, catching brief glimpses of an eye here, a leg there, an antler over there, never seeing the creature clearly, but getting an image from the scattered impressions. The image here was far less wholesome than any deer, and his head ached from the memory of it. He had a clear impression of limbs, too many limbs, some of them coiled and others bent in too many places.

Flatter spaces along the back, near the top, suggested wings flared in the act of taking flight, and both men cowered back slightly, afraid the stone monstrosity might indeed take to the air. Something about the way the statue narrowed just above its base spoke of clawed feet gouging the rock below them, as if impatient to leap free. But its face was the worst – hints of something long and vaguely bird-like, a massive hooked beak, yet Dietz was sure he had glimpsed row upon row of teeth as well. And the eyes; those he could not deny seeing. Small and faceted, several sets of them above where the beak would be, glared out at him. Most of the other features vanished again when he blinked, so that he could not find them a second time, but the eyes remained, their stare clearly intelligent, and just as clearly malevolent.

Though carved from stone, the surface glistened slightly in the dim light, as if covered in an oily sheen – as if damp with sweat or blood. Everything about the sculpture spoke of power and violence, and madness – a madness that beat at the back of your brain and threatened to burst free, over-running your senses and your sanity if you gave it a moment's opportunity.

'It's a thing of Chaos,' Alaric whispered, backing away farther and dragging Dietz back with him. Neither of them could take their eyes from the foul carving. 'I've – I've seen drawings like this, once before, back at the university. The master kept them locked away. A traveller had made them, sketches of sculptures he'd seen on his travels – through the Chaos Wastes!'

The story continues in

DAY OF THE DAEMON

By Aaron Rosenburg

1-84416-366-0

Available now from *www.blacklibrary.com*

DEATH, BLOOD AND CARNAGE — GRIDIRON STYLE!